# Marvels of the Underworld

OTHERWORLD TRILOGY BOOK 2

HERMIONE LEE

This is a work of fiction. Names, characters, places, and incidents are products of the author's imagination or are used fictitiously and are not to be construed as real. Any resemblance to actual events, locations, organizations, or persons, living or dead, is entirely coincidental.

**World Castle Publishing, LLC**
Pensacola, Florida

Paperback ISBN: 9781956788686
eBook ISBN: 9781956788693
First Edition World Castle Publishing, LLC, March 7, 2022
http://www.worldcastlepublishing.com

Cover: Hermione Lee & Karen Fuller
Editor: Maxine Bringenberg

## Table of Contents

# *Dedication*

For Grandma (Ama) and Uncle Bryan. Thank you both for playing such important roles in my journey of birthing this book.

# Acknowledgements

First, I'd like to thank my family, without whom this book would never have seen the light of day. I'm also immensely grateful for Maxine Bringenberg for her incredible editing skills and Karen Fuller of World Castle Publishing for accepting and designing beautiful covers for my books, especially for the Otherworld trilogy, which will always remain near and dear to me no matter how many books I write. Furthermore, I would like to extend my thanks to my writing mentor Wulf Moon for his selfless desire to help new writers, like me, become better. His help and advice considerably strengthened my writing skills. Special thanks to my writing buddy Candice R. Lisle, whose enthusiasm and encouragement kept me excited about my writing. Also, I am beyond thankful for Rae Lan and Yu-Hui Huang, two incredible professors who influenced my writing in different ways.

Apart from them, there is an important group of friends that deserve my heartfelt thanks—my fellow authors at World Castle. Thanks to Judith White for helping me gain exposure by doing free promotions for my book on her Facebook page, and to Abby Farnsworth, Alexander Semenyuk, Barna William Donovan, Blake Alb, Cheryl Peña, Elizabeth Hartman Seckman, G.A. Minton, Jess Blenkarn, Joy Ross Davis, Judith Ann McDowell, Julie Parker, Khaled Talib, Lou Aguilar, Maria A. Palace, Mark F. Geatches, Meenakshi Gautam Chaturvedi, Melissa Davis, and

Sheryl Doiron-Powers. All of them helped me grow as an author and a person in more ways than I'd ever imagined.

Last but not least, thanks to Cat Jenson, Ed Gonzalez, Gloria Lakritz, Johan Prinsloo, Kelly Lo, Phillip Charlier, Stephanie Chiang, and Stephany Yang for their help in spreading the word about the Otherworld trilogy. And of course, loyal readers, thank you all for picking up my book and choosing to embark on a new adventure with Alexandria and her fellow Otherworldians. *Marvels of the Underworld* is my favorite book in the Otherworld trilogy. I hope you will laugh with the protagonists, cry with them, cheer for their success, and mourn their losses in this emotional rollercoaster of a sequel. Thank you again for supporting me and my work!

# Chapter One

## The Message on the Violet Leaf (Alexandria)

A fiery serpent burst from the tip of my scepter, now slithering on the ground. It let out a menacing hiss, a fierce glint visible in its ruby-red eyes. With a wave of my scepter, it was levitated off the ground. The snake twirled gracefully in the air and spun faster and faster, resembling an orange whirlwind. Then, it erupted into a million sparks of fire.

"That was epic," breathed Eileen.

"Thanks. Learned any new tricks lately?"

Eileen nodded. She plucked a daisy from a potted plant, placed it on her palm, and jabbed it with her scepter—a ten-inch stick made of vines and leaves. The daisy's petals withered and shriveled, and soon, the wilted petals vanished, leaving a little green seed on Eileen's palm. I watched, amazed, as the seed germinated, sprouted leaves, blossomed, withered and shriveled, and once again, the dead petals disappeared, revealing a little seed. The new seed germinated, and the cycle continued on.

"Nice." I grinned at Eileen.

"Alexandria, Eileen!" Clarissa Dawson and Daphne Sinclair waved at us from the balcony upstairs.

Clarissa was wearing a mischievous grin, a yellow shirt, and navy-blue skinny jeans. Curly dirty-blonde hair that fell to her shoulders framed her round face. Her doe-brown eyes, as they had always been, were twinkling with joy. Daphne, on the other hand, had on her favorite black lip gloss, an indigo asymmetrical blouse, and black leggings. Her silky blue hair hung long and loose on either side of her face.

"What are you doing in the back of the school? Testing your elemental magic again?"

"Hey, Clarissa. Hi, Daphne." I grinned at them. I hadn't seen them for two weeks, for we had all been busy studying for our midterms. Ninth-grade examinations were a pain in the neck. "Eileen and I are having a little after-exam celebration. Want to come join us?"

A visit to the Otherworld last year in September had made the four of us inseparable friends who would do anything for each other. It was also the first time I met my parents—King Patrick and Queen Marianne, the rulers of the Otherworld. They sent the four of us and two of the Elders, their courtiers and advisors, to the Underworld on a mission to retrieve an artifact stolen by Alta and Alto—the tyrants that ruled the Underworld. This was because Clarissa, Eileen, Daphne, and I were the heiresses of the four Creators that founded the first magical world. Clarissa was the heiress of Zeru, the god of the sky; Eileen, the heiress of Fern, the goddess of nature; Daphne, the heiress of Walters, the god of water; and I the heiress of Ember, the goddess of fire.

"You seen Helen, Zack, or Lilith lately?" Daphne called to us from above. The three of them had been our teachers but were, in fact, Elders in the Otherworld who were keeping an eye on us and ensuring our safety during the school year.

I shook my head. "No. We've got Ms. Harris, Mr. Watson, and Mrs. Dickinson as our substitute teachers."

"You know what they're up to? The Elders?"

"Good question. Helen left for the Otherworld two weeks ago. Said it was an urgent call. I've been living with Eileen and her mom and dad since then. Not that I'm complaining, though. The Spencers are really nice, and Eileen and I had fun playing around with our elemental magic and doing all sorts of gimmicks."

"Same here," said Daphne. "Lilith went to the Otherworld

two weeks ago and hasn't returned. Lucky Clarissa's family was willing to take me in."

Daphne had been my foster sister, but she was sent to live with Lilith while I went with Helen, on King Patrick and Queen Marianne's orders. They also named Helen my godmother, which both of us were delighted about.

"Come down and join us," I said, beckoning toward them.

Daphne got out a trident carved from ice, the scepter she had inherited from Walters, and gave it a sharp jab. The winding staircase in front of her froze to ice. She drew a diagonal line in the air, and the stairs melted and formed an icy slide.

"Come on, Clarissa," said Daphne. The two of them slid to the first floor and got to their feet. Daphne made a zigzagging movement in the air with her trident and restored the staircase.

"Seems like Eileen and I aren't the only ones who've mastered some tricks."

"Yeah, I miss going on adventures and fighting in battles, though. Can you believe it? It's been one year and two months since our previous mission. Time flies."

"Well, it's not like we haven't been practicing magic," said Clarissa. "Though it's been some time since we last had our training sessions."

We used to have training sessions every day after school, practicing our elemental magic and enhancing our fighting skills; that was, before the Elders returned to the Otherworld. As the heiress of Ember, I was able to conjure anything related to fire.

"I've always wondered what it would be like to own a wand, like the Elders," said Eileen. "It'd be interesting to charm objects and make them move, shrink, and distend. I still remember how Zack managed to shrink his shield and our tent and keep them in his pocket on our last mission."

"That would be really convenient. Suppose it'd take some advanced magic," I sighed. "Come to think of it, I miss the Otherworld so much...."

The Otherworld was my one and only home, the place where I felt a sense of belonging. I missed the magical creatures that dwelled in the Otherworld; bearnixes, unibirds, kittenpillars, and dogfishes—the spirits of fire, sky, nature, and water. Among the four creatures, bearnixes were the most aggressive animals, with heads like bears and bodies like phoenixes. Unibirds, creatures that resided high above the clouds, were winged unicorns with the ability to fly. Kittenpillars, docile nature lovers, had bodies like caterpillars and heads like cats. Dogfishes were dogs with fishlike bodies that could breathe underwater as well as live on land.

"You're not the only one feeling nostalgic," admitted Eileen. "Remember Ella? The kittenpillar in the courtyard of the palace?"

Everyone exchanged knowing smiles. We all knew Ella the kittenpillar. She was a meek furry fellow with a mint-colored caterpillar body and a white head, with whiskers and triangular ears sticking out from either side.

"I wonder when King Patrick and Queen Marianne will send for us," Daphne said.

"Well, doesn't seem like today," I replied with another sigh. Today was just like any other day, perfectly normal, and sadly, with no signs of anything magical or extraordinary.

"But on the bright side, our exams are over, and we can enjoy the sunshine," Clarissa, ever the optimist, reminded us.

The four of us strolled past the buildings, the manicured bushes of flowers, and the lush green shrubs and small hedges. The campus looked lovely, even in chilly November, when it was supposed to be enveloped in mist. The afternoon breeze hummed, teasing the leaves as it swept through the trees. Birds that perched themselves on the tree limbs tweeted a fine chorus. The entire campus was alive with joy.

Eileen stooped to admire a tiny red ladybug among the blades of grass. "Hi, there."

"Beautiful weather, isn't it?" I said as we passed a pageant of vibrant roses, violets, lilies, orchids, and chrysanthemums in full bloom.

"It's like magic," agreed Daphne.

"It is magic," Eileen beamed. "Every day is spring when you're with the heiress of Fern."

"What do you mean?"

"I planted these flowers. I did it with my nature magic, which is why they can thrive in November. See," Eileen raised her scepter, "I take it with me wherever I go."

Clarissa withdrew from the pocket of her jeans a golden spiral that resembled a unibird's horn and ran her fingers over it. "Me too. I see you've also got your scepter, Alexandria."

"Of course. It's the only connection I have with the Otherworld." I said, tightening my grip on my scepter, a fiery orange stick made of lava.

"Same," Daphne piped up. "I keep my ice trident in my schoolbag at all times. Boris Davis saw it yesterday and thought it was a toy."

"Boris Davis? The skinny boy with glasses in Zack's homeroom?"

"Yeah, that's him."

"I thought he had a crush on you," I said, restraining a smile.

"Oh, did he?" Clarissa looked mildly interested. "No offense, Daphne, but I thought he preferred Eileen."

"I'm not going out with Boris Davis," protested Eileen, a flush of red contouring her cheeks. "He's an annoying slob. And he's been going out with three girls in the past two months."

"You just don't like him because he outperformed you in English," Clarissa said, half-amused, half-indignant.

"Says who?" Eileen raised her eyebrows. "I just don't like how he's always showing off in class like an arrogant know-it-all."

"That's true. But he's quite good-looking, though," said Clarissa with a dreamy expression on her face. "His beautiful eyes and straight—"

"Anyway, who needs Davis when Eileen's already got someone who's loads better?" I interrupted.

Clarissa and Daphne both giggled. Eric, my cousin who lived in the Otherworld, shared his first kiss with Eileen before we returned to the mortal world last time.

"You haven't forgotten Eric, have you, Eileen?" I teased

her. "I heard you murmuring his name in your sleep yesterday."

"Whoa, you had dreams about your sweetheart? How *adorable,*" Clarissa gushed.

Eileen actually frowned and smiled at the same time. "Oh, shut up, Clarissa. It's not funny at—"

But before she could finish, a fuzzy violet leaf trimmed with gold dropped from the branches above and landed on her shoulder.

"Wow." I took the leaf and examined it. "A *purple* leaf? Rimmed with gold?"

Clarissa gaped at the leaf in awe. "Maybe it's something magical."

*Magical....* Something occurred to me at that precise moment. *Surely it couldn't be...?* Excitement coursed through my veins as I turned the fuzzy leaf over. There, on the other side of it, was a message scrawled in fancy silver letters.

"It's from Eric!" Clarissa squealed, hopping up and down. "Is it a love letter for Eileen? Read it aloud, Alexandria."

"Hmm, it's not a love letter. It's addressed to the four of us.

*Dear Alexandria, Clarissa, Eileen, and Daphne,*

*I hope everything's fine with you girls. Things are getting a little complicated here in the Otherworld. Helen asked me to send for the four of you so that she can explain everything in person. Please come to the palace of the Otherworld. I will be waiting for you at the front gates. Set off as soon as possible.*

*Sincerely, Eric*

I looked up at Clarissa, Eileen, and Daphne, and saw my eagerness and ecstasy reflected on their faces. "So, what are we waiting for?"

Across the sports field, up the slope, past the administration office, and into the school courtyard, we went. There perched the large, white-bricked fountain—the portal to the Otherworld.

"I can hardly believe this," Daphne said, her voice quivering with excitement.

"Neither can I," I agreed. It seemed too good to be true. The thought of being back home in the Otherworld thrilled me, filling me with mirth beyond expression.

"And you're going to see the love of your life again, Eileen!" Clarissa hollered in a singsong voice, making Eileen's face redder than the beds of roses on the campus.

"You'd better stop teasing her, Clarissa, or she might send a self-running-flesh-eating-Venus-flytrap after you," I said, sniggering. "Let's hurry up and get to the Otherworld first. Come on." I clambered into the fountain.

Clarissa, Eileen, and Daphne followed suit. "I forgot how to activate this portal," Daphne said. "Do we have to shout our destination aloud?"

"I think—" began Clarissa.

But the rest of her sentence was drowned out by the screams that came from everyone else. The ground had rifted, and before we knew it, we were plummeting through a void of darkness and nothingness....

# Chapter Two

## HELLO AGAIN
## (ALEXANDRIA)

*Splash!*

"This has got to be the worst mode of transportation in the world." I cursed, trying not to drown as I climbed out of the fountain. "One day, when I'm the queen of the Otherworld, I'm going to block this portal."

Unlike our last visit to the Otherworld, it was sunny and warm here this time. The sun, framed by streaks of white clouds, was smiling at us in the sky.

"The village seems deserted." Eileen jerked her head at the residential area behind us.

"No way!" Daphne groaned. "Don't tell me that the Gem of Hope is stolen again! I'm not going to—"

"Relax, Daphne. It's not like last time. The weather seems pretty nice here," Clarissa pointed out. "Alexandria, did Eric give any details or mention anything else in the letter?"

I looked down at the violet leaf. "No. He only told us to get to the front gates of the palace as soon as possible. I bet it's something really urgent. We've got to get going. Clarissa, after you."

"Me? But I—oh...oh!" Clarissa's eyes widened with comprehension. She got out her scepter and pointed it at a cloud in the sky. "Descend," she muttered, her face contorted with concentration. A cloud sank to the ground. "Good thinking," Clarissa grinned at me.

We climbed on, and the cloud solidified as we sat down. It was like sitting on a mound of wet cotton, soft yet damp.

"Hold on tight," said Clarissa. She pointed her scepter at the cloud beneath us. "Levitate, to the front gates of the palace." Our cloud rose up into the air and drifted forward.

"So why is Eric sending for us?" Daphne said.

"Good question," Clarissa, who had eyes only for the scenery below us, muttered.

"I just hope I'll get to see Eric and Ella," sighed Eileen. "After practicing for months, I can finally conjure a wreath of daisies. I'm going to give them one each as a present."

"Practicing for months?" Clarissa goggled at her. "Are you that lousy at magic?"

Eileen made a face. "It's really complex, you know, but I think I've got the hang of it after spending countless weekends locked up in my room and trying to figure it out. Well, it gets sort of nasty after an unsuccessful attempt. Huge farting flowers sprout in my room each time I fail. At one point, my bedroom was full of that foul, disgusting stuff. Barely managed to remove them until yesterday."

Daphne grinned and shook her head. "Some magic, isn't it? I can't wait to see the expression on Eric's face when he hears this."

Clarissa and I were both howling with laughter. "Those farting flowers!" Clarissa said. "Did your mom and dad ever find out?"

Eileen shook her head. "Nope. They were both stuck at a seminar yesterday, and they've been so busy preparing for it during the past month that they barely had time to talk to me, let alone inspect my room. Say, Clarissa, done any experiments with your magic?"

"I sneaked out of the house when my mom and dad were busy, and I drew clouds from the window of my room and went for vacations in the air. It's been pretty awesome, drifting in the sky and watching everything from high above. I see meadows in the daytime and orbs of lights floating on the streets in the evening." Clarissa's lips curved into a dreamy smile.

"Any funny accidents?" Eileen asked.

Clarissa sat still for a moment. "Oh, now that you mention it.... Once when we had to write an essay comparing different terrains for homework in geography, I got so frustrated that I decided to go on a flight and see if I could, you know, get some inspiration. I made the huge mistake of taking my workbook with me, and I got so distracted by the meadows below that my—" She burst into a peal of laughter. "My workbook fell from the cloud and went soaring down into the meadows!"

Everyone roared with laughter. "Oh, I remember that!" Daphne managed to say between gulps of laughter. "Lilith Jackson exploded in front of the entire class."

"Didn't you try to clarify everything?" I asked.

"Well," said Clarissa, beaming, "that's what I did. Told her and all the kids in class that I was flying a cloud and daydreaming, and my workbook fell into the meadow below, and I couldn't find it. And guess what? Lilith didn't even give me a punishment. Simply shouted at me for five minutes for making up some cock-and-bull excuse for not finishing my homework. Humph, some temper she's got. But I'm lucky it wasn't my language arts workbook. Helen's awfully strict, and I have a feeling she's not as forgiving as Lilith. She would never have let me off the hook like Lilith did. Good old Zack wouldn't have minded, though. Come to think of it, he probably would've had a good laugh over the whole thing."

I visualized the whole incident in my mind and grinned. "I guess the whole class found it hilarious."

"Of course! They roared and cheered for my farfetched story and clapped me on the back during recess, treating me like a hero. They thought I was annoying Lilith on purpose. What about you, Daphne? You done anything interesting with your elemental magic?"

"Well, I did, but it's not that much of a laugh," said Daphne. "I can make the rain sing and dance. The raindrops make splashing noises rhythmically and zigzag in the air. They've got a language of their own—the language of water. Every drop of rain has its own story. Oh, besides that...." Her eyes gleamed with excitement. "I can build ice cabins."

"Wicked!" Clarissa yelled. "What else can you build? Ice skyscrapers? Ice castles?"

Daphne shook her head. "Those are huge projects. And you know, building stuff with magic is exhausting. But I'll try that and see how far I can go next time. Hey, look, I think we've reached the palace."

"Yeah, here we are."

Clarissa lowered our cloud, and the four of us hopped off. We found ourselves facing not only the wrought iron gates of the castle-like palace but also—

"Eric!" Eileen squealed.

"Hi, everyone! It's so great to see you again, all of you," Eric beamed at us. "Welcome home."

"I thought the drawbridge was the front gate," said Eileen. "We entered the palace through that entrance last time."

"That's the side gate. You haven't changed much, baby. Still charming, still beautiful." He planted a kiss on her forehead, and she let out a girlish giggle.

I noticed that Eric was wearing a lilac tuxedo. "You've joined the Elders?" I asked, amazed, as he reached out to shake my hand.

"Yeah. You've got to be sixteen or older to join the Elders. I filed my application on my sixteenth birthday, which was four months ago," he replied, puffing out his chest and squaring his shoulders. "Didn't even have to take the recruitment test. King Patrick, Queen Marianne, and Helen unanimously admitted me."

"Congratulations!" Clarissa and Daphne exclaimed in unison.

Eric grinned. "Thanks. But I did have to take etiquette lessons with the other newcomers. Helen taught us new Elders all about the formal dress code, table manners, and palace rules that'd take me a decade to write down. All that stuff about what we should do and what we shouldn't because it's...what was the term she used? Oh, right, *discourteous*. It's awfully boring." He sighed. "A precious hour of my life I'll never get back. Wish Helen could've done me the favor of sparing me those lessons."

"But you made it, Eric. You're now an Elder, and you should be so proud of yourself," Eileen said, giving his hand an affectionate squeeze. "Speaking of Helen, how is she?"

The big grin on Eric's face faded away. "Well...." He heaved a sigh.

"What do you mean?" I asked, concerned.

"Is she all right? She's not...hurt or sick or—or anything, is she?" Daphne said.

"And what about the others? Zack, Lilith, and Evonne?" Clarissa piped up.

"And my parents?" I added.

"They're all...well, doing fine. No health problems." But Eric's odd voice implied that something was indeed wrong. "It's complicated. I sent for you girls on Helen's orders, and she'll explain everything in person. Come on."

Eric turned to the gates, and I saw a slot with a purple button where the lock was supposed to be. He placed his wand in the opening, which bore the words *Wand Identification*. There was a beeping noise, and the button greened. The gates swung open to admit us. "Come along." Eric beckoned for us to follow him.

The pristine marble towers and turrets of the immense palace greeted us as we entered through the gates. Waves of nostalgia welled up within me. We made our way across the front lawn, which stretched on for about a thousand feet.

"How do you reckon they keep the exterior of the palace as good as new?" Clarissa asked. "I mean, just look at the pillars and everything. They're as white as snow."

"Magic, of course," Eric said with a laugh. "They clean the walls once a month."

Eileen stopped to observe the vibrant butterflies, which were weaving through the peony bushes and statues that dotted the lawn. The peonies in different shades of purple reminded me of what Lilith had said about the Elders' dress code. Regular Elders wore lilac gowns and tuxedos; Elite Elders were attired in lavender, and the Representative Elder in a rich, deep shade of violet.

Meanwhile, Daphne had stopped to admire a huge, dazzling fountain. Jets of water spouted from the dogfish statues' mouths. The water gleamed, gilded by the golden sunlight. I smiled. It felt great to be back home.

"Hurry up," Eric urged them. "I know you're all excited about the palace, but we mustn't keep the Elders waiting."

Eileen and Daphne hurried over to us. Together we crossed the lawn and went up the marble steps that extended from one side of the palace to the other. I craned my neck, surveying the intricate arcades on the walls and the golden embellishments on the slender white spires that seemed to penetrate the sky.

"Here," said Eric as we reached the top. He tapped his wand on the burnished double doors a couple of times, and cursed. "Got the rhythm wrong. Let me try again."

"Hasn't changed much, has he?" Daphne whispered to me, and I rolled my eyes at her.

"Makes me wonder how he's managed to get along with Helen ever since last September," remarked Clarissa. "She's so prissy and formal all the time, and she hates cursing, especially in the palace."

I beamed as a vision of Helen and Eric quarreling over a silly little matter crossed my mind.

"Yup, got the rhythm right." Eric's voice brought my mind back to reality. "Come in, everyone." He pushed the doors open, and we followed him into what seemed like the grand lobby of the palace.

It was a vast, resplendent hall with walls of milky white marble. Everything here, from the banisters of the imperial staircase to the ornate balustrade that ringed the second floor, was gilded. Thousands of golden candles squatted on the chandelier below the soaring ceiling. As I looked down, I saw that even the floor looked magnificent; the plush carpet emitted a sparkling silver glow, making it seem as though we were standing on a sea of diamonds.

Clarissa's mouth dropped open, at a loss for words. "This

is—"

"Marvelous," Eileen finished her sentence for her.

"Completely different from the palace of the Underworld," said Eric. "It's all black, from the exterior to the interior."

The sound of delightful music and people laughing and chattering wafted into the lobby.

"What's that?" I asked.

"Some party, I guess," said Eric. "King Patrick and Queen Marianne have been hosting thousands of those these days."

For some reason, I felt fishy about everything in the Otherworld. "Hold on for a moment, Eric. Why haven't we met any guards since we arrived? I mean, there ought to be some safety precautions set up around the palace. Anybody, including Alta and Alto, could've entered—"

"They would have to get through the wand identification and—"

"Well, they could fly in through the gates on unibirds, if you haven't noticed! Or they could destroy the gates with a spell or a bomb or anything. Don't you think it's crazy that we've got this kind of lousy security for a palace?"

"You're right, but under the current circumstances...." Eric shook his head. "Everything's been real bad lately. Let's discuss this later with the other Elders." He got out a map and studied it for a few minutes. "Yeah, we're here, and...all right, got it."

We followed Eric up the staircase and through a door. A maze of passages lit by purple torches greeted us, and after quite a few lefts and rights, we came across a magnificent spiral staircase that curled up for seven stories.

Eric led us to the fourth floor and turned right. "Room 401...the conference room, this one over here."

"I thought we were going to the Throne Room?"

"No. The Elders are in here." Eric knocked on the door. "It's me, Eric. I've brought the heiresses along with me."

"Dianthus, open the door, if you please," came a voice, unmistakably Helen's.

A man with silvery blue hair greeted us and motioned for us to enter. The conference room was semicircular, with a vaulted ceiling, a carved cornice, fancy gold-trimmed walls, and floors carpeted in beige. I could see the gates of the palace from an enormous floor window that punctuated the curved wall on the left side of the room.

"Whoa, what's all this about? Why are they here?" I heard Clarissa murmur to Eileen.

I transferred my gaze to the other side of the room and saw twelve Elders gathered around a circular table. All of them were garbed in gowns and tuxedos in various shades of purple. Four faces that could not have been more familiar smiled at us and showed signs of recognition—Helen, Zack, Lilith, and Evonne.

"Good afternoon, heiresses," said Helen. She looked as elegant as usual, with her long mane of wavy hair draped down her back like a lustrous shawl of ebony silk.

"Hasn't changed much either, has she?" Daphne whispered.

Helen glided over to a huge lilac poster on the wall, the heavy train of her velvet ball gown trailing behind her. I spotted an elaborate amethyst brooch with the curly silver words *Representative Elder* pinned to her waist, wondering why I'd never noticed it. "Come and put your names up here. Tap your scepter on this, and you'll see your name on it."

I walked up to the poster, which bore a few unfamiliar names. Wondering where all this was headed, I followed Helen's instructions, and the words *Alexandria Richardson* appeared. After Clarissa, Eileen, and Daphne had done the same, Helen motioned for us to sit down.

I took a seat beside an Elder with fair hair and doll-like features. She was staring ahead with glassy eyes, lost in her daydream. Clarissa parked herself beside me and surveyed the conference room with her large, curious eyes. I was uncomfortably aware of the fact most of the Elders were observing us with interest. A woman who wore her green hair in a braid gave each of us an appraising look, scanning us from head to toe, while a black Elder gazed at us with his jaw hanging ajar. But fortunately, they all devoted their attention to Helen instead as she spoke.

"Heiresses, we are now in the conference room in the west

tower. I suppose that you do not recognize most of the Elders who are present, so I'll make a brief introduction of everyone first. Most of the Elders here are newly recruited and are only sixteen, but we do have a few old hands. Of course, you are familiar with Zack, Lilith, and Evonne." Helen indicated the three Elders who sat on her right. "And this is Brian Lee, a sixteen-year-old genius." She gestured at the Asian Elder on her left. "William Johnson, or Willy." A handsome black man grinned hello at us, revealing neat rows of white teeth. "Sheldon Richardson—"

"That's me, your uncle, Alexandria," a man with curly brown hair piped up, winking at me. The laugh lines etched upon his face suggested that he was a jolly man who often smiled. "And this is Juniper, your aunt."

The woman with braided green hair nodded when her name was mentioned. She had a pretty face, but the color of her hair clashed horribly with her lilac gown.

Helen continued. "Connie Miller." A stout woman with a round, friendly face waved. "Cameron Miller, Connie's twin brother." A man with hair the color of chocolate inclined his head. "Dianthus Brown." The man with silvery blue hair that had answered the door flashed a confident smile at us. "And finally, Gidget Chase—"

"Did someone call my name?" The Elder on my left, who had snapped out of her reverie, said in a squeaky voice. She had pretty golden ringlets, soft blue eyes, bubble-gum pink lips, and was wearing a dainty lilac gown with silk rosettes blooming on the skirt. Her rosy cheeks, petite stature, and delicate features resembled a doll.

Helen locked her eyebrows. "Yes, Gidget," she said through gritted teeth. "It would be very nice if you stopped daydreaming during our meetings. I was just—"

"How come you're so tiny, Gidget?" Clarissa asked, her eyes glistening with curiosity. She muttered an "ouch" as I gave her a kick from under the table.

The Elder named Gidget, though, did not seem offended at all. On the contrary, she seemed to regard it as a flattering question. "I'm a half-dwarf!" she squeaked, looking delighted that she got an opportunity to show off this fact. "My dad was the king of a tribe of dwarves, and he married a human and had—"

"Elders," Helen cut in. "Meet Alexandria, Clarissa, Eileen, and Daphne, heiresses of Ember, Zeru, Fern, and Walters. I hope you will all get along well in the future."

"*You* are Alexandria? Heiress of Ember and princess of the Otherworld?" Gidget squeaked.

"Yeah, I am her—I mean, that's me."

"Really? You must be so proud of yourself! I've heard that—" Her voice faltered as she took notice of Helen's dour countenance.

"Thank you very much. Alexandria, Clarissa, Eileen, and Daphne. You may all be wondering why I've sought you."

The Elders seemed to know what Helen was about to say, and they apparently didn't like it. Evonne shifted in her seat, looking uneasy; Brian Lee pursed his lips, and many Elders exchanged significant yet somber looks with their neighbors.

As for Helen, she closed her eyes as though praying for courage to continue. "The Otherworld is in danger. Danger that most people remain ignorant of."

# Chapter Three

## Corruption (Zack)

"In danger? What do you mean in danger?" It was Alexandria who raised the first question. "And why would the Otherworldians not know if there's danger?"

"Does it have something to do with the Underworld?" Eileen said.

Helen replied with a grim nod. "It all started last Wednesday when Alta and Alto launched a series of attacks on the Otherworld. Many Elders and guards died in the attacks, but the rest of us kept fighting. Just when we were about to win, Alta and Alto called for a temporary truce. On the following day, the Underworld sent a messenger to the Otherworld, who was called into the Throne Room during the Elders' morning assembly. He gave Queen Marianne a letter Alta wrote, which claimed the Underworld wanted to make peace with the Otherworld. The messenger also brought a bag of gold as a gift of peace."

Clarissa's mouth dropped open. Eileen's eyes were as round as coins. Daphne blinked slowly as if having trouble with comprehending her words.

Alexandria, however, let out a snort. "Another one of their foul, dirty tricks. King Patrick and Queen Marianne weren't foolish enough to believe him, were they?"

The Elders lowered their heads. The room had become so quiet that one could hear a pin drop.

"Well...as a matter-of-fact, they did," I broke the uncomfortable silence.

Taken aback, Alexandria gaped at me. "No!" She surveyed the mirthless expressions of the Elders and realized the truth. "What were they thinking? Anyone with common sense would have known they were lying to lower our guard!"

"Yes and no," said Helen. "Alta and Alto kept their promise, and the attacks stopped. King Patrick and Queen Marianne have been having celebration banquets and balls and all sorts of events in the palace ever since the messenger's visit."

"Celebration?" Alexandria echoed, unable to conceal her utter consternation. "Celebrate...*what?*"

With a bitter expression, Helen said in scathing tones through gritted teeth, "The so-called reconciliation between the Otherworld and Underworld."

"R-Reconciliation?" Alexandria echoed. "You're not telling me they not only believed every single word of that making-peace nonsense but also had parties to celebrate—Wait a second, they *took* the gold from the messenger and *spent* it on those parties?"

"Exactly."

Alexandria's eyes were glazed with disbelief. "But couldn't you all talk some sense into them? I mean, you're Elders, right? They'd listen to you, wouldn't they?"

I let out a hollow laugh at her naivety. "You think we didn't do that? King Patrick and Queen Marianne, especially the latter, were over the moon about the news. Wouldn't hear a single word against Alta and Alto. After the messenger left, the king and queen announced that all morning assemblies, meetings, and training sessions would be thereby cancelled. And as you know, King Patrick and Queen Marianne have been having parties—Mind you, it's those luxurious ones that involve thousands of people I'm talking about. They invite the Otherworldians, those with higher social statuses. It's getting out of control."

"We saw the village when we were on our way here. It

was almost deserted," Eileen pointed out in a little voice.

"See?" I turned my palms skyward. "Solid proof of what I'm saying. They're all down there, in the ballrooms. Having feasts and balls and goodness knows what. I suppose they've spent an obscene amount of money on those. And to make matters worse, about ninety-five percent of the Elders followed their footsteps."

"But didn't they feel skeptical about the whole thing?" Clarissa asked.

"Perhaps they did, deep down," said Helen in a quiet voice. "But just think about it. Celebrating and relaxing every day, all play and no work. Would you rather stand up to the rulers or play along with them? It's much easier to just ignore the truth than face it, especially when the majority chooses to do so. Besides, after seeing what happened to us...."

"What's that supposed to mean?" Daphne asked.

I knew that Helen was reluctant to explain the details all over again, so I stepped in. "You see, after the last morning assembly, some Elders came straight up to me and Helen and expressed their doubts about the whole incident. Our consensus was that Alta and Alto were calling a strategic truce. It wasn't like them to want to make peace with the Otherworld. Anyone with an ounce of logic could tell that they had a goal—they were plotting something. They must have sent the messenger here to make peace with us and lure the Otherworld into a false sense of security so that they could assault us in the future when we were the least prepared. After a discussion, Helen volunteered to talk some sense into the rulers, and it didn't turn out well. Queen Marianne was furious. You know, she always wanted to reconcile with her siblings more than anything. Day and night, she dreamed of restoring her relationship with them, and now there they were, begging for eternal peace." I sighed. "People do silly things when what they've been hoping for all along finally comes true. They choose to believe what they want to, no matter how obvious the opposite is. You could imagine Queen Marianne's anger at the fact someone dared to question Alta and Alto's generosity. Queen Marianne even—" I shot Helen a wary look. "She even threatened to...to withdraw Helen's position as the Representative Elder and banish her from the Otherworld."

"What?" All four heiresses looked horrorstruck.

Alexandria looked as if she were about to slam her fist on the table any moment. "Banish Helen? They can't do that! They're believing what they want to and ignoring the truth."

"In fact, they can," said Helen. "They have every right to withdraw my position and banish me. As the rulers, they can do whatever they please. It's within their power."

I put my hand on top of Helen's to comfort her. The heavy shadow over her eyes shattered my heart into a million pieces. It was not until then that I truly understood her dilemma and felt the pressure and anxiety she had felt. It made me realize how important yet difficult it was to remain unwavering during turbulent times of corruption.

"This is outrageous," said Alexandria, burying her head in her arms in dismay so that her words came out muffled. "It's a scandal! A disgrace! What would the Otherworldians say? The royal family is becoming the laughingstock of the Otherworld!"

"And what happened next?" Daphne asked.

"We, all the Elders who were sensible enough to confront the truth, formed a war council to discuss the Otherworld's next step. That's us. All the Elders present." I indicated everyone sitting around the table. "We call ourselves the members of the Inner Circle, and today's our fifth meeting. We've been using this conference room as our headquarters."

"Why didn't you send for us earlier?" Alexandria asked.

"Queen Marianne made it clear in the last assembly that anyone who dared to question Alta and Alto's kindness might as well pack their bags and leave," Eric chimed in. "We didn't want you to get involved."

"And what made you decide to send for us?"

"We talked this over yesterday, and our conclusion was that since the four of you are also a part of the Otherworld, you have a right to know about the recent events. Plus, the Inner Circle could use some support." Eric shook his head. "We're trying to *help* the Otherworld, and the rulers think we're all rebels."

"Corruption," muttered Alexandria, breathing heavily

through her nostrils. "The rulers are the ones who are blind. Helen, I can't believe my mother did that to you. I'm sorry."

"You meant well, and we all agree you've done your best to warn Queen Marianne. It's not your fault she didn't listen." I knew that Helen, as a dutiful Representative Elder, would do everything for the Otherworld. It was ironic her firm loyalty was what caused friction between her and the rulers.

"Of course, it isn't her fault. Queen Marianne's the one who's losing her marbles," agreed Brian. "She's being absurd. Believe me, one day, they'll all regret not listening to us in the first place." With a sigh, he continued. "Come to think of it, it's only my first year in the palace, and already things are getting crazy and out of control. Nobody is in their right mind these days."

"You can say that again," Lilith chimed in. "I feel sorry for those fools down there. Dancing and partying when there's an imminent war. Bet they really fancied those feasts and trashing up the palace, now that King Patrick and Queen Marianne have given them a lame excuse to kick back and take it easy every day. Some party...the so-called peace." She tutted in disapproval. "You're right, Brian. They'll regret not listening to us one day. And mark my words, it'll be too late to remedy their mistake then."

"Honestly, we're lucky Helen hasn't given up," Sheldon said. "The Underworld's going to attack us, sooner or later. Anyone with common sense knows that. We'll all be fighting soon. Maybe today, maybe tomorrow, maybe the day after tomorrow. If our rulers can't lead us to defend the Otherworld, we'll do it ourselves."

"Yes, of course, we will. But...." Alexandria cast an uneasy look at Helen. "No offense, but Helen, aren't you worried about being withdrawn from your position? I mean, this is taking a huge risk, forming the Inner Circle and doing all this." Noticing the reproachful looks on the others' faces, she added, "It's not that I'm against the Inner Circle. Personally, I think it's incredibly brave of you—all of you—to acknowledge and face the truth, rather than shrugging it off like what they're doing. But this might mean paying a huge price for nothing, and it's just so unfair for you. For all of you," she ended in a small voice.

"I see where you're coming from," replied Helen. "You mean it's best to comply with King Patrick and Queen Marianne since they've got the power to remove titles and banish advisors."

"Yes—no. I mean, I didn't mean—"

"If I tell the rulers to stop fantasizing the truth, I'll likely lose my position. But if I play along with them and ignore my duties, it'll be a matter of time before the Underworld takes over. And in that case, there won't be any position to get withdrawn from."

"What do you mean?"

"Just use your logic. If Alta and Alto take over the Otherworld, they'd murder us Elders in fear of a rebellion. And in that case, none of us would stand a chance against them. Representative Elder or not, Alta and Alto will kill me, and the same fate will meet all the Otherworldians who refuse to join the dark side."

A murmur of agreement rippled throughout the other Elders.

"But I'm not going to let my parents—" Alexandria cut in.

"The truth is," Helen plowed on, raising her volume, "I don't care about whether I lose my position or not. Honest. To me, the 'Representative Elder' is nothing but a title, simply the name of the role I am obliged to play. What I truly value is the obligations and responsibilities that I, as the Representative Elder, must shoulder, rather than the honor and privileges of such a position. I must make decisions for the bigger picture, for the greater good, and most importantly, for the future of the Otherworld, at all times."

A tumultuous round of applause greeted Helen's words. I gazed at her, astonished by her resolve and courage.

"Well said," barked Lilith with some sort of fierce approval. "Let's get started right away. What should we do first today?"

"As you know, I've been in the Archive Room these days, flipping through old journals recorded by Elders who have gone on missions to the Underworld. Yesterday, I came across this entry—" Helen picked up one of the books stacked beside her seat and flipped through the yellowed pages. "Here it is. I found an interesting passage that suggests a theory, and it gave me an idea—a goal we could focus on. It mentions that since the terrains in the Underworld revolve around the palace—"

"That's true," confirmed Eric. "My mother—I mean, Alta used to keep me locked in the palace. Sometimes I would sneak out and run away when the servants were busy, and I'd find myself in strange parts of the Underworld. Once when I escaped, I saw that our palace was located in the middle of a tundra, and the next time I snuck out, I found myself surrounded by green mountains."

Sheldon and Willy exchanged whispers of skepticism, and Gidget cast a wondering look at him.

"But hold on for a moment," Brian chimed in. "So the Underworld *really* is a terrain-shifter?"

"It must be, but the problem is how they shift." Evonne cut in. "Might there be a pattern? A nexus between the change of the different terrains?"

"Don't be silly. That's not possible," Lilith said. "Everyone knows that Alta and Alto made the Underworld a terrain-shifter to confuse Otherworldians who entered their world. Every time we arrive at the Underworld, we face different terrains. I don't see why they would create a pattern."

"It could be a very complicated pattern none of us could figure out," suggested Sheldon. "Like what Eric said, I guess he—"

"Is telling a well-rehearsed tale that is far from convincing," remarked Juniper. She snorted and shot Eric a look of contempt. Juniper had never liked Eric, and she was the only one who protested against Eric's application of joining the Elders, though in vain.

Ignoring Juniper's sarcastic response, I asked Eric, "Do they have names? The mountains and rivers and all those savannas, tundras, and geographic landscapes?"

"Yes, but not all of them. Alta never trusted me with the top secrets of the Underworld, which involves the names and positions of the different terrains. She always made sure I was out of earshot while she and Alto and their subordinates were discussing top secrets."

"Tell me everything you know," said Helen, a look of deep interest on her face.

"Well, there's a valley called Evergreen Valley and a cape called Cape Evergreen somewhere near it. There's also a tundra in the Underworld. And of course, there's Mount Maravillas, a huge—"

"Maravillas...," Helen repeated, lapsing into silence for a few moments. "Isn't that the Spanish word for 'wonders'?"

"Right you are," said Brian with a smile, looking delighted that he had an opportunity to show off his knowledge.

"You've got a knack for foreign languages, Helen," said Alexandria, looking half-amused, half-impressed.

"As a language arts teacher who has managed to survive more than one year at a middle school, I daresay I have. Eric, please continue."

"There's a cobblestone path called the Foss Trail that leads to Foss Falls, a waterfall. It's the waterfall we jumped into last time. Well, that's all I know."

"Perfect," said Helen, examining her notes. "So, back to the topic, this paragraph over here suggests it's not impossible to decipher the transformation of the terrains in the Underworld. In other words, there might be a pattern. All we have to do is to figure it out."

"Meaning?" Juniper demanded, donning a mocking expression.

"Meaning we may be able to solve the mystery of the ever-shifting terrains of the Underworld," answered Helen in a crisp manner.

"And how exactly should we do that?" Juniper scowled.

"We draw maps of the Underworld and study the journals I found in the Archive Room."

"And why is that important, may I ask?" Juniper's scowl had become more pronounced.

"Here's a suggestion. Why don't you just get out and leave the room instead of questioning Helen?" I said, pointing at the door.

Juniper rounded on me. "Mind you, I would've happily walked out the door if— "

"Juniper, you promised," Sheldon whispered, shooting his wife a look and silencing her.

"Oh, come on." Juniper rolled her eyes in a dramatic fashion. "Aren't we supposed to be honing our battle skills or whatever and preparing ourselves for the invasion?"

"Really? I thought we were going to brainstorm some ideas and invent weapons or gadgets to fight against the Underworld," said Gidget. "You know, futuristic science-technology stuff like robots, mechanical gadgets— "

"Don't be ridiculous," snapped Juniper.

"I'm not being ridiculous. In fact, I've just started working on my draft of a dwarf-sized airplane."

Juniper snorted. "Oh, really? And what good will your great invention do us, may I ask?"

"Back to the point," Helen said, her voice raised. "I believe we've learned quite enough skills during the past few years of training."

"But what about newcomers like us?" Willy chimed in.

"I suppose you've been taught some decent skills when you were an Elder-in-training. Who was your mentor then?"

"Lilith, but— "

"Good, and I assume it's unlikely that someone as dutiful as she would teach her apprentice nothing," Helen cut in.

"We did cover some rudimentary skills and tactics," said Lilith, looking embarrassed by her protégé's lack of confidence.

"But how are we supposed to face Alta and Alto by using basic skills and—?"

"I assure you the senior Elders can take care of that during the fight. No, I don't think we ought to focus on battling skills and strategies, especially with the four heiresses here. We should devote our time to work out the terrain transformation of the Underworld instead. For starters, if we figure out the pattern of the terrain transformation, it will be much easier to break into the Underworld if we launch attacks on them in the future. Second, if we are able to fully navigate the Underworld, we can predict what lies ahead during our future missions, which means we can be prepared beforehand. Last but not least, we all know that Alta and Alto made the Underworld a terrain-shifter because they wanted to confuse and fluster Otherworldians. By solving the terrain transformation of the Underworld, we will gain more confidence and fight better in the final war."

"You're our best strategist, Helen. I don't know what we'd do without you," I said.

"You're just being modest. I'm sure you'd be able to handle the situation well, even without me," Helen gave me a rare smile, which made my heart skip a beat. "So, if nobody has a problem with this plan, let's all get started," she said, returning to her grim self. She passed a stack of journals to me. "Everyone, take one each."

I flipped to the first entry of my journal and scanned the page.

*Goal of mission: To locate the palace of the Underworld (failed)*

*Date of mission: 21st September 2000*

*Participants of mission: Ingrid Gates (leader), Ferdinand Myers, Andrew Moore, Lilith Jackson*

"Hey, Lilith, I see your name here."

"Really? When was that?"

"September twenty-first, two thousand."

"Ah, yes, I remember that one. Good old Ingrid Gates led that mission. It was the last mission she ever led. Pity, she didn't survive the next one," Lilith sighed. "Read it aloud, won't you?"

"Sure," I said, poring over the entry. "'As we left for the Underworld, we found ourselves transported to a valley with blooming flowers and cerulean lakes—'"

"Evergreen Valley," muttered Eric under his breath.

"Sorry?"

"Evergreen Valley," he said aloud. "I'm almost positive. I heard Alta talk about it when I was little. It's a place of eternal spring, the prettiest place in the Underworld. It's so beautiful there that it seems...surreal."

"Very well, I'll copy that down," said Helen, scribbling on a piece of paper.

"I think we were there on our last mission," said Evonne, casting a glance at Helen and then at me. I nodded, remembering the misty hills there.

"The most dangers often lie in the most beautiful places," Eric said in a strained voice. "Go on, Zack."

"'We then had a narrow escape when running away from some devils and devilines. After hurrying along the bank of a large river for a few hours, we ended up in a forest, and that was where we spent the night. The next day, we navigated our way through the forest and came across a huge magical swamp. We planned to ford across it at first, but as we were about to reach the opposite shore, the swamp immobilized and tried to swallow us. Fortunately, we got away in the end, thanks to our youngest member, who saved us by braiding the vines of a nearby tree and using it as a rope to save us. After that close call, we proceeded on and came to a cobblestone path. However, we were ambushed by a two-story-tall canary—'"

"The Chirpy Bird," Alexandria interrupted. "Wonder if it's the same bird we met last time."

"That's possible. I know for a fact there are two Chirpy Birds in the Underworld," Eric added. "Sorry, Zack. Keep reading."

"'However, we were ambushed by a two-story-tall canary. We put up a fight with it, and this time, we barely survived. Not only did it dominate us in size, but it was also invincible to weapons. The odds were against us. To make matters worse, two of our members got maimed by the bird. We had no choice but to run for our lives while dragging our injured companions. We couldn't continue our mission anymore since two of us were in no shape to fight. Finally, we managed to throw the bird off when we reached a dilapidated suspension bridge. After crossing it, we came to a savanna and spotted a fountain sitting in the tall tufts of grass. We tried it, hoping it would be the aquaportal to the Otherworld, but no luck. Just when we thought things couldn't get worse, a tiger-cat attacked—' Yes, Alexandria?" I noticed her raised hand.

"Not sure if you've realized, but the writer is talking about the savanna and cobblestone path we came across on our last mission. Same terrains, same monsters. Like Eric said, that's—"

"Foss Trail," finished Eric himself. "You copied that, Helen?"

She nodded and motioned for me to continue.

"'A tiger-cat attacked us. We ran away from it and soon found ourselves facing a haunted house that had a garden with black rose bushes. We spotted a fountain in the middle of it and fortunately made it back to the Otherworld this time. Our mission was a failure, but we were lucky none of our fellow Elders suffered permanent damage.'" I looked up from the journal. "So, what have we learned about the Underworld after reading this?"

"They were transported to Evergreen Valley and left the Underworld through a fountain portal in front of a haunted manor," Brian summarized the entry.

"But Zack," Alexandria piped up. "Isn't the Underworld supposed to be a terrain-shifter? Foss Trail led us to the suspension bridge the last time we went to the Otherworld. I thought the terrains mentioned in the journal should be different from what we saw on our last mission."

"I don't think so," Brian said. "The third entry in my journal corresponds with the terrains mentioned in the one Zack read."

"Read yours aloud," said Helen, scribbling a few more lines on her paper.

"*Goal of mission*—"

"Just tell me the terrains and landscapes mentioned in the journal," Helen interrupted him. "I want to confirm something."

"All right. The Elders were transported to a prairie by a forest. Then, they uh...sort of wandered to Evergreen Valley, and a deviline chased them to another prairie. They crossed a suspension bridge and came to a savanna. And after that, a tiger-cat attacked them. And here's my point—they made a run for it and reached the haunted manor. Just like the one Zack—"

"Where was the aquaportal that took them back to the Otherworld?" Helen cut in.

"Um...let me see...the fountain in the middle of a labyrinth of granite pillars. It was beside the haunted manor."

"A labyrinth? Goodness, might it be the one we...?" Helen, Lilith, Evonne, and I exchanged significant looks with each other. We had had a traumatic experience the last time we were trapped in the maze. Evonne had been maimed and lost her memory for six months. She had not recovered until last year when the Gem of Hope was restored and healed her.

"Yeah, I guess so," Brian said in a perfunctory manner. "Listen, I just had a theory. It sounds impossible and pretty ridiculous, but I think I could give it—"

"It doesn't matter," Helen cut in, waving her hand in impatience. "It's all right to make assumptions. Just carry on."

"Well...." Brian brushed his shoulder-length black hair out of his eyes and took a deep breath. "I think the Underworld is not a terrain-shifter," he started in a small yet firm voice. "The only thing that's changing is the portals—the entrances and exits to it. This is the only plausible explanation. Also, I don't believe the palace is the hub of the Underworld. The terrains are also changing around it."

His words were followed by the loudest silence I had ever heard.

"Or at least, that's what the evidence suggests," Brian added, wringing his hands in nervousness.

"I think he's right," said Alexandria in a hushed voice.

"But it's been confirmed that—" started Lilith.

"Confirmed?" Brian repeated. "Says who? Nobody has ever actually confirmed that. No offense, but there are no statistics, no evidence, and no theories about the Underworld being a terrain-shifter. I've been in the Archive Room with Helen and Zack during the past couple of days, and I found no proof from the journals, documents, and research books that confirms the Underworld is a terrain-shifter. What makes you so certain it is one, Lilith?"

"Well, we've always been told—"

"Been told? People can be misleading. From *our* point of view, the terrains in the Underworld are forever changing. But on the other hand, if we view things from the *Underworld's* point of view, we are the ones that are changing—or to be accurate, the portals that took us there are the ones that are changing. Know what I mean?"

"But Brian...." Helen scanned her notes, struggling to find proof to contradict his words. "A flawless theory," she admitted in the end. "Impressive, very impressive indeed."

A murmur of approval erupted throughout the Elders.

"In that case, we'll be able to figure out the positions of the terrains and the exact locations of the aquaportals," said Helen.

"Of course—but now I'm getting hungry." Alexandria rubbed her stomach. "What's the time now?"

"It's...." I checked my watch. "Oh, it's already seven. I suppose dinner's ready."

"Very well, then. We'll continue our research on the Underworld during our next meeting," decided Helen. "We're going to meet here at eight in the morning tomorrow. Meeting adjourned."

The Elders got to their feet and left the room in twos and threes, while Eric and the four heiresses stayed behind.

"Where are they going?" Alexandria asked me.

"Downstairs. To conference room 302. We've booked it all to ourselves, and that's where we'll be having dinner."

"Aren't you coming with us? You and Helen?"

"Um...." I glanced at Helen, who was jotting down notes and muttering under her breath, having no intention of leaving. "I'm staying here with her."

"Alexandria," a voice said. It was Evonne, with tiny Gidget by her side. "Care to sit with me at dinner?"

Alexandria beamed with pleasure. "Sure."

"Wonderful! I'd love to hear you relate your adventure in person." Grinning, Evonne skipped out of the conference room. Gidget cast an admiring look at Alexandria before following Evonne out.

"Oh Alexandria, got yourself some new fans, haven't

you?" Daphne teased.

Alexandria's face flushed red, but before she could answer—

"I'd keep my distance from them if I were you," came Juniper's cold voice.

"Hello, Aunt Juniper," Alexandria greeted her. Her warm smile faltered at Juniper's icy expression.

"As a member of the royal family, Alexandria, there's a very high chance you will join the Elders when you are of age. I suppose you're turning sixteen next year. You will be eligible to join us then."

"Yeah, I'd like that," Alexandria said.

"And in that case, you should be more selective about your friends. Trust me, you won't want someone indecent on your side."

"What do you mean?"

"Evonne Fitzgerald and Gidget Chase?" Juniper smirked. "You can do so much better than them."

"Don't be so mean," said Alexandria in a low voice.

Juniper ignored her. "Evonne is one of the worst fighters here in the Inner Circle, and Gidget the crackpot—"

"I am perfectly clear of who is a crackpot and who isn't, thank you very much," Alexandria retaliated, her voice dripping with contempt.

The corners of Eric's mouth twitched. He poked Eileen in the arm, and both grinned.

"Is that intended as sarcasm? Are you insulting your aunt?" Juniper demanded, whipping out her wand.

Helen stood up. "Juniper Richardson, do not threaten Alexandria in front of me."

Juniper raised her eyebrows. "I am her aunt."

"While I happen to be her godmother."

Recognizing defeat, Juniper shot Helen a withering look before turning on her heels and marching out of the conference room.

Alexandria's eyes followed her aunt as she left. "What's her problem?"

"Don't mind her. She's always been annoying," I said.

"Annoying? That's an understatement. She's a mean old cow, that's what!" Eric said, indignant. Then, catching a glimpse of Helen's expression, he muttered a quick apology.

"No need to apologize, Eric. You're right. I don't like her much. Come to think of it, she's my aunt...." Alexandria groaned.

"You don't have to talk to her if you don't want to," Daphne said. "I don't like her much, either. Come on, let's get going. I'm starving. We'll see you both around." She waved at Helen and me before following the other heiresses out of the conference room.

"And that leaves us." I scooted my chair closer to Helen. "What are you studying?"

"I'm trying to draw a map, but these descriptions aren't making sense at all," she said, crumpling the piece of paper she had been drawing on.

"We'll figure it out eventually," I assured her. "Let's go to the Archive Room. I saw a huge bookshelf there yesterday, and it's filled with books about the history of the Underworld. Perhaps we'll be able to find a clue or two."

"Good idea."

As Helen stood up to leave, she swayed where she stood and grabbed the back of a chair for support.

"Helen, are you all right?" I laced an arm around her shoulders to steady her. "You look paler than usual."

Helen closed her eyes and pressed a hand to her forehead. "Nothing, I'm just...dizzy. It's been going on like this for days." Then, seeing the concern on my face, she added, "I—never mind. It's been a long time since I had a full night's sleep. I stayed up for many days but still didn't manage to decipher anything."

"You need some fresh air? Or do you want to go to the infirmary? I can come along with you."

"Zack, it's...it's nothing."

"But...." I wanted to utter a reply, but words failed me. My brain was becoming fuzzy. For some reason, I found my mind randomly grasping details about Helen, like the bracelet of pearls I'd given her last month and the necklace with the amethyst teardrop pendant she had hardly ever taken off.

"Don't worry about me. Really, I'm fine," said Helen. "Let's go to the Archive Room straight away."

"You should rest first," I insisted. "We'll go to the Archive Room when you're feeling better. May I escort you back to your room?"

Helen hesitated for a fraction of a moment, but I couldn't help feeling a tingle of joy when she nodded.

# Chapter Four

## The Elders
## (Alexandria)

Dinner that night was a rather cheerful event. We joined the members of the Inner Circle for a delectable meal of assorted vegetables, broiled meat, rich gravy, cheese casseroles, and sparkling pineapple and blueberry smoothies. The vibrant colors and the alluring aroma of the food added to its delicacy. Dessert, which consisted of golden oranges, silver apples, blue and brown bananas, and bearnix-shaped cherry-and-almond tarts drenched in syrup, was served after the meal.

"What's with the bananas?" I asked, pretending to develop a sudden interest in them. I was glad to have a change of topic, for Evonne, Gidget, and Uncle Sheldon had been bombarding me with questions about my last adventure for the past two hours. Or, to be more accurate, Evonne and Uncle Sheldon were asking most of the questions while Gidget listened with a polite smile on her face. It turned out that the three of them were good friends. They were all interested in me, and I liked them in return. Evonne, Gidget, and Uncle Sheldon were very much alike, all cheerful and easy to be around.

"The brown ones are chocolate-flavored bananas, and the blue ones are peppermint-flavored," answered Uncle Sheldon.

"Chocolate and peppermint bananas?" I repeated. "How

do they taste?"

Uncle Sheldon looked as though he didn't know whether to laugh or not, and he finally compromised with a smile. "Well, like bananas mixed with chocolate and peppermint, obviously."

"Oh, don't be silly, Sheldon," said Evonne, suppressing a grin. She turned to me. "The brown bananas are coated with chocolate, while the blue bananas contain little chunks of peppermint candy inside." She peeled a blue banana and snapped it in half. "See?"

"Interesting. What do you think?" I asked Eileen, who was sitting on my right.

"What's the harm in trying one?" she said with a shrug, reaching for a blue banana.

"Wait a second, Eileen," said Eric. "Try this baby first. You'll love it. Here you go." He poked a small cherry-and-almond tart into her mouth.

"Eric!" Eileen protested with her mouth full, little crumbs dropping on her plate.

"Do you like it?" Eric asked.

Eileen chewed, swallowed, and nodded.

"Great. Then try this, too. You'll definitely like it," said Eric, handing Eileen a plump silver apple.

I watched her take a large bite of the sparkling apple. "How does it taste?"

"Like a mixture of my favorite fruits. Pineapples and oranges."

"That's funny. Isn't it supposed to be an apple?" I took another silver apple from the platter and took a bite. It had a delightful taste of crunchy, blended fruits. "Hmm, this is interesting...a mixture of my favorite fruits as well—grapes, peaches, and berries."

"I didn't know these apples come in different flavors," said Eileen, taking another bite. "They all look the same."

"You mean those silver apples?" Evonne replied. "The taste and flavor of a silver apple depends on the fruits the eater likes. It tastes differently according to everyone."

"Cool. Is it the same with golden oranges?"

"No. All the golden oranges taste the same, a rich combination of all the citrus fruits. Oranges, grapefruits, lemons, tangerines, and so on. Care for one?"

Since I had never been a big fan of citrus fruits, I passed.

Eileen, on the other hand, nodded. "Three, please," she said, passing one of the oranges to Clarissa and the other to Daphne, who was chatting with Brian.

"Thanks," Clarissa said, digging her nails into the golden orange to peel it.

Daphne and Brian were too immersed in their conversation to notice the fruit. She was asking about the meat dishes and how the Otherworldians managed to get their hands on pork, beef, chicken, and fish. Brian explained that they imported meat from the mortals every month since eating bearnixes, unibirds, kittenpillars, and dogfishes were forbidden in the Otherworld.

"Where does pork come from, anyway?" Uncle Sheldon asked, joining their conversation.

"Pigs," answered Daphne.

"Wigs? Or is it figs?"

"I said 'pigs,'" said Daphne, her voice trembling with giggles.

Uncle Sheldon framed the word with his lips. "Interesting. Then what about beef?"

"That's easy," Evonne cut in. "Anyone who's been in the mortal world knows beef comes from cows."

"'Cows'?" repeated Uncle Sheldon. "That word exists?"

"Of course, dummy," said Daphne. "Ever consulted a dictionary before?"

The three of them chuckled.

In other circumstances, I would have found their positivity contagious. But joking at inappropriate times like this irritated me. How could they have the heart to goof off when the Otherworld was in danger? Frowning, I looked away from them.

"Eric, do you know what's going on downstairs right now?" I asked. I still found it hard to believe that King Patrick and Queen Marianne were hosting balls and feasts and refusing to believe the fact that the Underworld was likely to invade anytime.

"Well, the usual stuff, you know. Some fancy event...the chefs have been exhausted these days, catering the food for them. Word's that one third are planning to resign from their jobs soon. The guards, on the other hand, have been sneaking out of the palace and enjoying life these days since they've got pretty much nothing to do."

"The chefs and guards? Kittenpillars?" Eileen said, her eyes widening.

"Not exactly. The kittenpillars in the palace work as chefs, doctors, nurses, and designers, while the bearnixes, dogfishes, and unibirds are guards. They also work as our messengers. They carry mail and parcels to the king and queen and the Elders."

"What about Ella?" I asked, recalling the adorable kittenpillar we had come across in the courtyard last time. "What does she do?"

"Ella is King Patrick's pet," said Eric, taking a huge bite of his cherry tart. "She doesn't have to work or do anything. Lucky her. But on the other hand, she doesn't get paid."

"The chefs, guards, and the others all have salaries and holidays, don't they?"

"Of course. They get paid as much as we regular Elders. King Patrick and Queen Marianne have always been very kind to the attendants in the palace." Eric looked slightly uneasy. "But the chefs are overworked these days because of the crazy stuff that's been going on."

"Ridiculous." I shook my head. "I'm going to talk some sense into King Patrick and Queen Marianne as soon as I meet them."

"But Alexandria, they won't listen—" Eric started.

"Well, I don't care about—"

"Where do you think they've gone?" Eileen whispered to us.

"How am I supposed to know where my mom—?"

"I meant Helen and Zack. Just wondering where they went for dinner or whether they'd skipped it."

"Oh." I surveyed the table and registered their absence.

"You're right. I didn't even notice before you pointed that out."

"They always skip dinner, the two of them," said Eric, restraining a smile. "I guess they've gone to the Archive Room to study the journals."

"What's so funny about that?" I asked.

"Well—oh, all right, don't tell them I said this, but I think they sort of...like each other, Helen and Zack."

"You're joking!" Eileen and I exchanged a look of incredulity. Clarissa's mouth dropped open, and Daphne choked on her pineapple smoothie.

"I understand why you're surprised," said Eric. "I mean, Helen's not the type that would go chasing after and swooning for boys."

Everyone roared with laughter, and even Brian, who had been listening to our conversation all along, cracked a smile.

"That's the most accurate statement I've ever heard," Clarissa said, gasping for breath between gulps of laughter.

"It's the truth," Eric remarked. "I wouldn't call Helen a beauty, but she's definitely graceful enough."

Brian pouted at Eric as though pretending to be angry with him. "Honestly, love is not as superficial as you think. It's far beyond that."

"Really?" Eric put on an amused expression. "Would you mind sharing some of your insights on that topic, great genius? What, in your brilliant mind, do you think true love takes?"

Brian rolled his eyes at Eric's immaturity. "Mutual support and admiration, obviously. The events two people have been through that brought their hearts together—Hey, look, the others are clearing out."

"What time is it?" I asked.

Brian glanced at his watch. "Oh, it's already nine-thirty, no wonder."

The four of us stood up to leave. Clarissa and Daphne took a few more blue bananas with them, and Eileen pocketed a cherry tart. We filed out of conference room 302 and into the corridor.

"Hey, girls," said a voice. It was Lilith.

"Hello," I greeted her as the others nodded. "Good to see

that you're in the Inner Circle as well."

Lilith sighed. "I never thought things would evolve to what they are today. The only bright side is how it's given us a chance to prove ourselves to King Patrick and Queen Marianne. Although I've always wanted the rulers to...to like me more, I didn't want any of this to happen."

A fount of pity for her welled up in me. "You said you wanted King Patrick and Queen Marianne to like you more?" I asked in a gentle voice.

Lilith nodded, her eyes sad like a puppy's. "They don't seem to value me much."

"Don't say that," said Eileen, placing her hand on Lilith's arm. "Why would they send you to the fountain and take us here last time if they didn't value you?"

"Well, they thought I knew you four the best, I guess," Lilith said. "Or maybe it's because they needed Helen and Zack more, so they kept them by their side."

"We need you as much as they need them," Daphne assured her. "You're one of our favorite Elders."

I was astonished to see Daphne comforting someone else. It was unlike her to offer solace to people in need. Nevertheless, it was more than heartwarming to witness her transformation.

Lilith smiled. "Don't get me wrong. I'm not jealous of Helen and Zack, though I admit it can be hard to remain this way sometimes. But there are times every person wants to be the best, right?"

Clarissa nodded. "Don't worry, Lilith. We support you."

Eileen, Daphne, and I echoed her sentiment, and Lilith beamed again. She gave us a wave before retiring to her room.

"Poor Lilith," said Clarissa. "She's so underrated. I've always suspected the rulers didn't like her as much as they liked Helen and Zack. Turns out I was right."

"I'd love to go on a mission with her," I agreed. "She would no doubt do a good job protecting us."

"You think she ever gets jealous of Helen?" Eileen said in a quiet voice. "The way she claimed she wasn't jealous of her and Zack.... I don't know. It sounded a bit unnatural to me."

"Oh, yes," said Daphne. "Of course, she envies Helen. I mean, who wouldn't? Zack's crazy about her. You all remember how the girls in our school never stop talking about how handsome he is? Blond hair like the sun, blue eyes like the sea— "

"Wait a minute, stop," said Eileen, the corners of her lips curling into a smile. "Why does it sound to me like you're the one who's in love with Zack?"

"I'm just stating a *fact*," said Daphne, stressing the last word. "I wouldn't want to fight Helen for him."

Clarissa thumped her on the head. "Girl, do you know what you're saying? He's thirty something, at least twenty years older than you. He could be your dad."

"Yeah," agreed Eileen. "Plus, Helen's going to kill you for that. Try her. I hate to imagine what a bloody mess you'd be after a duel with her, assuming that you survive."

"Blah, whatever," said Daphne, rolling her eyes. "So, are we staying in the palace tonight?"

Eileen let out a squeal of delight. "That'd be wonderful! Let's go find the Elders and ask them."

"Your Highness." A dogfish and a bearnix, both looking familiar, hurried toward us.

I recognized them as the guards outside the Throne Room. "Noir? Bessie? Is that you?"

"You remember us," Bessie said, smiling. I noticed four vials clutched in her vermillion wings. Noir bowed, and Bessie raised a wing in salute as the two of them approached us. The bearnixes, unibirds, kittenpillars, and dogfishes had their own language, but Noir and Bessie, being the guards, were trained to speak English.

"Your Highness, Miss Dawson, Miss Spencer, and Miss Sinclair," Noir addressed us. "King Patrick and Queen Marianne know about your arrival, and they invite you to spend a month at the palace. You will be staying in rooms 601 to 604, the first four rooms on the sixth floor. They've just been cleaned out. Oh, and your belongings have been transported there by magic—you'll find them in your rooms."

Clarissa, Eileen, and Daphne exchanged looks of glee.

"King Patrick also reckons it would be better if you all change into gowns and try to blend in with the other Elders," said Bessie. "This way, you'd attract less attention. Your new outfits will be ready in a week. Meanwhile, you might have to make do with the clothes you're wearing. Here." She handed us each a vial with limpid contents. "The thorough-cleaning concoction. Just three drops on your clothes, and they'll be good as new."

"Awesome," breathed Clarissa. "Then let's get going. I can't wait to see what our rooms look like!"

"Your Highness...may I have a quick word with you?" Noir asked.

"Sure." I turned to the others. "Just go without me. I'll catch up with you later."

They nodded, laughing and chatting as they mounted the spiral staircase.

"Yes, Noir?"

"Your Highness, do you know about the recent events?"

I uttered a heavy sigh. "Yes, Helen told us. The Underworld sent a messenger to make peace with the Otherworld, and King Patrick and Queen Marianne believed him. They've been hosting all sorts of fancy events in the Otherworld since then. Are you talking about that?"

Noir and Bessie nodded their expressions grave. "Your Highness, what do you plan to do?"

"What can I do? Anyone with common sense knows the Underworld's going to invade anytime. I'm going to work with the Inner Circle and focus on defending the Otherworld. Noir, Bessie, haven't you two tried talking some sense into the king and queen? You're supposed to be guarding the Throne Room, aren't you?"

"They're deaf to anyone who claims the Underworld is plotting to attack us." Bessie looked as if she were about to spout fire.

"You know what happened to Lady Helen, don't you?" Noir asked. "Nobody is foolish enough to follow in her footsteps and contradict the rulers these days. Better to sit back, shut our mouths, and let them be. Brave and wise Lady Helen was, but got herself into hot water with King Patrick and Queen Marianne."

"But Your Highness, we support you. Me and Noir. After all, it's better to accept the truth than believe a lie."

"Noir, Bessie, thanks. Please keep me updated in the future and report anything unusual to me. Good night to you."

"Yes, Your Highness. We'll take our leave."

As I ascended flight after flight of stairs, I thought about everything that had happened today. All I knew was that the Otherworld was doomed. The Underworld was more than likely to launch an assault on us anytime, and it would be impossible to fight back. Still numbed by disbelief, I didn't know what to think or feel. I yearned for someone to talk to, someone to confer with, someone who would understand....

Eric, a small voice in my head suggested.

***

"Sixth floor...sixth floor...," I muttered to myself. "601, 602...."

"Alexandria?" The figure of Eric emerged from the dim-lit corridor ahead. "Oh, here you are. I was just looking for you."

"Me? Why?"

"Thought you'd like someone to talk to. I'd be feeling very overwhelmed right now if I were you. Want to come to my room and have a chat?"

An upsurge of affection for my cousin gushed up inside me. "I'd like that."

"Come along, then." Eric walked to room 605 and stuffed his wand through the peephole. "Wand identification," he explained.

The door swung open, and I followed him into the living room. Three squashy lime armchairs surrounded a small table with ornate carvings. On it perched a potted plant with long blades of leaves, adorned with tiny white and turquoise flowers. Beneath our feet was a plush mint-green carpet with odd shapes and lines, like an abstract painting. A small chandelier that dangled from the ceiling illuminated the whole room with a warm glow.

Eric disappeared into another room and came out with a

plate of cupcakes. "Want one?"

I shook my head. "Not in the mood."

"Come on," said Eric coaxingly. "A cupcake a day keeps bad moods away."

"Well, all right." Not wanting to hurt his feelings, I chose a cupcake with blueberries, purple frosting, and white chocolate sprinkles. "Hmm, not bad."

"Okay, then," Eric said, plopping himself down in one of the armchairs and undoing his bow tie.

"What about Eileen?"

"What about her?"

"She won't get angry or upset if she sees the two of us here, will she?"

Eric laughed. "Of course not. She can't get in here, anyway. Not unless I open the door to admit her. Now, Alexandria, you must have a lot of questions. Spit them out when you're ready."

"I...." Doing my best to fight against the torrent of emotions, I forced myself to go on. "It's just that...you know, Eric, I've never had a true home or anything that makes me me before I knew about the Otherworld. It's the one and only place I belong, and I can't help but realize so much has changed. For some reason, everything seems so foreign and faraway. I feel lonelier than ever and as if I'll never be happy again."

"I know," Eric replied. "The whole making peace incident has changed pretty much everything. But Alexandria, you've still got us—me, Clarissa, Eileen, and Daphne, right? And Helen, Zack, Lilith, and everyone else in the Inner Circle."

"They've been acting really distant to us. Helen and Zack, I mean."

"Ah, well, of course, they're not too cheerful these days, under the current circumstances. Can't blame them. You know Helen. She values her duties as the Representative Elder more than anything. I suppose she's pretty overburdened these days. You see, with the king and queen frolicking all day long, Helen's left in charge of everything. Organizing defenses, leading the Inner Circle, deciphering the terrains...I wouldn't be surprised if the stress is wearing her down. Of course, I've volunteered to help a few times, but I'm just a new Elder, and I don't know much. As for Zack, he's trying to help her with all her duties and stuff since he's a senior Elder. But I think he's actually trying to win Helen's affection and court her like Brian said. I guess Zack's also been having a rough time. He probably wants to confess his love for Helen but can't because she's so stressed these days, and he doesn't want to pressure her even more."

I couldn't help laughing at his assumptions. "Some romance expert, are you?"

"Hey, cousin, there's a reason why I got my sweetheart before you did."

"Duh," I smiled. "How can you be so sure that Zack likes Helen, anyway?"

"You know…." A mischievous look flashed in Eric's eyes as he said this. "I saw him kissing Helen's hand the day before yesterday."

"Isn't that supposed to be a gesture of courtesy?"

"Come on," Eric said. "You don't see people kissing each other's hand nowadays just because of courtesy or whatever. You've got to admit it's super obvious. He likes her. Gosh, it's really hard to communicate with you people who don't believe in romance."

Grinning, I stuck out my tongue at him.

"Feeling happier?"

"Yeah, thanks."

"Hey, what are cousins for?" Eric winked at me. "Anything else you want to ask?"

"Speaking of cousins, having you been seeing Jacob and Samantha lately?" I said. Jacob and Samantha were my two other cousins who lived in the Otherworld.

"Um, not often. You know their mom, Juniper. She doesn't like me."

"What...? Oh, yeah. I forgot Juniper's their mother. Is she always that annoying?"

"Bit of a nuisance to be around, yeah. Juniper didn't want to be in the Inner Circle in the first place—she joined because of Sheldon, her husband. She really hates Gidget, by the way."

"Gidget? Why? I thought Juniper hated Evonne?"

"Juniper dislikes Evonne but hates Gidget. Feels jealous of her, more like."

"Jealous? How come?"

"Long story. For starters, Gidget beat Juniper in the Elders' recruitment test. You see, when an Otherworldian wants to join the Elders, he or she will have to first get a mentor among the current Elders and get trained for a year."

"But you—"

"I was allowed to skip the one-year training process and the test because the rulers believed I had gone on a mission and proved myself worthy of being an Elder. As for the others who want to join, a recruitment test will be held after their year of training. There are four categories in the recruitment test, twenty-five points for each. Only the top twenty are qualified to join the Elders."

"And what are the four categories?"

"Archery, swordplay, dressage, and spells."

"By dressage, you mean using unibirds as horses, right?"

Eric nodded. "To see how well the candidates can fly on them. Right, so back to the point. Sheldon has been serving King Patrick and Queen Marianne ever since they created the Otherworld, so everyone had very high hopes for him and, naturally, his wife, Juniper. They expected her to come in first in every category. Juniper's only advantage was dressage, and her performance in the other categories was lousy. However, she lost to Gidget in the dressage test, and because of this, she didn't make it into the top twenty. Juniper wouldn't have made the cut if Patrick and Marianne hadn't decided to accept ten more candidates this year."

Eric poured himself a goblet of silver potion from a flask, which gave off the impression of liquid metal. "Deluxe sparkling cherry wine," he said to the goblet. The silvery substance turned into a brilliant shade of red and gleamed as though rubies had been added into the drink. "Want some?"

"What's that?"

"Depends on what you want it to be." Eric filled another

crystal goblet with the silvery substance. "What's your favorite drink?"

"Um...iced grape tea with coconut jelly and a cherry floating on top?"

The silver liquid in the goblet turned into a vivid magenta with translucent blocks of jelly, and a big red cherry materialized on the top.

"Then iced grape tea with coconut jelly and a floating cherry it is!"

Taken aback, I stared at the beverage as though it had come from another planet.

"Well, drink up, silly," Eric said, grinning. "It's not poisoned."

I blinked and took a careful sip, letting the cool, sweet liquid caress my taste buds. "Interesting...."

"You can say that again," said Eric, taking another swig of his cherry wine.

"Yeah." I brought my goblet to my lips and ate the cherry. "Wait, where were we? Oh, right. So Juniper hates Gidget just because she beat her in the recruitment test? What a sore loser."

"Tell me about it. Juniper reckons that Gidget tampered with her unibird and made her fail the test."

"Hold on, Eric. Do you know how old Uncle Sheldon is?"

"Thirty-four."

"But Juniper looks no older than twenty."

"You know, there's another reason Juniper hates Gidget. Sheldon's first wife, Elysia Adams, was a clever Otherworldian who made great contributions in agriculture. Since Sheldon was a member of the royal family, everyone thought he'd marry another powerful Otherworldian after his first wife died. Much to everyone's surprise, though, he fell in love with the daughter of a rich businessman. Yes, that's her—Juniper Smith. She was neither as skilled at magic nor as talented as Elysia Adams. Now, let's talk about Gidget, an exceptionally talented Otherworldian. She had been inventing potions and crafting dwarf-sized weapons since the age of seven. Because of this, Juniper envied her potential. Plus, Gidget was very good friends with Sheldon, which reminded Juniper, even more of her predecessor. I've heard some rumors about Sheldon and Juniper. Word is that they don't get along too well."

"Yeah? Well, it's not Uncle Sheldon's fault. Anyone locked up in the same room with that old bat would go crazy. I don't think I'd mind if Sheldon divorced her and married Gidget, though. Gidget seems pretty nice, shy and sweet. I can't imagine anyone hating her. What do you think?"

Eric laughed. "You know, Alexandria, in fact, she reminds me of you a lot. Different, yet beautiful in your own ways. Like you, she always had unconventional thoughts. Gidget could think outside the box, which others couldn't. It made her seem odd, eccentric and rather crazy, different from ordinary people. But in fact, she was way brighter and cleverer than the fools who looked down on her."

"Does Gidget know the other Elders don't like her?"

"I think so. They're always voicing their disapproval of her. But I don't think she took the mean things personally. She's pretty detached, you see. She lives in a world of her own."

"I wonder what her family was like," I said. "Didn't she tell us her father was the king of a tribe of dwarves who married a human?"

"I know her family background. Rather a sad story, come to think of it. When dwarves used to roam freely all over the Underworld, the Underworldians forced them to relocate deeper into the mountains, and that was where they stayed for a few centuries. But Alta and Alto weren't satisfied. They thought of the dwarves as barbarians. They wanted to unify all the dwarf tribes and make them civilized, but when the dwarves refused to yield, Alta and Alto launched a genocide on them for their disobedience. Poor Gidget. She witnessed almost her entire tribe perish in the genocide, unable to help her people. She and her family were the only survivors."

I felt a dreadful mixture of pity and horror. "That's awful. You couldn't tell that by just looking at her. How did you know all those details of her background?"

"Overheard Helen telling Zack one night. I couldn't

believe it myself when I heard it. But Gidget's not the only one with a tragic past."

"What do you mean?"

Eric sighed. "As you might know, all the Otherworldians consider being an Elder a noble profession. The Elders are the only ones deemed wise and competent enough to serve the king and queen. Every year, countless young, talented Otherworldians who are of age want to join the Elders."

"Of age? Sixteen?"

Eric nodded. "Yes. Most Otherworldians are keen to join the Elders at first but end up resigning. Can you guess why?"

"Well...." Not wanting to look like a fool, I took a sip of my grape tea instead of completing my sentence.

"Many were eager to become Elders in the first place because of the honor, rights, and privileges. Being able to live in the palace like aristocrats, dressing up fashionably, having decent feasts...and so on. However, most newcomers choose to quit in the end, after experiencing the true life of an Elder and realizing how far from their expectations it is. We have to attend training sessions and meetings every day. Also, King Patrick and Queen Marianne send Elders on missions to the Underworld from time to time, and not everyone survives every mission...there could be deaths or injuries. Plus, the Elders are always the ones to fight at the front line in battles and protect the Otherworld during invasions. In those cases, it's not about having delicious meals or dressing up beautifully anymore. It's a matter of life and death, witnessing your companions die right in front of you, life wiped from their bodies in a blink of an eye. It's about the experience of knowing how it feels to be only inches away from your demise, realizing you might be facing your final moments right now, aware of the fact that making a simple mistake, a wrong step, a poor choice...and it's likely the last thing you ever do. Many Elders couldn't take the pressure and trauma, and so they left. I learned all this the hard way because of the attacks last week—the attacks that took place before the messenger's visit. It was awful. Seven Elders and ten guards were gone."

"But what about the other Elders? The ones who chose to

stay and fight rather than call it quits and run away like cowards?"

"Alexandria, only the ones who have suffered will gain strength and resilience. Take the members of the Inner Circle as an example. They all have their reasons why they chose to stay and fight. Gidget? She saw her own tribespeople killed right before her eyes when she was only a teen. She knew what extreme measures the Siblings would resort to, knew that they'd secure their throne and power at all costs. Brian? His girlfriend gave her life to save him when Alta and Alto tried to persecute them. Like Gidget, he saw how horrible the Siblings could be, how they would spare no effort to get rid of the people that stood up to them. Willy? He had had a few cousins who belonged to an organization of rebels. One of the members betrayed them and sold them out to the Siblings, and Alto tortured the rebels into insanity. Willy, too, knew exactly how brutal Alta and Alto could be. And Connie and Cameron, the twin brother and sister? They weren't actually twins; they were triplets. They had a triplet brother named Colin, who perished at the hands of Alta and Alto when he was only three. All of them, Gidget, Brian, Willy, Connie, and Cameron, they all knew what it was like, how it felt to be helpless, grief-stricken, witnessing their family or friends' deaths. They've all been there." Eric paused, an inscrutable expression on his face. "Terrible, isn't it?"

"Terrible," I echoed him, shaking my head. *How much blood has been shed over the past decades because of the Siblings? How many innocent lives have been destroyed? How many families have been torn apart? Would this ongoing tragedy end one day?*

"However," Eric's voice gradually got steadier, "this gave them something worth fighting for, someone worth avenging—their loved ones, who all suffered at the hands of the tyrants. It made them tough. It gave them strength. It united them, giving them a common goal. Because of their pasts, they gained the courage and momentum to fight against the Underworld."

Eric's words left me pondering. I felt as though I had beheld something horrendous, painful, yet sublime. Perhaps this was what history looked like—tragic yet epic, like the life of a hero.

"Sometimes," Eric went on, "I wonder whether Helen had a dark past of her own and why she's always acting so decent yet aloof. Why did she choose to fight for the Otherworld in the first place?"

"Devotion to the rulers, I suppose," I replied, contemplating the possibilities of what lay beneath Helen's fierce determination and unwavering loyalty.

"I heard that her father died when she was just a baby," said Eric. "Maybe it's got something to do with the Siblings."

"Really? I didn't know that," I admitted. "Helen would never tell us if we asked, anyway. Perhaps she had a very hard childhood."

"And Zack, too. He was always funny and easygoing, but I'm starting to wonder if he's as cheerful as he seems on the outside."

Eric's words kindled a spark of curiosity in me. I wondered if Zack had been concealing an unspeakable past of his own.

"You reckon he'll tell us if we ask him?"

"Definitely not. If he's got a tragic past that's been bothering him all along, he's hiding it pretty well. I'm getting sleepy." Eric yawned and glanced at the clock on the wall. "Oh, it's already twelve-thirty. We've got a meeting tomorrow with the Inner Circle."

"Oh, yeah...got to figure out the terrains and portals." I downed the remaining contents of my drink in one gulp.

Eric got to his feet and approached me. "Alexandria, you know, if you ever want someone to talk with in the future, you can always trust me, all right?" He gave me a pat on the back.

"*Always* talk with you?" I said, putting on a playful expression. "Are you making Eileen jealous on purpose?"

"No, but.... I mean—she's my girlfriend, but you're my family, my blood-related cousin. Family is forever. No matter what happens, I have your back."

I studied Eric, and for the first time, I acknowledged how much he had matured since our last mission. Yes, I could still see the shadow of his past self, the traits he had once possessed, but now, he seemed much wiser and refined.

"Thanks. You can also—I mean, if you ever want to confide in someone else other than Eileen, I'm here for you. Always."

"I know." Eric flashed a radiant smile at me and walked me to the door. "Good night."

"Eric?" I gave him one last look before stepping into the dark corridor. "I'm lucky to have you as a cousin."

# Chapter Five

## All Falls Down
## (Zack)

"So what do we know about the portals?" asked Helen.

"Um...." I found myself staring at Helen, unable to utter a complete sentence. She was attired in a ball gown with a portrait neckline today, baring her fine collarbones. On her slender arms were lacy white gloves that reached her elbows. A furry shawl sat on her lap, snow-white against dark purple. I couldn't help noticing how beautiful she was, though not by conventional standards. It wasn't how attractive her features were or how she did her makeup, but rather her stately demeanor, her regal bearing, and the prim way she always carried herself, with mien of royalty. Somehow I was sure underneath that mask of formality and harshness, there lay a soul infinitely gentle. At that moment, I registered my arm was touching Helen's. Wondering if she'd noticed, I cast a quick, cautious glance at her.

"According to what we discussed yesterday, we can leave the Underworld through the fountain by the haunted manor if we enter through Evergreen Valley," Brian piped up.

"Very well said." Helen surveyed the members of the Inner Circle, who were all sitting around the table. "Our goal is to figure out where the terrains and the aquaportals are. But now, we have a huge problem. The descriptions in the journals are getting confusing. The portals keep changing, popping up, and disappearing in different terrains. I'm starting to suspect that perhaps there isn't a pattern between the—"

*BOOM.* A deafening sound of an explosion blasted everyone's eardrums.

"What's going on?" Helen rose to her feet and hurried over to the door.

"Don't go out." I gripped her by the elbow. "It could be dangerous outside."

"Perhaps it's just some new Elder horsing around," suggested Eric with a shrug.

"Probably," Evonne agreed. "The guards will make an announcement if there's a huge accident or anything unusual. It's all right, let's carry on with—"

The door burst open, and in rushed Noir, looking bedraggled and filthy. His eyes were wide with fear.

"What's wrong, Noir?" Helen said. "And what happened to you?"

Noir was so petrified with fear that he couldn't speak.

"Are you all right?" I asked.

"They...they...." panted Noir. He was so terrified that he could not form a complete sentence.

Helen and I exchanged an unnerved glance with each other. I knew what she was assuming, and I hoped it wasn't true.

"Who's *they*?" Alexandria, who had also gotten to her feet, demanded.

"Underworldians," Noir gasped. "Invaded—palace—and—Alta and Alto—attacking—Elders."

"What?" A few others stood up, some clutching wands or scepters.

*Alta and Alto? In the palace of the Otherworld?* I felt as though the floor had been yanked away from under my feet. My ears were ringing, my mind was drawing a blank, and my heart was banging against my Adam's apple.

"But what about the other Elders? And King Patrick and Queen Marianne?" Alexandria said.

"They're trying to evacuate all the Elders!" Noir, who

seemed to have recovered from his shock, shouted.

"Evacuate? What do you mean evacuate?" Alexandria was now yelling.

"Alta and Alto brought an army with them and ambushed the Elders in the ballroom! They don't stand a chance against Alta and Alto, the Elders!"

Alexandria slammed her fist on the table. "Don't stand a chance? How is that possible? The Otherworld must fight back! Not run away like cowards!"

"And how are they supposed to fight back without their weapons, may I ask?" Noir bellowed, completely forgetting who he was talking to. "How can they even fight without getting changed? The Underworldians are already attacking them, and they don't have time to grab their swords, let alone—"

"Well, I don't care!" Alexandria roared. "They're Elders! They're supposed to be fighting at the first line no matter what!"

"Your Highness, please be reasonable—"

"I'm going down there," I said. I wasn't sure why I made that decision, but it was the only sensible thing to do at that moment. All I knew was that I had to protect the Otherworld, myself, Eric and the others, and most of all—Helen.

"What?" Helen whirled around to face me. "No, you can't! We need a plan—"

"And by then, it'll be too late!"

Without another word, I dashed out of the conference room. The arrival of this sudden impromptu exam of our ability to defend ourselves rendered me speechless. I sprinted down the nearest staircase, and to my horror, the third floor was already packed with Elders, guards, and Underworldians. The invasion had begun. It seemed to me that although many Elders had been evacuated, even more, chose to remain behind and fight. Most of the Elders had somehow retrieved their weapons; they stood their ground and fought, waving swords and spears at the invaders. I felt the pocket of my trousers, and fortunately, I had my sword and shield with me, both shrunken and hidden.

An arrow whizzed past my ear, and I turned, only to see a deviline—a female devil—with wrinkly green skin and huge turquoise horns sneering at me. I tapped my wand on my weapons to enlarge them and swung my sword at her, leaving a bloody gash on her neck. The deviline let out a howl of fury and fired another arrow to get revenge, which I deflected with my wand. At that moment, pain exploded across my senses. Another deviline had snuck up behind me and stabbed my left arm. A copious amount of blood was oozing from the wound, sapping my strength and energy.

"Leave him alone!" a voice shouted. Before I knew it, Alexandria leapt out of nowhere and tackled the deviline, pinning her to the floor. The two of them wrestled for a while, shooting arrows and hurling fireballs at each other, both desperate for dominance over the other. The deviline tried to attack Alexandria, but the latter was too quick for her. Alexandria grabbed ahold of the deviline's large horns, hoisted herself up into the air, and did a somersault, then shoved the deviline out of her way before bringing her spear to her neck.

"Thanks, Alexan—"

She seized me by the arm and pulled me into a nearby room, slamming the door shut.

"What do you think you're doing?"

"And what did you think you were doing?" Alexandria rounded on me. "What were you thinking, running away like that?"

"I—Alexandria, if you think I'm letting Alta—"

"Listen, Helen made me swear that I'd ensure your safety, in case you're wondering why I'm here." Alexandria walked up to the floor window and severed the draperies with magic. "Here," she said, looking less angry as she swathed the makeshift bandages around the wound on my arm.

"Thanks," I grumbled. "Does it look...bad?"

Alexandria hesitated for a moment. "It's a very deep cut. I'd be more careful if I were you."

"Where are the others?"

"You mean the Elders in the Inner Circle? They're all fighting out there. I suppose—"

*Boom*. The door was blasted open. "There they are!" An

army of devils and devilines forced their way into the room. They raised their bows and weapons, edging towards us as they savored the satisfaction of watching us trapped, helpless and terrified.

Alexandria looked desperately at me as though trying to communicate without speaking.

"What?" I whispered.

"Your shield," muttered Alexandria, trying her best to talk without moving her lips. "Smash floor window. Es—"

The army of devils and devilines advanced on us. Waves of arrows zoomed at me and Alexandria, who was doing her best to hold them off and buy me time. She conjured a fiery serpent, hurled fireballs and lavabricks at them, and aimed a swift kick at a deviline who snuck up behind her.

A stab of pain coursed through my body. A spear had pierced the wound in my left arm, and blood was seeping through the bandages. However, I had no time to dawdle or examine my injury. With my face screwed in pain, I bolted to the floor window and smashed my shield into the glass. The window shattered, and with a wave of my wand, the shards of broken glass rose into the air and sailed toward the remaining devils and devilines. High-pitched shrieks shattered the air as the glass pierced their wrinkly green skin.

"Come on!" Grabbing Alexandria by the wrist, I made a run for our only escape. The two of us jumped from the window and plummeted into the moat below.

Alexandria swore, kicking her feet and waving her arms. She inhaled a large gulp of water and coughed. My left arm stung and throbbed in the water, but still, I paddled toward the shore with all my remaining strength.

*Splash.*

I turned and saw a few devils and devilines plunge into the moat, swimming toward me and Alexandria. One of the devilines dived and grabbed me by the leg. Arms flailing helplessly, I sank deeper and deeper into the water. I tried to scream, but no sound came out. Only bubbles, a stream of bubbles wafting toward the lake of light above me, journeying to a place I longed to be in.

"Alexandria? Zack?" a familiar voice yelled from above. "Eileen, quick!"

Something long, tangled, and green dropped from the sky, swinging above me.

"Grab the vine, and I'll hoist you up!" a second voice yelled.

I felt something slippery clutching my hand, and I struggled to break free.

"It's me, Zack!" Alexandria's voice shouted. "Take my hand!"

I kicked the deviline's face with my free leg and heard a muffled howl of fury and anguish in the water.

"Here, hold onto this," said Alexandria. "The vine over here. Eileen will heave us up onto the cloud."

A sudden twinge of pain in my left arm seemed to penetrate my body. The wound was killing me. My fingers slipped, and I lost my grip.

"I can't...," I moaned as I felt the energy draining from my body.

"Clarissa, lower the cloud!" Alexandria yelled.

Two hands grasped each of my arms, pulling me upward and onto something moist and fluffy that solidified as soon as I sat down.

"Take that, you fools!" Clarissa gave her scepter a swish, and a streak of lightning struck the devils and devilines in the moat. They sank into the waters and vanished.

"Neat," Daphne grinned. She looked unscathed, except for a gash on her cheek. "What happened to you, Zack?"

"Ran into an army of devils and devilines. They almost killed me and Alexandria," I mumbled, delirious. Waves of pain clouded my brain, making it impossible for me to think.

"Your sleeve's drenched in blood," said Eileen, looking worried. She withdrew a little vial filled with golden substance from her pocket. "Here." She dabbed some on the wound. "Willy got a few vials of the newly-invented healing ointments from the infirmary and gave them to us."

"Newly-invented?"

"Yeah, well, they can numb the pain but can't heal cuts. They can come in handy in battles, though. I've got two, one for you."

"Thanks." Now that the pain was subsiding, my mind cleared once again. "You seen Helen and Eric?"

"They were fighting Alta and Alto with a trio of Elders when I last saw them," said Eileen. "We also saw the Chirpy Bird."

Clarissa waved her scepter, and our cloud zoomed toward the palace. Below us, clusters of Elders and Underworldians, all fighting to kill, were swinging swords and blocking blades with everything they had. Noir, the dogfish, followed by Bessie the bearnix and a few others had also joined the fight. They pelted icicles and spouted fireballs at the invaders.

"We're now hovering above the front gates, and I'm going to land us in the middle of the front lawn," announced Clarissa.

"Now, all we have to do is to get there," Alexandria pointed at the marble steps way ahead of us. "And then we can go upstairs—"

"And face the Chirpy Bird, huh?" Daphne said with a nervous grin.

"Honestly, Daphne, it's just a stupid old bird with a shrill, annoying voice. I don't get why you're scared."

"Yeah, an annoying two-story-tall canary with humanlike fingers who is invincible to weapons. Would be real easy to take—"

Cries of warning and screams of pain cut across her. A sea of arrows soared through the air and zapped at us.

"Follow me!" I zigzagged around several bushes and statues and decided to take refuge behind a statue of a yawning dogfish. "Get down," I whispered to the others.

"What were you doing, running around all those bushes?" Clarissa hissed, dabbing some ointment on her arm. "One of the arrows grazed my—"

"I was trying to confuse them. Bet you anything, the monsters won't find us that easily now."

"Monsters? Devils and devilines again?" Alexandria, who

was crouching beside Clarissa, asked.

I nodded. Alexandria raised her scepter.

"No, not now." I laid a warning hand on her arm. "Don't do anything." I stood up while making as little noise as possible, peering at our enemies from the opened mouth of the dogfish statue.

What I saw almost gave me a heart attack. There were about fifteen devils, devilines, bearnixes, unibirds, kittenpillars, and dogfishes, all fully armed. They skirted around three shrubs ahead of us and blasted a bush to pieces.

"How can they destroy nature like that?" said Eileen through gritted teeth. "It's so disrespectful!"

"Shh, now's not the time to talk about that," Daphne whispered.

The enemies edged closer to our hideout, their weapons raised. Any time.

"What's wrong, Zack?" Alexandria asked.

"We're outnumbered. There's about fifteen of them. What should we do?"

"Play for time," Daphne said at once. "Zack, Alexandria, fight and distract them. Buy us as much time as you can. I'll make a few catapults, and Clarissa and Eileen, can you help me with the ammunition?"

They both nodded.

"And I'm going to conjure a self-running-flesh-eating-Venus-flytrap," added Eileen.

"Good," I muttered, sneaking a glance at the enemies. "They're coming. We'd better run before they blast this statue apart and get us killed. Now!"

The five of us took off in different directions. Our opponents were quick; they had already split into teams of three and were each in pursuit of one of us. I ducked behind a bush of lilac peonies, firing streaks of light at them between the leaves. One of my spells hit a dogfish, and it collapsed into a shrub. As I was gloating over my success, an arrow brushed past my ear. I turned and found myself face-to-face with a devil. He stabbed his knife at me, and I dived out of the way, aiming a kick at his knees and knocking him to the ground. The devil stood up and raised his blade to attack, but I slammed my shield in defense and gave him a violent nudge in the stomach.

Just then, a ball of scarlet fire zoomed at the devil and hit him smack in the face. He let out a howl of wrath as his body melted in the scorching flames.

"Thanks, Alexandria."

She nodded. "Should we make a run for it and hurry into the palace? Or should we deal with these monsters first?"

"Deal with them. We don't want to leave them here and give them the chance to attack more Elders and guards."

Just then, a gigantic green plant came hurtling toward us. It smacked its huge jaws, revealing innumerable rows of teeth.

"Alexandria, Zack! Watch out. It's my Venus flytrap!" Eileen yelled from nowhere.

"Oh, I hate this thing!" Alexandria yelled, raising her scepter.

"Don't blast it apart!" Eileen's voice squealed. "It's on our side!"

Mayhem reigned. Our enemies seemed desperate to get rid of us, for they were now firing arrows at everyone they saw, friend or foe. I leapt from statue to statue, bush to bush, trying to avoid getting struck. I dodged an arrow and took cover behind a statue of a unibird.

Meanwhile, Daphne was standing by the huge fountain, twirling her scepter and muttering commands. The water in it rose up into the air, forming a large wave. Daphne stood on her tiptoes, waving her scepter as though conducting a choir. The tide of water grew and grew, doubling in height and width. A group of bearnixes made the mistake of darting past the fountain, and that was when Daphne's hand dropped. The waves crashed onto the bearnixes. Bellowing and roaring, their bodies melted on making contact with the water.

"No!" An angry dogfish lunged at Daphne, and I fired a jet of purple light to distract it. Unfortunately, the dogfish came for me next. I bolted across the lawn, firing spells as I glanced behind. The dogfish didn't seem at all injured. All I had managed to do was agitate it even more. I passed Alexandria, who was dueling hand-in-hand with a devil. Eileen, who was chucking more ammunition into the catapult, was a few feet ahead.

I flicked another look over my shoulder and saw that Eileen's Venus flytrap had joined the chase. It was only a few feet behind the dogfish. The flytrap snapped its large jaws at me, and at that moment, a crazy plan formed in my mind. Given the distance between the dogfish and the flytrap, there was a high chance it would work, but if it didn't.... Anyway, I had to take the risk and give it a try. I hurried toward a tall shrub and crouched behind it. The angry dogfish followed me. As it drew nearer, I got up, leapt over the shrub, and bolted in the direction I'd come from. I clenched my fists, not daring to look back to see if my plan had worked.

*Chomp*! I turned, and to my relief, I had succeeded. The dogfish, too slow to turn around, had run headfirst into the shrub, giving the Venus flytrap enough time to catch on. The flytrap clamped its jaws on the dogfish as it howled in agony.

"Nice one, Zack! I saw what you did over there!" a voice called out to me from above.

I looked up, just in time to see Clarissa summon a powerful streak of lightning. Daphne, who was also sitting on Clarissa's cloud, flicked her ice trident; a clean spray of water erupted from the tip. Together, they annihilated two devilines.

"Mission accomplished," announced Clarissa, lowering her cloud and hopping off.

Alexandria, Eileen, and I hurried toward them.

"Any more monsters?" I asked them.

"Eileen made a poison ivy trap, and I set it on fire," said Alexandria, grinning. "Five enemies smothered."

"Ingenious. You used that trick last year, right?" I recalled how the foolish bearnixes had burnt themselves in Eileen's traps on our last adventure, causing the poison to spread and kill the other prisoners.

"Wasn't she awesome?" Alexandria said, slapping Eileen on the back.

"Indeed," I said, and Eileen beamed with pleasure. "Come

on, everyone. Back to our mission."

***

We passed the ornate double doors and entered the grand lobby of the palace. Even though I had been here countless times, the grandeur of the official entrance never failed to amaze me. The imperial staircase, the magnificent crystal chandelier, the soaring ceiling and the incandescent plush carpet was a spectacular sight to behold. I felt an immediate rush of gratitude at the fact that the lobby had not been ravaged by war yet. I led the others up the imperial staircase, and Lilith emerged from a corridor flanked by Brian and Evonne. A nasty cut was etched upon Lilith's face, and the ruffles on her gown were ripped. Brian's sleeves were singed and torn. Evonne was drenched with sweat, her damp blonde hair plastered to her cheeks and forehead.

"Zack, it's you! We just won an epic fight against ten bearnixes on the grand staircase!" Lilith called out to me.

"That's great, but how are the others?"

"Not good. We just sent a few Elders to the infirmary—"

"Then you'll be sending more!" a voice behind us announced. Ten devils and devilines appeared from the right corridor and advanced on us. Before I could react, one of the devils charged at me. He drew his spear, slashing sideways and aiming for my stomach. I intercepted the blow with my sword, and the blade connected with the devil's arm instead, butchering its slimy turquoise flesh. The devil let out an inarticulate yell of rage and whipped out a knife. I would have been killed if Evonne hadn't fired an arrow at him at that instance. The devil sank to the ground, clutching his bleeding eye.

I ran to the balcony and scanned the massive hall, searching for the others and seeing if anyone needed help. Alexandria and a deviline were fighting. She flung a fireball at the deviline but missed, and the deviline plunged her spear into Alexandria's arm as revenge. Clarissa, who happened to sprint by, brought her sword to the deviline's neck and delivered a fatal blow. The deviline moaned as she sank to the floor. Almost dying, she made a final snatch for Alexandria's leg, but a pointy icicle soared across the room at that moment and pierced the deviline's forehead. She now resembled a unibird with an icicle for a horn.

Brian, who had sustained a nosebleed, was in the middle of a duel with a devil. Alexandria sent a ball of fire flying at the devil, who dived out of the way and retaliated by flinging his dagger at her. She deflected the blade, and it cut into Brian's leg instead.

"Sorry!" Alexandria squeaked, terrified. She hurled another fireball at the devil but missed.

Eileen sprinted down the staircase, flicking her scepter and shouting commands. Sticky vines sprouted from the devil's nostrils; they grew in length at a rapid speed, entangling his whole body and immobilizing him.

"Thanks," said Brian thickly, blood dribbling from his nose and splashing the front of his shirt. Eileen handed him a vial of healing ointment and rushed over to Lilith and Evonne, who were fighting a group of devils and devilines. It was difficult to tell who the swords, spears, and shields belonged to, for all of them were waving weapons at each other at the same time. I wanted to provide assistance more than anything but dreaded the thought of hurting, or worse, killing someone on my side by accident.

"Zack!" Alexandria raced over to me. "I got an idea." She whispered her plan to me, and I frowned.

"Are you sure it's going to work? What if we hurt—?"

"We must give it a try," said Alexandria, her face lit with fierce determination.

I didn't know why it hit me at that particular moment, but for some reason, I acknowledged the resemblance between Alexandria and Helen. They did have a lot of differences—Alexandria, impetuous and impulsive; Helen, decent and dignified—yet they shared the same fierceness and tenacity when it came to protecting fellow Otherworldians. A strong torrent of affection and respect for both of them flooded upon me.

"Zack, are we going to do it or not?"

Weighing my options, I looked at the group of fighters below and then up at the chandelier. "All right, then, we'll put your plan into action. Do it on my command. We must make sure we won't hurt anyone on our side."

I watched Evonne fire dozens of arrows at a devil who was about to attack Brian. Lilith slashed her sword at another and ducked as a knife sailed over her head.

I signaled Alexandria. "Do it."

Leaning over the balustrade, Alexandria pointed her scepter at the crystal chandelier dangling above the hall. "Sever!"

The chandelier crashed to the floor and smashed right on top of the group of fighters, glistening fragments of jagged beads splashing everywhere. The devils and devilines howled and shrieked wrestling and thrashing each other as they tried to escape from the weight of the chandelier.

Lilith, who leapt out of harm's way at the last second, remained uninjured. She looked around to see who had done it. I winked at her, and she caught my eye and laughed. "What were you trying to do, Zack? Kill me?"

"Well, the plan worked. Alexandria's idea, in fact."

Lilith cast her an admiring look. "Very clever. You are a genius, Alexandria."

"It was pretty dangerous," admitted Alexandria. "And it could've hurt one of you, but we had to take a risk. We can't spend the whole day here fighting these devils and devilines. Why do they always seem to multiply out of thin air? Oh no, there goes another one."

Alexandria hurtled after Evonne, who was in pursuit of an unscathed deviline that had been lurking under the staircase. She hurled a fireball at the monster and hit the target.

"Nice aim, Alexandria!" Evonne shouted.

"I haven't been in a real fight for fourteen months, but I'm starting to get back on track," said Alexandria, flashing a proud grin at her. She healed the wound on her arm with another blazing fireball. Being the heiress of Ember, she was not only immune to fire, but it also healed her injuries.

"Now what?" Clarissa said, joining us in a huddle.

"Finding Eric and Helen," I reminded her. "Lilith, where did you last see them?"

"In ballroom 408, on the fourth floor. They were fighting

Alta and Alto, but the two cowards escaped in the end, and a large canary took their place in the fight."

"Oh boy...the Chirpy Bird," said Daphne, shaking her head. "Not again...."

***

The winding passages beside the lobby were lit by the torches on the walls. Dim flames in various shades of purple flickered feebly on the tip of the torches.

Alexandria swore. "Where's the spiral staircase?"

"No idea," I said. Even though I had lived in the palace for almost a decade, I still couldn't figure out how to navigate the labyrinth of passages on the first floor, which, after all, had been designed to confuse intruders. Every path looked identical, bathed in hazy hues of lilac, lavender, and deep violet.

Alexandria snapped her fingers, and a ball of fire blazed on her palm. "Here," she held up her hand. "So you can see better."

Hurrying through dozens of passages, we turned right, then left, and came to a dead end.

"Let's go back there and take the right one," Evonne advised.

We did, but still no luck. Weaving through the endless maze, we came to three more dead ends.

My patience was running low. "Now, what do we do? We don't have time for this."

"Maybe we should find the courtyard first," suggested Lilith. "As long as we find the courtyard, we can get to the spiral staircase by turning left and then right."

"Good plan." Allowing my intuition to guide me, I set foot on another passage that curved and twisted like a snake. As if an invisible force was conspiring against us, we were greeted by another dead end. I heaved a sigh. The frustration in me was reaching its boiling point.

"This is getting annoying," said Brian. "Eric told me he had a map of the labyrinth of the passages here. Darn, I should've borrowed it from him before—"

"Look! What's that?" Alexandria pointed her finger at the left passage ahead of us. A ray of sunlight slanted into the dark.

"The courtyard?"

Sure enough, we found ourselves in the courtyard of the palace as we proceeded forward.

Evonne gasped. "What's that monster? And is that—?"

Willy, who was fighting what seemed like a gigantic flying ant with a human face, saw me. "Zack? What are you doing here—? Ouch!"

The giant ant slammed Willy to the ground, and he landed hard on his back. Brian forced him out of harm's way as the ant made another attempt to attack him. Eileen and Daphne dashed toward the flying ant, thorny roses and jagged icicles zooming from their scepters. Clarissa summoned a cloud, got on, and advanced on the monster, impaling and slicing off one of its wings.

"Lilith, Evonne, stay here," I told them. "Go find help if things get bad for us." Without another word, I dashed into the battlefield. I fired a streak of light at the ant's right eye but missed. "Why are you standing there, Alexandria? Do something!"

She put her index finger to her lips, her eyes focused on the battlefield. "I'm biding my chance and looking for a good angle to attack its weak spot—its stomach. I need your help."

"Fine, but what's your plan?"

"We'll close in on the ant on my command. Zack, you take its right side, and I'll take its left. Three, two, one, now!"

The two of us pounced on the monster. Alexandria tried to plunge her spear into its stomach, but the ant seemed to know exactly what she had in mind. Something pink sprayed at her from its large antennas, and Willy cried out a warning, "it's formic acid! It'll make your skin itch and swell!"

Alexandria leapt out of the way to avoid it. Meanwhile, something white and green and furry emerged from a yellow rose bush. My heart gave a jolt as Ella, the kittenpillar, wriggled toward the gigantic ant, hissing. A jet of pink liquid zoomed at the little kittenpillar.

"Not Ella!" Eileen screamed, deflecting the pink liquid with her scepter and causing it to drench a devil who had entered the courtyard at that moment. His wrinkly green skin swelled and reddened, now an ugly shade of brown.

Daphne summoned a flurry of snow and cursed as millions of feathery white flakes glided down from the heavens.

"What are you doing?" Brian demanded. "Now's not the time to play with snow!"

"I'm trying to start a hailstorm," she wailed. "But I can't!"

"That's all right, just leave it to us," Evonne said. She shot an arrow at the ant's head and pierced the target. However, the dazed ant began swaying left and right, trying to regain its balance.

"Alexandria, run! It's either going to squash you or crush me!" I turned on my heels and fled.

"No, not yet! Your sword! Be prepared!"

"Are you insane?" I roared at her. "What if it loses its balance and crashes on top of me?"

Alexandria heeded my advice and took a few steps backward, keeping a safe distance away from the tottering ant. Just as I thought she was going to flee, she flung her spear at the ant's stomach as it swayed to the right side. At the same time, Evonne fired another arrow at the ant's chest. It slammed to the ground, where it moved no more.

Sighs of relief echoed among the others as we congregated at the passage.

"Willy, you all right?" I asked.

Beads of sweat glistened on Willy's forehead. "I'm fine," he said, clutching Brian's shoulder for support. "I want to come along with you guys. Where are you going?"

"The ballroom on the fourth floor. To help Eric and Helen."

"And how do we get there?"

Lilith pointed at the passage ahead of us. "Turn left and right, and we can get to the spiral staircase."

We followed her through the passage and up the staircase. "Now, we should do a quick rehearsal and—"

"There they are!" a voice shrieked from below.

"Get down!" Lilith screamed.

A wave of turquoise light soared above us, slamming into the wall on our left and blasting it apart. Daphne sprang to her feet and chucked an ice boulder at whoever was trying to ambush us. However, her foot slipped, and she lost her balance, tumbling down the staircase and falling to the floor, where she lay motionless.

"Daphne!" Eileen screeched. Both Alexandria and Clarissa's eyes widened in terror.

"We must split," I said, looking at the others. "Brian, Evonne, Willy, take Daphne to the infirmary. One of you must carry her while the other two look out for lurking enemies trying to ambush you."

"But what about Helen and—?"

"That'll be our job." I cut across Evonne. "Just take Daphne and go. You may come back and fight if you want to. See you guys later. We've got to get going."

We sped up the winding staircase, Lilith and I bringing up the lead and the heiresses at our heels. The spiral staircase made me feel dizzy, as though running in endless circles. My lungs protested, aching and screaming for more air as I gasped for breath; every muscle in me twitched in protest. Unendurable pain flooded every inch of my body, begging me to stop. However, it was the dreadful thought of losing Helen and Eric that kept me moving. The nightmarish notion brought agony neither sword nor injury could inflict upon me. I pinched myself hard, trying to take my mind off the innumerable possibilities of what may have happened to them during my absence.

"Fourth floor, yes, we're here," said Lilith.

I could see the reflections of the Elders and monsters in the glossy marble floor of the ballroom. The purple curtains, tattered and torn, were hanging haphazardly by the windows. The gilded mirrors were askew, dangling precariously on the walls. I straightened them with a flick of my wand in fear that they would crash down on the fighters below.

A torrent of shrill laughter sent a chill down my spine. I turned and saw the Chirpy Bird towering over Helen, Eric, and Connie. Helen fired streaks of light at the bird while the others punched it, but the bird remained unharmed. The Chirpy Bird picked up a random shield that was lying on the ground, and one of Helen's spells backfired and struck her instead. Injured, she sank to the floor.

"Ha! Serves you right!" The Chirpy Bird let out a shriek of ecstasy at her misery.

Alexandria, Clarissa, and Eileen, who had been conferring since we had entered the ballroom, charged at the Chirpy Bird.

"You'll pay for that!" Alexandria bellowed, lavabricks shooting from her scepter. Eileen gave her scepter a twirl, and spiky roses zoomed toward the bird.

Meanwhile, I dashed to Helen and knelt down by her side. "Are you all right?"

"I...I think so." A deep gash a few inches below Helen's left collarbone glared at me. She winced, pressing a palm to the cut.

"You're hurt. Come on, I'll take you to the infirmary," I insisted, helping her up.

"I'm not going. I've got to stay here and fight until the—"

The rest of Helen's sentence was drowned out by a roar of mirth, which came from no other than the Chirpy Bird. I looked up, and my stomach gave a jolt as I saw Lilith crumple to the floor, unconscious.

"No!" Still pressing the wound with her hand, Helen hurried to Lilith's side and bent down to check on her. She grabbed one of her arms and hoisted her up. Brian, who had darted into the ballroom moments ago, took Lilith's other arm.

"I'll do it," I volunteered.

"No. You're more experienced than I am. You've got to stay and fight," said Brian. "Helen and I can take Lilith to the infirmary."

"But—"

"We'll be fine," said Helen, putting on a brave expression.

Giving them one last look, I turned and bolted over to the others. Alexandria, Clarissa, Eileen, and Eric were the only ones left fighting the Chirpy Bird, who was busy dodging the fireballs, golden sparks, spiky roses, and turquoise fireballs zooming from their scepters and wands.

"Where are the others? Dianthus? Sheldon? Juniper?" I

hollered.

"They were chasing after a group of bearnixes!" Eric shouted.

The Chirpy Bird caught a spiky rose and chucked it at Eric, scarring his bare arm.

"Hey, you silly bird!" Clarissa shouted. "Why pick on him? Why not pick on an heiress with elemental magic, huh? Are you that big a coward?" She raised her sword.

"No, Clarissa! It's invincible, remember? The Chir— "

But it was too late. She had made the huge mistake of swinging her sword at the Chirpy Bird. The blade bounced off its neck and rebounded on its owner, scarring Clarissa's arm. The force threw her off balance, and she landed on the ground with a loud *thump*.

The Chirpy Bird tightened its grasp on a bloody dagger and shoved Alexandria and Eileen out of its way. It looked at Clarissa, eyes gleaming with madness. "You! Aren't you the little hero who knocked me out with lightning last year?"

"That's right," said Clarissa, getting to her feet. "Scared, birdie?"

I immediately sensed the danger and seriousness of the situation, but Clarissa, who was always too bright and naive, did not. I wanted to cry out a warning, but right at that moment, the Chirpy Bird planted the dagger into her stomach.

*Shock. Disbelief. A rush of panic.*

Alexandria and Eileen, both bruised and battered, raced to Clarissa's side at top speed. Eric, clutching his bleeding arm, tottered toward them.

The Chirpy Bird guffawed, "Time for the teary farewell!"

"You wish!" I growled, aiming a streak of purple light at the bird, who dived out of the way. Vengeance fueled me, eclipsing every rational thought that remained in my mind. Insanity roared in me like a furious beast. All I wanted was to quench my thirst for revenge, to punish the bird for almost taking Clarissa's life, to cause it as much harm as I could. Tear it apart, blast it to pieces—

"Come quick, Zack," Alexandria said in a quivering voice.

The Chirpy Bird grinned and left the ballroom, screaming

with laughter.

"Come back, you coward!" I shouted.

"Zack, drop it!" Eric shouted. He sounded as though he had been crying.

An ominous feeling rose in my chest. "Clarissa?" I hurried to her side and crouched down.

Blood was gushing profusely from Clarissa's abdomen, which the dagger had sliced into. Her pale lips formed a weak smile as she saw me.

"Clarissa—" Alexandria began.

"Family...," muttered Clarissa, her gaze traveling from Alexandria's face to Eileen's, then to mine.

"Yes, yes," Alexandria said, starting to panic. "Don't worry. We'll send you back to your family in the mortal world soon. No more fighting, I promise."

Clarissa shook her head. "Beyond healing...."

"Don't say that." Tears were leaking from Eileen's eyes and splattering onto the marble floor. Clarissa brushed the tears from her face with a thumb. She shivered, and Eileen shrugged off her jacket and wrapped her in it.

"Zack, do you have the ointment with you? I've used mine up," Eileen implored me with her teary gaze.

I did, but Clarissa was right—she was beyond healing. It was the exhaustion and the innumerable wounds all over her body that were killing her, sapping her stamina, and now, her vitality. Plus, the ointment could only relieve her pain and not heal her injuries.

"Clarissa...." Eric's eyes welled up with tears.

"Eric...." Clarissa fixed her gaze on him.

Eric's lips twitched as he reached out to stroke her hand. "You're like a sister to me. Always were."

With trembling fingers, Clarissa pressed her scepter into Eric's hands. It glowed as his skin made contact with it. "Take this."

"But I don't—" Eric's voice faltered on meeting Clarissa's pleading gaze. A look of understanding seemed to pass between the two of them as he accepted the scepter like an obedient child.

Clarissa looked eerily relieved as her expression relaxed. "And...and...tell them...tell Daphne...and Helen...I said... goodbye."

"You're not dying!"

Clarissa spoke again, her voice now a feeble whisper. "Family...."

"I know. We'll take you back to the mortal world. You'll see your mom and dad again very soon," said Alexandria. There were tears in her eyes.

Clarissa shook her head again, this time with great difficulty. Life was draining out of her. "You...all of you...my... true family."

Her eyes, once sparkling with curiosity, were losing their usual mischievous twinkle. A stray final tear escaped her left eye and careened down, colliding with the marble floor. I watched, in utter disbelief and horror, as her pupils dilated, becoming glassy and vacant.

*No, not Clarissa, never Clarissa.* Clarissa, artless and enthusiastic, the shining ray of light that never seemed to fade...I could not confront the cruel reality, could not bear myself to digest the brutal truth that Clarissa was gone, once and for all. *How was it possible? She was too young, only fifteen. She had a bright future waiting ahead of her....*

Alexandria remained as still as a statue, tears flowing down her cheeks. Eric and Eileen sobbed in each other's arms. I knelt there by Clarissa's side, not knowing what to say or do.

An arrow zoomed at us from nowhere, brushing past Alexandria's neck. Everyone snapped out from their trances.

"Eric, Eileen," I said. "Take Clarissa to...." The words got stuck in my throat.

"The infirmary," finished Alexandria, wiping the back of her hands across her tear-stained cheeks. "They're laying the fallen ones in a small room there." Tentatively, she closed Clarissa's eyes with two trembling fingers.

Eric and Eileen obeyed, not showing even the slightest sign of protest. My gaze followed them as they left the ballroom, carrying Clarissa's body.

"Come on, we've got to find the Chirpy Bird and kill it," said Alexandria. She was no longer crying. Her hands were balled into fists, and I could see flames sizzling in her pupils.

She aided me to my feet and led me through the ballroom. As we made our way past the combatants, I spotted Helen among a group of Elders, fighting a gang of bearnixes. Though still numbed by shock, I couldn't help feeling a tingle of relief when I saw her safe and sound.

However, it was the sudden emergence of a tall figure that completely shook me out of my grief and drove every thought out of my mind. She had hair like a flow of lava, which bore a striking resemblance to Alexandria's; however, her eyes, unlike Alexandria's, were crackling with hatred and bloodlust. Her cheeks were hollowed, and her mouth was twisted into a malicious smirk.

*Alta.*

Alexandria, too, was gaping at her. Yet Alta had no intention of killing her niece. She was regarding me with a look of insanity, eyes bulged with elation, pure venom oozing from every inch of her face.

"Zachary, my old friend." Her voice was silky in a murderous way. "How have you been?"

I had to move. I had to get myself away from her as soon as possible. My legs were screaming with the need to escape, but I could not move them, could not even will them to move. Fear had spun a chrysalis around me. I was trapped.

Alta edged closer and closer, her face alight with a fanatical, almost cynical grin. Something zoomed toward me from her raised bow, and in a fraction of a moment, I knew what had happened.

But before I could react, a blur of black and violet flew toward me, and the next second I was pinned to the ground. I closed my eyes, not daring to look. Something wet and warm splattered onto my clothes and pooled on the floor beside me. A coppery tang that filled the air told me it was blood.

*Is dying painless? Or have I lost all my senses?*

Slowly, I opened my eyes. Something was tickling my

neck. I brushed off a cascade of wavy black hair. With my heart beating an inauspicious rhythm against my chest, I managed to get into a sitting position.

Only to find Helen sprawled beside me, her body limp, her eyes closed.

Something invisible extracted the remaining air from my lungs. Terrified, I whispered, "Helen?"

No answer.

# Chapter Six

## Salvage (Alexandria)

It was as though the world had melted away. Time seemed to solidify like ice. Everything was taking place in slow motion. Voices roared, weapons clinked, and jets of light zapped in every direction, illuminating the ballroom with hues of purple and turquoise. However, I was blind and deaf to all the sounds and sights around me.

"Helen!" Dodging and ducking the beams of lights, I ran for her.

"Please...no, don't...." Zack was kneeling beside the unconscious form of Helen. Her face was as white as marble, and she barely seemed to be breathing. Drops of blood trickled down from the corner of her mouth. My stomach lurched as I saw that the arrow had pierced Helen's shoulder, a few inches below her left collarbone and above the bodice of her gown. The earlier fight with the Chirpy Bird had already left a deep gash there, and the second blow of the arrow only made matters worse. It hit home when I realized how much blood Helen had lost—even her skirts were soaked.

*Please don't take her....* Praying to the heavens, I placed a shaking hand to Helen's neck to feel her pulse. A powerful surge of relief gushed up inside me. "Zack, take her to the infirmary right now. It might not be too late."

Zack did not wait for me to finish. He threw his jacket around Helen's shoulders and pressed a hand to her wound to staunch the flow of the blood. Scooping her up into his arms, he dashed out of the ballroom.

Meanwhile, Dianthus, Willy, and Connie were dueling Alta three-on-one, firing streaks of purple light at her. Alta retaliated almost lazily, flicking her scepter and causing their aims to go awry. A jet of turquoise light shot from the tip of her scepter. It hit Willy on the chest, and he doubled over.

"Dianthus, keep fighting!" Connie shouted, rushing to Willy's side and bending over to check on him.

"Yeah, yeah. Come on, little boy, give me your best shot," Alta jeered at Dianthus in a singsong voice, waving her sword and deriving immense pleasure from watching him dodge left and right.

"Having fun?" I roared, chucking a ball of fire at Alta. She let out a shriek of mirth.

"Alexandria, my niece! How is your godmother?"

"You will not touch her again!"

Alta simpered. "You don't sound very confident, do you? Dear, dear, is she going to reunite with your beloved Clarissa soon?"

Concentrating with all my might, a fiery serpent burst from the tip of my scepter. It hissed and coiled its body into a spiral.

"Go!" I egged the snake on, waving my scepter and motioning for it to attack Alta. Flames spouted from its jaws, scalding her arm.

Alta gave her scepter a sharp jab, and to my horror, the serpent dissolved into ashes. She let out a sneer. "Pathetic. You are so naive, so foolish to think you stand a chance against me. But if you really are brave enough to try...." She unsheathed her dagger, and I raised my spear, ready to fight anytime.

Before I knew it, Alta struck, fast and fierce, leaving a deep gash on my arm. I made an attempt to take defense, but she blocked my spear with her shield and feinted with her right hand, leaving another cut on my arm.

"The hero of the Otherworld who has never failed in a battle," said Alta. Her voice trembled with mirth and triumph as her chest rose and fell in wild excitement. "Are *you* having fun? Still naive enough to believe—"

"You evil witch!" a furious voice squeaked. Gidget was standing in the doorway, fury radiating from her tiny figure in waves. "Alexandria, leave! She's mine!"

A devious grin spread across Alta's face. "Gidget Chase, is it? Long time no see. I believe you have already gotten used to witnessing your friends die, haven't you? I still remember the day I met your tribespeople. Serve them right, those miserable midgets who died at my hands." Alta let out a scream of maniacal laughter. "Take that!" She flung a spear at Gidget, who dodged it.

Gidget advanced on Alta and plunged her knife into her lap, savaging her flesh. Alta roared in agony and dropped to her knees. Gidget towered over her. "You dare speak of them, my tribespeople? The innocent lives you've taken by force?" Her voice was no longer a squeak but rather a snarl of wrath and anguish. She slapped Alta in the face with all her might.

"Get off me, you foul, disgusting—"

"Leave our mistress alone, or I'll kill him!" a bearnix roared. He was supporting an unconscious Dianthus and pressing a dagger against his wrist. After a moment of hesitation, Gidget took a step backward.

Just then, a unibird with a glowing turquoise horn swooped into the ballroom through a shattered floor window.

"About time." Alta leapt to her feet and mounted the unibird. "Now, now, my boy, easy on him."

The bearnix released Dianthus, who collapsed with a thud.

"I think we've done enough damage to the Otherworld today. Don't forget, we are just giving them a taster this time."

The bearnix saluted Alta before leaving the ballroom.

"Don't just run away like a loser! Fight me! Fight me back!" I screamed at Alta, unleashing a round of fireballs at her, which she converted to ashes with an idle jerk of her scepter.

"Don't worry," said Alta with a devilish grin. "The worst

is yet to come."

Before Gidget and I could close in on Alta, she raised her scepter, made a slashing movement in the air, and dissolved into a cloud of turquoise mist.

Shocked silence.

Gidget exchanged a fearful look with me. "The worst is yet to come...," she repeated in a faint voice. "What does this mean?"

I surveyed the crimson stains on the shards of glass and scattered remains in the ballroom. The floor windows had been blasted away. The chilly wind swooped down on me, slapping my face and clawing at my shirt like an angry cat. I made my way through the rubble, kicking away chunks of debris and clearing a path.

Kittenpillars were grazing peacefully on the verdant fields and mountains that surrounded the palace. Two dogfishes were frolicking and splashing water at each other in a lake by the fields. The sky was speckled with unibirds; they flapped their wings, gliding past the fields and lakes below. The village halfway up the adjacent mountain was filled with activity; Otherworldians bustled around in the little town, their voices and laughter blending into a muffled chorus. They appeared to be oblivious of the fact the Underworld had just launched an assault on the palace nearby. Further and above the village, little green and white specks, presumably wild kittenpillars, dotted the plateaus in the mountains. The ill-lit sky was overcast, crammed with morose clouds in monotonous shades of gray. It was just like the day I had first entered the Otherworld. Everything gave off an eerie sense of tranquility, as though the pre-apocalyptic calmness before another brutal storm.

"This may be the first assault, but it won't be the last."

Strong, doleful gusts of wind howled in the distance. Torrential rain began pouring from the vortex of clouds—the prelude to a violent storm. A thick film of darkness loomed over the fields and village.

"Alexandria?" The urgent footsteps that sounded behind me announced the arrival of Eileen. Her voice sounded odd and croaky. "Come quick. It's Helen."

I obeyed without the slightest hesitation.

Outside the palace, thunder roared, and a streak of lightning split the sky.

***

The pungent scent of blended ointments filled my nostrils as Eileen and I set foot into the infirmary. Apprehensive whispers were audible from the Elders that were gathered beside every bed. There were grazes and cuts all over their faces, evidence that they, too, had been fighting for the Otherworld.

"There." I spotted the figures of Zack, Eric, Brian, and Evonne further ahead, all looking somber and stricken. Zack's face was shadowed with pain and remorse. He was grasping Helen's hand as though he could revive her by just doing so.

Eric's head jerked up as he saw us. "Oh, Eileen! You're not hurt, are you?" He hurried toward us, and before Eileen could react, he swept her into a tight embrace.

"I'm fine," said Eileen, draping her arms around his back.

"Alexandria." Eric turned and gave me a hug. "Thank goodness you survived."

I nodded. "How is Helen?"

This apparently was the wrong thing to ask. Eric lowered his head, Brian let out a sigh, and a sob of distress escaped Evonne's lips.

"They've managed to stop the bleeding and bandage the wound. Helen lost a lot of blood, but that's nothing compared to the arrow...." Brian cringed. "It was poisoned. Missed her heart by only inches."

Eric's eyes were bloodshot. "Roxanne managed to clean the wound and get the poison out, but Helen's still...weak."

As I drew nearer, my insides plummeted. There Helen lay on the bed beside him, thick tresses of her hair spilled across the pillow. Her eyes were closed, her face was emaciated and ashen, and her breathing seemed shallow.

"Couldn't you use the healing ointment to heal her?" I looked at Eric, who shook his head.

"It wouldn't work. It's the poison and the blood loss that's weakening her," he explained. "Roxanne asked us to...to be prepared for the worst."

"She'll make it through." Brian put on a brave face. "Even Roxanne admits it was a miracle Helen wasn't killed right on the spot. She might...get lucky again." But even as he said this, his bottom lip trembled.

A horrible mixture of uncertainty and apprehension sank to the pit of my stomach. Fear lanced my heart, piercing me like a sharpened blade and numbing all my senses.

Uncomfortable silence loomed upon all of us for a few minutes until Zack broke it, looking for words to fill the air. "What...what exactly happened after I left?"

"Helen dashed out of the conference room and went after you," I replied. "She was so worried you'd get hurt or killed by the intruders."

"We were all surprised," admitted Eric. "Helen wasn't like herself. You know she would never act without a plan. But right after you left, she was so distraught that she went after you without a second thought."

"I think you meant a lot to her," Eileen said in a timid voice. "She really cared about you, Zack."

The royal doctor, Roxanne the kittenpillar, wriggled her way toward us. She cast a worried glance at Helen. "Still unconscious?"

"Will she…?" Zack's voice faltered. He avoided the word as if saying it aloud would be all it took to make it happen. "Will she be all right?" he rephrased his question.

Roxanne did not answer, but the silence itself spoke volumes. I saw a flicker of fear in Zack's gaze. He reminded me so much of a lost toddler. Insecure. Alarmed. Frightened.

"Yes. She will," I broke the silence. These words I said, partly for him, and partly for myself. "Anyone else in the Inner Circle hurt?" I murmured in a hushed voice after Roxanne had moved on to the next bed.

"Daphne broke her right leg and cracked a few ribs," Eric replied.

"Cameron was knocked out by a huge canary," added Brian. "Lilith and a couple of others are also hurt, but they're in no immediate danger."

"But the Chirpy Bird," Evonne said between heaving sobs. "It...it gobbled up most of the Elders in the ballroom."

"That monster," I muttered, my hands clenched into fists. "I'm going to kill it. But what about the others? Uncle Sheldon? Willy?"

"They're fine. I just met them. Alexandria, have you seen Clarissa?" Brian asked. "She was with you when I last saw her."

Brian had no idea that Clarissa had been killed. "Well... Clarissa—" The words got stuck in my throat. I could not bring myself to talk about Clarissa's death. Saying it out loud would make this terrible truth a fact, an unchangeable, irreversible fact.

"The Chirpy Bird killed her," whispered Eric.

"No way!" Brian gasped. He clapped a hand to his mouth. Evonne wept harder into her already saturated handkerchief.

"We were there. We saw it happen," Eileen said, tears pooling in her eyes.

"And Clarissa—she gave me her scepter moments before she died," Eric said, mopping his eyes. "It sort of glowed when... when I took it."

"Which means you are now the heir of Zeru, the god of the sky," said Zack, who had remained silent ever since Roxanne's departure.

"Me? The heir of Zeru?"

"By giving you her scepter before dying, Clarissa has made you the second heir of Zeru. In other words, you have inherited Clarissa's elemental powers."

Eric gazed at the scepter that resembled a unibird's horn, his expression forlorn. Almost reluctant, he picked it up and gave it a wave. Golden sparks emitted from the tip of his new scepter.

"It recognizes you as its master," said Brian.

"But I already have a wand, a wand I can use to perform Underworldian magic."

"Your magical powers got transferred to this scepter the moment you inherited it from Clarissa."

Eric said nothing but continued to devote his attention to his new scepter.

A tiny fair-haired girl approached us. It was Gidget.

"How's Dianthus?" I asked.

"Better," Gidget replied, pursing her lips. "What are we going to do without Helen? The Inner Circle, I mean. Are we going to keep having meetings and discussing the portals and terrains?"

"Play it by ear, I suppose," replied Brian. "Anyway, I don't think we'll have to carry on with this Inner Circle thing. King Patrick and Queen Marianne have learned their lesson this time."

"Pity. I enjoyed our meetings," said Gidget, lowering her head.

The lavender figure of another Elder approached us, and as he neared, I recognized him as Uncle Sheldon. "I heard the news about Helen. Thought I'd like to come and visit her in person. How is she?"

"Not that good, to be honest," answered Brian. "Who told you?"

"Juniper," said Uncle Sheldon. "Oh, and she also said Patrick and Marianne want all the surviving Elders to gather in the Throne Room at one in the afternoon."

"All the surviving Elders?" A lump formed in my throat. "Uncle Sheldon, how many Elders...didn't make it?"

"Around thirty," he sighed. "Dreadful, isn't it?"

"Thirty?" Zack, Evonne, Brian, and Eric exchanged thunderstruck looks.

But before they could resume their conversation, Noir the dogfish came hurrying into the infirmary.

"Lord Zack, Lord Sheldon, Lady Evonne, Lady Gidget, Lord Brian, and Lord Eric," he bowed, addressing them. "King Patrick asks all the Elders to congregate in the Throne Room right away. Only those who are severely injured may be excluded."

"I thought it was two hours later, at one in the afternoon?" asked Uncle Sheldon.

"They've changed the time, and they expect everyone to be there in ten minutes," said Noir. "No time to change outfits. Most of the Elders are already there. I suggest you all come as soon as possible." With another bow, he exited the infirmary.

"Come on, then," said Gidget.

"But what about our clothes?" Brian tapped his wand on the torn sleeve of his tuxedo again and again. "I can't fix the darn thing by magic."

"No, no, no. It's a flick, a jab, and a zigzag. Like this," Gidget corrected him, demonstrating the correct movement and mending his sleeve for him. "There you go. It also works for removing blood stains, scorch marks, and singed skirts. We'd better hurry up and leave the mending until later. Eight minutes to go."

"What about Helen?" Zack asked in a strained voice.

"We'll stay with her. Me and Eileen," I said. "She'll be fine with us."

"I'm not leaving her," said Evonne tearfully. Her whole body shook as her sobs rattled her lungs. "She must've sat by my side for days and nights when I was attacked on the last mission. I want to be here for her like she was for me."

"We'll come back after the assembly." Zack aided Evonne to her feet and patted her on the shoulder. "Alexandria, Eileen, I'll see you around."

"Let's all go and visit Daphne when I'm back, shall we?" Eric, who lingered behind for a few moments, asked.

"Sure."

He nodded at us before following the other Elders out.

When they were gone, I vanished the smears of blood on Helen's gown with the charm Gidget had demonstrated. With a sigh, I transferred my gaze to her face, still empty of expression.

"I wish you were here with us," I said, though I knew she could neither hear my voice nor sense my presence. "We miss you, Helen. We need you."

From the corner of my eye, I thought I saw her hand twitch, though I could not be certain. My mind wandered to all those memories we shared and all the things I should have told or asked her but neglected to. Whether she had a favorite song. A favorite color. A favorite food. Shame flooded me as I realized how little I knew about Helen, even though she was my godmother. What if I never got the chance to know her better?

What if I never saw her alive again?

Everything seemed so surreal. One day we were at school, celebrating the end of our examinations and rejoicing at the sight of the leaf letter, and the next, we lost Clarissa, thirty Elders, and probably…. I looked down at Helen, banishing that awful possibility from my mind.

Something flickered in Eileen's eyes as she cast me a look. Was it concern? Or was it sympathy?

***

We spent the next five days in the infirmary. The storm continued on for days as if it would never relent. Eclipsed by clouds in melancholic tones of gray, the sky seemed to reflect our moods.

Helen had been in a coma since the invasion, and Zack, Eric, Eileen, and I sat by her side, flipping through old journals day and night in order to kill time and numb the anxiety and fear of losing her. Such efforts ended up in vain, for none of us could fully concentrate. Every now and then, my gaze would wander to Helen's chalky face and blank expression. I wondered when she would regain consciousness, or perhaps worse if she ever would.

The Elders' meetings and training sessions were all cancelled for a month, and the members of the Inner Circle paid daily visits. Even Juniper came, though she did look rather reluctant sometimes. As for Zack, he barely spoke these days. I knew he blamed himself for Helen's accident, but I did not know what to say or do to alleviate his feelings of guilt. I felt like an intruder to his sorrow, powerless over his pain. Every minute, hour and day drifted away in creepy silence.

***

"Ignite."

I pointed my scepter at the golden candelabra beside Helen's bed. A flicker of flames emitted from the tip then extinguished. I cursed. The damp weather was starting to annoy me. The incessant rain and moisture the storm had brought during the past five days made it more difficult for me to conjure fire. Focusing on the color and shape of the element I harnessed, I tried again and succeeded. Orange flames blazed vigorously on the tips of the three candles, painting my journal yellow. I turned to page twenty, the one that had a bearnix-shaped bookmark, and perused the entry.

*We traveled through a forest with trees that had crimson leaves, soaking wet and exhausted. An earlier fight with a Chirpy Bird had slashed our stamina. Heavy rain was pouring down from the clouds miles above us. Blinding streaks of lightning took occasional peeks at the forest, brightening the trees ahead of us. Thunder roared in the sky like a furious bearnix. It was probably foolish to remain in the forest during a thunderstorm, but after several failed attempts, we had no choice but to give up on finding the exit. Just then, a peculiar oak tree ahead caught our attention. Magical candles blazed on its branches, unfazed and undisturbed by the continuous rain. An arch-shaped door was carved in the trunk of the tree, where an eerie red glow seemed to emit from behind it. Cautiously and curiously, we approached the door, pushed it open, and saw –*

"Zack?"

"Helen?" Three other heads jerked up in surprise.

"Oh, Zack! Are you hurt?"

I'd never seen Helen like this before. Her eyes were fearful and her voice frantic.

"Relax, Helen. We're all fine," said Zack. "How are you feeling?"

"Better, now that I know you're not hurt." Helen stirred, attempting to sit up. Zack helped her into a sitting position, and she took notice of Eric, Eileen, and me. "You're all here?"

I nodded. "Of course. Everyone in the Inner Circle's visited you in the past few days. Evonne and Brian just left for a shower. They'll be pleased to know you've come round."

Helen grimaced and pressed a hand to the bandaged wound.

"Does it still hurt?" Eileen asked, concerned.

"I—" Noticing the pained expression on Zack's face, Helen improvised, "not that much."

"I'm sorry, Helen. I'm so sorry. I never wanted you to risk

your life for me. How could I have let that happen?" A glimmer of light sparkled in Zack's eyes as he took Helen's hand. "Forgive me...please."

"It had nothing to do with you," said Helen, placing her other hand on top of Zack's to console him. "It was my choice, and I don't regret it." With what seemed like a huge effort, she forced a feeble smile.

"You always ask too much of yourself."

Helen patted Zack on the shoulder and turned to the rest of us. Although she said nothing, the turbulence of emotions was clearly reflected in her expression. "I...I've been meaning to ask this for a while...." She paused as though dreading to hear the answer.

I knew what was coming, and I didn't like it.

Helen swallowed hard. "How many?"

"Sorry?"

"How many Elders went down in the battle?"

"Um...thirty," I answered, shifting my weight from one foot to the other in uneasiness.

Helen inhaled deeply, then exhaled as if preparing herself for the worst. "And the members of the Inner Circle did any of them...?"

The rest of us exchanged looks of uneasiness.

"Helen, I'm really sorry to tell you this, but—"

"That's enough, Alexandria," Zack snapped, his tone stern. "She shouldn't be hearing—"

"Well, she'll have to face it sooner or later."

"But not now. The news would overwhelm her. She can't take another blow like this."

"Please," Helen's tone was almost imploring. She closed her eyes, and I thought I saw a tear glistening under her lush black lashes. "I *need* to know. Who was it?"

There was a moment of silence before I broke it. "Clarissa. The Chirpy Bird killed her."

Helen looked at Eric and Eileen as if expecting them to convince her otherwise.

"We witnessed it," said Eileen in a quiet voice.

I half-expected Helen to burst into tears or faint from shock, but she remained perfectly still, as though refusing to believe the truth. "Why Clarissa? She had a whole life ahead of her...." Her voice trailed away. "She was only fifteen, too young to suffer such a horrible fate."

"I know. I know." Zack draped an arm around her, tears surfacing in his eyes.

I felt as though I had relived the memory of Clarissa's death. The stab of realization and finality cut me fresh, paining me like a knife to the heart. I would never see Clarissa's smile again. I would never hear her cheerful voice again. She had become nothing more than a cold corpse void of warmth and emotion. Gone. Just like that.

Both Eric and Eileen turned away from the Elders, identical expressions of grief etched upon their faces. We, including Daphne, who was sound asleep five beds away from Helen's, all knew, yet none of us dared to voice aloud, that four would never become five again. The four of us were an incomplete puzzle. A fragment had been snatched away forever by the cruel hands of fate, never to be relinquished.

A figure emerged at the entrance of the infirmary and neared us. "Lady Helen, Lord Zack, Lord Eric."

"Noir?" I looked up, recognizing his voice.

"It is me, Your Highness," replied Noir, bowing.

"What brings you here?"

"King Patrick and Queen Marianne are planning to hold a morning assembly three days from now. Same time, same place." He exchanged a knowing look with the Elders. "Your Highness, Miss Spencer, and Miss Sinclair are also invited."

"Alexandria and I will be there, but Daphne's in no shape to go," Eileen replied at once.

We had visited Daphne earlier this evening. Her broken ribs and leg made it impossible for her to leave the infirmary in the next week. Also, she had to take the Curing Concoction five times a day—a gooey blue substance that, according to Daphne herself, had a salty taste of seawater.

"And Lord Zack, the rulers ask you to temporarily replace

Lady Helen as the Representative Elder and take over her duties," Noir went on.

"What? They still think she's being ridiculous?" Eric said, frowning.

"No, my lord. King Patrick and Queen Marianne have witnessed the destruction caused by the Underworldians and will no longer blame the Inner Circle. They wish that Lady Helen will continue to serve as the Representative Elder after she has made a full recovery."

"Oh. Finally doing something sensible, are they?" Eric grumbled. "Why have they scheduled a morning assembly all of a sudden?"

"King Patrick and Queen Marianne want to confer with the Elders and figure out the Otherworld's next step."

"All right," Eric shrugged. "Makes sense, I guess."

"Then I'll take my leave." Noir bowed and left.

"This is ridiculous," remarked Eric, shaking his head. "But they're starting to see sense, and I guess that's an improvement."

"I reckon they'll consult us, the Inner Circle," said Zack, glancing at Helen.

"Tell them everything we've discovered," she replied.

Some of my thoughts must have reflected on my expression, for Eileen asked, "What's the matter, Alexandria?"

"I've been thinking that...I think we should take action as soon as possible."

"Take action?" Zack repeated. "What do you mean?"

"Look," I explained, "we've been flipping through old journals and drawing maps and stuff, but we're not getting anywhere. We already know the Underworld is not a terrain-shifter. All we need to do now is to figure out the portals and terrains and where they're located. This is risky, but...."

"Go on," Helen said, a curious expression on her face.

"We need a mission," I finished. "We must go and navigate the Underworld in person."

Whatever they were expecting, it was not this. The silence that followed my words had become so loud that for a moment, I thought it would last forever.

"I know it's dangerous, and we might have to go through a lot of unexpected terrains in the Underworld." I gave Eric a harsh look as he opened his mouth to interrupt me. "Yes, there's a very slim chance we would survive this mission, but we can't spend every day stuck here reading the journals. The first invasion's already taken place, and it won't be the last."

"So you think something worse is going to happen?" Eric, Eileen, and Zack all stared at me.

"Positive." I suddenly remembered I hadn't told them Alta's final words before leaving the Otherworld. "Listen, after Helen collapsed...." And then I related to them everything I had witnessed.

"What?" Eric said. "But that's—"

"I second your thoughts, Alexandria." Helen's expression had become pensive rather than curious. "It hasn't ended. And it's only going to get worse."

Somewhere in the distance, the growl of thunder filled our eardrums. The storm had not yet ceased. The sky, still hemorrhaging with rain, showered the castle grounds with furious downpours and waterfalls.

"Haven't seen a thunderstorm like this for years," Helen said in a would-be steady voice, staring at the window opposite her bed. "Turbulent times have come."

***

About ninety percent of the Elders were already gathered in the Throne Room for today's assembly. Everyone was appareled in black silk, lace, or chiffon rather than purple, for it was the first assembly after the disastrous invasion that claimed the lives of many. The Elders all looked handsome in their gowns and tuxedos, but their haughty expressions and vain demeanor did not make them seem at all likable or approachable. Eileen and I were both dressed in identical understated black gowns, which made it easier for us to blend into the crowd.

I devoted my attention to the Throne Room as we followed Eric in. It was the same as I had last seen it, with towering walls sheathed with white marble, a fancy chandelier, and a carpeted aisle that divided the opposite rows of smaller thrones occupied by Elders.

"Over here," said Eric, indicating the vacant little thrones beside his.

Eileen and I took our seats. I turned, half-expecting to see Clarissa on my other side, but was then brutally reminded again that she was gone. Forever. Both Eileen and Eric were quiet; I had a feeling the three of us were sharing the same thoughts—mourning in silence for Clarissa, who should have been here with us but wasn't and would never be.

The absence of Helen aroused ripples of murmurs throughout the other Elders. Rumors were flying all over the palace. Some claimed that Helen was so upset about the rulers' disregard of her warning that she left the palace, yet others believed she was being held hostage by Alta and Alto, and they were using her as bait to lure the Elders to go and rescue her. Nobody apart from the Inner Circle seemed to know the truth. Elbowing and whispering to their neighbors, every one of them looked rather delighted to have her gone.

Well, screw them, I thought savagely, gritting my teeth and glaring at the cruel, ignorant Elders. White-hot anger licked my insides as I resisted the temptation to burn the Throne Room to the ground.

"Don't mind them," said Eric, though he, too, was glaring at the group of Elders who were guffawing and buzzing with conversation. "They're a mean lot."

The doors opened, and in came Bessie the bearnix. The talking died down as if a show was about to start.

"What's wrong?" I whispered to Eric.

"The king and queen have arrived. They're waiting outside the doors. Bessie's going to notify the Representative Elder, who's about to give commands. Look."

I looked in his direction and saw Bessie whispering something to Zack, who nodded. Although he was the deputy Representative Elder, he had, perhaps deliberately, left Helen's seat unoccupied.

"Elders, your attention, please," announced Zack. "All rise for the king and queen."

A hush fell upon the room. Everyone rose to their feet, and Eileen and I followed suit. Bessie hurried to the doors and opened them. Sure enough, King Patrick and Queen Marianne, both bedecked in fine black satin, entered the Throne Room and made their way down the aisle. After they had settled in their thrones, the Elders turned to face them.

"Greetings, Your Majesties," the Elders chorused, bowing and curtsying. Eileen and I did the same.

"Rise," King Patrick commanded. "You may take your seats, Elders."

"What next?" I murmured to Eric as I sat down.

"The Representative Elder will do a roll call in alphabetical order. All you have to do is raise your hand when your name's called and say—"

"Spare the roll call for today," said Queen Marianne, waving her gloved hand as if dismissing him. Then, in a more serious manner, she addressed her audience. "Elders, you all know why I have summoned you here today. We have made a grave mistake, neglecting the threat of the Underworld and endangering not only all of you, but also the Otherworldians. Patrick and I offer our sincerest apologies and deepest regrets for our unwise judgement. Thirty Elders and seventy guards have lost their lives in the invasion. As some of you might know, a funeral will be held the day after tomorrow to commemorate the fallen ones who rose valiantly to the occasion and sacrificed themselves while defending the Otherworld."

There was a murmur of agreement.

"However, the past is in the past. No matter how much we regret the occurrence of the tragedy, we do not have the power to alter it. We can only look forward to the future, and we must have faith. We will defend our compatriots—the men, women, elderly, children, and all the creatures in our realm. We haven't lost. It's just that we haven't won yet. We," Queen Marianne's voice intensified in both strength and volume as she continued to exhort the Elders, "will never surrender. This is not just a slogan. It's a spirit everyone should have. Our enemies may outnumber us in people, but not in unity or concordance. We mustn't let darkness separate us, for our hearts beat as one, always and forever."

"Bunch of baloney," Eric muttered to Eileen, who bobbed her head up and down in agreement. "Alexandria, can you cut her off and begin your speech right now?"

"A few more minutes," I whispered back.

We had rehearsed this speech quite a few times yesterday. I would first explain our newest discovery, then make a request for a mission to the Underworld to navigate the terrains in detail. However, I didn't want to be rude and interrupt Queen Marianne so soon.

"Now, there are some unsung heroes I would like to credit. A group of Elders, known as 'The Inner Circle,' have been doing research and attempting to help the Otherworld. The group is led by none other than your Representative Elder, Helen Edmunds. She stood her ground and held on to her beliefs, despite the continuous disdain and discrediting of others."

"Funny how Queen Marianne forgot she's the one who's been 'disdaining and discrediting' Helen all along," Eric muttered, his voice juicy with sarcasm.

"Helen Edmunds performed a noble act of bravery during the invasion, sacrificing herself for the safety of a fellow Elder. Our thoughts are with her, and we wish her a speedy recovery."

Another ripple of murmur broke throughout the Elders. Eric nodded a cue, and I seized my opportunity and raised a hand.

"Yes, Alexandria?"

Heads turned. Every Elder focused his or her gaze on me.

"Your Majesty, as a member of the Inner Circle, I hope to shed light on some facts we've discovered."

Both rulers nodded. "You may," said King Patrick.

"For the past few weeks, we've been taking old journals out from the Archive Room and studying them, and we have come to a conclusion: the Underworld is not a terrain-shifter. The only thing that's changing is the portals to it."

The Elders broke into whispers of skepticism, or to be more accurate, contradiction.

Queen Marianne blinked. "But...Alexandria, it's been confirmed that—"

"With all due respect, Your Majesty, nobody has ever actually confirmed that. There are no statistics, no evidence, and no theories about the Underworld being a terrain-shifter. However, two corresponding entries from two separate journals have proved our theory of the changing portals and non-changing terrains—"

"Your Highness," an Elder who I recognized as Kerry Jenkins chimed in. "Forgive me, but this theory of yours seems so...ridiculous." She let out a simper. "I find it very hard to believe what you just claimed to be a fact. Are you saying that you have evidence to—?"

I felt my temper rising. "Evidence? Yeah, I've got plenty of that. Just ask any member of the Inner Circle, and he or she will answer your pointless questions. We've done all the research, and this is our conclusion."

"Oh please, of course, they would say—"

"Why would I lie to the king and queen? What good will that do to the Otherworld?" I retorted. "For your information, I've brought the journals here with me. However, I think it's unnecessary to waste time on explaining a solid fact in detail only because some—"

"Are you insulting me?" Kerry Jenkins demanded, her face turning blotchy red.

"Enough from you, Jenkins." It was King Patrick who spoke this time. "Alexandria, I believe you."

A surge of gratitude for my father filled me. "Thanks," I replied. "Your Majesty...about the facts we've discovered...may I make a request?"

King Patrick and Queen Marianne exchanged a look in silence.

"Please, Your Majesty. Although we have discovered the truth about the changing portals, it would be impossible for us to have a full understanding of the terrains of the Underworld by merely reading journals. It is my request that we go on a mission to the Underworld and navigate everything in person."

King Patrick and Queen Marianne gazed at me, stunned.

I glanced at Eric and Eileen, and it was their looks of encouragement that goaded me into speech. "This may not seem urgent or important, but in fact, it is both. If we have a clear picture of the terrains in the Underworld, it will make missions much easier for the Elders who go to the Underworld in the future. They will know the exact positions of the aquaportals, entrances, and exits and will no longer have to spend time searching for the portal to the Otherworld on their way back. Also, we will be able to predict what challenging terrains lie ahead, and that will definitely boost our confidence. Plus, we'll be able to pay the Underworld back for what they did to us last week—"

"Pay them back?" King Patrick questioned. "What do you—?"

"They're not giving up, Alta and Alto. They sent a messenger to the Otherworld, pretending to reconcile with us while actually luring us into a false sense of security. There will be a war sometime soon in the future, Your Majesties. A chaotic final war that shall determine the rise or fall of the Otherworld. Either we win and defeat the Underworld, or we lose and relinquish our world to Alta and Alto. I don't know what will happen, but I am positive the Otherworld and Underworld will both spare no effort to face off."

"You believe there will be a final war, and navigating the terrains in the Underworld is essential?" Queen Marianne asked in a solemn manner.

"Yes."

For a fleeting moment, our eyes met—King Patrick's, Queen Marianne's, and mine. Between the three of us, there passed a look of deep understanding.

"Very well, then. Request granted," King Patrick boomed, nodding his approval.

I blinked, assuming the convincing part would have taken much longer than just a few minutes.

"Zack and Eric, I would be more than grateful if you both go along on the mission," King Patrick added.

Eileen's brown eyes widened. "Excuse me, Your Majesty,

but could I—?"

"Eileen, as the heiress of Fern, your elemental magic may not be powerful enough to help you survive."

"But Your Majesty, Eric—"

"I understand. But this is a dangerous mission that will probably take a few days to complete. There is a high possibility you will not survive, and we will not take the risk of losing another heiress," said Queen Marianne with a gentle yet firm touch of finality. "Every Otherworldian matters, Eileen. I hope you understand that."

Eileen's head drooped, and her shoulders sagged. "Yes," she muttered.

Lilith raised her hand. "Your Majesties, may I join them?"

Kerry Jenkins let out a snort of laughter. "You! Don't make me laugh, Jackson."

King Patrick frowned. "Lilith, I don't think that's a good idea. You barely know anything about archery or swordplay."

"I'm good at spells. I'm sure they'd also come in handy during a fight."

King Patrick shook his head. "I'm sorry, but we can't risk losing another Elder."

Lilith nodded, crestfallen. It hurt me to see her head bent like a wilted flower. Why didn't the rulers have faith in her?

Jenkins smirked at her misery. It took all of my willpower to not stick out my middle finger at her.

"Zack, Eric, I only permit the most powerful and competent Elders to participate in this mission." As Queen Marianne said this, her resemblance to Helen was striking. "Please do not fail me."

"Yes, Your Majesty."

Queen Marianne uttered a sigh. "Helen would've been my first pick, but I suppose she's still too weak to leave the infirmary...."

"I won't disappoint you, Your Majesty," I assured her. "And neither will Zack and Eric. I have faith in them."

Queen Marianne was silent for a while. "Very well. You may begin your journey on the day after tomorrow when the funeral ends. I suppose...." Her voice quivered a little, "I suppose you'd want to pay your respects and say goodbye to Clarissa Dawson. She was your loyal friend and companion, after all."

"Thank you, Your Majesty," I said.

"Elders, that marks the end of today's assembly. You are all dismissed."

"Rise," commanded Zack. All the Elders stood up, bowed and curtsied, and filed out of the Throne Room, buzzing and chattering.

"Alexandria," Queen Marianne called my name.

"Meet us in the infirmary. Helen's bed," Eric muttered to me.

I nodded and waved at him. "See you."

After the last few Elders had left, I walked up to the gigantic thrones. "Your Majesties."

"Alexandria, what made you decide to request a mission?" asked King Patrick. I was taken aback to hear that he sounded more concerned than astonished.

"For the future of the Otherworld," I replied without hesitation. "We have to put a stop to it. Sooner or later, the Underworld will launch an attack on us again."

"Are you aware of the high stakes of the upcoming adventure?"

I nodded. "I know there's a slim chance I'll make it back alive, but I'm dead set on this." The memory of the peaceful village and grazing kittenpillars occurred to my mind at that moment. "I have to do my duty to the Otherworld."

Queen Marianne gazed at me, a soulful look in her emerald eyes. When she spoke, her voice was surprisingly soft. "Alexandria, you are indeed a noble and courageous Otherworldian. I want to give you my blessing and full support on this mission. I want you to be proud of yourself, to fight for your beliefs, and to be welcomed back as a hero. But Alexandria...." She paused, fighting against her emotions. "It's just so, so hard for me to yield, to let go. I am the queen of the Otherworld. I want the Otherworldians to be safe and all Elders reunited with their families. But at the same time, I am also your mother. Granting your request is like sending a lamb to the slaughter, and I can't help worrying about the dangers that lie ahead of you. You're our only child. We can't afford to lose you."

I fixed my gaze on one of the iridescent opals on Queen Marianne's necklace so I wouldn't have to look into her eyes and feel the pang of guilt. Her words got to me. When I had come to the Otherworld, I had planned to confront Queen Marianne as soon as I met her for neglecting the threat of Alta and Alto and putting the Otherworld in danger. But now, I just couldn't.

"I know it's hard, Your Majesty. But think of the fallen Elders and guards who gave their lives to defend the Otherworld. They fought, even though some of them probably didn't stand a chance against the most powerful and evil Underworldians. They were also mothers, fathers, sisters, brothers, daughters, sons, wives, and husbands to their families, but that didn't stop them from fighting. Every life is worth the same, and it wouldn't be fair for them if I was out of harm's way while they were out there, risking their necks and sacrificing their lives for the Otherworld. Plus, the Otherworld is my home, the only place where I belong. I can't stand being locked away safely, watching my home collapse before my eyes when I could've made a difference and kept it safe. As the princess, it's my duty to protect the Otherworld."

Queen Marianne observed me, an unfathomable expression playing on her face as if she were pondering over something inexplicable. "Then at least promise me something," she said after what seemed like an hour. "Take care of yourself."

"I will. Goodbye, Your Majesties." I curtsied, bowing my head as deeply as I could to avoid their gazes.

"Rise," King Patrick said. "And...Alexandria."

"Your Majesty?"

He closed his eyes, looking as though pleading with himself. I could have sworn I saw his bottom lip trembling. "Good luck, my daughter. I'll be waiting for you."

I nodded, not knowing what to reply. Words were unnecessary in times like this. Before leaving, I gave my parents one last lingering look and forced a reassuring smile at them.

***

Two days had passed since the assembly. The storm had finally ended this morning. Zack, Eric, and I stepped into the courtyard, the chilly breeze whispering in our ears. Twilight had tinted the sky pale pink and littered it with silver stars and streaks of clouds. Glistening dewdrops clung onto the blades of grass like tiny diamonds playing hide-and-seek. I surveyed the courtyard and gazed up at the immaculate towers and spires of the palace, wondering if I would ever come back alive and see them again.

"Ready?" Zack asked.

Eric and I both nodded. We all knew what we were getting into the moment King Patrick and Queen Marianne approved of my request.

Without a word, the three of us clambered into the three-tier fountain together and raised our wands and scepters. "Three... two...one...the Underworld!"

The ground rifted open, and we felt ourselves engulfed by a tunnel of coolness and darkness.

# Chapter Seven

## MORS MANOR
## (ERIC)

*Splash*!

Behind me, I heard Alexandria and Zack splashing water and coughing.

"Where are we?" Alexandria asked.

Small waves lapped at my waist as I struggled to get into a standing position. "I think we're in another fountain in the Underworld. Here, take my hand." I grabbed Alexandria's clammy fingers, and together, we climbed out of the fountain.

We found ourselves transported to the strangest garden I had ever seen, conspicuously dark and somewhat insidious. Obsidian sculptures of bearnixes, unibirds, kittenpillars, and dogfishes dotted the olive-green lawn. Black bushes and hedges with blooming maroon and burgundy roses littered the garden, giving off a viscous sense of foreboding. A thin, dreamy film of mist floated in the air, wisps of white vapor clinging onto the ebony bushes in smokey swirls. In front of us, half-shrouded by the fog, there perched an ancient, derelict manor with three stories.

"What are those? Oversized bats?" whispered Alexandria, pointing at the purple sky.

Squinting, I managed to make out the dark silhouettes of

a flock of black unibirds soaring above us, flapping their bat-like wings and cawing.

"A species of unibirds. They're a creation of Alta's dark magic."

"Do they attack people?" Alexandria asked.

The curious look in her eyes reminded me of Eileen, who had always been interested in flora and fauna. I wondered what she would say if she were here with us. Subconsciously, I felt the lump in my pocket for the silver locket Eileen had given me before we left for the Underworld.

"Eric?" Alexandria sounded scared. "Do they...do the unibirds attack people?"

"Huh? Oh, uh...I don't think so. Look, they're flying away."

"Kind of an eerie place to begin our journey, isn't it?" Alexandria said, surveying the garden. "It looks pretty Gothic around here."

"God...Godic? What's that?"

"No, no. Gothic," corrected Zack. "It's an expression mortals use to describe things that look dark and mysterious."

"That's interesting. I didn't know someone coined a word for—Alexandria, don't!" I grabbed her arm as she touched a burgundy rose.

Too late. The petals snapped shut, trapping Alexandria's finger.

"Get off me!" she cried, struggling to free her finger. Zack and I tugged the petals, but the stubborn rose refused to open.

"Sever." I pointed my scepter at the petals. However, all it managed to do was to make the rose growl and tighten its grasp on Alexandria's finger.

"What on earth are you doing, Eric, killing me?"

"Sorry. Let me try a different one. Blast!"

The rose clamped its jaws on Alexandria's finger, chomping into her flesh and puncturing her skin. She let out a howl of pain and cursed.

"I'm sorry! I don't know—"

"Since violence won't work, what about we try something different?" Zack stroked the rose with his wand. The petals opened in a wide yawn, releasing Alexandria's finger before closing shut again.

"That was clever." I gave Zack an admiring look.

Alexandria conjured a ball of fire and healed her finger with it. "Sorry for causing so much trouble in the first ten minutes of our mission."

"That was a bad omen," said Zack. "We should get out of here as soon as possible. Eric, can you summon a cloud?"

Just then, a tiny drop of water splashed onto my nose. Before I knew it, the rain was drizzling over the three of us.

"Darn, it's raining," Alexandria said. "Let's find a shelter for tonight."

"Good idea," agreed Zack. "It's getting late. We'll carry on with our mission tomorrow." He pointed to the manor up ahead. "We could stay there for tonight, in that house. I think it's empty."

"But—" I started.

The rain was intensifying at a rapid speed. In less than five seconds, we were drenched by the torrential showers, now pouring over us like mad. My clothes were sodden, and to make matters worse, the water was seeping into my boots and socks.

"Fine, we'll go into the house and wait for the rain to stop," I gave in, disgruntled at the cursed weather.

Sloshing through overflowing puddles, we raced to the veranda of the desolate manor, raindrops whipping our faces. I inhaled lungfuls of the damp, chilly air as I gasped for breath. Zack and Alexandria were also bedraggled and soaking wet.

"Here." Alexandria dried my clothes with a fireball when we reached shelter.

"Thanks." I cupped my hands around the blazing orange ball of flames perched on her palms. I was trembling from head to toe with cold or fear. I wasn't sure which.

"You okay, Eric?"

Desperate not to act like a coward, I nodded. "Some first night, isn't it? We get transported to a garden clearly full of dark magic, then we're supposed to spend tonight in a strange, abandoned house. It seems as if everything's against us," I said with a shaky laugh, trying to make the series of misfortunes sound like a joke. "What are you looking at, Zack?"

He was riveted by a golden plaque on the wooden door, as still as a statue.

I walked up to him and studied it. "*Mors Manor*.... Is that the name of this house?"

"Maybe," said Zack. For some reason, he looked troubled and distracted.

"What's wrong?"

"I'm thinking that.... I hope I'm wrong, but I think this may be *the* 'haunted manor.'"

My heart skipped a beat. "The one we've read about in the journals?"

Zack nodded, a grim expression etched on his face.

"Is it?" Alexandria let out a laugh of relief. "Well, I don't remember the journals mentioning any paranormal activity in this house. I guess it's safe to stay here for tonight. Anyway, it's not like we've got an alternative. Come on." She pushed the door open as it creaked and moaned. "I'll go first," she volunteered.

Wand and scepter raised in caution, Zack and I followed her. Ice crept down my spine as I set foot in the manor. It was unusually chilly, and even though the door was closed, I felt cold air whispering and whooshing behind me. Everything was dark. I could only make out the frames of the furniture around us. An ominous feeling bubbled in my stomach. "Is it only me, or does it feel a bit cold in here?"

The rain was still thundering outside, pounding the roof and walls, its volume muffled by the confines of the manor. Any hope of spending tonight outdoors was out of the window.

Alexandria lifted her lava scepter and pointed at the rusty chandelier hanging from the ceiling, where stubby candles squatted snugly in the sockets. "Ignite."

A warm glow illuminated the house, and we found ourselves in the living room. Cobwebs sparkled beneath the ceiling, dotted with three tiny spiders. Dust lay thick as snow on the antique furniture. Woodworms had almost destroyed the large bookshelves that sat in the corner of the room. The carpet was moth-eaten and littered with tiny particles of filth and balls of fuzz. There were scorch marks etched on the singed velvet curtains, and the wallpaper was peeling.

The dining room was right behind us. On the lacquered table perched piles of dishes, all smeared and soiled. Countless furry little gray balls licked the grease, hopping up and down on the plates like children bouncing on trampolines.

"What are those?" Alexandria reached out a hand to touch them.

"No, don't," I said, grabbing her arm. "Those are filthers, the most disgusting creatures in the Underworld."

"Filthers?"

"They're scavenging animals. They feed on leftovers and all sorts of rotten food."

"And decayed bodies," added Zack, looking as though he had watched someone vomit.

"Well, all right. I won't get closer to them," said Alexandria. She flicked the filthers a curious look before turning to leave.

I caught sight of a small room on the left of the table, presumably the kitchen. The room was cluttered with junk, making it impossible to gain entry. A crowd of filthers bounced out from a worn armchair in the kitchen, a huge gray blur of fuzzy balls.

"Not in the best condition, huh?" Alexandria said, her tone serene and conversational, as though she were talking about what to have for dinner rather than the furnishing of a haunted manor.

"No," Zack agreed, striding up to the stairwell. "There's a second floor," he said, pointing at a wooden staircase that ascended into darkness. "Suppose it wouldn't hurt to navigate the rooms upstairs, would it?"

"Good idea," said Alexandria. "I don't think the rain's going to stop until tomorrow. It's best to check this place thoroughly before we settle down and sleep. I'm going first." She set a foot on the creaky wooden planks.

"Together," Zack corrected her.

I had an awful feeling about heading upstairs, but I gritted my teeth and followed the two of them.

"Take my hand if you're scared," whispered Alexandria in my ear. For the first time in my life, I was glad to have someone to hold onto for support.

The wooden planks beneath our feet moaned and groaned as we made our way upstairs. My skin prickled with goosebumps. I did my best to keep my hand steady as I raised my scepter, ready to attack any creatures lurking in the darkness.

"I think we've reached the second floor," said Zack.

A long, endless corridor unfolded before us, half-swallowed by inky darkness.

Alexandria ignited the chandelier dangling beneath the ceiling with a swish of her scepter. "Come along."

Unmoving portraits with spectral glares stared at us as we proceeded along the corridor, guided by the pools of light above. The floorboards cackled beneath our feet like a sinister witch.

"Let's see, three rooms and a bathroom," said Zack, his tone falsely cheerful. "A master bedroom, a guest room, and...a nursery."

"Then let's go and take a look at that one first." Alexandria pointed to the room at the end of the corridor.

The door groaned open, and we were greeted by a stale, musty smell. The master bedroom was overloaded with discarded furniture, all caked with thick films of dust. A few shabby cabinets stood by the door, the painted surfaces peeling off in strips. In the corner of the spacious room, I saw an old-fashioned bed with a canopy. Black brocade curtains embroidered with gold hung loosely around it. Five crates lay scattered on the bed, containing moldy sheets and clothes either damaged, stained, or tattered.

"Definitely not my dream room." Zack forced a smile.

"Nor mine," Alexandria said, closing the door as we left. "Want to take a look at the bathroom?"

As soon as she opened the door, the unbearable stench of urine and filthers' droppings assailed my nostrils. I gagged, pressing a hand to my tortured nose.

"Seems like we won't be setting foot here tonight." Alexandria slammed the bathroom door shut.

"Lucky I showered this morning." I scanned the long corridor. "Two rooms left."

"What about this, Alexandria?" began Zack. "Eric and I will sleep in the guest room together while you're in the nursery. Since you're a girl, I think it's best if we separate."

"Jolly good," answered Alexandria, smiling. "A whole room to myself. All right, let me go and check it out." She disappeared behind a large black door.

Zack and I wandered along the corridor and came to the guest room, which was opposite the staircase. The rusty hinges creaked as we pushed the door open. I had expected to see a mess, but to my surprise, the guest room was quite fit for living. A tufted white bed with dusty sheets and pillows stood across from the door. Two rustic nightstands with vases of wilted flowers rested on either side. A large gilded wardrobe with a cloudy mirror was erected by the door, and a couch covered with patches sat opposite from it, the stuffing spilling out from a crack. The gray silk curtains behind the couch were marred by large black blots of ink but otherwise looked in fine condition.

"Perfect," said Zack, even though the room was far from that. "I mean, compared to the other rooms," he explained.

"Yeah, at least it looks...okay," I said, heaving a sigh. "You can have the bed to yourself, Zack. I'll take the couch."

"Are you sure? The couch doesn't look too comfortable. We could share a bed if you don't—" Zack paused in mid-sentence.

"What's wrong?"

He brought an index finger to his lips.

A few seconds of stillness and silence. Moments later, a strangled scream shattered the serenity of the house.

"Who? What?"

"Alexandria," was Zack's curt reply. Without another word, he dashed out of the guest room. I raced after him, and into the nursery, we ran.

The grayish-blue curtains were twisting and tangling themselves around a struggling figure, who flailed her arms and shrieked in a muffled voice. Zack and I rushed to the curtains, pulling and tugging at them to free Alexandria. However, the curtains, which seemed to have a mind of their own, shoved me and Zack out of the way and wrapped themselves more tightly around her.

"Get off me! Help!" Alexandria clawed at the curtains like kittenpillars did when they were under attack. "Do something, Eric!" Her face was turning purple.

Recalling the biting roses we had encountered earlier, I stroked the curtains with my scepter. However, all it did was agitate them. The curtains whacked me in the face with the force of ten people, knocking me to the floor. Before I knew it, a wisp of fabric wrapped itself around my torso, tightened itself, and soon immobilized my body, trying to throttle me like it had done to Alexandria.

Thrashing against my bindings, I kicked and fought against them to escape. However, the more wildly I struggled, the more firmly the curtains anchored themselves around me. My lungs constricted as I gasped for breath. I tried in vain to stomp on the hem of the curtains and free myself; a tuft of fabric slithered to my legs like a snake and started trapping my feet.

"Sever," said Zack, pointing his wand at the curtains.

Nothing happened.

"No...no, let him go...," I wheezed as another wisp of fabric wound itself around Zack's waist. The curtains were now squeezing my neck. I could feel my eyes bulging and every last bit of air leaving my lungs. I felt as if I were drowning, sinking into an ocean of endless darkness....

"SEVER!" I heard Zack shout.

*Thump.* The heavy curtains finally released the three of us, collapsing into a heap on the floor. The grayish-blue mound grappled with itself, wrestling and twisting its wisps of fabric. I saw a hummock of toy blocks, a pink stuffed bearnix, and a wooden unibird hobbyhorse on the other side of the room. The curtains flapped on the floor, edging toward the stuffed bearnix and twisting themselves around its neck.

"Run!" I heard Zack shout.

I didn't need reminding twice. Flanked by Zack and Alexandria, I sped toward the door. With a loud bang, we kicked it shut.

"Are you all right?" I asked Alexandria, massaging my neck.

She nodded, gasping for air. "It—it was horrible. I'm never going into this room again."

"What happened when you first went in?"

A shudder ran through Alexandria's body. "It was cold. Very cold. Not the windy sort of cold, but freezing, as if a blizzard was coming. I was sure I felt something weird in the room."

"Did you see anyone?" I asked.

Alexandria shook her head. "No, but I could sense someone. It was an odd feeling. An intuition, more like. I felt as though somebody was...monitoring me."

"And what happened next?"

Sweat dotting Alexandria's forehead, she continued in a timid voice. "A lot of strange things happened at the same time. I turned to see if anyone had come into the room, and I saw the wooden unibird rocking all by itself, the toy blocks hovering in the air, and the stuffed bearnix—" Alexandria gulped. "It growled, and its eyes glowed red."

Zack's hand flew to his mouth.

"I was about to make a run for it, but that was when I heard someone whispering. I couldn't make out the words, but I could tell it was coming from behind the curtains. I went up to check if anybody was hiding there, and the curtains twisted themselves around my body and tried to strangle me. I'm not going in there a second time."

"Then you'll be sharing a room with us tonight. Come on."

The three of us returned to the guest room. "It's getting dark in here," said Alexandria. "Any candelabras or lanterns?"

"Haven't found one yet," answered Zack, opening the wardrobe. "I think we'll manage to find one of those in this huge pile of mess." He rummaged through the mountain of random objects in the wardrobe and chucked a brown snuffbox onto the bed. To my astonishment, the snuffbox jumped and ran across the mattress. With a nimble somersault, it landed on the floor.

"Cool," said Alexandria, grinning in surprise.

Zack tossed a leather-bound book with loose bindings onto the floor, and it began singing off-key in a shrill, unpleasant voice. Alexandria and Zack covered their ears, and I ran to the book and slammed it shut. After a moment of silence, the three of us looked at one another and burst into peals of laughter.

"Life's always filled with surprises, isn't it?" Alexandria said. "Let me see if there's more of them." Still smiling, she trotted to the wardrobe and flung a few more objects onto the bed. "Ah, just what we need—three lanterns and a few candelabras."

Alexandria gave her scepter a gentle wave. Several golden orbs of light fluttered from the tip and landed on the lanterns and candelabras, bathing the room in a gentle orange glow. She set the rusty white lanterns on the two nightstands, one on each. "Better, isn't it?"

I nodded.

"I'll leave the other lantern and the candelabras on the floor," she announced. "I don't think we'll be needing them, or at least for now."

"Put them back in the wardrobe, then," said Zack.

Alexandria did. Just as she was about to close the door, three more snuffboxes jumped out and bounced onto the bed, doing backflips and cartwheels as they hopped down to join the first one.

"Interesting." Alexandria beamed at the dancing quartet of snuffboxes. "Is it safe to keep them?" she asked Zack.

"You want to take them back to the Otherworld?" I said, raising my eyebrows.

"It wouldn't really count as stealing, would it? Since nobody lives here anymore."

"I don't think that's a good idea. Don't forget, we're in a strange old manor. We shouldn't meddle with anything here. We never know whether it's been cursed or not." Zack stifled a yawn, "I'm going to bed, and I think you should all take a rest. Tomorrow's going to be a very tough day."

"All right," I said, tearing my gaze away from the snuffboxes, which were now performing an impressive series of gymnastics. "Alexandria, you can have the couch to yourself.

Zack and I can share a bed."

"Thanks," she said, dimming the lanterns and candelabras with a twirl of her scepter. She curled herself on the couch like a cat. "Goodnight."

"Same to you and Zack." I removed my boots, climbed onto the bed, and pulled the covers up to my chest.

It was a still and silent night, everything in profound repose. I fixed my gaze on the dancing shadows of the flickering candlelight projected on the ceiling. Lying flat on the bed, I sank into meditation. I thought about our impossible mission—navigating the Underworld. *How big is this place? How many terrains will we have to go through? How long will we have to stay in the Underworld before leaving? Could there possibly be a shortcut yet unbeknownst to us?* Contemplating all those possibilities made me dizzy. I shook my head to clear my thoughts.

A sigh at the other end of the bed told me I wasn't the only one lying awake. I looked at the couch and saw Alexandria resting her head on a yellowed cushion. She didn't seem disturbed by the looming terror of our mission at all. But then again, she was the one who had insisted we go on this mission in the first place. I liked Alexandria very much, but she could be reckless and impulsive at times. Had it not been for her, we would still be in the Otherworld now, safe and sound. I wondered whether Alexandria was aware of the risks we were taking, whether she knew what she was doing. We could lose our lives any moment, expose ourselves to the Underworldians and get killed, or—

"Eric?" Zack whispered.

"Yeah?"

"What are you thinking about?"

I stared at the dusty cobwebs above, glistening in the weak candlelight. "Nothing."

Zack smiled. "I often let my imagination run wild while tossing and turning in bed. I call it my reflection time." He let out a chuckle. "Do you often lie awake in bed and dream about the impossible?"

"The impossible?" I said, my gaze focused on a spider prowling on the cobwebs. "Like what?"

"Have you ever wondered...about...you know, your father?"

I did not answer. I did not want to tell him I had spent almost every day of the past decade wondering about my father, who he was, whether he was still alive or not, and where he could possibly be now. Perhaps I would meet him one day. Perhaps he was hiding in the Otherworld. Or perhaps he was among the guests that got invited to the countless balls King Patrick and Queen Marianne had hosted over the past few weeks. I wondered what his name was. I wondered if he knew about my existence at all. I wondered why he had abandoned me in the first place, leaving me with that horrible Alta. Perhaps he, too, had been abused by that lunatic. Perhaps he, too, had been tortured and enslaved by her. She might have tricked him into falling in love with her and had me.

"I'm sorry, Eric. I didn't mean to ask," Zack said gently. "That must be a sensitive topic for you. Just pretend I didn't—"

"No, it's okay." I rolled onto my right side to face him. "In fact, I often think about him when I'm alone."

"How much do you know about your father?"

I shook my head. "Not much. Alta wouldn't let me ask questions about him. But I do know he and I were a lot alike. Alta always said I reminded her of my father, which I guess is why she hates me so much."

"Then...were you curious about him?"

"Very. I wonder who he was. What his name was. When he left Alta and me. Why he left us. Where he might be at this moment. Come to think of it, I don't even remember his face. Have I ever met him in the flesh before? Maybe he left me even before I was born."

Zack's expression was enigmatic, unreadable. "Would you want to get to know him one day? Search for him in the future?"

"We've got a war to fight."

"Then maybe after the war?"

My lips parted to speak, but my voice failed me. The complicated feelings I had for my father swirled in me like a tornado. Yes, I had always been curious about him; however, at the same time, I felt an undeniable wave of resentment for him. Had it not been for his departure, I wouldn't have had to go through such a dark and traumatic childhood.

"Honestly, Zack, I...I don't know. I really don't. Sometimes, I wish I did."

"What do you mean? Weren't you always curious about him?"

"I was. I want to think the best of him. I want to imagine he was a kind and wonderful father figure, like you. But in the end, he was the one who left me with Alta. I can't help wondering if he cares about me or if he knows I exist." After a few moments, I added, "Perhaps he's happier without a burden like me. Perhaps that's why he chose to leave in the first place."

"I know how you feel, Eric, but don't say that. That's not... that can't be true. No father would think that way." Zack looked heartbroken for me. There were even tears in his eyes. "I'm so sorry."

"It's fine," I lied, staring up at the ceiling and pretending it was no big deal.

Silence drew upon us like a curtain. I wondered what Zack had meant when he said he knew how I felt. Did he lose his father at a young age, like me? Or was it his mother? I had never heard him mention either of his parents, after all. I peered across the musty sheets to look at Zack, who was studying the embroidered dogfishes on his black velvet cloak.

"Nice cloak," I said, a brave attempt to ease the tension. "I've never seen you wearing it before."

"Gift from Helen," replied Zack. "She gave it to me two months ago as a birthday present. Did the designing, cutting, and embroidering all by herself, without magic."

Although it was dim in the room, I could see Zack's expression softening. "You like her, don't you?" I asked, trying to sound innocent and curious.

"Who doesn't? She's always been a great leader to us."

"You have a crush on Helen."

Zack neither admitted nor denied this. When I thought he was going to ignore me, he spoke. "More than that. I adore

Helen, respect her, trust her, look upon her as a sister, and regard her as my family. I want to be there for her when she needs me."

My gaze dropped to the intricate patterns on his cloak. "I think she's pretty fond of you, too."

Zack, however, seemed to be oblivious to my words. A subtle smile flitted across his face. "I still remember the first time I met her when I first set foot in the palace of the Otherworld."

"How long ago was that? The first time you met her?"

"Nine years ago. King Patrick named Helen my mentor when I was an Elder-in-training. I was attracted to her at first sight, not by her appearance but rather her elegance. She was always strict with me and never smiled, and I used to think her cold and distant. But as I got to know Helen, I realized she was a wonderful person."

"Took you long enough," I joked, grinning.

"Helen took me under her wing, coaching me day and night, even though the other senior Elders made fun of my lack of potential. She was the only one who showed faith in me when they suggested for her to give up. I passed the Elders' recruitment test the following year, under her guidance, and became an Elder. We went through so much and faced so many challenges together. And I just couldn't help it...my admiration for her mounted into affection, which eventually became love. And my love for her grows every day." He paused, lost in his thoughts. "Eric, is this how you feel when you see Eileen?"

I thought of the countless times Evonne, Willy, and I had joked about Zack falling in love with Helen. I recalled how I had made fun of the two of them, telling the heiresses that Helen was 'not the type that would go chasing after and swooning for boys', and how everyone had then laughed at my statement, myself included. However, I did not laugh now. I couldn't. This was too deep, too serious a matter to joke about. Brian's words occurred to me: *Love is not as superficial as you think. It's far beyond that.* Perhaps he had been right all along.

"Yes," I said. "I think it's time you confess your feelings for her, Zack."

No response.

"Zack?"

A snore told me he had fallen asleep.

I rolled onto my left side and felt my pocket for Eileen's locket. I imagined her reaction if I told her about Zack's confirmed fondness for Helen. Eileen would smile, of course. I was certain it would be a knowing smile rather than a disdainful one, for she knew how it felt to be in love. At that moment, a strong upsurge of affection for Eileen gushed up in me. I thought of her angelic face, her silky brown hair, her sweet voice.... I wondered what she was doing at this precise moment. Pondering over the countless possibilities, blissful dreams took me.

In my dream, Eileen and I were waltzing in the courtyard; she in a silky azure dress, I in a white suit. She giggled as I spun her around and around and gave me a swift kiss, pecking my cheek with her glossy pink lips. Ella, the kittenpillar, emerged from a yellow rose bush, wriggled up to us, and nuzzled Eileen.

"Look, Ella thinks we're a cute couple," said Eileen, a beautiful smile on her face.

"We are," I replied, stroking the kittenpillar's furry white head. "Eileen, don't you think we'd make a perfect family? I'm the dad, you're the mom, and Ella's our little girl."

Eileen blushed. "Then what would it take to get the dad to say 'I love you, my sweetheart' to the mom?"

"You are so naughty." I hooked a finger under her chin and kissed her on the lips. "I love you, my—"

Just then, an excruciating, unearthly howl split the air, shattering my eardrums and tearing through my slumber. It sounded like the wail of a tortured demon, a cry that came from the bowels of hell.

I jerked awake and sat bolt upright in my bed. "What happened? What was that noise?"

"You heard it too?" Alexandria, who was also awake, whispered. "Who could be screaming at one in the morning?" She raised her scepter and pointed it at the door.

Zack looked from Alexandria to me. "We're not safe in here." He slid off the bed and grabbed the lantern on the nightstand. "Eric, take the one beside you. Alexandria, where's the last lantern?"

"I have it with me." Alexandria stepped into her shoes and raised the final lantern. "What should we do?"

"Leave this place. As soon as possible."

***

The three of us hurried down the moaning staircase and dashed past the living room. I overtook Alexandria, bolted toward the front door, and wrenched the handle, desperate to leave—

*Only to find it locked.*

Fear flooded in me. I turned to Zack and Alexandria. "What should we do?"

"There must be other ways to leave," asserted Alexandria, eyes darting from the kitchen to the living room. "We could try the windows." She hurried to the scorched velvet curtains and cleaved them apart, revealing a huge floor window. The ambient candlelight danced on the glassy surface.

"Let me try," I volunteered. With a flick of my scepter, a wave of turquoise and gold sparks zoomed at the window.

Nothing happened.

"Perhaps it can't be destroyed by magic. I've got an idea." Alexandria ran to the dining room and came back with a few moldy plates. "Stand back." She hurled them at the huge window with potent force, but the dishes smashed into pieces while the window stood there, intact, as though mocking us. Not even the tiniest crack appeared on the glass panel.

At that moment, another bloodcurdling howl reverberated throughout the manor. The three of us stared at one another, petrified.

"It's a monster," said Zack. "We must search every corner of this house. As long as we kill it, we can spend the rest of our night here and figure out how to leave in the morning."

"Okay," said Alexandria. "But what should we do now?"

"For starters, we've got to split."

I felt a jolt of terror at the thought of having to navigate the dark rooms on my own.

"Have you got your lanterns?" Zack went on.

"Yes," Alexandria and I chorused.

"Good. Alexandria, search the first floor while Eric takes care of the second. As for me, I'm going to check the attic."

Alexandria nodded. "See you guys later."

Zack and I mounted the stairs, and darkness closed in on us. Before our feet unfurled the endless corridor.

Zack laid a hand on my shoulder. "Eric, stay safe."

"You too."

He exchanged a would-be reassuring look with me, and we headed off in separate directions. Taking a deep breath, I treaded along the hallway, my scepter grasped in hand. Little flames flickered on the stumps of candles in the sockets of the chandelier, illuminating the corridor with a hazy, muted glow. It was quiet. Not the peaceful kind of quiet, but utter, complete silence. I could almost sense the ambiguous threats prowling around, perhaps only inches from me.

Holding my breath, I tiptoed past the guest room and into the nursery. The door moaned open as I drew nearer. *Is it my imagination, or is something lurking in the shadows?*

A shiver of terror ran through my body, and I felt an ice-cold sheen of sweat breaking across my forehead. I raised my lantern and saw the heap of curtains that had almost strangled us, now lying inert on the floor beside the pink stuffed bearnix. Piles of toy blocks lay scattered by the beige unibird hobbyhorse. A soiled white closet and a crib stood beside the window. The walls, I noticed for the first time, were painted pale green. An array of faded crayon drawings plastered to the wall by the crib snagged my attention. Most if not all of them included a small boy in a turquoise shirt and jeans.

A sudden rustling that came from the closet brought me back to reality. I glanced sideways at the source of the noise but saw nothing. Assuming it was just a filther, I ignored it and went back to studying the drawings. I frowned. There was something funny about them. The position of the little boy had somehow changed in all of the pictures. Spooked, I decided it was best to leave the room as soon as possible. Stepping back into the dim corridor, I made my way to the master bedroom. Right at that moment, a faint, muffled whisper broke the silence.

"Zack? Alexandria?"

No response.

I took a few deep breaths to calm my nerves. The floorboards below weren't helping matters. Every creak and cackle sent bolts of terror down my spine. Gingerly, I approached the master bedroom and pressed my ear to the door, certain that the whispers were coming from behind it.

"Who's there?" I demanded, pushing the door open.

Only to be confronted by the sibilant whispers of the wind. For a few moments, I stood there, staring into the void of endless darkness.

Nothing.

It was deathly quiet, as still and silent as the ocean at night. My gaze roamed the room, flitting between the cumbersome chunks of furniture, sleuthing for anything unusual. The only sound I could hear was my own breathing. Though skeptical, I convinced myself that the room was safe to enter. I searched from the dusty cabinets to the crates piled on the bed, scrutinizing every little corner for the slightest movement, for any hint a monster was lurking around here. Parting the brocade draperies, I checked if anyone was hiding behind them.

Nobody.

I frowned and noticed something tickling my hand. Several silky stray strands of gossamer were clinging on to my fingers. I brushed them off.

"Eric? Where are you?" Alexandria called out. Her footsteps drew nearer and nearer.

I hurried back to the corridor. "Yeah?"

"Oh, there you are." Alexandria emerged at the top of the stairwell. "Zack, I've found him."

"Great." Zack descended the stairs, and the three of us convened in the corridor.

"I found nothing in the attic. How about you two?" Zack asked. "Any luck?"

Alexandria and I both shook our heads.

As though a gust of wind had swept through the corridor,

the candles went out at that moment, and before we knew it, everything plunged into inky blackness.

"What's happening?" I grabbed Alexandria's arm.

"I don't—hold on, Eric." Alexandria's gaze dropped to the ground.

"What are you looking at?"

"What's that by your feet?" She stooped and picked up a yellowed slip of paper. It was crumpled and stained with brown spots as though torn from the pages of an old book.

"Are those...words?" Zack squinted his eyes at the squiggly penmanship on the paper.

Alexandria raised her lantern and studied the words. Absolute horror worked its way through her features.

"What?" Zack and I crowded over her shoulder to see what was written on the paper. The ink was smudged and faded, but I could make out two words.

*Any time.*

I felt a spasm of terror. "Any time? What does this mean?"

But before either of them could answer me, a dark shadow loomed over the three of us. I looked up and screamed. A devil with green skin and glowing red eyes was leering at us.

"Scatter!" Zack hollered. He made a run for the attic while Alexandria sprinted down the stairs. As for me, I took off running along the corridor. The pounding footsteps behind announced the proximity of my pursuer. I had no choice but to hide and take refuge in one of the rooms.

"Ouch!" I tripped over a snuffbox that was jumping about on the floor. An agony of frustration flooded me. Cursing, I struggled to get to my feet. A hand seized a fistful of my hair and wrenched me upward, yanking me like a puppet. I whipped out my scepter to make a counterattack, but the devil snatched both my scepter and my lantern away before I could even utter a command. He pinned me to the wall, a murderous glint in his crimson eyes. I squirmed and wriggled, fighting back with all my might, but he overpowered me in strength. Then, still clutching my hair, he slammed me headfirst into a wall. A volcano of pain erupted in me. Every inch of my body roared in protest. My vision was blurring, narrowing, receding to nothingness as I clung on to the last shred of my consciousness with my eyes closed, determined not to pass out. I felt the devil release me. He probably thought I was dead.

*Dead....* An idea occurred to me. Peering through my eyelids, I saw the devil examining my scepter, waving it and trying to get it to obey his commands. I lay as still as a statue, feigning death. Once every few seconds, I would sneak an occasional peek at the devil, who was getting more and more frustrated as the scepter continued to fail him. He stomped at the floor, snarling incomprehensible words as he glowered at my scepter.

Now was the perfect moment. I seized the devil's legs, lifting him up into the air and backflipping him. He landed hard on his head, moaning. I wrenched my scepter out of his grasp and sprinted into the master bedroom, slamming the door shut.

Everything was shrouded in complete darkness. Panting for air, I collapsed onto the floor, nursing my forehead, where I felt sure a bruise was starting to bloom. I could hear the devil blundering in the corridor, floorboards moaning beneath his feet.

*Stomp. Stomp. Stomp.* Every stomp sent jolts of terror coursing through my body. Any moment and he would come barging into the bedroom. I groped in the darkness, rounded a heavy cabinet, and pushed it to the door, blocking the entrance. *Bang.* I crouched down behind the cabinet and saw the ugly green feet under the cracks of the door. Another bang, this time followed by a groan. I saw the devil crumple to the floor, unconscious.

I exhaled a sigh of relief and stood up, ready to leave. But what I saw next almost gave me a heart attack. A buttery yellow lantern was floating in the darkness—a disembodied enemy.

*Did it hear me? Can it sense my presence?* Holding my breath, I sought the sanctuary of the shadows and retreated into the darkness, edging as far away from the lantern as I could. I crouched down and crawled on the floor in fear of tripping or knocking over something by accident. Skirting around the lumpy objects around me, I bumped into something hard and solid. I traced its silhouette with my hand. A cabinet. Making as little movement as I could, I stood up and saw the lantern drifting away from the corner of my eye.

A swell of relief blossomed in me, and I wiped the beads of sweat from my forehead with trembling hands. Slightly relaxed, I leaned on the cabinet and sank to the floor.

"Hello."

My blood froze to ice. I was face-to-face with a person who mirrored my appearance. A doppelgänger. No, a clone. My clone. The lantern in his hand tinted his face a waxy yellow.

A frenzy of panic seized me, yet I stood there, dumbfounded, gaping at my clone. I ought to have screamed or run away in fear, but I had gone rigid with shock instead. For a moment, all was silent, except for my throbbing pulse.

The clone glared at me with fierce, unblinking eyes, like a predator regarding its prey before swallowing it raw. "Give it to me."

Still transfixed with horror, I stared at him. "What...what do you want?"

His lip curled. "What's mine."

Before I could react, he lunged at me and made a snatch for my scepter.

"Harm!" I shouted intuitively, shutting my mind and focusing on the command itself. A stream of yellow sparks flew at my opponent but soon ceased as my concentration broke. The clone dived out of the way at the last moment. I seized my only chance when he was distracted and leapt onto the bed. I wanted to summon Underworldian magic to get rid of him once and for all, but I couldn't focus hard enough to conjure anything. Gathering all my strength, I lifted one of the heavy crates and brought it down on his head. A yell of pain told me I had enough time to escape. Not daring to look back, I bolted for the door and pushed the cabinet away with all my might, but it wouldn't budge. I directed my scepter at the cabinet and yelled my best hope aloud. "Blast!"

The wooden boards cracked, but my spell wasn't powerful enough to reduce it into pieces. To make matters worse, the clone, now snarling and yelling abuse, was staggering toward me. I wrenched the boards from the cabinet's frame and flung them at the clone; one hit him on the head, and he collapsed. I kicked the now dilapidated cabinet away, knocking it into a mountain of junk. Not wasting a moment, I fled the room.

At the foot of the door sprawled the unconscious devil, my lantern lying by his arm. I took it back and tiptoed down the corridor. The candlelight coming from the guest room painted the walls and furniture orange; Alexandria's magical flames were still blazing in there.

Making as little noise as I could, I walked in, finding the room empty. Slumping on the couch, I took out Eileen's locket. I opened it and gazed at her picture, drinking in every little detail of her face as I carved her image into my mind. After barely escaping from a life-and-death situation, I couldn't help fearing I'd never get to see her again. Flashbacks of our last mission replayed in my mind, the vivid images floating before my eyes. I remembered breathing in the sweet scent of Eileen's hair, remembered her blushing scarlet and beaming at me, remembered her emerald eyes, greener than the young blades of grass under the gentle sunlight in spring. I clasped the locket to my heart, the only connection I now had with Eileen. I wished she were here with me. Perhaps she was thinking of me at this moment. Perhaps she missed me as much as I missed her....

A chilly breeze glided across the room, extinguishing all the candles. Now that the candlelight was snuffed out, I noticed a pearly white glow issuing from the mirror. I closed the locket and stuffed it back into my pocket. Curiously, I stood up and approached it. Nothing unusual. Only my reflection staring back at me. I frowned, wondering what hidden powers the mirror concealed as I continued to stare at it.

Then, to my utmost terror, a gnarled hand hovered in the air and landed on my shoulder.

I whirled around, but nobody was there. The only sound I could hear was my own breathing. I blinked and looked back into the mirror. My heart gave a jolt. I was no longer looking at my reflection. In the mirror, my skin greened, my eyes turned scarlet, and my features contorted into the face of a devil—the exact same devil I had fought off earlier. Before I could react, the image of the monster leapt out from the mirror and pounced on me. I blasted him out of the way with my scepter, snatched my lantern, and bolted into the corridor. However, the devil was too quick for me. He wrestled me to the ground and pushed me into the nursery. Seizing his large turquoise horns, I dragged him into the room and kicked the door shut.

The devil hurled a ball of turquoise fire at me, which I barely dodged. I grabbed a few toy blocks lying on the floor and chucked them at him; one hit him on the head, leaving a bloody cut. He retaliated by flinging a knife at me, scarring my right arm. I kicked the unibird hobbyhorse at the devil, who tripped and fell face-first into the heap of curtains. The curtains curled themselves around the devil's neck, and the more he struggled against his bindings, the harder the wisps of fabric wreathed themselves around his body. The devil clutched at the air wildly with his gnarled hands. He caught my leg, and I tripped, but just then, the curtains wound themselves around the devil's arm. I felt his grip on my leg slacken. Twisting myself free, I raced out of the room and slammed the door shut.

Weak-kneed, I leaned against the door and sank to the floor. I was still in shock; I couldn't believe I'd made it out of there alive. Taking a few shaky breaths to calm myself, I dabbed some healing ointment on my arm.

"Eric Williams!"

An orange lantern appeared on the other side of the corridor, and the figure of Alexandria came into view.

"Alexandria!" A torrent of relief bloomed in my chest as I saw her.

Before I knew it, she stormed up to me and slapped me across the face.

I gaped at her. "What are you doing?"

"I was about to ask you that question!" Alexandria snapped, pointing to a cut on her sleeve. Her face was white with anger. "You attacked me with no reason at all, and now you shrug it off like nothing happened?"

*Had she lost her mind?* "Me? I attacked you?"

"Oh, forgotten about how you growled in my face and sliced my arm with a knife, have you? Or was it your twin brother I just ran into?"

"What? I—I—" A moment of epiphany dawned on me. *I wasn't the only one who had run into the clone.* "Alexandria, I—" I froze as a sudden thought struck me like lightning. Without hesitation, I pinned her to the wall and directed my scepter at her heart.

"Are you crazy? Let me go!"

"Tell me, how was Evonne Fitzgerald revived last year?"

"That's not important. Get off me!"

"I will jinx you if you don't answer me in five seconds!" I roared.

"Fine!" shouted Alexandria. "She was resurrected by the Gem of Hope! But that's not—"

I relaxed my grip on her. "Sorry. I had to check if you were the real Alexandria. Listen, there are clones running around in here."

Alexandria's anger melted. "Clones?"

"Exactly. I just ran into one of them." And I told her my version of events since we had split.

"This is terrible," whispered Alexandria after I had finished. "We've got to get out of here right now."

"Eric, Alexandria." The footsteps that thundered down the stairs announced the arrival of Zack. Both Alexandria and I pointed our scepters at him.

"Whoa, what are you two—?"

I took a menacing step forward. "How many years have you known Helen Edmunds?"

Zack backed away from us. "Why is that important? We've got to leave this house before—"

"Answer him," snarled Alexandria.

"Well, I don't know. How could I remember—?"

"I'm giving you one final chance," I bellowed. "Tell me."

"I've told you, I don't remember how many—"

"Harm!" I ordered my scepter. A streak of lightning burst

from the tip and jetted toward Zack, or what looked like him. He lost his balance and tumbled down the stairs.

Alexandria cast a worried look at me. "Are you sure he's a clone?"

"Positive. Zack himself told me tonight. He's known Helen for nine years."

"But then, where's the real him?"

My gaze hiked up the flight of stairs that ascended into darkness, leading to the attic. "We're about to find out."

With Alexandria tagging along behind me, the two of us hurried up the stairs. The attic was consumed by darkness. I fumbled around and stumbled over what seemed like a large chest with three rows of keyholes. Swearing under my breath, I felt my grazed knee and noticed that my fingers were stained with blood.

"Careful." Alexandria tapped her scepter on her palm and conjured a ball of fire. Now that the room was brighter, I could see heaps of worn-out armchairs, cushions, tables, and shelves crowded in the attic.

"Any lanterns or candelabras here?" I asked. "I left mine in the guest room."

"Hmm, let me see...." Alexandria squatted on the floor and removed two stacks of old books. "Here, I found one. Ignite."

I took the lantern from her and surveyed the attic. Large cobwebs gleamed, stretching between the beams above us. Ghostly shadows of the furniture danced along the walls and the ceiling. An elliptical mirror stood behind the hill of broken chairs, spiderwebs veining the surface. Recalling what had happened downstairs minutes ago, I shuddered.

"Looks like nobody has been here in de—"

I screamed. Somebody had seized my neck from behind and pinned me to a wall. It was a deviline with long black hair and pale skin.

"Get off him!" yelled Alexandria. She withdrew a shrunken spear from her pocket and enlarged it with her scepter. The deviline bellowed and shoved me out of the way. I crashed into a bookshelf and slid to the ground. Pulsing waves of pain took over me as tears pooled in my eyes.

Meanwhile, Alexandria had put up a duel with the deviline. Both of them struck without mercy. Alexandria slashed her spear at the deviline, who intercepted it with her shield. The deviline then maneuvered with her left arm and struck with her right. The two of them fought, but it was obvious the deviline was more powerful.

Just then, two arrows sailed across the air, one brushing past the deviline's arm and the other piercing her leg. Alexandria seized her opportunity when her opponent was distracted, thumped the deviline on the head with one of the books on the ground, and slammed her into a cabinet.

I turned to see who our benefactor was. A figure cloaked in violet was standing at the top of the stairwell, a bow in her hands. She threw off her hood, allowing her wavy hair to flow to her waist.

"Helen?" Alexandria and I gaped at her, stunned.

She nodded and pointed her wand at me. "How many Elders are in the Inner Circle?"

"Thirteen, myself included. Well, seventeen, if you count the four heiresses."

"Correct." Helen pointed her wand at Alexandria.

"I can vouch for her," I said quickly. "But...but how on earth did you—? Do King Patrick and Queen Marianne know?"

Helen nodded. "Left them a note before I set off."

Beaming, Alexandria dashed over to her godmother and enfolded her in an embrace. "It's wonderful to see you, Helen."

"Great to see you, too, Alexandria," said Helen, draping her arms around her.

"But you're not supposed to leave the infirmary yet, are you?" I asked.

"I'm fine," Helen insisted. "I had to come along to make sure that...that you didn't get yourselves killed." She managed a smile. "Where's Zack, by the way?" she said, her smile fading.

"We were just looking for—"

"Helen?" I recognized Brian's voice coming from downstairs. Alexandria exchanged a look of surprise with me on hearing his voice.

"Have you seen Alexandria and Eric?" Brian shouted. "We've found Zack."

"The real one?" yelled Helen.

"Yes. We checked his identity."

I saw my own relief reflected on both Alexandria and Helen's faces.

"Any idea where the others are?"

"They're with me, Brian." Helen turned to us. "Come."

"Who else is here?" I asked as she ushered us down the stairs and all the way to the first floor.

"A couple of volunteers who insisted upon coming along with me. Brian, Evonne, and—"

"Eric!" I heard a voice I knew only too well. "You're safe!"

The next moment, the lovely figure of Eileen emerged from the dining room, garbed in a white floral scarf and a viridian cloak. She gave me a heartfelt smile of delight that I would give anything to see again.

"Eileen, it's you! It's really you! I thought I'd never see you again." I choked up as I saw her safe and sound. I flung my arms around her little frame, overjoyed that she wasn't a mere mirage.

Eileen wrapped her arms around my back.

"I missed you so much."

"I missed you too, Eric. And oh, Alexandria!" Eileen pulled Alexandria into a hug.

"I can't believe you're here." Alexandria beamed at Eileen. "How did you guys know where we were?"

"We got transported to a fountain in a spooky garden in front of this house, and we saw streaks of light coming from the windows. We thought there was a battle raging in here, and you were attacked by monsters. We were worried to death!"

I saw Brian and Evonne assembled in the dining room, he in a blue cloak, she in a lilac shawl. Brian caught my eye and waved at me.

"How did you get into the house?" I heard Alexandria ask Eileen. "The front door locked itself when we tried to escape."

"There's a back door." Eileen pointed to a dilapidated

wooden door by the kitchen. "It was Brian's idea. He's such a genius."

Meanwhile, the Elders were done catching up with each other and were now in the middle of a serious discussion. Helen and Brian were doing most of the talking. I noticed Zack kept stealing looks at Helen during the whole time, glancing at her with a mixture of delight and admiration. I couldn't help wondering if Helen had already noticed Zack's obsession with her.

"So, where did you guys find Zack?" I asked Eileen.

"He was knocked out and dragged into the kitchen by a clone that looked exactly like him, according to what he told us," she said, shivering. "Scary, isn't it? Just imagine running around in a haunted house and meeting yourself."

"You can say that again," I agreed. Alexandria and I exchanged a wink, as we both knew I learned that the hard way.

"The kitchen was packed with junk and strange little gray furballs, and we had to blast our way through it. We were all so scared of hurting Zack by accident. Gosh, we were lucky he came round and shouted at us before we wheeled a table straight into his face!"

Alexandria and I laughed. Everything seemed ten times funnier now that we were safe and reunited.

At that moment, a loud crash upstairs filled our eardrums, followed by the thundering of footsteps. A hush descended upon the Elders.

"They're coming," whispered Zack, his eyes darting at the stairwell. Fear rippled across his pale, sweat-beaded face.

Helen walked over to the back door, pushed it open, and peered into the darkness. "Coast clear. Come along, everyone. There's a forest behind Mors Manor, and I think we should stay—"

"A...a forest?" A chill traveled down my spine. "That doesn't sound too...cozy. Are you sure we should go there?"

"Anywhere is safer than Mors Manor," Zack cut in. "After you, Helen."

***

As we proceeded further into the dense forest, I edged

closer to Eileen, allowing the tufts of her long brown hair to brush against my arm. She was the light that banished all my insecurities, leaving me with a sense of protection instead. Warmth radiated in my chest as I cherished her presence like never before.

# Chapter Eight

## Into the Forest (Helen)

All was silent. The only audible sound was the dried foliage cracking and snapping under our weight. Ahead of us, around us, tall, ghostly trees veiled by night towered over our figures like giants. The only brightness that guided us was the alabaster moonlight, luminous between the tangled leaves overhead. Tiny circles of light and shadow danced across the faces of my companions as we plunged into the depths of the forest. It was probably foolish to venture into the thick, inauspicious-looking forest, but it was the safest place I could think of.

"Uhm.... Where are we heading? Do we have a destination?" It was Alexandria who broke the eerie silence.

I wiped the sweat on my forehead with the back of my hand. "As far away as we can get from that house."

The wound below my left collarbone stung in protest as I hurried deeper into the woods. It had almost healed over the past week, leaving nothing but a thin red scar, which Roxanne said would fade away in the coming months. The pain had receded, but there were occasional bursts of throbbing. It did not bother me much, though, as it was nothing compared to losing Zack. A shudder ran through my body as I thought of how narrowly we had escaped from the haunted manor. I didn't dare imagine what the consequences would have been had Eileen, Brian, Evonne, and I been a few minutes later. Immersed in my thoughts, I tripped on the hem of my cloak and stumbled. Two strong arms clasped my shoulders and caught me as I fell.

"Be careful," said Zack. He released me after I had regained my balance.

The heat rose in my face. "Thanks," I mumbled.

Zack nodded. Was it my imagination, or did I see a hint of concern in his eyes? A quick glance at him told me he was wearing the cloak I had gifted him two months ago for his birthday, the one embroidered with silver dogfishes that I had spent a week making. I suddenly became aware of the remaining warmth of his hand on my shoulders. For some reason, a bout of dizziness invaded my mind.

"Helen," Brian's voice punctured my reverie. "Did you... did you hear that? That scratching noise...."

I paused for a few moments and frowned. "It sounded like someone sharpening their knife. I think it came from that tree over there."

"This one?" Alexandria and Eileen approached the tree with great vigilance. "Who's there?" Alexandria called out, a ball of fire blazing on her left palm.

"Cut it out! We don't want to draw attention to ourselves," Eileen whisper-scolded.

"All right, fine." Alexandria snapped her fingers, and the ball of fire dissolved into ashes.

Eric went further ahead, rounding a few trees and crouching behind several shrubs. "Nobody. Not a living soul," he affirmed, turning to us. "Alexandria, what are you looking at?"

"These weird carvings on the tree." Alexandria edged closer to the trunk, raised her glowing scepter, and scrutinized it. "There are words carved on the trunk. Let me see...."

"What words?" I said.

"They look as if they've been here for decades." Alexandria squinted at the letters. "I can't make them out."

I motioned for the other Elders to come along as I neared

the tree. "It says...beware, Otherworldians...."

"How does it know we're here?" This was Brian's first question.

"Maybe it's just fooling around with us," Zack suggested.

Eileen gasped and clapped a hand to her mouth.

"What's wrong, Eileen?"

"What's...that?"

Ignoring the mounting fear and trepidation in me, I looked in the direction her finger was pointed. Something odd was hanging from the branches of the trees. Something gashed and filleted, gleaming crimson in the moonlight. I felt a mixture of repulsion and nausea as I realized what it was.

"A dead bearnix," said Alexandria, who had also noticed it. Both Zack and Evonne recoiled in disgust as they caught a glimpse of the grotesque sight.

"I'm scared." Eileen let out a whimper and skirted closer to Eric, who patted her on the back.

"But why is it draped on the branches?" Brian said, edging closer to observe it. "Don't you think it's really bizarre that—?"

"Now's not the time to discuss this," I interrupted him. "We've got to get out of here right away." I raised my wand and drew a gleaming purple circle on the tree that bore the carved words. "Let's go. I'll mark every tree as we pass so we won't get lost. We'll find our way out soon."

But as though the woods had comprehended my words, we couldn't find our way out no matter how far we went. We were lost in the boundless labyrinth of dark, identical columns and ever-lengthening shadows.

*You pompous, attention-seeking fool,* an annoying voice nagged in my mind. *You came all the way from the Otherworld to be the hero and ensure the others' safety, and now look at what you've done. You led them into a wicked forest and probably straight into a trap set by the Siblings. It's a miracle you haven't been killed yet.*

Unnerved, my eyes darted from tree to tree, scanning for lurking enemies. Everything seemed possible in the creepy woods. Any creature could swoop down on us from above or attack us anytime. Panic rose in my chest as I felt my heart slamming against it. My pulse thudded in my ears, and my stomach churned as I tried not to contemplate the possibilities of the horrifying events in store for us.

*If anything happened to my companions – no.* I pinched myself hard. I would not allow this dreadful thought to form in my mind. Still, a nasty parasite seemed to twitch and grow in me as many unpleasant what-ifs formed in my mind and replicated like bacteria.

"Helen?" Alexandria said in a strained voice.

"What?" I felt guilty and unable to look her in the face. After all, I was the one who had acted irrationally and guided all of them into this sinister, secluded forest. I stared straight ahead at the endless rows of trees, avoiding Alexandria's gaze.

"Look." She raised her scepter, illuminating a tree in front of us. As I drew nearer, I saw the same carved words on the trunk. However, there was no sign of the purple mark I had drawn earlier.

"Well...," began Alexandria, shifting her weight from one foot to the other in uneasiness as though afraid I would explode with frustration. "There's the body of the dead bearnix over there." She pointed at a nearby tree.

"Wait a second, we've been running around in circles?" Eric gaped at the words on the trunk.

Brian and Evonne were deep in discussion, and on hearing Eric's words, they rounded a tree and checked another one beside it.

"Impossible," said Zack. "We came all the way here...from there." He pointed to where we had entered the forest.

"That's right." Brian and Evonne emerged from behind the tree. "We just saw another unmarked tree that's got the exact same words on its trunk, and Evonne and I saw a bearnix's body hanging from the branches on the one beside it."

"What does this mean?" Alexandria asked in a small voice.

"I think this forest.... It's full of identical, carved trees and bearnix corpses," surmised Brian. "This can explain why we're seeing the same things over and over again."

"But...why would a forest be full of those...those horrible...

things?" Eileen sounded terrified.

"Maybe the forest's trying to confuse us and stop us from leaving where we entered," replied Eric.

"Perhaps they're designed to frighten us," I suggested. A horrible mixture of guilt and mortification washed over me as I met the stares of my companions. "Listen, I'm...." My voice faltered. "I'm sorry for everything. It's my fault we're now lost and stuck here."

"No, it's not," said Evonne, taking my hand. "You didn't want this to happen, either."

"And if we'd stayed behind, we'd have been killed by those monsters by now," agreed Zack.

Gratitude for both of them gushed up inside me. "Maybe we should go find a place to camp out for tonight. We'll figure our way out tomorrow morning."

"Good idea," said Evonne, rescuing me from my plight of embarrassment.

"Let's move on, then."

Dodging trees and branches obscured by darkness, I noticed something floating ahead, something misty white and swirling.

"What on earth...?" I turned to the others. "Stay here and don't move. I'm going to—"

"No, you're not. I'm coming with you," Zack cut in.

"Me too," Alexandria seconded him.

The words of refusal withered on my tongue as I saw the determination and earnestness in their gazes. "All right, then. Brian, Evonne, keep an eye on the others." Before they could answer, I approached the airy, floating creature with Zack and Alexandria following closely behind.

"It's a sheet of mist," said Alexandria. She reached out a hand to touch it.

"A very thick *cloud* of mist," Zack corrected her. "I reckon it's concealing something."

"Mist.... Tiny drops of water. And water...the nemesis of fire...." It took Alexandria a few more moments to put two and two together. She pointed her scepter at the cloud of magical mist. "Dissipate."

The mist dissolved at once, revealing a small wooden cabin alight with yellow lanterns. Brian's hand flew to his mouth, and Eric and Eileen exchanged a scared look.

Evonne took a sharp intake of breath. "A cabin in the woods? Are we seeing illusions, or have we gone mad?"

Alexandria, the only one who didn't seem at all taken aback, neared the window on the right side of the door. Standing on her tiptoes, she announced, "Don't be afraid. It's safe."

"What's in there?" said Zack.

"Just an empty cabin with no rooms. Nobody inside. No beds or anything. What should we do, Helen?"

Seeing the weary expressions on the others' faces, I decided. "Let's spend our night here."

"Awesome," Alexandria pushed the creaky door open and gave the rest of us a reassuring smile. "So, what are you guys waiting for?"

One by one, we tiptoed into the cabin. As if we had set foot into a shrine, nobody spoke or made even the smallest noise.

"I suppose everyone must be exhausted from all that exploring. Brian, Evonne, get the sleeping bags out and extend them to normal size."

"What about night watches?" asked Evonne. "One of us must stand guard outside the cabin in case—"

"I'll take the full watch," I volunteered, hoping to compensate for my mistake of leading them into the forest.

"And I'll do it with you," Zack chimed in. "I slept for quite a few hours last night," he added as I opened my mouth to refuse. "Anyway, it's too dangerous for you to guard the cabin alone." He turned to the others. "Goodnight, everyone."

"Goodnight," I echoed him.

Both Alexandria and Eric gave me smiles of encouragement before closing the door. Brian and Evonne busied themselves with the sleeping bags. Eileen was huddled in a corner of the cabin, entertaining herself with a baby cactus she had conjured.

"Helen," said Zack, sitting down on the stone steps outside the door. "Thank you for coming to our rescue. We wouldn't have survived if you and the others hadn't shown up and bailed us out."

I parked myself beside him. "I knew I had to come, for some reason." I averted his gaze as I said this, for I couldn't bring myself to tell him the truth—that all I wanted was to see him safe and sound. Instead, I devoted my attention to the dark sky. Streaks of clouds were visible, illuminated by the pearly beams of the full moon. "She would've wanted me to prioritize my fellow Elders' safety over mine like she sacrificed herself for him," I thought without realizing I was saying it aloud.

"Who?"

"My mother."

Zack was silent for a while. "You told me about her before. She was the reason you became an Elder. You wanted to take revenge on Alta and Alto because they killed her after she'd defied them."

"They, Alta and Alto, didn't want to kill *her* in the first place. It was because of a man. She gave her life to save a young man. One day on her way home from work, my mother saw a young man being accused of treason by an officer, a subordinate of Alta and Alto's. The Siblings had imprisoned his only living family, his grandmother, after discovering she had been plotting against them. The man fought back, claiming he was innocent, and so was his grandmother. He begged in vain for the officer's mercy and attracted a huge crowd. The officer tortured him and humiliated him in public. As the man fought back and attacked the officer, he was jinxed into a coma."

Zack let out a gasp.

"That was when my mother, one of the bystanders, shielded the innocent man from further harm. The officer and his colleagues threatened to kill her if she didn't stop interfering, but she did not give in. So they attacked and maimed her. She was sent to a hospital right away, and...." I looked away from Zack so that he wouldn't see the tears in my eyes. "She died the next morning. I still remember her last words. She made me promise I would do my best to spare the innocent from harm and not let the tragedy Alta and Alto caused repeat itself."

"Your mother...." Zack sounded breathless and seemed to be having difficulty speaking due to astonishment. "What was her name?"

"Valerie. Valerie Edmunds."

Shock registered on Zack's face. "That's *her...*," he said. He closed his eyes and muttered to himself. "It really is her. Valerie—"

"What do you...?"

"Valerie Edmunds. She's...the one who saved me."

"The one who saved you...." It took a while for his words to sink in. Comprehension dawned over me. "You were the man my mother saved?"

The answer was etched in his expression. Flustered by his confession, I found myself at a loss for words. Was the universe playing a trick on me, on us? My mother had given her life to save not a random stranger but the man I would mentor and grow to love in the future. What did this mean? What did our entwining fates imply?

"You must hate me," Zack said in an injured voice.

"Why would I?"

"Your mother would still be alive if it weren't for me."

"That's not true. You didn't ask her to sacrifice herself for you."

"So you don't hate me for...telling the truth?"

I shook my head. "It was brave of you to confess that." The compliment came out easier than I had imagined. "I don't know if I'd have the courage to confess if I were you."

"You really think so?"

I nodded. Zack's expression relaxed in relief.

A chilly breeze fluttered throughout the forest, and the neighing of a unibird sounded from a nearby tree. A few minutes drifted by in silence.

"Is that why you chose to come along to the Underworld and help us, to honor her memory?"

"Yes." The lie escaped from my lips with such an air of truth that I almost believed it.

No, a voice in my mind contradicted me. *You've always*

*loved Zack as a little brother, or maybe more than one. He was always there for you when you needed him, showing his silent yet strong support. You couldn't stand not knowing what dangers he'd face on this mission. That was why you insisted upon coming to the Underworld, as well as the reason you took the poisoned arrow for him. You would go to any lengths to rescue him. Admit it. You love him.*

Ignoring the voice in my mind, I continued. "The sudden invasion made me realize how fragile life is. Nothing can last forever. We can never predict what's going to happen tomorrow. I want to make the most of my life, to protect the other Elders and the people I care about while I can."

"You said the sudden invasion made you realize.... But you did assume there would be an invasion, didn't you? We all knew for a fact the Underworld was bound to attack anytime."

"Yes, but I wasn't expecting that many casualties. Thirty Elders dead, Zack. Thirty."

"I know," he said, his voice dropping to a brisk whisper. "And the fallen thirty...it could've been any of us. Me, Lilith, Brian, Evonne...."

"Or me," I added.

Zack winced. "Don't say that. You wouldn't—"

"There's no use pretending it's impossible," I interrupted him. "You know what I'm saying is a solid fact. I came close to death when that poisoned arrow almost killed me."

"You have no idea how scared I was when that happened," replied Zack in a small voice. "Why did you do that?"

*Because I love you*, I thought, though determined to keep my feelings for him concealed in case my romantic interest went unrequited. I stroked the milky stones on my pearl bracelet, admiring their glossy sheen. It was a gift from Zack last month; he had had my name engraved on one of the pearls.

"How am I ever going to forgive myself if you died for me?" He grimaced, as if the utterance of that word pained him like a physical wound. "You risked your safety to ensure mine when you could've kept yourself out of harm's way—"

"And let a fellow Elder leave me when I could've stopped that tragedy from happening?" I finished the sentence for him.

Seeing that he remained silent, I plowed on. "And how could I live with myself if I did that? My mother would've wanted me to keep my promise and spare the innocent from harm. Not stand aside and watch them perish."

*You know, deep down, this is not the full reason. You love Zack. You love him with all your heart. He was the one who aroused the tender feelings buried deep within you,* the nagging little voice said in me. However, I couldn't bring myself to tell him that.

*But he doesn't love you,* another voice reminded me. *He looks upon you as a role model because you're the Representative Elder. Yes, perhaps he admires you, but admiration does not equal love. You know perfectly well he regards you as a sister. Nothing more.*

"She would've been proud of you," said Zack in a quiet voice. "Your remembrance for her...." His voice trailed away. "But my son—"

A serious realization struck me at that moment. "*Your* son?" I repeated, stunned.

"Since you've trusted me and told me about your mother...." He sighed. "Helen, promise me you won't hate me after learning this. Please."

I nodded, an invitation for him to continue.

"I once had a relationship with Alta. We were both very young; she was twenty-four, and I sixteen. I doubt I knew what love was back then. Our relationship lasted for four years. I left her as soon as I discovered she'd been lying to me."

I did my best to conceal the astonishment of learning the truth. "And...that's all?"

Zack shook his head. "You can't imagine how Alta was then. She was as normal as any other person even had a charm of her own. If she had a rotten core and a mind of a demon, it was hidden very well. Her sister's departure and her parents' death changed everything. She lost faith in everyone, disdained people who still cared for her, insisting the so-called love between family members was nothing but a joke. She didn't even care when Marianne returned and apologized two years later. The seed of hate had already been buried within her. Alta still looked normal on the outside, but deep down, she had become a monster. Nothing mattered to her anymore except gaining wealth and power. She hated her sister so much she lost her belief in humanity and converted to the dark side; she and Alto studied evil spells and practiced black magic, becoming so obsessed with them they vowed to rule the world in the future and turn it into a realm of darkness. And all those years, Alta had been lying to me, concealing her true nature. As soon as I realized who she really was, I decided to leave her. We quarreled, and we dueled. Alta couldn't take it anymore. She wanted to control me, but I wouldn't let her. Then, she attacked me and knocked me out."

I listened to Zack's story, a horrible fascination bubbling in me.

"Alta locked me up, but I managed to escape in the end. The whole incident made me realize that Alta Williams was no longer herself but a demon I didn't know. She was insane, and I could no longer reason with her. I severed ties and hoped never to have anything to do with her in the future. Several months later, Alta and Alto took over the throne by force. The Siblings' worshippers, advocates of their immoral leadership, became officers. They tortured, killed, and imprisoned anyone who was suspected of plotting against the government. I thought Alta had already forgotten about me, and I paid the price for my naivety."

"She imprisoned your grandmother and accused her of treason."

Zack nodded. "She was my only living relative. My parents both died when I was a baby, so my grandmother took me under her wing. She was the only one I had. I promised myself I wouldn't let anyone hurt her. When I learned that the Siblings had taken her, I decided to confront Alta and bring my grandmother home. But on my way to the palace, the officers cornered me. It was as if they knew exactly what I had in mind. I would've died if Valerie Edmunds hadn't come to my rescue.

"After that incident, I was willing to do anything to overthrow Alta and Alto. I knew King Patrick and Queen Marianne were planning to create another world of magic. Tempted as I was to join them, I was sure Alta would hunt me down if I did, which would mean great danger for both me and my family. Instead,

I fled to the mortal world with my grandmother and went into hiding."

"And what happened after you left the Underworld?"

"My grandmother was never the same since Alta imprisoned her," said Zack in a low voice. "She was so horrified that she wouldn't tell me what Alta had done to her. Whatever it was, it must have been traumatizing. She became mentally ill after that incident, and I took care of her until she died."

"I'm sorry," I said, pretending not to see him wipe a tear from his cheek.

"Excuse me." Zack took a quick moment to collect himself. "I've kept this to myself for almost a decade. Six years later, when I was sure Alta would leave me alone, I went to the Otherworld and became an Elder, determined to take revenge on the Siblings. They took everything away from me, and I was going to make them pay. But the shocking news soon reached me—Alta had given birth to a son the exact same year I had fled the Underworld."

"But it could've been the child of another man."

"I had my doubts on who the boy's father was until the day I met Eric Williams."

"Are you saying Eric Williams is...your son?" I could not force myself to grasp the possibility of such an inconceivable fact.

"Do you remember what Eileen said when we first came across Eric? She said his blue eyes and straight nose looked just like mine. She called him my doppelgänger."

"Eric's *your* son? Which makes Alexandria your...your niece?" I half-expected Zack to burst into laughter at my foolishness for believing this farfetched tale. However, something in his tone and expression convinced me he wasn't lying. I recalled all the events that had taken place last mission, searching for hints. "Is this why you vouched for him in the first place, persuading me to accept his pledge?" Everything was starting to make perfect sense.

"Listen, Helen, I—I just couldn't leave him." Bitterness brimmed up in Zack's voice as if the words he uttered pained him to the bones. "He didn't deserve to be treated like that, as though he was less than worthy of affection."

I saw the hurt in Zack's eyes. For some reason, I felt his agony as though it were my own. "I would've done the same if I were you, taken him back to the Otherworld and protected him from Alta."

"I had to compensate. I had to make it up to him the moment I realized who he was," Zack went on. "Not a day goes by that I don't think of Eric. He deserved so much better than that. Every time I see him, I think of how much he must have suffered because of me and how much I owe him. But what hurts the most is the ignorance in his gaze. The fact he doesn't know who I really am. He's my child. *Mine.*"

Guilt, remorse, and anguish; it hurt me to see him waging an internal war against these emotions.

"Why didn't you tell him?"

"I've been aching to. All along. But I couldn't. I cringe whenever I think of Eric's reaction when he learns who I am. He would never have been mistreated if I hadn't left him with Alta in the first place. I've been haunted by guilt ever since I discovered Eric. I owe him, owe him too much. I couldn't bring myself to face him."

"Don't beat yourself up," I said, holding his hand. "After all, it wasn't your fault in the first place. You didn't know Alta was pregnant then, did you?"

"I didn't."

"Eric is a sensible boy. He won't hate you as long as you tell him everything and be honest about it." After a moment of hesitation, I added, "I suggest you tell him the truth as soon as possible."

"Why?"

"It all goes back to what I said about life. We can never predict what will happen tomorrow."

"You're right." Zack broke the silence that followed my words.

"Everything will turn out fine between you and Eric, I promise. Now that he's with us, I will protect him at all costs, even if it's the last thing I do."

He nodded. "Thank you, Helen. I hope you know how much your words mean to me. I've never confided in anyone apart from you. They wouldn't understand, none of them. They're not like you. You're so different. There's something special about you that makes me feel I can trust you."

"Really?" I managed to say in a steady voice, ignoring the rising heat in my cheeks and the rapid throbbing of my heart.

"I found trust and solace in you. You were my best friend and companion, but...." For the first time, he seemed to be struggling with emotions too complicated to be articulated.

I held my breath, waiting for him to finish. My heart was now galloping against my chest so loudly I swore he could have heard it.

"But Helen, having you as a best friend and companion isn't enough. It was not until I almost lost you that I realized how deep my feelings for you were. You are the bravest, strongest, and most noble person I've ever met in my life. Getting to know you was the best thing that ever happened to me." He gave a brief pause, then continued. "All I want to say is...I love you, Helen. More than anyone or anything in my life."

A collision of emotions. Completely overwhelmed, I did not know whether I was in a state of euphoria or astonishment. *It could not be true*. He was making fun of me; he had to be.

"But...you deserve someone else." These words I said, suppressing my true feelings on one hand and testing him on the other. "Me? I'm forty-one this year. Too old for you."

Zack shook his head. "I used to believe in true love as a kid, believe that as long as I trusted people and was kind to them, I'd be treated the same way. But I lost all my beliefs after realizing who Alta Williams was. I swore never to fall in love again, never to even believe in it. But Helen, it was you who ignited the ashes in me, you who moved my mind, you who changed my heart. You made me believe I could regain the courage to love again. All those years, we've fought, side-by-side, shoulder-to-shoulder. All those events we've gone through together, the ups and downs. You've been with me ever since I joined the Elders. I started off liking you as a friend, then growing to admire and respect you as a mentor, but finally, I couldn't help falling for you. I've never had such strong feelings for anyone, but you are unique. I'd do anything for you, anything to be with you. It's you I want, Helen, nobody else but you." His voice, unlike usual, was filled with unmistakable desire and longing.

"Zack, the truth is...." The words of confession clung to my tongue but escaped my lips at length. I could no longer conceal my feelings for him. "I love you, too." It came out more naturally than I had thought.

"Really?" Zack's eyes lit up like an excited toddler, and a soft grin of relief spread across his face.

"I've always heard that true love is when you care about whether someone lives or dies more than you do about yourself. I've never felt that way before meeting you. You made me understand what it's like to love someone as if they're your other half."

Zack's fingers intertwined with mine as he pulled me close to him. The intimacy dazed me, making me giddy and lightheaded. "You have no idea how long I've kept this a secret. I love you. For your wisdom, your classy temperament, and your depth of character. How poised and elegant you are, and how you willingly sacrifice yourself for others, even when it's not your duty. Your presence is a gift, Helen."

Words failed me. His gentle utterance of my name sent torrents of affection gushing through me. I tried to analyze my feelings for him, but for the first time, I failed to. I had never before felt emotions this tender, this thrilling, this tantalizing. It was inexplicably deep and irrevocable; it was a peculiar sensation I had never felt before. Was it infatuation, or was it love? Whatever it was, it had overpowered my consciousness and dictated my usual sensible self.

Zack spoke again, his voice a gentle murmur. "It felt bittersweet, every time I thought of confessing my feelings for you; sweet because the thought of you always makes me smile; bitter because I was worried you didn't feel the same way about me, and you'd never want anything to do with me in that case. I thought you'd reject me."

"Reject you? I'd never do that."

"I thought I wasn't good enough for you."

"That's not true. You are worth so much more than you know. You were the one who told me it wasn't my fault when Evonne lost her memory, the one who stood with me when almost all the Elders lost faith in me, the one who took my side when Queen Marianne and I had a row. You gave me the strength to carry on when I was vulnerable, guided me through the darkest of times, and provided unconditional support when I stood alone. I need you."

"I need you, too." Zack's voice was soft. "I loved you as a sister, or perhaps, more than one. If I know what felicity is, it's because I met you." A smile curled his lips as his eyes sparkled with joy. "I never thought I'd live to tell you all this."

His words sent a frisson of fear coursing through me. I shivered, but it had nothing to do with the chilly weather.

"What's wrong?" Zack tightened his grasp on my hand.

"I was so scared I would never get a chance to talk with you. What if you hadn't made it out of Mors Manor alive? What if I'd been too late?"

"It's in the past," he consoled me.

"No, it's not." I felt a lump rising in my throat. "It's this lingering uncertainty about the battles. One day I'm here, and maybe the next day, I'm not. I—we could all be dying anytime. We have to acknowledge the fact every day might be the last one of our lives. I don't know how much time I've got left, especially after Clarissa passed away. She was only fifteen. The next time tragedy strikes, it will be any of us. I'm so worried about you, Alexandria, Eric, Eileen, Lilith, Brian, Evonne, and all the other Elders."

"Don't think that way. You're the best leader we have in the Otherworld. We'll survive the war under your guidance. But Helen...." Zack placed his palms on top of my hands. "I want you to know you're not alone. I'm here for you. Always am."

Relaxing against him, I rested my head on his shoulder, allowing his soothing words to caress me and give me the strength and hope I never needed more.

"We're in this together," Zack assured me, giving my hand a squeeze.

"Together...," I echoed him. Unable to tell him how much his words meant to me, I nodded to show my gratitude.

We spoke in silence, our gazes conveying more words of affection. He looked profoundly at me with those haunting eyes that melted the core of my bosom; they twinkled under the gentle moonlight, having all the brightness of a sapphire yet none of its iciness. I gazed back into the depths of his soul; all I saw was my own reflection. For a fraction of a moment, I had an intuition it was all he wanted to see.

Was it fate, or was it destiny? It was as if some sacred, celestial force was determined to link me to him and him to me, bestowing upon us so many inexplicable connections and coincidences to strengthen our bond. Did soulmates exist in reality? I'd never believed they did until today. The crossroads I shared with him convinced me the universe created us just for each other.

"Never leave me, Helen," said Zack, his voice low, intimate, husky.

I edged closer to him, sealing the gap between us. He slipped an arm around my shoulder, and the proximity set my heart racing.

"Never," I promised him. My voice was a mere whisper, yet audible to him.

And there we sat, drinking each other in as we waited for the nocturnal sky to crest into dawn.

# Chapter Nine

## The Sorceress and the Shortcut (Alexandria)

Troubled dreams reigned my sleep.

A haughty-looking woman with flaming red hair sat on an obsidian throne in a room of bare black marble threaded by ivory veins. She addressed the four devils and devilines kneeling in front of her, "Anderson, Scott, Lowry, and Jones."

"Your Majesty?" whispered one of the devils.

Alta was in an ugly mood. "From what my scout has reported, the Otherworldians entered the Underworld last night."

"Who did they send this time, Your Majesty?" the other devil asked.

"My ignorant niece, my traitor of a son, and my old friend, but four more Otherworldians entered the Underworld last night—the foolish Representative Elder, the heiress of Fern, and two junior Elders."

"What do you reckon their goal is, Your Majesty?" said the first devil.

"What do you think, Anderson?"

The devil named Anderson gulped. "Your Majesty, we must be careful. According to our scout, they have already discovered the secret of the Underworld. They now know it's the portals that are changing, rather than the terrains. They've come to the Underworld in order to figure out the positions of the terrains, and I fear they will succeed."

"That is correct." Alta pursed her lips, her eyes staring out of focus.

"But Your Majesty," a deviline spoke, "as long as the Otherworldians don't know about the Control Center, we've got nothing to worry about, do we?"

"That does not mean we can lower our guard, you foolish girl!" Alta snapped at the deviline. "They're planning to navigate the Underworld, and it's likely they'll come across the Control Center by accident. In that case, we mustn't let them break in. Anderson, Lowry, keep the Control Center guarded. I demand the highest security."

"Yes, Your Majesty."

"The Control Center's the place where all the secrets of our world lie, with hidden weapons and the most technological instruments ever invented. You must *not* fail."

"Yes, Your Majesty. We'll do our best," Lowry promised her.

"But it's unlikely the Otherworldians would scale Mount Maravillas if they didn't know about the Control Center—" The deviline who had defied Alta broke off in mid-sentence on catching sight of her stern expression.

"Edith Jones, I'm giving you one final chance. Do not let me hear one more ridiculous theory from you. Scott, you and Jones are to take your troops around Mirabilia District and patrol it. Ambush and maim, or better, kill any Otherworldians you come ac—" Alta stopped all of a sudden and turned to face my direction. She glared at me as though she could sense my presence. I held my breath as she reached out a gloved hand to touch my face. The next thing I knew, a blinding flash of light exploded right before me—

My eyes blinked open. The others were still asleep and perhaps, dwelling in dreams of their own as well.

Chilly air and moist mist greeted me as I stepped out of the cabin. I looked back at our hut and surveyed the woods, which was shrouded by a thick veil of drizzling fog. It was an enchanting sight to behold, a little cabin sitting in the middle of a misty forest, like the setting of a fairytale in reality. However, I didn't have the heart to enjoy the scenery. I sat on the stone steps, ruminating over my dream and letting it replay once again in my mind.

*The Control Center.* Alta looked almost frightened of the possibility of us breaking into the Control Center. According to her, it was the place where all the secrets of the Underworld dwelled, with hidden weapons and the most technological instruments ever invented.

"What are you doing out there alone?"

I glanced over my shoulder. "Zack?"

"Is something wrong?" He looked concerned. "You can tell me if you need someone to talk to."

Zack was such a nice person. So kind, so considerate, so easy to trust. But I didn't want to let him in on the details of my dream.

"Alexandria?"

"Oh, well...nothing," I lied.

Zack gave me a look as though wanting to ask more but then thought better of it. "Then come in, and let's have breakfast."

As I stood up and followed him back into the cabin, I recalled how Alta had addressed him—*my old friend.* Was she being her usual sarcastic self? Or, like Eric and I had discussed a while ago, did Zack have a dark past that involved Alta?

"Hi," said Eileen rather tentatively as I passed her.

"Huh? Oh, good morning."

"You look troubled," she observed.

"Are you all right?" Eric, who was sitting beside her, asked.

"Yeah. Yeah, I'm fine," I shook my head and snapped out of my thoughts. "So, what's for breakfast?"

"Vegetable sandwiches and meat pies the Elders brought along with them yesterday," replied Eric. "There. Helen and Brian are handing them out."

I walked up to Helen and took the last sandwich and pie from the box she was holding. "Could we talk?"

"Alexandria," Helen looked up at me. "I'm sorry."

I blinked. "For what?"

"Not having a proper talk with you ever since you came to the Otherworld. Come to think of it, I've been a horrible godmother so far."

"No, don't say that. I never thought so."

"It's just that...I—we've...." Helen rubbed her eyes. "All of us, we've been going through quite a lot these weeks."

"It's all right, I understand. Could I tell you something?"

Helen nodded.

"I had a dream last night, a weird one about Alta and her minions. They...they know what we're up to. They know we've figured out the Underworld isn't a terrain-shifter."

Clunk! The now empty box Helen was holding dropped to the floor.

Everyone's heads jerked up. "What's the matter?"

"Excuse me," muttered Helen, picking up the box and pretending to act normally. I could see apprehension working its way through her features. "Let's talk this over during the meeting after breakfast, all right?"

"Good idea. This way, everyone will know."

I sat down beside Eric and Eileen, took a bite of my sandwich, and chewed slowly, still reviewing the details of my dream.

Helen was busy whispering to Zack, who had shrunken all the sleeping bags to finger-size with his wand and was now stuffing them into the pouch of his cloak. He frowned and glanced at Helen after she had finished. "That's very bad.... We must talk it over with the others."

"Look what I've got!" Brian ran over to us with a wooden box in his arms.

"A box of cupcakes?" Eric said, his gaze hopeful.

"Even better," Brian grinned and produced a crystal decanter of silvery potion from his box.

Eric squealed in delight. "Excellent!"

Brian filled seven goblets with the silver substance and handed everybody one each.

"What's this?" Eileen said.

"Whatever you want it to be," I replied. "Iced grape tea with coconut jelly and a cherry on top," I said to my goblet and took a sip after the liquid had turned into that very beverage.

"Pineapple and orange smoothie," Eileen commanded. Her drink turned into a bright shade of mustard yellow, unpleasantly reminiscent of the Chirpy Bird's feathers.

"How does it taste?" Eric asked, taking a swig of his cherry wine.

"Delicious." Eileen smacked her lips.

Helen cleared her throat. "Your attention, everyone," she announced. "We need to have a meeting right now and figure out today's schedule."

"Shoot," muttered Eric.

"I don't think Helen would mind if we drank this during the meeting, would she?" Eileen asked, taking her goblet along with her.

Everyone gathered around the stack of notebooks Helen had piled in the middle of the cabin, forming an irregular circle.

"As Alexandria told me earlier, she had a dream about Alta." Helen looked at me and nodded, indicating it was my turn to speak.

"That's right. In my dream, Alta was talking to her minions. She told them a scout reported to have seen us enter the Underworld."

"A scout?" repeated Eileen.

"Could be one of the monsters we met in Mors Manor yesterday," said Eric. "Go on."

"Alta looked very mad. She asked one of her devil minions for advice. The devil told her the scout knows that we know the Underworld isn't a terrain-shifter, and we're here to navigate the terrains."

Eric and Eileen stirred in uneasiness, and I saw Helen and Evonne exchange a nervous look.

"I hate to suggest this, but is it possible that...we've got a spy?" Brian said quietly, voicing the assumption I had had but didn't dare to mention.

"A spy? What makes you think so?" asked Zack.

"It just seems so unbelievable this scout of Alta's knows so much about us, the facts we've figured out, the goal of our mission...."

Everyone turned to look at Helen. "You're right, Brian," she said in a solemn manner. "I'll report this to King Patrick and Queen Marianne as soon as we get back to the Otherworld and tell them to be more careful from now on."

"But who could it be?" Zack said. "There are tons of suspects."

"Could be anyone," agreed Helen. "And the problem is, we can't ask the rulers to investigate further and find out who it is."

"Why not?" I asked.

"Interrogate every single Elder in the palace and search for the real spy? We can't, and we're not going to do that. The Underworld might launch a second invasion on us anytime, and we can't start fighting amongst ourselves. Like it or not, we must trust each other, especially in times like this."

Zack nodded. "Well said."

The details of my dream occurred to me, and I felt reminded again of how Alta had called Zack her *old friend*. And the spy Brian just mentioned...the scout that had tipped Alta off and provided her with information about the Otherworld and our plans. My stomach gave a jolt. Could Zack be the spy?

While I was lost in my thoughts, Helen asked, "Anything else in your dream?"

"What? Oh, right.... Alta got all upset about our figuring out the terrains, and one of her deviline minions said as long as the Otherworldians don't know about the Control Center, they've got nothing to worry about."

"What's the Control Center?" Evonne piped up.

"Judging from the rest of the conversation, it sounded like a very important...um, building? It's on Mount Maravillas. Alta reckons if we're here to navigate the terrains of the Underworld, we'd likely come across the Control Center by accident. She demanded that her minions keep the Control Center secured."

"Interesting...," muttered Helen. "Seems like Alta is terrified at the possibility of us breaking into the Control Center. "

"Right. Alta also said the Control Center is the place where all the secrets of the Underworld lie, with hidden weapons and the most technological gadgets ever invented."

"All the secrets of the Underworld?" Brian said. "You don't think...we can see a map there or something that can help us figure out the terrains?"

"Maybe. I think it's worth a try," I answered. "We'll find out all the answers to the questions we've been wondering about for ages. So, how do we get there? Cloud-flying?"

"Hold on for a moment," Helen cut in. "I know everyone's all excited about this, but it's a dream, Alexandria, just a dream. It may not mean anything."

"No, I don't think it's just a dream," I said. "It's more like a...a vision. I'm positive it's true."

"But if it really is true, why would you have this sort of... link that can make you see visions of Alta?" Eric asked. "Unless you can see—"

"*See,*" I repeated. The word rang like a bell. It was as though someone had opened a door in my mind. "That's it, Eric. As the heiress of Delphia, I can foresee the future. That's probably why I had that vision."

"What?"

"Haven't I told—oh, right...King Patrick made me promise I wouldn't tell anyone. It's supposed to be a secret between him, Queen Marianne, and me. The ancient seer, Delphia, like the four Creators, also chose an heir before she passed away. Delphia was a member of the Richardson family, and the ability to foresee the future passed on from one generation to the next. When King Patrick and Queen Marianne were fighting for the Otherworld, Alta struck King Patrick with a spell, which damaged his seeing ability. He's never been able to tell complete prophecies since then. He can, however, sometimes see or sense illusions from the future. He made two predictions about me before we went on the mission last year, and both came true in the end."

Stunned silence.

"And...have you inherited his damaged seeing ability?" said Helen, though it was clear from her taut expression that she already knew the answer.

I nodded.

Helen tightened her grasp on her notebook. "So the vision and the conversation between Alta and her minions might be true. It may even be taking place at this very moment." She took a deep breath. "Then we must set off right now. To the Control Center on Mount Maravillas."

Eric's mouth fell open. "You can't be serious, can you?"

The others, also flabbergasted by this sudden decision, stared at Helen. It couldn't have been clearer. They were all feeling worried for her sanity.

Helen gave Eric such a stern look that he closed his mouth. "I'm serious. If there's a Control Center that houses all the secrets of the Underworld, we must go and see for ourselves."

***

The mist had grown thinner as we left the cabin and stepped out into the forest. The Elders were whispering to each other and discussing how to leave. Strangely, the carved words on the trees had all vanished, and the bearnix corpses were also nowhere to be seen.

The cloudless sky was in the color of smoke, serving as a backdrop for the dark silhouettes of the tall trees and skeletal branches around us, black against pale gray. The stripes of trunks in the distance were enveloped by mist and had faded into the sky...all except for a shadowy figure that penetrated the fog ahead, nearing and approaching us—

"What's that?" Eric, who had also noticed it, called for the Elders' attention. He pointed in the direction of the black figure, and to my horror, it had triplicated. There were now three figures coming in our direction.

"Cloaked monsters." Helen and Evonne withdrew their bows.

A sea of arrows sailed at the approaching enemies. Now that they had drawn nearer, I saw there were ten of them. A cloaked bearnix hurtled toward me; I whipped out my spear and stabbed it. The bearnix yowled in anger, and chomped at my arm, but I dived out of the way and aimed a kick at its rump. Eric raced toward me, a ball of turquoise fire blazing in his hands—

"No, Eric! Don't! Remember, we're in a forest! You might lose control and burn this whole place to the ground!" I yelled before he could toss it at the bearnix.

Eric tapped his scepter on his palm, and the ball of fire dissolved into ashes. An arrow soared through the air and pierced the bearnix's wings, and I seized my opportunity and managed to escape. Though injured, the bearnix chased me around as I attempted to throw it off. I dodged trees and ducked under branches, swerving my way through the forest. Gritting my teeth, I snuck a glance behind my shoulder and saw Eric following the bearnix closely. He raised his sword, ready to strike—

Distracted, I tripped over a tree root protruding from the ground. The bearnix's snarls of fury told me I had no time to run. "Eric! Do something now!"

Eric flung his sword at the bearnix. It roared, exhaling flames before falling to the ground with a thud. I extinguished the fire with my scepter before it could burn down the trees and gave my cousin a high-five.

"Well done!"

"Thanks. Where are the others?"

"I thought they were over there...." My voice trailed off. "Wait, where are we?"

I surveyed our surroundings and saw nothing but countless rows of identical trees. A stab of horror lanced my heart. "Are we lost?"

"We came in that direction, didn't we? Perhaps if we follow—"

"Wait." I held up my hand, certain I had heard the cracking of leaves and twigs nearby—someone's footsteps. Eric edged closer to me, tightening his grip on the hilt of his sword.

"Who's there?" I yelled, raising my scepter.

"Oh, it's you, Alexandria." The figure of Brian jogged into view. His cheeks were grazed, and there was a deep cut on his forehead. "I just got away from a crazy dogfish. Barely escaped." He let out a weak chuckle.

"Where are the others?" Eric asked, his voice strained. "Have you seen Eileen?"

"She was dueling with a devil the last time I saw her," said Brian, applying some ointment on the cut on his forehead. "Pretty clever, that Eileen. She got another dogfish tangled up in vines before picking up a duel with that devil."

"And the Elders?" I asked. "What were they doing when you last saw them?"

"Helen and Evonne were firing arrows at the enemies, and Zack was sword-fighting a unibird, a real tough opponent to— Hold on...." Brian had suddenly gone as still as a statue. "Do I hear someone coming this way?"

"Eric? Brian? Alexandria?" a high-pitched voice called from nowhere. "Oh, there you are." The figure of Eileen appeared from the mist ahead, rounding trees and leaping over bare roots as she sped toward us.

"What happened to you?" Eric asked.

Eileen's sleeve was torn, and her right arm was gashed and scratched. "A deviline with long talons did this to me. She was chasing me all over the forest, and I got away by conjuring a self-running-flesh-eating-Venus-flytrap."

"Good thinking," Eric said, grinning. "I remember how you tripped the Chirpy Bird last year by cutting off a tree when it—"

"There they are!" a voice yelled. "Charge!"

The four of us stood our ground as an army of bearnixes, unibirds, and dogfishes advanced on us. The dogfishes seemed to be avoiding me because of my elemental powers, but with a few good aims, I managed to wipe out four of them with my fireballs.

"Alexandria, watch out!" Eric hollered as an arrow sailed over my head.

I turned, only to see a furious unibird with a bow clutched in its wings. Without thinking, I conjured a fireball and lunged at it, ready to hurl—

I froze in my tracks. It was the first time I'd been face-to-face with a unibird since Clarissa's death. Although I knew I had to kill it before it did me in, I could not bring myself to. At that moment, three other unibirds zapped me with their horns. The force was so powerful it threw me off balance. Before I knew it, I soared through the air and slammed into a tree. Stars swam in my vision as my head spun out of control.

"Are you all right?" Eric's frantic voice called out to me. He hurried over to my side and aided me to my feet.

"I'm fine. Where's that unibird?"

"I zapped it with my scepter, and it flew away."

A deviline charged in Eric's direction and drew her sword to fight.

"Eric, behind you!"

Eric intercepted the deviline's blade by swinging his sword at her. The deviline's weapon sliced into a nearby tree. Furious, she hissed and pinned Eric to the ground, grasping a handful of his hair.

"Let go of him!" I shouted, impaling her arm with my spear. The deviline yowled, clutching her wound, and released Eric. "Quick!" Grabbing his hand, I bolted in the opposite direction, getting us as far away as we could from the injured deviline.

"Thanks," said Eric, gasping for air and massaging his scalp.

"Have you seen Eileen and Brian?"

Eric pursed his lips. "A quartet of bearnixes chased them away from my sight when I was fighting that unibird earlier. Let's go and find them."

"Alexandria, Eric!" screamed a voice. "Run!"

The next second, Eileen emerged from behind a tree, her eyes wide and her face pale. "One of the bearnixes burned down my poison ivy trap, and the forest is on fire!"

"What? Where is it? I can go and extinguish it before it burns down all the—"

"You can't! The fire's spreading all over the forest like crazy! We must find our way out before the fire finds us! Follow me!"

We took off running, leaping over roots and skirting trees. The rising heat engulfed us as we dashed through the forest.

"Eileen, where's Brian?" I yelled.

"I don't know! We split the moment we saw the bearnix burning down the trap and setting fire to the trees! I told him to go and warn the other Elders while I came to find you!"

"Oh no!" Eric, who was the slowest among us, hollered. "The fire's right behind us!"

I glanced behind my shoulder, and sure enough, the smoke, ten times thicker than the drizzly mist I had seen this morning, was right behind us. The trees, once lush and green, were burning in columns of charcoal. The branches and trunks were choked by orange and yellow flames that sizzled and burned with a kind of savage, malicious enthusiasm. Cinders, ashes, and dying embers flew from the scorched limbs of the trees, falling and flying like huge bats. I felt the humid air clinging on to all my senses, my vision now clouded by smoke. Even though I was immune to fire, I knew I had to leave as soon as possible, for we couldn't afford to lose anyone. Every second we lingered in the burning forest meant a huge risk of losing my friends.

"Keep running!" I sprinted toward a section of the forest not yet consumed by the flames. To my relief, the smoke was thinning and dissipating up ahead.

Panting and sweating, I came to a stop and found myself surrounded by trees with leaves the colors of autumn—vermillion, amber, and gold. But as I neared, they blushed and deepened into a vivid shade of red. The crimson leaves and burgundy trunks were a peculiar yet beautiful sight to behold. Sunlight seeped through the shade of scarlet above, casting pink polka-dots of light on the ground, which was carpeted by fallen leaves.

"Phew, that was a close call, wasn't it?" I glanced over my shoulder. "Eileen? Eric?"

Nothing.

Panic flooded me, coursing through my veins and taking over my senses. I ran from tree to tree, looking around and calling their names in hope of coming across one of them.

I hopped across a little stream with only a few inches of

clear water and mossy rocks. Crimson leaves floated around them like boats, blanketing almost every inch of the brook. Rounding a few more trees, I stopped.

A towering oak that stood out among the others caught my attention. Ivory-yellow candles squatted on the hollow parts of the burgundy trunk and gnarled roots, scarlet flames blazing on the tips. I looked up and saw the ancient branches weaving around one another as though arms reaching out to touch the sky. However, it was a carved door etched upon the trunk of the tree that piqued my curiosity. I was sure the oak tree had an empty heart and was probably home to someone or some mysterious creature. With great prudence, I approached it, taking one step at a time. An eerie red glow seemed to emanate from within the oak tree. A tendril of crimson smoke drifted from the carved door, and a figure emerged. I whipped out my scepter and found myself face-to-face with a young sorceress with soft features. Curly auburn hair flowed around her shoulders. Her eyes were the color of fire; they glowed warmly as they studied my face. Underneath her billowing red cloak was a black chiffon dress.

"There's—there's a fire in the forest," I stuttered. "I—I was running away from it, and—and I stumbled across your oak tree. I was just admiring it," I explained, lowering my scepter. "I come in peace."

"A fire? In this forest?" said the sorceress in a floaty voice.

"Um, no...the trees there, they were...normal...green, I mean."

The sorceress nodded. "I see. You will be safe here. Nothing can cross the invisible barrier I drew between the Scarlet Forest and the Elec Forest."

"Excuse me?"

"The Elec Forest is the neighboring forest with green trees. It's behind Mors Manor."

"What about humans? I mean, I crossed the barrier. You're not going to attack me, are you? I was just running away from the fire and ended up here by accident."

"Not the first one," she said, a curious expression on her face. "You are Alexandria Richardson, princess of the

Otherworld." It was a remark and not a question.

"I am." I registered the fact she addressed me by name, which I preferred much more than "Your Highness."

"It's dangerous out there, especially for an Otherworldian like you. Come in."

My curiosity getting the best of me, I obeyed and followed her into the hollowed tree trunk. Enchanted by the spectacularity the moment I set foot into the oak tree, I gasped. The interior was far more spacious than what it seemed from the outside. Millions of tiny orbs hovered below the vaulted ceiling, emitting warm, rosy hues of yellow, orange, and pink.

"Have a seat," the sorceress said, jerking her head at a crimson pouf beside a tree stump, which I assumed was a coffee table.

"Thanks, but who are you?" I mumbled, trying my best not to sound silly.

"Ruby. They know me as the Scarlet Sorceress."

"They?"

"People who know about my existence. I'm on your side, and I am just like you. Fighting against Alta and Alto."

"Well...all right," I said, not knowing what to reply and uncertain whether it was wise to trust this stranger.

"The Siblings are cruel and foolish. They've been trying to persecute me for ages. Never managed to succeed, though," Ruby smirked. Then, in a much more serious tone, she asked, "Alexandria, what were you thinking, entering the forest like that?"

"I got lost. I was chased by a couple of monsters, and the woods got burned down, and the next thing I knew, I was in this forest with red trees."

"Why did you even enter Elec Forest in the first place?"

"Me and my friends barely escaped from Mors Manor, and Helen led us to the neighboring forest—" I stopped in mid-sentence, wondering if I had told her more than necessary.

"You came with the Elders?" Ruby gazed at me, a look of dawning comprehension on her face.

"Yes, I—"

"What did you come here for?"

"We—um, well—" I stammered, playing for more time and silently hoping she would stop gleaning information about me.

"You don't trust me, do you?"

"Well, no…yes…I mean—"

"What about this—I'll tell you how to leave this forest in order to prove I'm on your side." Ruby turned and rummaged in a wooden crate, snatching things out and setting them aside. I saw a golden necklace, a ball of red yarn, a brooch with rubies, a crown of maple leaves, a tartan shawl, a fringed scarf, and—

"Ah, yes." Ruby handed me what looked like a red silk ribbon. "A magical ribbon that will guide you out of the forest."

"Thanks," I said.

"Lost travelers...," Ruby shook her head. "Alexandria, it was a very unwise decision to enter this forest. Remind your friend Helen for me, won't you? Many people wander into Elec Forest, but *none* ever leave."

"None?" I repeated, stunned.

"It's bewitched, this forest. Anyone can enter, but *nobody* ever leaves. Alta and Alto have sent countless subordinates into Elec Forest. None ever returned."

"Dead?" I guessed.

"Driven into insanity. Seeing the same trees and running into the same...things over and over again. They go mad in the end. Blabbering nonsense, seeing hallucinations, claiming they witnessed murders that never occurred."

I remembered the carved words on the trees and the bearnixes' corpses last night. "But I didn't see those strange things this morning."

"They only appear in the evenings."

"So...nobody can leave Elec Forest no matter how hard they try?"

"They can't. That is, without the help of a magical artifact only I possess," Ruby pointed a painted nail at the ribbon in my hand. "I've helped some lost Elders that are fortunate enough to stumble across my oak tree. Sadly, very few do."

"Then why don't you leave your tree and help the other lost travelers?"

"Me? Leave my hiding place when the rulers are doing me a huge favor by failing to find me for decades?" Ruby laughed without humor. "Enough about me. What about you? Why have you come to the Underworld?"

I told her all about how we had come to navigate the terrains. "I had a dream yesterday about Alta. She mentioned a place called the Control Center, and that's where all the top secrets of the Underworld are kept. We're trying to locate it and break into it."

"It's on Mount Maravillas," replied Ruby. "Got an idea of where you're supposed to find the Control Center? Which peak?"

"What? I don't know anything about 'peaks.'"

"Mount Maravillas is a huge mountain with four peaks. The north peak is the highest one, as well as the tallest point of the Underworld. All the rivers and waterfalls in the Underworld originate from the north peak. The melting snow and ice keep the rivers flowing. The south peak is the lowest one, and it's the easiest to scale. The east peak is home to the most exotic species of flora and fauna in the Underworld. Very few people dare to scale it in fear of encountering beasts they've never imagined existed. And finally, there's the west peak, the one that's known for its picturesque scenery and the beautiful hiking trail that leads to the summit. The Control Center is on the west peak, which is where your destination lies."

"Oh...oh!"

"There is a room in the Control Center called the Control Room. You will find all the information you need there, details about the terrains and everything you need to know about the Underworld. I would be more than delighted to provide you with the information you need, but I don't know more than you do about the terrains, having taken refuge and lived here in the oak tree ever since I was your age."

"I can't thank you enough, Ruby," I said. "But how can you be sure about the exact location of the Control Center if you've never been there in person?"

The sorceress's eyes twinkled. "I have my own way of knowing things. Now, you must go on and complete your mission. I suppose your friends are searching for you at this moment."

"We...we got lost," I recalled, a nasty feeling sinking to the pit of my stomach.

Ruby unlaced the locket she was wearing, pressed a finger to the crystal pendant, and held it on her palm. "What are their names?"

"Eric Williams and Eileen Spencer."

The crystal locket shimmered, and an image began to take place. It was Eric and Eileen.

"We've searched all over the woods, and we still can't find her!" Eileen was on the verge of tears.

"We've got to keep searching until—hold on. Is that you, Alexandria?"

"Eric? Eileen?" I called out to them in disbelief.

"Where have you been? And why are we seeing you on a thin sheet of mist?"

"I'll explain later. Where are you?" I asked.

"In a strange forest full of trees with red leaves."

"All right. I'll go and join you as soon as possible, and I'll explain everything. I've got loads to tell you. See you later."

The image of Eric and Eileen faded away.

"You have an important mission to complete, and I must not delay you," said Ruby, who walked me out to the entrance. "You'll see your friends there. The fifth tree ahead."

"Thank you." I grasped for a word to express my gratitude but couldn't. "Thanks," I repeated. "You know, Ruby, you could join the Elders in the Otherworld one day if you want to. You look like a very powerful sorceress."

"I would love to, but any Underworldian who joins the Otherworld will get their family into trouble, and I cannot take the risk of losing my siblings. There is a possibility they might find and kill them one day."

"They're doing that?" I asked, horrified. "Killing off and torturing people just because their family went to the other side?"

Ruby nodded, a grave expression etched upon her pretty face. "This is because Alta is ashamed of the fact her own son betrayed her and pledged allegiance to the Otherworld. Furthermore, thousands of Underworldians fled to the Otherworld during the past year."

"Alexandria? Where are you?" I heard Eric's voice in the distance.

"Goodbye. Oh, and I must remind you, the Siblings have placed a very powerful protection charm on the west peak of Mount Maravillas, so any form of elemental magic will not work there. Good luck to you." With a final nod, Ruby disappeared behind the carved door of the oak tree.

"Oh, there she is, Eric!" a girl's voice shouted. Before I knew it, I was swept into a tight embrace by Eileen. "Alexandria, we were worried sick!"

"Eileen, let her breathe," said Eric, beaming with relief.

"Where in the world were you? We were looking for you, and all of a sudden, a thin sheet of mist materialized in front of our eyes, and you—"

"I guess my story can wait. Let's find the Elders first."

"What are you three doing there?" a voice, unmistakably Brian's, hollered.

We whirled around and found ourselves face-to-face with the four Elders. Brian had sustained a wound on his arm, blood was oozing from a gash below Evonne's right eye, and there were grazes and cuts all over Helen and Zack's faces.

"We thought—we thought they'd gotten you!" said Helen, pressing a hand to her heart. "Thank goodness you're all safe. What happened after we'd split?"

With the combined efforts of Eric and Eileen, the three of us told them everything that happened since we had parted ways.

"...and then Alexandria disappeared when we were running away from the fire," finished Eileen.

"Right. I couldn't see anything ahead of me because of the thick smoke, but then...." Quickly but clearly, I clarified my encounter with Ruby and everything about Elec Forest and

Mount Maravillas. "I've got proof," I added, showing them the red silk ribbon.

Eric gaped at it in awe. "So it's true."

"What's true?"

"Ruby the Scarlet Sorceress. Rumor has it she's the most powerful Underworldian. Alta wants to get rid of Ruby because she's terrified of her. I had no idea she was lurking in this forest all along." Eric gazed at the rows of trees, a wondering look on his face.

"What do you think?" Zack turned to Helen. "Should we trust this sorceress?"

Staring at the ribbon in my hand, Helen remained silent for a while. "We'll see where this ribbon takes us. If the sorceress is telling the truth, we will proceed to the west peak and break into the Control Center, like she suggested."

"Good plan," said Evonne. "And what should we do with this ribbon?"

Gingerly, I set it on the ground. The ribbon curled itself and turned into a snake. It looked at Eileen and hissed.

"Blast it to pieces!" Eric shouted, pointing his scepter at it.

"No," said Eileen. "The snake told us to follow it."

The snake nodded and slithered through the forest, the seven of us on its heels. As we hurried after it, I noticed the trees around us were growing younger.

The colorless sky blued as soon as we came to a clearing. I looked over my shoulder and saw, with a pang of astonishment, that the entire forest had vanished. The snake turned and hissed at us.

"Thanks," said Eileen, patting it on the head with a finger.

The snake hissed again, this time turning to face me. I reached out to touch it, and the snake transfigured back into a red ribbon.

"Amazing," breathed Evonne.

I pocketed the ribbon. "I'm going to keep it as a souvenir," I explained to the others, who, judging from their expressions, thought I had taken leave of my senses.

"We must begin our journey to the west peak right away,"

said Helen.

"But where in the world are we now?" Evonne asked.

We were in a glade surrounded by green hills. Small hummocks perched in the distance, the frosty peaks of taller mountains and buttes visible behind them. An arbor embellished with mint-green and ice-blue roses stood on our left. Behind it was a flight of stone steps that led up the hill and out of the glade.

"Are we in Evergreen Valley?" said Brian.

"No." Helen tightened her grasp on her wand and bow and approached the arbor. "There are words carved up here. *Hiking Trail to West Peak of Mount Maravillas.*"

I felt a jolt of excitement. "This is it. We're here."

# Chapter Ten

## Mount Maravillas (Eileen)

For a solid minute, we all stood there in silence, mesmerized by the trail that led to the mysterious building which held the deepest and perhaps darkest secrets of the Underworld.

"Come on," said Helen, shrinking her bow and arrows with her wand and stuffing them into the pouch of her cloak. "To the Control Center."

"But hold on for a moment. Don't you think this is a bit... strange?" asked Brian, frowning. "I mean, there must be some sort of shortcut around here or some alternative way that'll get us to the west peak. Anyway, we can't follow this trail all the way to the end. For starters, we don't know how long this thing is. We might spend days and probably weeks trying to scale this thing. Second, we don't know what dangers we'll face along the way. Third—"

"You can give me as many reasons as you like, Brian, but you *may* have realized there is no other option," Helen interrupted him, her nostrils flaring.

"We could fly a cloud to the Control Center," suggested Eric. "That'd save us a lot of time."

"You're forgetting something," I piped up. "According to Ruby, we can't do elemental magic here." I gave my scepter a wave, and nothing happened. "See?"

Eric muttered a cuss word that made Helen frown in disapproval.

"And," I plowed on, "since any form of elemental magic won't work here, I don't think any bearnixes, unibirds, kittenpillars, or dogfishes can attack us with *their* elemental powers, either, which will make things a lot easier for us."

"What do you mean?"

"Just put it in this way. A bearnix wouldn't be much of a threat if it couldn't spout fire."

"But there are still plenty of ways the Underworldians can stop us from reaching the—"

"We're not getting anywhere," Helen cut in. "There's no point in speculating. Since we've got no other alternative, our only option is to hike up the trail and do it the hard way."

"I agree," said Zack. "The Underworldians already know we are navigating the terrains. I don't think they'd be foolish enough to design a shortcut to the Control Center in case we find it by accident. *This* is the one and only route."

"But there's no evidence to prove that a shortcut to the Control Center doesn't exist," protested Brian. "Surely it'd be—"

"And that's exactly what the Siblings would want us to do, to search for an easy way that doesn't even exist," said Helen in a harsh voice. "We'd be wasting days or weeks or months on that and still not reach our destination."

"But what if there really is one?"

"Even if there really is a shortcut, there's a high chance we won't make it to the Control Center alive by going that way. It'll be twice as risky and dangerous."

"How do you know?" Brian questioned.

"Most people fail to realize this, including you, Brian, but not everything has a shortcut. Hard effort and honest work, though often underestimated, are the only ways to succeed. I don't expect people as superficial as Alta and Alto to appreciate this, and that is their biggest flaw. They will assume we are going to look for a shortcut to the Control Center, which gives them the perfect opportunity to ambush and kill us by setting traps along the shortcut. So, the only safe route is to follow this hiking trail all the way up to the Control Center."

"Well, I guess that makes sense," Brian gave in, turning his palms skyward. "So, what next?"

"After me," said Helen, setting foot on the stone steps. Zack and Evonne tagged along with her, and the rest of us followed. I watched Helen curl her long hair into a tight bun and secure it with a silver hairpin, thinking her new hairstyle suited her stern personality better. Shaking my head, I smiled, wondering why in the world these random little thoughts always popped up in my head in random little moments like now.

We had a sweeping view of the sloping meadows, which were blanketed in innumerable shades of green. The hills in the distance were tinted turquoise, fading into blueness and assimilating with the clear, cloudless sky. A carnival of sporadic yellow flowers blossomed, sunbathing on the lush meadows. A viridescent wave rippled through the tall blades of grass as a breeze traveled by, humming and whispering in my ears. Below us, a silvery blue creek gurgled, leaping over craggy rocks as it weaved its merry way through the chartreuse-green hills like a shiny ribbon with sequins. Dogfishes with shimmering scales frolicked in the creek, chasing after each other and splashing water like dolphins. Large ripples and white foam marked the spots where they landed.

We ascended higher and higher above the meadows and hills. Viridian pine trees stood sentinel along the trail ahead of us, like soldiers guarding a secret passage. I saw a family of kittenpillars grazing by the trail. All of them had fuzzy lime-green heads and emerald-green bodies with black spots. A few of them stopped and turned to stare at us as we passed. Alexandria tightened her grip on her spear, ready to attack anytime, but the kittenpillars seemed uninterested in fighting us. They merely gazed at us with interest, as if we were aliens from another planet.

"How odd," said Alexandria, jerking her head in the direction of the kittenpillars. "They seem rather gentle."

"Definitely not Alta's minions," I agreed.

"Of course, we aren't! We hate her as much as you do,"

one of the kittenpillars said in indignation as it wriggled its way toward me.

I blinked, taken aback. "You...you can speak English?"

The kittenpillar shook its head. "No, heiress of Fern. You are the only one who can understand us."

"What are you doing, Eileen?" asked Alexandria. "Are you...are you talking to this kittenpillar?"

Frowning, I looked at her. "Can't you...?"

"She's the heiress of Ember. She can't understand our language," said the kittenpillar, shooting Alexandria a frightened look.

"Lower your spear, Alexandria. You're scaring it." I turned to the kittenpillar, "You said you hate Alta as much as we do. How come?"

"She destroyed our homes and built fortresses, castles, and palaces for herself and her nasty brother," growled the kittenpillar. "I used to live on the south peak of Mount Maravillas until the Siblings started building fortresses there. They've also built a Control Center on the west peak. Who knows what they're going to do next?"

"Come on, Eileen," Zack called out to me. "We've got to stick together."

"Good luck on your mission," meowed the kittenpillar before wriggling back to join its family.

"Goodbye." I waved at the kittenpillar. "All right, I'm coming." I ran over to the others and caught up with them.

Alexandria, Eric, and Brian cast curious looks at me. "So, what was that all about?"

I told them everything about the conversation I had with the kittenpillar. Eric didn't seem surprised at the fact the kittenpillars hated Alta as much as we did.

"A lot of magical creatures in the Underworld are against her," he said.

"I can definitely see why," remarked Alexandria. "Pretty kittenpillars, aren't they? I've never seen polka-dotted kittenpillars."

"Those are wild kittenpillars," explained Eric. "They're

harmless."

"Unlike the unibirds we saw at Mors Manor?" Alexandria asked. "The huge, black, bat-like ones."

"Bat-like unibirds?" I asked. "I didn't know there were different species of unibirds and kittenpillars in the Underworld."

"Of course," Brian piped up. "Among the four creatures—bearnixes, unibirds, kittenpillars, and dogfishes—there are four species of each. Wild, dark magic, ordinary, and camouflage."

"So, what's the difference between the four species?" I asked.

"Different species have different colors. For example, ordinary dogfishes like Noir have brown heads and yellow fish bodies. But wild dogfishes have white heads and blue bodies. As for camouflage dogfishes, they change color depending on where they are. Also, ordinary, wild, and camouflage dogfishes aren't as aggressive as their dark magic counterparts."

"What do they look like?"

"Dark magic dogfishes have black heads and violet fish-bodies. But since we're on a hiking trail, we'll get to see all four animals in wild colors."

A chirping noise drew our attention. I saw a flock of unibirds sailing above us, spreading their feathery white wings. They had brown heads with a splash of ivory between their eyes. Their golden horns glowed fiercely under the sunshine.

"Wild unibirds," said Brian, pointing at them. "Brown heads and white bodies. They're the only species of unibirds that can make chirping sounds. And in case you're wondering, we might see some wild bearnixes soon. Auburn heads and red bodies."

"Interesting," I said. "What do they eat? The wild bearnixes and unibirds."

"All unibirds feast on dead bodies of other animals. As for bearnixes, they prey on others for food."

I frowned. "That's so cruel."

"It's the cycle of nature," replied Brian with a shrug. "You of all people should know, Eileen."

"How did you know all this?" Alexandria said, looking

impressed. "It's no wonder they call you a genius."

"Nah," replied Brian with a smile. "I just like reading about the animals in the Underworld."

The trail was now leading us into a jungle. It wound its way through an array of large natural skyscrapers, some plump and stout, others slender and lanky. Soon we found ourselves surrounded by an impressive palette of trees, shrubs, and undergrowth. Shafts of sunlight streaked through the soaring emerald canopy of leaves above, bathing the vegetation in a soft green-and-yellow glow. Kittenpillars gazed down at us from the branches with droopy eyes, yawning and stretching their long bodies. Vines coiled themselves around the trunks like snakes. The ground below us was slippery and carpeted with moss. Everything was a verdant, vigorous green. I gazed at the jungle hungrily, feasting my eyes on the beguiling beauty of nature as though I could never get enough.

"Bit slippery, isn't it?" Alexandria said. "The ground, I mean."

Brian got out his wand and pointed it at the ground. With a wave, the moss vanished, baring the stony hiking trail. "Better?"

"Yeah. Nice wand you've got there," I said.

Brian ran his fingers over his wand, a glossy lilac stick carved from marble. "Thanks."

"How do they work, those wands?" I asked. "How do you Elders manage to charm objects and make them move, shrink, and distend?"

"Oh, it's easy. We don't have actual charms or spells. We perform magic by giving our wands commands and making the correct movement. But most importantly, we rely on our willpower to cast spells. The more focused we are, the more powerful magic we can perform. For some experienced Elders they can will objects to obey them by pointing their wands at them without saying anything or making any movement. It requires very strong concentration."

"What happens if you're not concentrating hard enough?"

"You'll only get half the effect you want."

"Why don't you fight in battles with wands? They look

much more convenient than weapons."

"That's because the spells cannot do enemies much harm. With wands, we can only inflict or heal minor injuries or fire streaks of light to warn each other. They're not meant to be used as weapons, you see. Wands are mostly used to perform simple magic like blasting obstacles apart, enlarging or shrinking things, removing smears from clothes...small stuff like that."

"Then why do you keep your wand with you all the time?"

"It's easy to carry around, and like you said, less cumbersome than swords or shields, which we usually keep shrunken and hidden in pockets. Plus, I'll need it to enlarge my weapon when fighting—Oh, look, wild bearnixes."

Sure enough, we saw a cluster of bearnixes traipsing around the fern bushes on our right. They gazed at us with sad, miserable eyes, probably sulking about being unable to perform elemental magic in Mount Maravillas.

"Won't they burn this jungle down?" Eric asked, his eyebrows knitted.

"They can't do magic here, don't you remember?" I reminded him. "Poor bearnixes.... Imagine what life's like for them."

"Well, all they need to do is to leave Mount Maravillas," said Alexandria. "How long do you reckon this hike will last, by the way?"

"About two or three days, I suppose," answered Brian. "We'll have to find a place to stay for an evening. An inn or something, if we're lucky enough to come across one."

"And what if we don't?"

"Evonne and I each brought a tent. We could find somewhere to camp out for tonight."

"I hope you didn't bring any porridge with you," quipped Alexandria.

"Oh, did you guys have porridge on the last mission?" Brian asked, looking interested. "Was it awful?"

"The worst."

Brian laughed. "Yup, the notorious porridge. Every Elder knows that. It's sort of a tradition to have porridge for dinner during missions. But rest assured, we didn't pack any with us. Nope, only meat pies, vegetable sandwiches, and two decanters of Mystery Potion."

"Mystery Potion?"

"The silver drink that takes the form of whatever you want it to be. Best drink on Earth, if you ask me. It'd make mortals green with envy." Brian laughed.

I was starting to like Brian a lot. He was not only intelligent but also much more approachable and interesting than Helen or Zack.

"Brian, I've got a question, but I'm not sure if it's...polite," began Alexandria in a hesitant voice.

"Sure, just ask."

"Why don't you...?" Alexandria's voice faltered. She cleared her throat and started again. "Why don't you get along with the other Elders?"

"Who told you that?" Brian said, looking strangely amused at her assumption.

"Well...no offense, but why are you talking with us instead of joining Helen, Zack, and Evonne?" Alexandria jerked her head at the figures of the three Elders, a little further ahead of us.

"Ah, well...they're older, you know. And they've been close friends long before I joined the Elders. Not that I don't get along with them, mind you. It's just that I don't feel like a part of them. Both Zack and Evonne had been Helen's apprentice in their years of training. Plus, Zack likes Helen. See? There's not much of a place for me."

"I see. You reckon they're in love, Helen and Zack?" I said, changing the topic.

"Positive. Or, to be more accurate, I'm sure Zack's in love with Helen. I've no idea whether she likes him back or not."

"Aren't they a wee bit old to get into a relationship?"

"Forty-one and thirty-six? Not really. It's not uncommon for Otherworldians to live to a hundred and fifty, you see. Helen may be the oldest among the Elders, but actually, she's not *that* old. Pretty experienced, though. I wouldn't dare question her ways of thinking or challenge her authority."

"You guys really respect—Hold on, why are they stopping?" I asked.

Helen, Zack, and Evonne had stopped walking and were now in the middle of a discussion. "Where are the others?" Helen turned. "Hurry up. We've got a problem here."

The four of us raced over to join them. "What's the matter? Oh...."

The trail had led us to the edge of a tall cliff. I had expected to see a creek bed, but instead, a small valley yawned below us, unfurling into the distance. Enormous trees the size of apartments stretched their long, gnarled, lichen-coated limbs as though giants flexing their muscles menacingly. The thick branches thinned into twigs at the ends, like talons clawing at the air. Large, jagged rocks clad in vivid green moss squatted below the huge trees. An almost dried-up brook swerved through the narrow, labyrinthine passages between the stones. On the other side of the valley stood another cliff, where the hiking trail meandered on.

"Look." Brian pointed at the scattered remains of a wooden bridge lying at the feet of the trees.

"So, how should we cross this?" Evonne frowned at the fragments of the broken bridge below. "It's beyond repair."

Helen, however, was not paying attention to her. She leaned forward and observed the landscape in front of us. "These are no ordinary trees."

"Not ordinary? What do you mean?" Eric asked.

"Just use your common sense," snapped Helen. "Look at the splintered planks of wood in the valley. Do you think the bridge broke by accident? Somebody must have come here before us and destroyed it to stop us from reaching the Control Center."

"They ruined the bridge?" I said. "But then nobody, including their fellow Underworldians or Alta and Alto, can get past it."

"So there must be a second way to cross this valley. I bet we've got to interact with the landscape." Helen fixed her gaze on the large trees, studying them up close. Then, she pointed her wand at the knobby branches. "Reveal."

Thick verdant vines sprouted from the knuckles of the

branches, cascading down before us like streamers.

"Clever, those Underworldians," muttered Helen to herself, scrutinizing the vines. "I thought we'd have to perform some complex magic or enchantments to cross this valley, but all it took was one simple command instead."

"But why would they do this?" asked Zack.

"The simplest things are often the most overlooked. In this case, the Underworldians are testing our logic and intelligence rather than our magical ability and skills. The question is not how difficult the magic is, but rather *which* command to use and *what* object to charm."

Brian nodded fervently, drinking every word in. "Very wise theory."

The blank expressions on Eric's and Alexandria's faces told me I wasn't the only one who didn't understand.

"Yeah, you're right," agreed Zack. "But how should we get past these vines?"

"We're not supposed to use elemental magic here," I chimed in. "What should we do?"

"It's obvious, isn't it?" Brian cut in. "We swing our way through the valley. I say we'd make it to the other cliff in about... eight swings."

"What?" Eric and I gaped at him, fearful for his sanity.

"It's the only way," said Helen, pursing her lips.

Eric stared at the innumerable vines dangling from the trees. "How can you be sure it's safe?"

"It must be," Helen assured him. "There must be at least one safe way to get through this valley, in case Alta and Alto want to check on their Control Center. So who's going first?"

"Me," I volunteered.

"You?" Alexandria, Eric, Helen, and Zack looked at me, astonishment etched on their faces. I had a reputation for being timid and shy, unlikely to volunteer first on anything. However, swinging on vines and crossing a valley was way too tempting for a nature lover like me.

"Well, come on, then." Helen stepped aside to let me pass.

I closed my fingers around the nearest vine, then grasped

it with both hands. Taking a deep breath, I kicked off the ground, swinging out toward the opposite cliff.

An airy, divine, ethereal sensation of flying. The rushing sound of the wind filled my ears, blurring into a quiet roar. I knew I ought to be terrified; had the only cord my life depended on snapped, I would've plummeted to my death. However, it was hard to feel frightened while swinging in the light breeze. Cold air brushed against my cheeks, sending thrills of excitement tingling in me. I wrapped my legs around the vine as I soared in the vast green valley, swinging back and forth, as light as a feather.

"Move on, Eileen!" I heard Eric shout.

"Oh, right!" I had forgotten what I was there for. As the vine swayed to the other side, I made a lunge for the next one. Eric grabbed ahold of the first vine as it swung back. From the corner of my eye, I saw Helen, Zack, Evonne, Alexandria, and Brian forming a line behind him. I reached for the next vine, but the huge gap made it impossible for me to move forward. A mixture of frustration and panic burned in me.

"Hold on there," said Eric. "I've got an idea. Eileen, hold on tight. Don't let go no matter what."

"What are you going to do?"

"On the count of three, all right? One, two...three!"

"Ouch!" I screamed as a hand pushed me forward with potent force.

"Go! Grab the next one!"

I seized the thick, curly vine in front of me as soon as it was within reach. With a tremendous effort, I managed to get past a few more vines. Now that my stamina had been greatly reduced, it was more about persevering and gathering my remaining strength to proceed rather than the joyful, floating sensation of swinging. My arms were sore and aching, and I could feel my muscles protesting. Summoning all my willpower, I clung to the penultimate vine with my sweaty hands as I suppressed the urge to look down. I could see the trail on the other end beckoning to me. Just another swing and I could land on the cliff. I looked over my shoulder and saw Eric, Helen, Zack, Evonne, Alexandria, and

Brian, each struggling to maintain a tight grasp on their vines.

"Eric, could you—?"

Panting and sweating from fatigue, he shook his head. "Can't...," he moaned, his knuckles white from clutching his vine. Eric's pale forehead was beaded with sweat. He closed his eyes, his body hanging almost limply on his vine.

"Eric?" I whispered with urgent effort.

"I'm fine, just...just go." His fingers slid down a few inches, and I knew I couldn't rely on him anymore. I gazed desperately at my destination, debating with myself on what to do. A sudden thought flashed across my mind. It was dangerous, and the consequences could be worse than death. But anything was better than being suspended in midair, dangling on a vine, and waiting for the remaining strength to drain from me. I concentrated on my goal, which was a little beyond reach. Counting to three, I let go of my vine and made a dive for the next. Relief welled within me as my fingers curled around the final vine. Hoisting myself up into the air, I took a leap, and my feet landed on the cliff.

"Whew!" I nursed my sore hands and dabbed some healing ointment on my blistered fingers.

Eric reached the cliff a few seconds after I did, his breathing labored. He landed on the ground, fell to his knees, and collapsed on the silky grass. "I'm...I'm never going to do this...again. That was the most horrible—"

"Be grateful you survived," gasped Helen, the third to arrive. She leaned against a tree trunk and sat down, catching her breath.

Zack, Evonne, Alexandria, and Brian joined us, one by one.

"You okay, Eileen?" said Alexandria, massaging her arms. Her long locks of red hair were plastered to the sweat on her forehead and brows.

I nodded. "Still alive, and I guess that's something to be thankful for."

***

It took everyone a while to regain energy. A quick late lunch of sandwiches and pies made everyone groggy. Had Helen not been persuading and coaxing everyone to pull themselves together and carry on, we would have happily and lazily spent the whole day relaxing.

"I'm not going to get up if there's another darn jungle ahead," declared Brian, lying on the ground and having no intention of continuing our journey.

Helen shot him a look that reminded me of a wrathful bearnix about to spout fire.

"Cheer up, Brian. I think I see a streak of light up ahead," Evonne said, standing on her tiptoes. "Might be a clearing or something."

"Oh, fine, fine.... I'm getting up," groaned Brian, gathering himself and standing up.

"Good," said Helen. "Then off we go."

We set off on the rocky hiking trail, with Helen, Zack, and Evonne taking the lead once again. The trees around us thinned, and the trail led us across a clearing ringed with pine trees.

I took a deep breath and closed my eyes. The bright sunlight painted my eyelids red, and for a while, that was the only color I could see.

"What are you doing, Eileen?" Eric's voice asked.

"I'm *feeling*. Feeling the nature aura here," I replied.

Eric asked no further questions. He simply took my hand and guided me forward along the hiking trail. It was a symbol of the strength and depth of our love that he did not make fun of me.

"Oh, Eric, I almost forgot," I said, opening my eyes. I groped in the pouch of my cloak and got out a wreath of daisies.

Eric looked amused. "For me? Don't you think it looks a bit...too cutesy?"

"Nonsense, it'll suit you just fine," I said, levitating the wreath with my scepter and making it land on his head. "Hmm. You don't really seem to appreciate this little gift."

Eric laughed. "What are you talking about? Of course, I appreciate it. I like whatever you give me."

I perked up at his words. "You do?"

"Yeah. Not because it's pretty or expensive or whatever.

You know, Eileen, it's you and your thoughts that really count."

He stole a glance at me, and our gazes met. A look of understanding passed between us. Blushing, I looked away from him and instead fixed my gaze on an odd rock in the shape of a kittenpillar.

"How did you learn to make this?"

"I taught myself and practiced for months. Locked myself in my room and did elemental magic, hiding from my mom and dad. Barely got away with the farting flowers."

"Farting flowers?" Eric's eyes widened, and his brows lifted in interest.

"Huge farting flowers sprout in my room every time I fail," I said, doing my best to keep a straight face.

"Oh, that does happen sometimes when you're experimenting with advanced magic," Brian piped up. He devoted his attention to the wreath of daisies on Eric's head. "But well done, Eileen, you seem to have mastered it."

I nodded a thank-you at him. "I miss elemental magic. Don't get me wrong. I do like it here in Mount Maravillas, the greenery and everything. It's just that...." I ran my fingers over my scepter sadly.

"Same," Alexandria echoed my sentiment. "I wonder why the Underworldians built the Control Center on the west peak of Mount Maravillas."

"Let's think," said Brian. "According to Ruby, the north peak is the highest of the four, as well as the tallest point of the Underworld."

"They could've built it there," Eric pointed out. "Highest peak, tallest place in the Underworld. I can't see why they didn't choose the north peak."

"Can't you?" asked Brian. "Building something this important on the highest peak would make it inconvenient for Alta and Alto to go and check on their latest inventions."

"Fair point," replied Alexandria. "But what about the others?"

"Let's see, the south peak...that's the lowest one, right? The easiest to climb? That wouldn't be much of a challenge, would it?

Building the Control Center there would be like saying hello to anyone who wants to invade it."

"The east peak is a good option, though," I said. "Remember what Ruby said? It has a variety of exotic flora and fauna. 'Very few people dare to scale it in fear of encountering beasts they've never imagined existed.' Not that I'm complaining, but why didn't they choose the east peak? That'd be my first pick to build a secret fortress."

"Mine, too," Alexandria agreed.

Brian lapsed into thoughtful silence, then finally spoke. "Maybe that's why they didn't. Because it's too obvious. We all know the east peak is the most dangerous one. As for the west peak, it's neither the tallest nor the most dangerous, but it's also not too easy to scale, right?"

"'Known for its picturesque scenery and the beautiful hiking trail that leads to the summit,'" Alexandria quoted Ruby.

"Yeah, I guess that's why Alta and Alto chose the west peak," surmised Brian. "It's just like any ordinary mountain, with scenic landscapes and a nice hiking trail. Also, because of this, people are likely to underestimate the dangers along the way."

"You mean those huge trees?" Eric asked.

"Right. That must be one of the precautions Alta and Alto set."

"*One* of the precautions?"

"Oh, yes. There might be many more along the trail. I doubt the Siblings would be foolish enough to let their guard down. After all, they are the masters at scheming and setting traps."

"You really seem to enjoy figuring out this logical stuff," said Eric, eyeing Brian with admiration.

"Of course. I always get excited when solving things like this. I like to put myself in Alta and Alto's position and try to guess how they'd conspire against us."

"We're lucky we've got you and Helen, our two best strategists."

"Helen? No, no, no. I've got nothing on her. She's the wisest among the Elders, and I'm just a sixteen-year-old."

"But you're a genius," I said, looking curiously at him and trying to guess what was hidden in that ingenious mind of his.

"I *may* be clever. I'm pretty analytical and observant, and I do have an excellent memory about almost everything, but cleverness and wisdom are very much different. Cleverness can help you out of a dangerous situation, but it is wisdom that can truly benefit one in the long run. Wisdom accrues with age and life experiences, and I have very little of both."

The trail had terminated once again ahead of us. Plunging and thundering from the top of a cliff was a breathtaking five-story waterfall. Dappled boulders crouched in the bluish-white lake beneath the mural of water, swift currents swishing over them like a white veil. The air was cold and moist, damp with tiny specks of water that pecked my cheeks. As I neared, an earthy, fresh scent filled my nostrils—nature's perfume. For some reason, an inexplicable surge of calmness and tranquility rose in me, despite the constant roaring of the waterfall. I could sense the palpable power of nature in the magnificence of the falls and the depth of the lake.

"What a great surprise...," Eric voiced my thoughts.

"But how should we get past it?" Zack glanced sideways at Helen.

"Well...I could give it a try." Helen pointed her wand at the lake. "Reveal."

Nothing happened.

"Concentrate harder and try again," advised Zack.

Helen did, but still no luck. The waterfall continued its monotonous rumble as though mocking her efforts.

"Should we use the waterfall as a climbing wall and try to scale it?" Evonne suggested.

Both Alexandria and Brian frowned. "Of course not. That doesn't even make sense."

"Then how—?"

"Don't panic," said Helen. "Interact with the landscape, remember? Let's see...there's a huge waterfall, a cliff, and a lake here. What else?"

"Boulders," I replied. "There's a huge one over there, by

the lake."

Looking crestfallen, Helen sighed. "That's not much, to begin with. Even if we did 'reveal' on all of them, it probably wouldn't help us scale the waterfall...." Her voice trailed away as she gazed at the rocks.

"Hold on," Brian piped up. "What if there are clues hidden in the rocks?"

"Brilliant assumption," said Helen, her expression brightening. "I'll do 'reveal' on the big boulder and see what happens." The rest of us followed her to the gigantic rock. Examining it, she ran her hand over the uneven surface and directed her wand at the stone. "Reveal."

Nothing happened.

"Hmm." Helen knit her eyebrows. "Not this one. What about...?" She scanned the boulders by the lake, and her gaze fell on the smallest one, a plain, weathered rock. "Yes, that's exactly what the Siblings would do...the littlest one," she murmured to herself.

The seven of us made our way to the small boulder, and Helen raised her wand. "Reveal."

A collective gasp echoed among the others, and I immediately knew why. Inky black words formed on the lumpy surface of the boulder; the letters etched themselves into the stone as though carved into it by some unknown force.

"Whoa," whispered Alexandria in awe.

A hush fell upon us as we studied the words.

*Roaring and flowing, a wall of water*
*In the depths of the lake, something slumbers*
*Sealed underwater, a wheel of lumber*
*Ever concealed, yet revealed on order*

"So, a riddle, huh?" Brian said, grinning. "I love those. Especially original ones like this. Not the hackneyed ones like what-goes-up-and-never-comes-down."

"Right," said Helen. "Let's figure it out. Roaring and flowing, a wall of water...." She looked up at the curtain of water ahead of us. "The first line's referring to the waterfall, no doubt."

"*In the depths of the lake, something slum*—What's this *something* that slumbers under the lake?" I asked.

"A wheel of lumber, according to the third line," Eric said.

"How do you know that?"

Eric rolled his eyes. "That *something is in the depths of the lake*, which means it's *sealed underwater*, big genius."

"And what's the fourth line supposed to mean?" Zack squinted at the tiny words. "*On order*? What's this order?"

"Like a command, I guess," answered Helen. "We might have to point our wands at the waterfall and say the *order*. I reckon we've got to figure this *order* out."

"A command?" Brian said, his eyes widening.

"Yes. So what might this wheel of lumber be?"

"Let's brainstorm. Maybe a wooden Ferris wheel?" I guessed.

"That's likely, but how's that going to help us—?"

"Rise!" Brian almost shouted.

Everyone turned to look at him.

"That's the answer, rise!" Brian clapped his hands.

Helen blinked. "Rise? How did you figure that out?"

"Acrostic," said Brian proudly. "The first letter of the first word in each line. Roaring. In. Sealed. Ever. R-I-S-E, see?" He pointed his wand at the lake under the waterfall. "Rise."

Before we knew it, there was a seismic shaking and a deafening rumble.

"An earthquake!" Helen shouted. "Get down, everyone!"

Speechless with fright, we crouched down, edging as far away from the tall boulders as we could manage, in fear they would collapse and crush us. Eric grasped my hand tightly, and I could feel his nails digging into my palm. He pulled me tighter and closer as I buried my face in his shoulder. All of a sudden, the shaking and rumbling ceased. Stillness descended on us again.

"What were you doing, Brian?" I frowned at him. "You almost got us—"

"Look behind you," Brian interrupted, beaming.

I turned, and what I saw made my jaw drop. A water wheel

had risen from the lake. It was massive in width and exceeded the waterfall in height.

*"A wheel of lumber,"* said Evonne, breathless with surprise. "Wow."

"Wonderful, Brian." Helen's voice was softened by reverence. "Now, all we need to do is to figure out how to reach the top by using the water wheel."

"But how?" Brian walked up to the riverbank to get a better look at it. "What about...reveal?" He pointed his wand at the water wheel.

The levers started growing in size. I watched, in utter astonishment, as the lumbers connected with one another, forming small doorless compartments. The water wheel had transfigured itself into a Ferris wheel.

"Well, that makes things much easier," said Helen in her usual brisk manner. "I suppose...two to three people could share a compartment. Come on."

Helen and Zack got into one of the compartments. The Ferris wheel rotated, and Brian and Evonne got into the second one. Eric took off the wreath of daisies and slipped it into his pocket before joining Alexandria and me. The three of us crowded into the third compartment, and we rose up into the air.

"Magical, isn't it?" breathed Eric. "Everything that happened today."

"You can say that again," I agreed. I poked my head out of our compartment, bathing in the constant drizzle of water as I admired the hugeness of the waterfall. The pool below us shimmered under the radiant beams of the sun like a lake of melted diamonds.

"I'm glad we don't have to swim across this thing," remarked Alexandria. "I'd probably drown, and I'd hate to miss out on the rest of the journey if I did."

"So would I," agreed Eric. "Wonder what's in store for us ahead of the trail."

I watched the vertical drop of the waterfall sink as our compartment ascended higher and higher, jolting to a stop after half a minute.

"I think we've reached the top," said Alexandria.

Six wide wooden planks formed a walkway, guiding us to the top of the waterfall, where the Elders stood waiting for us. I could see the hiking trail curving around lumps of little green hills and hummocks behind them.

Alexandria hurried across the walkway to join them. Just as I was about to set foot on the wooden bridge, the terrifying memory of our last mission flashed across my mind. Recalling the suspension bridge with planks that cracked without warning, I froze on the spot, too afraid to move forward.

"Let's go together," suggested Eric. He took my hand gently yet firmly and led me to the other side.

"Thanks." I gave his hand a squeeze to show my appreciation.

"Some adventure, isn't it?" said Zack, beaming at the water wheel.

Helen almost smiled at his words. "Some adventure," she agreed, tucking a tuft of her hair behind her ear. "Definitely the craziest adventure I've ever been on. Let's carry on with our mission, everyone. I can't wait to see what marvels lie ahead of us."

I couldn't help smiling at the dry humor in her last sentence. Eric, who also found it amusing, grinned.

The seven of us proceeded along the trail. This time, I noticed that Evonne had chosen to join us, leaving Helen and Zack alone. We passed a lagoon as clear as crystal, the vast, glassy surface mirroring the viridescent hills and fir trees that stood nearby. A cool gust of wind glided through the lawns, stirring the grass and rippling the waters.

Brian's shoulder-length locks flapped around him. "Darn, I wish it was long enough so I could tie it in a ponytail."

Alexandria giggled. "That'd be cool. I've never seen men with long hair, but you do look quite handsome this way."

"Why aren't there any wild kittenpillars here?" I asked.

"The altitude is higher," answered Brian. "Kittenpillars prefer warmer climates."

"Brian," Helen beckoned to him. "Zack and I would like to

hear your opinion. And Eric...." She pursed her lips and hesitated. "Yes, you'd better come along as well."

"Talk to you guys later," said Eric in a low voice. Brian winked goodbye at us, and he and Eric trotted up to Helen and Zack.

"Wonder what the Elders are talking about," Alexandria muttered.

"Recruitment, I suppose," replied Evonne.

"Recruitment? You mean recruiting new Elders?" I asked.

Evonne nodded. "Fewer and fewer people are willing to join the Elders since that invasion. Recruitment's becoming a huge problem for us. There used to be hundreds of Otherworldians and Underworldians pining for the vacant positions, but now...." She heaved a heavy sigh.

"Underworldians?"

"Right. Underworldians who managed to escape from Alta and Alto and wanted to take refuge in the Otherworld. Zack, Brian, Gidget, Willy, Connie, and Cameron had been Underworldians before they became Elders."

"What's life like as an Elder?" asked Alexandria. "I've always been curious."

"We get up at six in the morning on weekdays and have breakfast at seven in the Purple Room with King Patrick and Queen Marianne."

"The what room?"

"The Purple Room, also known as the one and only dining hall in the palace. We have our three meals there with the king and queen. Talk about formal and stifling. Then, we have to attend the daily morning assembly in the Throne Room at eight. It usually lasts for an hour. After the assembly, the Representative Elder and the Elite Elders will have a meeting, while regular Elders like Brian, Eric, and I get to enjoy three precious hours of free time." Evonne smiled at that mention. "At noon, all the Elders will gather in the Purple Room again for lunch, which is much fancier than breakfast. As for the afternoons, that's when our training sessions begin. We change outfits at one, thirty minutes before the classes start."

"Where do you have your training sessions?"

"On the training grounds, a large field behind the palace."

"And how do you train?"

"The senior Elders teach us archery, swordplay, dressage, and spells, one hour for each."

"Who's in charge of the four lessons?"

"Helen for archery, Zack for swordplay, Sheldon for dressage, and Lilith for spells. We have a one-hour rehearsal battle after the four hours of training. We practice and demonstrate the skills we learned that day during the rehearsal battle. Then, we return to our rooms, wash up, and change into our formal attire once again—evening gowns or tuxedos—for dinner, which starts at seven-thirty. It's a pretty decent meal, and the food's as good as the New Year Gala's. Dinner ends at nine, and we convene in conference room 403 afterwards. Helen will give us advice and feedback on our performance during the rehearsal battle. The meeting goes on for an hour, and we're allowed to go to bed after that."

"What about the weekends?"

"Everything's the same on Saturday, except we have a weekly review during our training sessions. King Patrick and Queen Marianne will be there to inspect us and see how well our mentors have taught us over the past week. Saturday night is the highlight of each week, as well as every Elder's favorite night. Evening banquets take place every Saturday, and the Elders' families are also invited. As for Sundays, we all have three hours of free time after the morning assembly. After lunch, King Patrick and Queen Marianne will take all the Elders to the towns and villages to check on the Otherworldians. Every week, we visit a different province or district, talk with the residents, and fulfill their basic needs to make life easier for them. Dinner on Sundays is preceded by a meeting that begins as soon as we return to the palace. We discuss our newest policies and the ways to improve the quality of life for the commoners. Then, after dinner, Helen, Zack, Sheldon, and Lilith will go off to prepare for the following week's training sessions, while the rest of us are free to do whatever we like for the rest of the night. I usually hang out with

Eric, Willy, Brian, and Gidget in the Elders' Lounge, which is sort of like a living room for all the Elders, except we can order drinks and snacks from the kittenpillar waiters. I like Sunday evenings. Gives us a great time to relax after a tiring week and recharge for the next. Sometimes I go to the courtyard and play with Ella the kittenpillar, but only if I can convince Helen to come with me."

Alexandria and I were both silent for a while, but I had a feeling we were sharing the same thoughts.

"That's far from what I expected, life as an Elder," I said. "All those meetings and training sessions."

"You're not the only one. Many Otherworldians envy us for the privileges we enjoy, but hardly anyone knows how difficult it is, being an Elder. It's easy to judge but hard to understand."

"Do you get salaries?" asked Alexandria.

"Twenty-five emeralds a month for regular Elders, fifty for Elite—"

"What? You get paid in emeralds?" I exclaimed. "Don't you have cents and quarters and dollars?"

Evonne shook her head. "No. We Otherworldians have our own system of currency—rubies, topazes, emeralds, and sapphires. Fifty-two rubies to a topaz, thirty-nine topazes to an emerald, and twenty-six emeralds to a sapphire."

"Why not use amethysts?" I asked. "I thought purple was the color of the Otherworld."

"Right, but amethysts are too rare. Only Elite Elders and above or members of the royal family are allowed to own them. In case you're wondering why sapphires are the largest denomination, it's because blue is the closest color to purple."

"Then why four denominations?" said Alexandria.

"Four is a number of balance in the Otherworld. The four gems—rubies, topazes, emeralds, and sapphires—symbolize the four kinds of elemental magic, the four Creators, and the four creatures."

Alexandria's eyes widened. "Interesting. I never knew that. Do you mail the money home to your family? Or do you store it in your bank account?"

"I mail half of my monthly salary home and keep the rest.

We don't have banks in the Otherworld, but each Elder has a vault in the palace."

"Where are the vaults? I've never seen one."

"In the basements of the palace. Basements one to twelve. The entrance is always guarded."

"But is it safe? Didn't the Underworldians break into the vault and steal the Gem of Hope last year?"

Evonne laughed. "I guess King Patrick and Queen Marianne must have learned their lesson that time. After that incident, they increased the number of guards and forbade us Elders to go down to the vaults unless we want to withdraw money."

"Withdraw? So you can actually spend them in the palace?" asked Alexandria.

"You can't buy pets, can you?" I said. "Kittenpillars, for example?"

"No. You can only buy them in the Underworld, where the bearnixes, unibirds, kittenpillars, and dogfishes are treated as slaves. On the other hand, King Patrick and Queen Marianne believe in equality, and 'buying animals' is strictly forbidden in the Otherworld. We can only hire them and pay them to clean our rooms, do chores, deliver mail to our friends and families, and... well, you get the idea. I don't recommend hiring them to deliver mail, though. Balloon mail's much cheaper, quicker, and safer, as I can't be sure whether the mail carriers have been peeking at our letters," said Evonne with a chuckle.

"Balloon mail?"

"We write letters or pack parcels and put them in inflated balloons. Then, we activate the balloons, tell them who the recipient is, and they'll find their way to the person. Right, simple as that."

"Cool. But how on earth do you spend money in the palace, then?"

"We can purchase outfits, shoes, accessories, jewelry, furniture, and necessities from the boutique, and weapons, wands, and anything related to training in the armory. Both are run by kittenpillars and are located on the second floor of the palace."

Silence fell upon us after we had exhausted the subject of the Elders' lives.

"Hey, Evonne," said Alexandria suddenly. "You still remember the time when you taught language arts at our school?"

Evonne smiled. "I sure do. I enjoyed my time working as an undercover teacher. It was fun. It made me feel like I had a secret identity. Of course, I came close to accidentally exposing myself a few times. The mortal teachers got suspicious when I said words like 'bearnixes' and 'dogfishes,' but Zack and Lilith always came to my rescue and covered up for me during those embarrassing moments." She let out a giggle.

"You were Helen's apprentice before you joined the Elders, weren't you?" I asked, remembering it was she who replaced Evonne as our language arts teacher after Evonne had lost her memory.

"Oh, yes, I was. I like her very much, and vice versa. She once permitted me to go on a mission with her, even though I was still an Elder-in-training."

"You mean that time you were trapped in the labyrinth and got attacked?" said Alexandria, her voice dropping to a whisper.

Evonne shrugged. "Well, yeah. Although I lost my memory for...how long was it, six months? Anyway, I'm grateful I was allowed on a mission."

"So you don't blame Helen for the accident?" Alexandria asked.

"Of course not. She didn't want this to happen, either. I'm not sure who told you the story and how you heard it, but Helen didn't use me as a shield, you know. Neither did Lilith or Zack."

"But asking you to go on a mission when you were just an Elder-in training?"

"I enjoyed it. Honestly, I did. It gave me an opportunity to broaden my horizons. I got to know what it's really like out there, to be on a mission, and I also got to test the skills I learned and put them into practice. Perhaps this will sound crazy to you, but I like going on missions. Do I know it's dangerous, and I might lose my memory again if a monster strikes? Yes. Do I know the Underworld's full of prowling dangers? Yes. But I don't like being stuck in the palace for endless days, weeks, and months. It's boring. So much etiquette stuff and rules to bear in mind as if we haven't gotten enough on our plate. Plus, there's the cursed dress code. We're supposed to wear gowns and heels in the palace, and we only get to change during the training sessions. I'm not exactly the sweet-and-lovely type." Evonne cocked her head. "Well, I could be," she added as an afterthought. "But...not that much. I'm more adventurous than you think."

"Cool," I grinned. "I thought you were a shy introvert. I had no idea you could be this cute and bubbly."

Evonne beamed. "I had to act shy in front of my students because I was afraid of saying things I shouldn't. But now, you'll get to know me as I am. Evonne Fitzgerald, and not Ms. Fitzgerald anymore."

"I really like you, Evonne," said Alexandria. "And Brian, too. You're both lively and interesting."

"Same, Alexandria. What did you think of me when I taught you? Was I a convincing language arts teacher?"

As the two of them chatted animatedly, I devoted my attention to the landscape around us. The narrowing trail was snaking up a steep slope that spiraled all the way up to a tall plateau. On our left was a kaleidoscope of voluptuous hydrangeas—azure, lilac, and bubblegum-pink. The globular flowers flaunted their flawless petals, as smooth as silk, as soft as satin. Behind the line of hydrangeas, I could see the cyan lakes and lush fields in miniature, unfurling under the gentle glow of the sunset. The word picturesque came to my mind as I savored the beauty of Mount Maravillas, relishing every moment.

After what seemed like five minutes but was actually thirty, we reached the top of the plateau. The hiking trail did not break off but instead skirted around a lake and threaded further into the depths of the mountains that ringed the left side. Small, stark columns of pinnacles and buttes erected on the plateau; they looked like rocky fingers reaching out to touch the sky. All of the pinnacles bore marks of the years, decades, and centuries they had been through.

The fresh, sweet aroma of flora lingered in the air, teasing my nose. I looked down and saw the ground sprinkled with luscious wildflowers. Unlike the dainty hydrangeas, they bloomed boldly in vivid hues, like a colorful explosion of confetti—crimson, vermillion, amber, and magenta.

"Look," Evonne pointed at the sky.

In the distance, I saw the evening horizon—streaks of yellow, orange, pink, and purple clouds against the pale blue backdrop, stretching far and wide in a chorus of pastel hues. It was a dreamy, whimsical scene to behold. I moved closer to the edge of the plateau, expecting to see an overview of the lakes and fields below. However, I found myself greeted by a swirling sea of layered clouds that shrouded the world beneath us. Ignited by the sun, they glowed like a fiery ocean of fire, waves crashing on waves of flames.

"Cool," breathed Eric. "It's as if heaven and hell met."

Words failed me. It was far too sublime, too spectacular a sight to describe.

***

The weary Elders decided to call it a day and camp there for tonight, which I was ecstatic about. Two purple tents—one for Zack, Brian, and Eric, and the other for Helen, Evonne, and Alexandria, were now perched on the plateau. After dinner, I announced my decision to volunteer to not only take the first watch but also sleep on the grass for the whole night.

The loud snoring of my companions told me I was the only one awake. Smiling, I tiptoed out of the tent and sat down on the moist grass.

A flush of scarlet reigned the sky, dyeing it a bloody burgundy-red. I watched, enchanted, as a faint tint of purple invaded, deepened, and slowly took over. Crimson and lavender struggled for dominance, yet the latter prevailed. Silver against the darkening violet, the universe of stars gleamed in the sky as though celebrating the downfall of crimson. A hint of amber lurked beyond the skyline, peeking at the world. Then, all was silenced, extinguished and drowned out by the blackness that spilled over the sky like a bottle of ink. More and more stars revealed themselves in the ebony sky. Like scattered pearls, they illuminated the evening with a charming white glow.

An epic drama. I had witnessed an epic drama.

"Eileen?" said Eric, crouching down beside me.

"How come you're not asleep yet?"

"I wasn't tired, so I did some research with Helen. Studying the journals and the notes she took. We've just finished, and I decided to come check on you. Go take a rest. You must be exhausted."

"A little, but more exhilarated than exhausted, though. As horrible as the Siblings are, you've got to admit the marvels of the Underworld are pretty fascinating."

Eric smiled. "Then share your thoughts with me tomorrow. Now all you need is a good night's sleep. Sweet dreams."

"Same to you."

A gust of wind swept across the plateau, caressing my cheek and fluttering in my hair. Eric removed his coat and draped it over me.

I lay in silence, gazing up at the heavens. In the moonlit lake, the star-strewn sky admired itself, duplicating its tiny silver orbs in reflection. Finally, I succumbed to my fatigue and closed my eyes. Listening to the lullaby of the humming breeze, I drifted into a world of dreams.

# Chapter Eleven

## The Control Center
## (Eric)

"Zack confessed *that* to you on the first night of your mission?" Eileen said, her eyebrows lifted in surprise. Brian and Alexandria were also staring at me in disbelief.

"He did," I replied. "Told me he fancied Helen. And I think she also likes him. See the black cloak he's wearing? Helen made it herself."

We had set off early in the morning and were now walking along the trail, following Helen, Zack, and Evonne, as we had yesterday. I was beginning to feel annoyed and fed up with all this hiking. However, I had to admit that gossiping with Alexandria, Eileen, and Brian did make the walk more or less tolerable.

Brian chuckled. "See, didn't I tell you guys? And now it's officially confirmed. By the way, what are you grinning about, Eileen?"

"Oh, just thinking about Helen and Zack as a couple. That'd be great, wouldn't it?" A dreamy sigh escaped Eileen's lips. I could tell from her vague expression and innocent smile that she was lost in her daydreams.

"Great?" repeated Alexandria. "You call this great? They're...we're—all of us—we're supposed to be defending the Otherworld in times like this, not flirting and falling in love! Oh,

Zack, what were you thinking?"

"Who cares about fighting when a romantic love story is about to bloom?" Eileen sighed.

"Spoken like a true hopeless romantic," I said with a grin.

"You don't know what you're talking about, Eileen," Alexandria groaned, looking as though her birthday party had been cancelled.

"Don't get too worked up over it," said Brian, laying a consoling hand on her shoulder. "I *know* Helen. She's the most decent and sensible person I've ever met. Trust me, Alexandria. Helen won't let her emotions sway her. She's not the type that gets distracted and carried away by romance."

"And Zack?"

"Well...." Brian gave an awkward pause. "I can't say the same for him. You know he's a romantic, and he's a bit impulsive and—"

"Maybe more than just a bit?" I suggested. That made everyone crack up.

"I wonder if they'll get married one day," Eileen gushed. "It'd be wonderful to go to their wedding. I'm getting excited just visualizing it."

"As much as I agree with Alexandria that we should prize the safety of the Otherworld in front of everything, I do think it would be a special event," said Brian, beaming. "You see, Helen and Zack would be rewriting history if they got married. A wedding between two Elders would count as a royal wedding, and believe me, you'd never want to miss out on a grand event like that. It would be a veritable wedding of the century."

"I wonder if we'll make it till that day," said Alexandria, a dark cloud looming over her face. She sighed. "With all these battles and everything...."

We threaded into a vapory cloud forest, where the trail wound on and on, fading away and disappearing into the dense fog ahead. The forest was engulfed by mist, which floated in the air like drifting tendrils of gossamer. Unpleasantly reminded of the garden in front of Mors Manor, I shivered. Eileen, however, seemed to be enjoying herself. She gazed at every single tree and bush with wide, wondering eyes.

"What do you think it's like, the Control Center?" Alexandria asked us. "Have you ever pictured it in your mind before?"

"No idea," I answered. "What do you think?"

"It must be huge. I guess it'd look like a fortress with thousands of secret passages and hallways. Perhaps a bit like Mors Manor, creepy and ancient."

"You think so?" said Brian.

"Yeah. It could also be like a palace," added Alexandria as an afterthought. "With glossy black marble floors and obsidian walls."

"Really?" Eileen piped up. "I thought it would be an industrial-style kind of building. You know, with wood and metal. Maybe it's an old warehouse."

"But wait a second," I said. "I don't think an old warehouse would be filled with hidden weapons and technological instruments. Plus, we're supposed to find out all about the terrains there. How will that—?"

"Am I the only one who thinks the Control Center might look like a large wooden cabin on the outside?" Brian cut in.

"A cabin? Why?"

"So it'd look less suspicious, silly. Darn it, why is the fog getting thicker?"

We could barely see a foot ahead of us. The fog was almost opaque and had swallowed the entire forest. The air, pregnant with moisture, was dampening my clothes. I could see nothing but the blurry gray outlines of the trees around us. It was as though we were in a spotless white cocoon.

"Should we keep going?" Alexandria asked, her eyebrows knitting together in a frown.

"Just follow the Elders," I said, trying to make out the billowing cloaks of the three figures ahead in the dense fog.

"Look!" Brian pointed to the end of the trail, where sunlight slanted into the shimmering mist.

"Is that a clearing?" Eileen and I exchanged hopeful looks.

"The Control Center! There it is!" Zack's voice shouted.

"Shh," Helen silenced him. She turned to us and mouthed the words, "Come quietly."

The shroud of mist dissipated the moment we stepped out of the forest, and the weather became clear and sunny all of a sudden. The trail had terminated once and for all, leading us out of the cloud forest and to—

"Oh my."

In front of us stood a huge spherical monolith of latticed glass and white steel. The sun flared in the cerulean sky, radiant beams dancing and reflecting on the glazed façade of the building. It looked like a gigantic three-dimensional puzzle of millions of glass triangles, rhombuses, and quadrilaterals, all pieced into a great, glittering, glassy orb.

"Quick, get down!" whispered Helen.

"What? Why?"

"The guards, if you haven't noticed!" she hissed.

A devil and deviline rounded the Control Center and appeared on either side of the spherical building.

"No Otherworldians?" the devil asked.

The deviline shook her head. "I don't think they're here yet. Honestly, I don't even know why we're wasting our time standing guard here. The Otherworldians might not even know about the Control Center."

"Now what do we do?" I whispered to the others. "Helen, Evonne, can you two shoot them?"

The two of them exchanged a look, and both shook their heads.

"Too far," said Helen. "I don't want to risk it and expose ourselves. We must kill them if we choose to attack, or they'll run away and report us to Alta. In that case, we'll all be doomed."

"Perhaps one of us could trick the guards and make them come closer while the others ambush them?" Brian suggested.

"Oh, very clever plan," said Helen in a sardonic manner, rolling her eyes. "You, Zack, and Eric are Underworldians who switched their allegiance and fled to the Otherworld. Alexandria's the most wanted person in the Underworld. And as for me, the Siblings would love this opportunity to do me in. So how in the world are we going to do that?"

"You're right," replied Brian, grinning. "But you're forgetting the others. What about them?" He gestured at Eileen and Evonne.

Poor Eileen looked flustered at being the center of an unwanted situation. "Me?"

Brian's grin widened. "Yes, Eileen. You and Evonne. The Underworldians are most unlikely to recognize you two among the seven of us."

"Nice plan," said Evonne, clapping her hands. "I'm all for it. So what should we do?"

"The two of you must go up to the guards and pretend Alta sent you. Tell them Alta has captured the Otherworldians—which means us—and is now waiting for them to join her at the palace of the Underworld, where she's planning to execute the Otherworldians. Then, try to lure them to the hiking trail, our direction, and we'll ambush them."

"What?" Eileen's mouth dropped open.

"This is crazy." Helen shook her head. "So much relies on luck. What if they attack Eileen and Evonne? What if they recognize them?"

"I know the stakes are high, but we've got to do something. We'll never make it into the Control Center if we keep hanging back here forever. We must give it a shot."

"And if your plan fails?"

"Then we fight to kill."

After a moment of hesitation, Helen gave in. "You're right, Brian. That's our only way."

"Very well, then." Brian glanced at Eileen and Evonne. "Ready? Let's go through everything again. Go up to the guards, tell them Alta sent you here, and she's caught the Otherworldians and imprisoned them. Then, lead them to the hiking trail—our direction—so we can attack them."

"Got it," said Evonne as Eileen nodded.

Helen gave Evonne a hug and a pat on the back.

"Good luck," I whispered to Eileen, squeezing her hand.

Carefully, the two of them made their way to the Control

Center.

The deviline was the quickest to notice them. "Otherworldians?" she demanded, raising her spear.

Alexandria, Helen, Zack, Brian, and I watched, holding our breaths.

"No," said Evonne with a calm smile. "Alta—I mean, Mistress Alta sent us. She's got the Otherworldians, and she wants us back at the palace."

"Aha!" the devil hollered. "She's got 'em, hasn't she?"

"Get a grip on yourself, Anderson," snapped the deviline. She shot Eileen and Evonne a look of skepticism. "Mistress Alta's got them? But why didn't she inform us sooner?"

Eileen and Evonne exchanged a nervous look. "Well—" Eileen began.

"The Otherworldians put up a fight with her, you see," Evonne cut in. "They killed a few of her bodyguards, but Alta intercepted them before they could do further damage."

"They put up a fight with her? But they can't do elemental magic in Mount Maravillas."

"They fought with weapons, not magic," explained Evonne, almost too quickly.

"Well, they *could* use elemental magic if they reached the Control Center...," the deviline murmured to herself.

"But me doubt they is clever enough to notice the ban's bin lifted up here," said Anderson, smirking.

I turned to the others. "The elemental magic ban is lifted here?"

Alexandria tapped her scepter on her palm, and her eyes widened in astonishment as a blazing ball of fire bloomed. "Whoa. Why would Alta and Alto lift the ban?"

"Probably so they can sneak vile creatures up here and attack us with elemental magic," surmised Brian.

Helen brought a finger to her lips and motioned for us to pay attention to the guards.

"Who are you two, by the way?" The deviline narrowed her eyes. "I've never seen you before."

"We're—" Eileen squeaked.

"Servants in the palace," Evonne finished.

"Not imposters, are you?" The deviline paced up and down on the front lawn of the Control Center.

My heart skipped a beat.

"Oh, come on, Lowry," Anderson chimed in. "Stop wasting our time and questioning them! Me wanna go back to the palace and blow those foul Otherworldians up! We'll miss the fun if you—"

"Well...." Lowry eyed Eileen and Evonne with suspicion, as though deciding whether to believe them or not. "Fine. Off we go." Lowry walked up to the back of the Control Center.

"Why don't we go this way?" said Evonne, jerking her head in our direction.

"What?" Lowry turned. "The shortcut's this way." She pointed at the back of the Control Center.

From the corner of my eye, I saw Brian and Helen exchange a look.

"Oh...well, we thought it'd be nice to...to enjoy the scenery, you know," said Eileen in a fake, cheery tone. "It's beautiful down there."

Anderson grumbled. "But me wanna go the fastest way to—"

"Shut up, Anderson," snapped Lowry. She turned and followed Evonne and Eileen to the hiking trail.

"Any time," whispered Helen, tightening her grasp on her bow. "Zack, Brian, take Evonne and get to the entrance of the Control Center as soon as we attack the guards, got it?"

"But Helen—"

"Now!"

We leapt out of our hideout, and Lowry shrieked. "There's someone hid—" she screamed again as Helen's arrow brushed past her arm.

"Alexandria, get her!" I shouted as we closed in on Lowry together. Alexandria knocked the deviline's weapon away and pinned her to the ground.

"Take this!" A turquoise fireball of Underworldian magic issued from my scepter and struck Lowry. With a groan, her eyes snapped shut.

"Where are the others?" asked Alexandria.

My gaze darted around the battlefield. "There! They're chasing after Anderson!"

Helen and Eileen were sprinting after the devil. Eileen hurled a spiky rose at him but missed.

"Here!" I shouted at Alexandria, dashing in the opposite direction and waiting for Anderson to collide into me. The devil noticed my trick and made an attempt to change his direction. At that moment, one of Helen's arrows scarred his leg, and he tumbled to the ground.

Alexandria and I raced up to the devil, and she pressed the long hilt of her spear to Anderson's neck while I pointed my scepter at his heart. Helen and Eileen joined us, their weapons raised as well.

"You nasty imposters!" Anderson spat at us, struggling to escape. I raised my scepter—

"DON'T KILL HIM!" Brian's voice roared.

"What?" We looked at him, stunned.

"We can't get into the Control Center! The entrance is locked. We'll never know the passcode if you kill him."

Helen directed her wand at the devil's heart. "Give us the passcode, or—"

"Me ain't sayin' nuthin'!"

"Oh yeah?" I raised my sword—

"No!" Alexandria shouted, grabbing me by the wrist. "We should interrogate him and torture him until he gives us the passcode."

Anderson's expression melted into one of contempt. "Three gals and one lad, eh? You guys ain't much of a threat, ain't—OUCH!"

I had pressed the blade of my sword into the devil's neck. Green beads of blood oozed from his wrinkly turquoise skin.

"Oh...fine, fine!" Anderson moaned. "It's zero six zero two three seven! Now can you let me go?"

"Not until they get into the Control Center."

"Wrong passcode!" yelled Evonne.

Eileen jabbed her scepter at Anderson's chest. "Give us the real one."

Anderson stuck out his tongue. "Don't think you can frighten me, you evil little—"

Eileen gave her scepter a flick, and a thick vine sprouted from the tip and coiled itself around Anderson's torso.

"No—no! I...I'm sorry!" He sputtered, gasping for air. "Let me...let me go! It's one zero four zero six seven!"

I saw Zack tapping on a device installed on a pair of steely white doors. A turquoise light flashed, and they yawned open, revealing a pair of revolving doors.

Eileen snapped her fingers, and the vines split.

"Now, your mistress wouldn't be too pleased to see you, would she? Get yourself out of here this instant and find a place to hide," Helen ordered.

Alexandria, Eileen, and I stared at her, our mouths rounding in protest, but neither of us dared to defy her. Among us, Helen always had an inexplicable soft spot for monsters. Last year she let a group of dogfishes walk away unscathed after they had tried to kill us all. I remembered how surprised I had been, as it was the first time she'd displayed her gentle side since I'd joined the Otherworld.

"Thank...thank you," wheezed Anderson, massaging his bloody neck and getting up. He left the clearing, blundering into the cloud forest.

"What if he reports us to Alta?" Eileen looked worried.

"He wouldn't dare," asserted Helen, leading us up to the Control Center.

Eileen and I exchanged a look and a shrug.

"Hey, guys." Zack, Brian, and Evonne grinned at us. "You were awesome."

"You did very well yourselves," Helen complimented them. "And let's not forget Eileen and Evonne. We'd never have made it here if it hadn't been for them."

Evonne blushed. "I've always wanted to be the hero and save the day. It's just so—" Her smile faded, and her expression twisted into one of horror. "Behind you, Helen!"

We whirled around and saw Anderson the devil, a glint of fury and triumph in his eyes. He raised his axe and—

I blinked. Before I knew it, Anderson had doubled over, the gleaming purple hilt of a sword protruding from between his two horns. Green liquid was seeping from the wound.

"Helen, are you all right?" asked Zack, his voice anxious.

Helen turned to look at him, then at the devil. Her gaze dropped to the sword. "Zack…? How did you…? Why…?"

"Why? Because you did the same for me," answered Zack, sauntering forward to retrieve his blade. All of us knew without saying it aloud that there was more to it.

Taken aback at his act of gallantry, a flush of crimson rose to Helen's cheeks. "I—Thank you," she said, struggling to gather herself.

"No problem." Zack gave her a pat on the shoulder. "Now, haven't we all got a mission to complete?" He flashed a confident smile at the rest of us.

As we entered through the revolving doors, Brian winked at Alexandria, Eileen, and me. I looked over my shoulder and wasn't surprised to see Helen and Zack holding hands.

The entrance led us to a circular atrium. We could see our reflections mirrored upside-down on the glazed white floor. A large anti-gravity waterfall stood before us; the tall, levitating curtain of water leapt upward instead of plunging down from the top, emitting a faint, ominous glow of turquoise. Everything here was either made of glass or white steel, giving off a futuristic feel. Silver asymmetrical patterns were etched on the walls opposite the waterfall. Like the façade of the Control Center, they formed countless geometric figures. The atrium stretched up for five stories. High above us, the sun gazed down through the glazed roof, sunlight filtering through the domed ceiling and making us seem as though standing in a cave of white light. I noticed a wide, modern staircase to the right of the anti-gravity waterfall. The frameless glass railing of the staircase stretched all the way up to the balustrades that ringed the annular balconies on each floor. Like ripples in a pond, the balconies rounded all the way up to the glowing ceiling.

"Wow." I was captivated by the spectacularity of the atrium.

"Wicked," Evonne whispered.

Brian craned his neck to have a better look at the upper floors. "That was far from what I'd expected. Prettier, and much more avant-garde."

"We must find the Control Room as soon as possible. After me." Helen turned to us. "And don't forget your weapons. Keep your guard up at all times."

We skirted around the waterfall and followed her up to the second floor. I looked around and saw a curving white wall stretching behind the balcony.

"Here." Helen pointed at two lacquered white doors that stood in front of us; one with a green sign marked *entrance,* the other with a red one marked *exit.* She walked up to the entrance door and flung it open.

A wide corridor with black walls unfolded before us, guiding us toward a void of darkness. The dark corridors and shadowy rooms of Mors Manor flashed across my mind, and a chill journeyed down my spine.

"What the...?" The floor glowed electric-blue as we set foot on the corridor, giving off the strange impression of us standing on a pool of glowing water.

"I got a bad feeling about this," I heard Eileen murmur.

"Just follow me," said Helen, her voice not betraying the slightest hint of fear. "Let's navigate the second floor and see if the Control Room's here."

We moved along the corridor and into the rooms, checking for anything unusual. It was like a huge museum, one spacious room after the next, with many walls to separate the rooms, yet no doors. I felt a sense of foreboding as I saw my own face staring back at me in the glossy black walls. The rooms here were the complete opposite of the atrium. Everything, from the faces of my companions to the ceiling, was painted a mysterious shade of blue by the glowing floor beneath us. There were no windows or anything else to provide light or ventilation. It was as though we were traveling through an endless abstract tunnel of sapphire-blue light.

"How odd...." Helen seemed to be talking to herself. "I've never been anywhere like this."

"Neither have I," Zack said in a small voice. "Some technological building, isn't it?"

"What's that?" I heard Alexandria ask. She pointed at an eerie wall of turquoise light issuing from one of the rooms ahead.

As we drew nearer, I realized it was a floor-length aquarium tank. A community of fish wove in and out of the colorful weeds and corals at the bottom. Large phosphorescent-teal blobs were swimming in it, drifting up and down lazily. I edged closer to the tank and squinted at them. One of the teal blobs wheeled around and stared at me.

"No way...glowing dogfishes?" Brian breathed.

"I think you're right."

The dogfishes had teal heads and neon-blue fish bodies. A few of them caught sight of us and bared their teeth like sharks.

"What's with the fish in the tank?" said Alexandria.

"Food for the dogfishes, I guess," replied Zack, as a dogfish opened its large mouth and swallowed three yellow fish in one gulp.

Eileen took a sharp intake of breath. "Look!"

"What?" I asked.

She took my hand and guided me to the tank opposite the dogfishes. Glowing kittenpillars with acid-green heads and turquoise bodies were grazing on a manufactured field of grass and wildflowers, highly reminiscent of the plateau we had come across yesterday. Behind them was a backdrop with an artificial setting sun. The kittenpillars shot us glares of malice as Eileen and I approached their tank.

"Can you talk to them?" I asked Eileen.

"They don't want to talk to me," she said. "I've tried. They hate humans."

"That's because Alta and Alto created them and locked them up here. Or at least, that's what the bearnixes told me," said Alexandria, who had wandered off to the next room.

"What do they look like? The bearnixes?" I asked.

"Fluorescent-orange heads and pink bodies. Come along."

I followed Alexandria to the next room and saw a large group of bearnixes pressing their faces against their glass tank. A huge volcano with lava erupting from its mouth towered behind them; rivers and streams of magma trailing everywhere, splitting and slicing through the rocky land beneath the bearnixes.

On the other side of the room was another glass tank, this one designed to look like the sky. Tendrils of clouds drifted in front of the blue backdrop, where unibirds flapped their wings and glided a few inches above the ground.

"Unibirds with blond heads and glowing yellow bodies?" Evonne frowned at the weird sight.

"These are genetically modified animals, all of them," said Brian. "The bearnixes, unibirds, kittenpillars, and dogfishes here. Alta and Alto might have created them with magic."

"But why? Why would they need—?"

"Take a look at this." Brian pointed to a black sign with gleaming words plastered to the wall and read the words aloud. "Genetic Modification Animals room: housing the most venomous, aggressive animals in the Underworld that can kill with just a bite. These phosphorescent animals can fight in darkness and—"

"Let me guess," Alexandria cut in. "They're inventing new species of animals and using them to fight against us?"

"Must be," affirmed Helen. "We're lucky they haven't set them free and taken them to the Otherworld yet."

"They might be planning to," replied Zack, a cloud of gloom on his face. "Remember what Alta said last time before leaving? The worst is yet to come. Anyway, let's get out of here. I don't like all these weird animals staring at us."

"But I like it here," said Brian, observing a glowing unibird who flapped its fluorescent-yellow wings menacingly at him. "It's like an indoor zoo with glow-in-the-dark animals. It's pretty cool."

"It is not cool at all!" Eileen interjected. "The animals are locked up when all they want is to get out of here!" She turned to Helen. "Couldn't we smash the glass tanks and set them free?"

"Are you mad?" Brian asked. "They could kill us all in one bite! They've probably got venom in their fangs and—"

"Why would they attack us if we freed them?" Eileen pleaded, looking at Brian with her large brown eyes. "They're not stupid, they know—"

"Enough," Helen interrupted, silencing both of them. She scanned the four tanks and pursed her lips as though struggling to make a decision. "Now's not the moment, Eileen. We've got urgent business. I don't think the Control Room's here, so let's go. Whoever's closest to the bearnix tank, please open the door beside it."

Zack wrenched the door open, and a chord of light bleached the room. He poked his head out. "Awesome. We're only a door away from the staircase."

"What? How come?" The rest of us crammed through the door to see for ourselves. Right before us was the annular balcony. A white door marked *entrance* stood on our left, and in front of the door was the modern staircase that had brought us up here.

"We've been going in a circle?" I frowned.

Helen nodded.

"I'm confused."

"We went from there," Helen pointed to the revolving doors in the atrium below. "To the waterfall, all the way up the staircase, along the dark corridor." She indicated the door beside us. "And into the rooms with black walls and glowing blue floors. The rooms form a circle," she traced her finger around the balcony, "and now we're back to where we started."

"So this is the exit door we saw before entering the corridor?"

"Yes." Helen pointed to the red exit sign hanging above the door. "We've got to give the third floor a quick try and see if the Control Room's there. Come with me."

"Aren't they clever, Alta and Alto?" Brian muttered to himself as we made our way up the staircase. "The design of the Control Center.... It's ingenious."

"Brian, don't you think it's weird?" I said. "There are

probably tons of technological gadgets and cool machines and stuff like that upstairs. Why didn't Alta and Alto use them during the last invasion?"

"Maybe these inventions are still in the experimental stage. In other words, Alta and Alto aren't that confident about the gadgets here. Perhaps they're worried their inventions would malfunction and backfire on them during battles. It's also possible they want to keep a few tricks up their sleeve, or...maybe more than a few. They want to save it till the final war."

"Where do you reckon the Control Room is?"

"Good question. I guess we'll have to comb every floor to find out."

"Search every floor...," Alexandria mused. "I've got an idea. Helen, why don't we break into groups? It might be more efficient—"

"And how are we going to let each other know if there's an enemy or monster?"

"We could fight them off and—"

"No, I won't risk losing anyone. I say we all stick together, the seven of us," said Helen with a touch of finality. I saw her shift closer to Evonne and reach for her hand, and knew she was worried about losing her former apprentice again.

We reached the third floor, rounded a wall that bore a sign with the words *Chemistry Inventions*, and came across a massive room. Unlike the rooms downstairs, the walls, the ceiling, and the carpet were all dazzlingly white and spotless. All about us were countless rows of glass shelves occupied by arrays of flasks, vials, jars, and containers of all shapes and sizes, filled with potions in various colors. The liquids smoked, sizzled, fizzed, and bubbled in their containers as if clamoring for attention. Small vials of glowing powder lined the highest row of the shelves. Tiny colorful specks danced in them like little flies.

I noticed a few semicircular columns protruding from the walls like roofless towers. White counters and colorful test tubes could be seen through the windows.

"Are those laboratories?" said Alexandria.

"Maybe," replied Brian. He wandered through the rows

of shelves and studied the little vials.

"Any idea of what these potions can do?" Eileen asked as she followed me to the first row.

I scanned the labels on the potions. *Dehydrating Draught, Coughing Concoction, Bleeding Brew....*

A vial of glittery black substance drew my attention. I squinted at the label and read the words aloud. "Puking Potion, newly-invented. One drop can cause the drinker to vomit for... what? Two hours straight?"

"Check this out." Alexandria pointed at a vial half-filled with limpid contents. Eileen and I crowded over her shoulder to have a good look.

"What—? Oh...." One glance at the label told me it was poison. Gingerly, I took the tiny bottle and uncorked it. "It looks like it's been opened before."

"Exactly. And look here." Alexandria pointed at the label. A tiny row of words was crammed below the word *Poison*. "'Still inventing. Can weaken victim and put victim in a coma for a week.'" I looked up at Alexandria and Eileen, and something told me we had the same assumption in mind.

"Remember the poisoned arrow that almost killed Helen?" Alexandria said. "Bet you anything this little vial did it."

"You're looking at the potions, aren't you? Look at this one I found," Evonne walked over to us, clutching a flask with magenta liquid. "'Hallucination Potion. Can cause victims to have delusions and hallucinate.'"

"Keep it, Evonne," said Brian, who emerged at the end of the row. His cloak was bulging with jars and vials of potions. "I found tons of Healing Potions on that one over there." He pointed at the sea of glass shelves. "Oh, and I guess we'd better take those as well." Brian snatched the Puking Potion and poison from me and shoved it into the pouch of his cloak.

"Are you sure you can handle all of them?" I asked.

"Oh, of course." Brian traced the silhouette of the pouch with his wand. "See? I just sealed it with magic. The potions are safe with me now. Come to think of it, we can nick a few more—"

"What are you doing?" demanded Helen, breezing down

the aisle toward us.

"Stealing this stuff before the despicable Underworldians can use it on us," replied Brian.

"No way," snapped Helen, a steely edge to her voice.

"You wouldn't want the Underworldians to use it on us, would you? We'd better destroy everything here in case—"

"No, we can't," Helen cut in. "Alta and Alto will know somebody's trespassed into the Control Center if we steal all these potions."

"Does that make a difference?"

"Of course it does. All we've got to do is sneak up to the Control Room, take notes on the terrains of the Underworld, and get out of here as soon as possible before—"

Croak! A loud croak interrupted the two of them. Everyone glanced around the room, looking for the source of the sound.

"I think it came from there," said Eileen. "Those tanks behind the shelves of potions."

Right she was. Strange creatures trapped in tall aquarium tanks filled with turquoise liquid were staring at us. Among them, I saw a cyan horned bullfrog with violet eyes and a forked tongue, a squid with unblinking golden eyes, a white hamster with gills and metallic wings as sharp as blades, a seahorse whose body changed colors every five seconds like a chameleon, and uncanny creatures of all kinds. Every tank was labeled *Aggressive*.

"Brian's right, Helen," I said. "The Underworldians created everything here—from the genetically modified animals to the potions to these weird creatures—in order to overthrow the Otherworld. We must destroy them, or else it'll be the other way round."

After a moment's silence, Helen gave in. "You've got a point. But everything can wait until after we get to the Control Room and figure out the positions of the terrains and portals. After all, that's the point of our mission. I reckon we should all stop dawdling and focus on finding the Control Room first. Now, don't stop to check on anything, all right? Just follow me."

The seven of us moved on to the next room, which looked as bright and immaculate as the previous one.

"Look at that." Brian pointed to a row of enormous white crates and wall-mounted shelves. What looked like hundreds of diamonds glistened in one of the crates. He squatted down to look at the white plaque attached to it. "Interesting. *Multifunctional Diamond Devices. Used for contacting others, taking notes* – "

"Keep going," said Helen briskly, leading everyone past the boxes.

"Here, Eileen." Brian gave her a handful of diamond devices and sealed the pouch of her cloak with magic. "Figured I'd work out how to use them as soon as we get back to the Otherworld," he added with a playful wink.

I spotted a black crate filled with small blue rockets labeled: *Rocket Missiles – missiles disguised as rockets. Can burn metal and steel.* Brian crouched down and nicked a few of them before catching up with us.

"What are those?" Eileen said, looking at another row of crates filled with small transparent orbs. "*Oxygen-producing bubbles. Can guarantee you an endless supply of oxygen for a hundred minutes.* Cool, I'll take the lot," she said, bending down and retrieving as many orbs as she could.

Alexandria shot Brian a look of amusement. "I think you've had a bad influence on her."

We passed rows of white racks, all crammed with small brass and silver instruments, then another few lines of towering glass cabinets with jars of red and orange slimy blobs that twisted and wriggled in the containers like jelly. I glanced at the plaque and saw the words: *Liquid Detonating Devices.*

"Detonating devices? These gooey red and orange... things?"

"We'll destroy the lot later," said Brian. "And what's this in front of us?"

There were no more rooms ahead. Instead, we found ourselves confronted by a wall of floor-length mirrors, like a dance studio.

"Is this a trap?" Eileen wondered aloud, frowning at our reflections.

"There's a plaque here, at the foot of the mirrors. Let me

see." Helen crouched down, her hair flowing to the ground like a curtain. *"Mirror Gateways. The fastest mode of transportation in the Underworld. Step into this mirror and get transported to its twin. These mirrors form a passage to the fourth floor."*

"I guess there's a matching mirror upstairs," said Brian. "To reach the fourth floor, we have to enter through this one."

"Is this safe?" asked Evonne, scrutinizing the mirror as though hoping to see the fourth floor through its glassy surface.

A pale glow seemed to emit from the mirror. It looked so familiar, but I couldn't recall why. Then, something in my mind clicked into place. "I got it!" I clapped my hands. "That's how the monsters got into Mors Manor without us knowing. They came in through the mirrors!"

"Good thinking," said Zack, looking impressed. "I guess it's safe, then. Who's going first?"

"Me," Alexandria and I said in unison. We looked at each other and laughed.

"We'll go together," Alexandria decided. "Now what should we do? Step into the mirror?"

"I suppose so, but I'm not sure how this thing works." Looking at the reflection of the spotless white floor, I lifted my right foot and brought it to the mirror. To my utter astonishment, my leg penetrated the glass. I felt my foot hit solid ground. Everything around me began to spin, slowly at first but then faster and faster. For a moment, all I could see was a blur of white, the ceiling, the walls, and the floor all jumbled together—

Then, without warning, everything stopped. Dazed, I blinked and looked around. I was transported to a strange room reigned by mirrors. They sprawled across the ceiling, the four walls, and even the floor.

"Where are we?" Alexandria, who arrived a few seconds after I did, asked.

I looked back and saw the image of Brian appear in the mirror. "This must be the fourth floor," he said, stepping out into the room.

Moments later, we were joined by the others.

"Everyone here?" asked Helen. "All set? Then let's hurry

up and go search for the Control Room."

"But how do we leave this mirrored room?" I asked. "There's no door—"

Helen directed her wand at the mirror opposite from us, and a door revealed itself.

Alexandria's eyes widened. "How did you...?"

"A silent revealing spell," said Helen. "Cunning Underworldians. They concealed the door with magic."

We followed her out the mirrored room and into a large hall with a soaring ceiling. The walls on our right looked like large, boundless screens, displaying abstract animations of symmetrical neon-blue lines forming, duplicating, triplicating, then all merging into one before disappearing into blackness, and finally reforming.

"How did they manage to do that?" asked Alexandria, observing the walls with a smile of amazement. "I thought the Underworldians didn't know anything about technology."

"No, of course, they don't," answered Helen. "These are not real animations. It's all magic rather than technology. In other words, the walls here are simply bewitched to display looping animations."

"Come to think of it, magic and technology are kind of the same thing, aren't they?" remarked Eileen. "Before I came here, I'd call these weird gadgets magic. But now that I've seen them in the 'flesh,' I know they exist for real. What sounds like magic to us now may be dubbed technology in the future."

"Nice theory," said Brian. "I think we might be close to the Control Room." Something caught his interest, and his eyes narrowed. "Are those...robots?"

Right he was. Robots of all colors, shapes, and sizes stared at us from the other side of the room. Some were tall and slender and had glossy white arms, resembling real-life humans. Others were small and had mechanical wings with laser beams. There were even robot bearnixes, unibirds, kittenpillars, and dogfishes. They glared at us with fixed stares, but none of them attacked.

"Are they real robots?" said Eileen. "Or are they the products of an enchantment conjured by magic?"

"Good question," replied Brian. "I wish I knew the answer."

"How do Alta and Alto activate the robots?" Alexandria asked.

"With their scepters, maybe," said Brian. "They could've found a way to link them together."

We saw several high-tech contraptions used for shrinking and enlarging robots in the next room.

"This way," said Helen, pushing open the frameless glass door. A familiar modern staircase greeted us as we followed her out of the room and to the fifth floor. "It's got to be up there."

A horrible thought floated to the surface of my mind as I felt a knot twisting in my stomach. *What if there is no Control Room at all? What if we were lured into the Control Center? What if Alta and Alto wanted us to show up here so they could murder us with their technological weapons?* My trepidation mounted with each step I took.

Now that we had reached the topmost floor, I could see the atrium in miniature below. Leaning over the railing, I spotted a thin, rectangular glass tank hanging upside down from the ceiling opposite us, where the anti-gravity waterfall foamed at the top, pooling upward into the tank of turquoise liquid that never seemed to spill.

"Cool, isn't it?" said Brian. "Can't wait to see what the Control Room looks like. I suppose there it is." He jerked his head at the pair of metallic double doors in front of us.

Helen pointed her wand at them, probably performing a silent spell. The doors swung open, and I felt a sudden drop in the temperature. I slipped an arm around Eileen as she shivered.

Behind the doors was an enormous pentagonal room carpeted with tiny hexagonal tiles dotted with orbs of blue light. A heptahedron counter made of glass perched in the middle. Innumerable neat rows of rectangular panels were inset on all five walls, a few of them reflecting the electric-blue glow that lit up the whole room. On either side of each rectangle was a small square that shone fiercely turquoise; they looked like microchips embedded in the walls. Like the rooms in the Genetic

Modification Animals section, the ceiling here was also black and glossy, reflecting our figures from above. I turned to the others, only to find them staring at a glass sign hovering an inch below the ceiling. On it was three silver words: *The Control Room.*

"The Control Room.... We're here," said Brian, his mouth agape in awe.

"Wonderful." Helen turned to us. "Now, we should split into two teams. Zack, Alexandria, Eileen, and Evonne, the four of you must guard the doors outside the Control Room. Notify us if you see or hear anything unusual while Brian, Eric, and I search this place."

Alexandria frowned. "Are you sure that's safe? I thought you were against the idea of us splitting up."

"Yes, but we have no alternative now."

"Helen, couldn't we all stay in here?" said Zack. "I want to know what's going on with the terrains and everything as much as you do."

"I know, but you're better at fighting. Plus, we need a couple of people to stand guard—"

"What about this," suggested Alexandria. "The four of us can keep a lookout from the inside of the Control Room. This way, we can hear your discussion and at the same time monitor the situation outside."

Helen pursed her lips. I could tell she didn't like Alexandria's plan much, but she didn't want to spend time arguing with her, either. "All right. Close the doors, just in case anyone out there hears our voices," she ordered. "Eric, Brian, come with me."

I followed Helen and Brian across the room, my stomach queasy. It felt like Mors Manor all over again, only this time we were in a weird, technological building with unknown threats rather than a spooky manor with supernatural beings.

Helen stopped as we came to the heptahedron counter. She ran a hand over it and tapped the counter with her wand. "Activate."

A white screen formed on the smooth, glassy surface. Three black words appeared on it: The Control Panel.

Helen, Brian, and I looked at each other. "What next?"

"Use your wands, silly," Evonne called out to us from the doors.

"But which command?" I asked.

"Anything."

Helen directed her wand at the screen. "Reveal."

Nothing happened.

"Activate."

A row of words took place: *How may I help you?*

The three of us glanced at one another again. "Try talking to it," said Brian.

"You've got to be demented," decided Helen.

"Well, if you won't do it, I will." Brian cleared his throat. "Control Panel, show us the terrains of the Underworld."

We gazed at the screen, waiting for something to happen.

*Which district?*

*Mirabilia District*
*Villam District*
*Urbano District*

"Districts? There are three districts in the Underworld?" We exchanged looks of utter bewilderment.

"What are they called?" asked Alexandria.

I read the three names aloud.

"Give the first one a try," she suggested. "I heard Alta mention it in my dream."

"Show us the terrains of Mirabilia District," said Helen to the Control Panel, getting out her notebook and pen.

A map with five vertical columns and three horizontal rows manifested on the screen.

"Wow.... An overview of all the terrains. Hey, it says down here the map only registers the major landscapes and omits small rivers and little forests."

"That's fine." Brian pointed his wand at the screen. "Magnify." Little words appeared in each box.

I squinted at them. "Mount Maravillas...Elec Forest...Mors Manor. Hmm, aren't these the places we were at yesterday?"

"And I see Foss Trail and Foss Falls on the left side of the map. Hold on, Eric," Brian said, closing his eyes. "Yes, that fits...if there are three districts and all the terrains are gathered in one...." His eyes blinked open. "What if...?" He looked from Helen to me, eyes alight with excitement. "What if we've been running around in Mirabilia District all along?"

"So?" I stared at him.

"What if the aquaportals can only transport us to different parts of Mirabilia District? What if we've never been anywhere outside of this place? This can explain why all the terrains we know are shown on this map."

"Excellent theory, Brian. We'll ask the Control Panel more questions later, but first, let me copy down the terrains and their positions." Helen withdrew a pen from the pocket of her cloak. "Activate."

"What's this?" I pointed at it. "Does it do anything magical?"

"My auto-transcribing pen. Cost me a hundred sapphires, but I think it's worth much more than that. It transcribes whatever people say and writes it down. Also, I don't need a wand to activate it. Just a command, and it'll know what and when to start writing."

"Cool," Brian chimed in. "Could I do it? I want to read the map aloud."

Helen nodded. "Transcribe begin." She motioned for Brian to speak.

"Terrains of Mirabilia District of the Underworld," Brian said in a loud, clear voice. The pen rose up into the air and scribbled on the pages of Helen's notebook. "Five columns and three rows are on the map on the Control Panel. I'll refer to the column on the farthest left A, the one next to it B, the one in the middle C, and so on. As for the rows, the first row above will be 1, the middle one 2, the bottom one 3. The coordinate says the right side of the map is north, the left is south, the top part is west, and the bottom is east. Now, I'll begin with box A-1, the highest one on the furthest left. Foss Trail in A-1. Foss Forest and Marais swamp in B-1. Foss Falls and Foss Woods in C-1. Shamo Desert in D-1, framed by an oasis in the same box. Selva Jungle in E-1. Now, for the second horizontal row. A bridge called Kenzania Bridge across the Kenzania River in A-2, leading to Foss Prairie. Evergreen Valley in B-2, a wide river called Evergreen River leading east, all the way to Box B-3. Foss Woods and Evergreen Prairie in C-2. Mount Maravillas in D-2. Tyhdepa Tundra in E-2. Now, for the third horizontal row. Kenzania Savanna in A-3. Cape Evergreen and a beach in B-3. From west to east in C-3 is Nadi Creek, a tributary of Evergreen River in B-2, Mirabilia Peninsula, and the Mirabilia Archipelagos. A labyrinth of granite pillars surrounded by trees in D-3. Elec Forest in E-3, which sort of stretches to Box D-3, and finally, Mors Manor in the east of the forest."

Helen's pen stopped scribbling. For a moment, silence fell over us like a curtain.

"I haven't the foggiest idea of what you're talking about or what the Control Panel's talking about," said Zack, a half-smile on his lips.

"The Control Panel's making perfect sense," explained Helen. "Take our last adventure, for example. We got transported to Kenzania Savanna on A-3, then crossed Kenzania Bridge in A-2 and got to Foss Prairie, where we met the devils and devilines disguised as boys. Then, we walked along Foss Trail in A-1, met Eric and the Chirpy Bird, and got chased into Foss Forest in B-1. Then, we went through the forest and jumped from Foss Falls in C-1 and camped there for a night. The next morning, we got chased into Shamo Desert in D-1 by the Chirpy Bird, and then a group of unibirds saved us and brought us to the oasis in the south of Shamo Desert, where we had our rehearsal battle. After that, we went diagonally through Foss Woods in C-2, found the Gem of Hope, and had our final battle on Evergreen Prairie, also in C-2. Then, after Alexandria's resurrection, we got chased to C-3 and left the Underworld through Nadi Creek."

"I thought we came and left through the same bridge and river," remarked Alexandria.

"No," said Helen. "They were just identical."

"Hang on for a moment," I said. "Do you remember the desert? How come it suddenly swallowed the oasis around us?"

"Maybe the terrains sometimes shrink or expand of their own accord?" Helen surmised. She asked the Control Panel if this was true and got a positive reply.

"And what about the terrains we went through this mission?"

"We got transported to Mors Manor in E-3, took refuge in the Elec Forest, then moved diagonally to Mount Maravillas in D-2, and all the way up to the west peak."

"What about the Scarlet Forest?" Brian recalled. "How come it isn't on the map?"

"Ruby may have hidden it with an enchantment," guessed Alexandria. "Remember how she said the Siblings were trying to persecute her for ages but couldn't? Perhaps it's because she hid her forest with magic so Alta and Alto couldn't find her."

"Maybe she came here before us and meddled with the Control Panel," Brian suggested. "That'd explain why a recluse like her would know where the Control Center is."

"Hey, that's a cool theory," replied Alexandria.

"Back to the point," Helen announced. She scrutinized the

map again and frowned. "We should have gone north to Kenzania Savanna after leaving Mors Manor. Then, we wouldn't have to waste our time in Elec Forest. I see a clear path between Mors Manor and the labyrinth, but I swore I'd never set foot in that cursed maze in my life again." Helen shot a concerned glance at Evonne as though fearing she might disappear the next moment.

"Right," answered Zack, though he didn't seem to comprehend Helen's words. "But at least we know the terrains won't change, right? As long as we've got them copied down, we'll be able to predict whatever lies ahead of us in our future missions, which, after all, is what we're here for."

" I just thought of something," said Helen. "Something in an entry in one of the journals." She closed her eyes. "The Elders on that mission crossed a suspension bridge, came to a savanna, got attacked by a monster, and ran to the haunted manor. I think that's A-3 and E-3."

"So?" I asked.

"Do you think Column A and Column E might be neighbors? In other words, do you think it's possible the five columns form a circle?"

Brian cast an admiring look at Helen. "I think you're right."

"You're a genius, Helen," said Evonne in a hushed voice. "I couldn't have worked out any of this, but you solved it. Now, we can go back to the Otherworld."

"No, wait. We haven't figured out the portals yet. And I think it's best to confirm the exact location of the palace."

"That's easy," I said. "Control Panel, where's the palace of the Underworld?"

*It changes once every two months, moving from A-2 to B-2, from B-2 to C-2, from C-2 to D-2, from D-2 to E-2, then back to A-2.*

"No wonder I always found myself in different parts of the Underworld when I ran away," I mused. "Where is it now?"

*B-2.*

Helen made a note. "And one last question. Show us where the aquaportals to the Otherworld are and how they change."

*Otherworldians are transported randomly to the five entrances to the Underworld. Each entrance has its own corresponding exit. One can only leave through the exit paired with the entrance that transported them here. The five pairs are shown as follows:*

*(A-3, C-3)*
*(E-3, A-2)*
*(D-3, B-2)*
*(B-2, E-3)*
*(C-2, D-3)*

Helen read the words on the screen aloud, and her auto-transcribing pen copied them down on her notebook.

"What does this mean?" I asked, staring at the screen.

"It's showing us the entrances and exits of the Underworld," explained Brian. "We got transported to Mors Manor, right? That's E-3—"

"So we must take the corresponding aquaportal in order to get back to the Otherworld.... That'll be the Kenzania River in A-2," I reasoned, the gears in my mind spinning.

"Exactly." Helen glanced at everyone in the Control Room and smiled for the first time in months. "Mission accomplished," she said slowly, as though savoring the words.

A cheer erupted among the seven of us.

"What a weird feeling!" Alexandria laughed in relief. "I haven't the faintest idea of what you guys were talking about, and suddenly, our mission's over!"

"I sort of understand," Eileen piped up. "I'll explain to you when we get back to the Otherworld."

"Settle down, everyone. Settle down," said Helen, still beaming. "Now, we must leave the Control Center before the Underworldians catch us. Eric, we'll need you to cloud-fly us to Kenzania River."

"Sure," I replied, grinning. I walked over to the metallic double doors and pushed them.

*But they wouldn't budge.*

"Wait.... We're locked in?"

Everyone froze in their tracks. A torrent of maniacal laughter issued from outside.

Nobody spoke, nobody moved. Eileen clutched my arm, Alexandria clapped a hand to her mouth, and the Elders exchanged horrorstruck looks.

"So you think you can trespass into the Control Center without my knowing." The nightmarishly familiar voice blew right through me like a gust of chilly wind.

"Get behind me," ordered Helen. "*Now.*" She was trying her best to suppress it, but I could tell from the tremor in her voice that she, too, was unnerved.

Scepters, wands, and weapons all pointed at the door, we held our breath.

I saw a blinding blade of light stab into the Control Room as the door burst open—

# Chapter Twelve

## Pandemonium
## (Eric)

That face. The twisted features, the murderous eyes, the sallow cheeks. I had hoped never to see that face again, the bestial face that had traumatized me when I was only a child, the face that belonged to someone ten times more terrifying than the contorted features. However, there she was, standing in front of me, flanked by a group of bodyguards. My nightmare. Alta.

She didn't speak. Instead, she gloated at the seven of us, allowing the tension to build and build.

"Of course," drawled Alta, her voice soft with implied danger. "Of course, I should have thought of that. With the most cunning Elder along with you...." Her gaze came to rest on Helen's face, and Zack tensed. "No wonder you didn't take the shortcut. Too obvious, isn't it? I was starting to think my scout was lying to me after I'd guarded the shortcut for nearly two days while waiting for you seven to show up. I decided to come to the Control Center to see in person if you were already here, and—"

"Wait, your scout?" I demanded, hoping to catch her off guard so that she'd reveal who it was by accident. "What are you talking about?"

Alta smirked. "You foolish Otherworldians trust each other so much that you never suspect anyone of leaking secrets to my side. Yes, my son. There's a spy among your fellow Elders, a double agent who has served me quite well during the past year, passing me important information every day by using this." Alta withdrew from the pouch of her turquoise cloak a multifunctional diamond device like the ones we had seen downstairs.

A mixture of panic and horror boiled in me. A spy? Alexandria mentioning the spy in her dream was one thing, but now, it was officially confirmed. There was indeed a spy among the Elders. My mind whirred with innumerable possibilities. *Kerry Jenkins? Galen Benson? Or perhaps even Juniper Richardson? Or...?*

"That's a lie," asserted Helen. "A vile, pathetic attempt to make us implode. I know the Elders. I know every one of them. They'd never do anything like that."

"You reckon so?" Alta sneered.

"I believe so." Helen stared down at her, confidence etched upon every inch of her face.

"You believe so." A creepy smile crept onto Alta's lips. "Do you really know all the Elders? Or do you *think* you know them? And I thought you were supposed to be wise, Helen Edmunds. But I like it better this way, you refusing to think badly of your fellow Elders. Noble of you, but ignorant. Very ignorant."

"You keep insulting her, and I'll attack you," said Zack, his wand raised. Helen gripped his arm and shot him a look of warning.

"You want to attack me?" Alta burst into a fit of laughter. "I could have killed you that time, sixteen years ago, if you hadn't run away like a coward rather than deal with the consequences of your actions and betrayal! "

"Keep her talking, but don't agitate her," I heard Helen mutter, her voice almost inaudible. "Then, we catch her off guard and attack, and we can get out of here."

Zack caught Helen's eye and gave her a subtle nod. "The hiking trail," he said aloud, this time in a calmer voice. "Why would you destroy the bridge that led across the giant trees if you were so sure we'd take the shortcut?"

"I had to set up some precautions, just in case," answered

Alta. For some reason, she didn't seem agitated or infuriated at all, even though we had outsmarted her and found the Control Center before she could kill us. On the other hand, she looked smugger than usual. "You don't seem scared at all, now that you're trapped here."

"There's nothing to be scared of," said Evonne. "We're not going down without a fight."

I felt someone tugging on my sleeve. It was Alexandria.

"What?"

"Wait for Helen's signal. Attack the bodyguard on her left, and I'll take the right one. Eileen, Evonne, and Brian will be in charge of the rest of them, one each."

"Got it," I whispered.

Alta sneered. "You think you've won, don't you? You barged into my Control Center and stole the top secrets of the Underworld. But you'd never have imagined I would send an army to the Otherworld in your absence."

"What do you mean?" A ghostly pallor worked its way through Helen's face, yet she stood her ground.

"The second invasion has taken place, of course," Alta grinned. "Half of the Otherworld will be in ruins when you go home. That is, if you make it out of the Control Center a—"

"Do it," said Helen in a carrying whisper.

Pandemonium erupted. I blasted Alta's bodyguard out of the way and bolted out of the Control Room, followed by Alexandria, Eileen, Brian, and Evonne.

"Down the stairs!" yelled Evonne, ushering us down the staircase.

"What?" Alexandria asked. "No! The others are still in there!"

"Helen told us to go first," said Evonne.

"But what's she doing? And where's Zack?" I asked.

"They're both trying to keep Alta busy," replied Brian. "Listen, now that we're out of the Control Room, we've got to destroy as many gadgets as we can while running around in the Control Center."

"But won't they—?"

"It doesn't make a difference!" Brian hollered. "They're already here! The Underworldians will attack us with those gadgets if we don't destroy them! Yes, right here, right now! We must—"

Evonne gasped. A row of crossed swords had blocked our way down the staircase, making it impossible to get to the fourth floor. We found ourselves face-to-face with five devils and devilines.

Brian and Evonne drew their swords, and each lunged at one of them, and Alexandria and Eileen flung fireballs and spiky roses at another. One of the devils decided to make a run for it and hurried down the stairs. Dodging and ducking swords and shields, Alexandria rushed after the devil.

I summoned a turquoise fireball and attacked the deviline on the right, but my hands were shaking so much that I missed. The two of us wrestled on the landing. The deviline roared and smacked me with her shield with such force that I fell, hitting my head on the glass panels of the banister. My head throbbed and seared as pain took over my senses. The crimson stains on my fingers and the burning agony told me I was bleeding. The deviline towered over me, sniggering at my plight. Staggering to my feet, I summoned my concentration and hurled another fireball at her. She dodged it narrowly, just as a stumbling devil stood on her large feet by accident. She shrieked, lost her balance, and toppled backward, falling off the banister of the staircase. The deviline clung onto the frameless glass railing with her gnarled fingers, her huge feet dangling in midair. Impassive, I watched her struggle.

Meanwhile, I could see the tiny figure of Alexandria in the atrium below, dueling one-on-one with a devil. With a well-aimed blow, she knocked her opponent into the anti-gravity waterfall. The helpless devil flailed his arms in a vain attempt to escape from the curtain of water. I watched the relentless current carry him all the way up, ignoring the wild protests of his limbs. The devil "landed" upside down in the glass tank on the ceiling, like an ugly green fish in a tank of turquoise water.

"Save me!" the deviline wailed, still clutching the railing

with all her might. I had forgotten about her existence.

"Save me, please!"

I smirked. "As if you won't kill me as soon as I do."

"I—I don't want to die," the deviline implored as her fingers slipped. "I—I promise I'll fight for you! I'll switch sides and help you Otherworldians out of the Control Center, but only if you save me!"

I hesitated for a fraction of a second, then grabbed ahold of the deviline's sweaty arms and hauled her up. She was a lot lighter than I had assumed. The deviline straddled the glass railing and let go of my hands.

"Thanks."

"Now, are you going to help us out of—?"

Before I knew it, the deviline seized my arms and shoved me over the fence of glass. I screamed, grabbing ahold of the only thing within reach—the railing. I shook like a leaf, my feet swinging in midair. My stomach gave an unpleasant lurch as I looked down at the atrium, four stories below me. I wanted to haul myself back up more than anything, but I barely had any strength left. The deviline gloated over me as I struggled to hold on.

"Idiot boy," she snarled. "I'm going to do away with you right now."

"You liar! I saved your life!" Every inch of my body was trembling, and the icy sweat pooling from my palms only made things worse.

"No need to be so nervous," said the deviline in a silky voice, prying my fingers away from the glass panel.

"What are you doing?" I was now clinging on for dear life with only my right hand.

"Ending your struggle once and for—"

"NO!" A thick vine shot out from nowhere and wreathed itself around the deviline's neck.

"Ouch, I—I can't breathe!" the deviline gasped. She let go of my hands and tugged at the vines around her neck.

Eileen grabbed the deviline by her horns and blasted her away. She tumbled down the stairs, still wrestling and thrashing against the vines.

"Eric, take my hand!" shouted Eileen.

"I'm trying to! But it's slippery!" Beads of sweat invaded my eyes as I managed to hold on.

Eileen looked around, then closed her eyes and took a deep breath as though debating with herself. "I'm going to try something risky. Don't let go of my hand no matter what. On the count of three...two...one!"

I felt something sticky coiling itself around my wrist and screamed as I was hauled up into the air. With a somersault, I fell, not plummeting four stories down into the atrium but safely onto the landing beside Eileen.

"Are you all right?" she asked.

I nodded, panting. She had conjured a thick vine and tied it around my wrist, using it as a rope to hoist me up. "Thank you."

Eileen and I looked into each other's eyes, and the two of us locked lips. Everything seemed surreal, like a beautiful dream. I breathed in the unadorned fragrance of Eileen's skin, drinking her in. Her lips were as soft as petals, as light as butterflies; every touch sent tingles of thrills down my spine—thrills of excitement mingled with horror. I knew a battle lay ahead of us, and I couldn't stop thinking about the possibility of this as our final kiss. How I wished time could have stood still and frozen right at that moment, leaving the two of us glued with each other for an eternity.

"Sentimental little heroes, eh?" A drawling voice punctured my fantasy. Eileen and I broke apart, only to see a devil holding a jar of red liquid that twisted and wriggled in its container—a detonating device. Just a simple command and we would be dead before we could even leave the Control Center.

Eileen and I tried to make a run for it, but the devil was quicker. "Activa—"

Blast! The small glass container in his hand shattered into a million pieces, and the devil crumpled to the floor, an arrow protruding from his chest.

I looked up and saw Helen and Zack. "You...you escaped

from the Control Room?"

"We knocked Alta out cold," said Zack. He and Helen raced down the stairs to join us, and the four of us walked down to the fourth floor together. "Have you seen the others?"

"Alexandria's in the atrium, but I don't know where Brian and Evonne are. They mentioned something about destroying the gadgets on the third floor—"

"What? We haven't got time for that!" Helen looked horrified. "The Otherworld's under another invasion, and we're supposed to get out of here as quickly as possible and leave the Underworld! Eric, Eileen, stay here while Zack and I find the others."

"Stay safe," said Zack, laying a hand on my shoulder.

"Same to you two." I watched them hurry down to the lower floors. "Eileen, should we help—Eileen?"

She looked straight through me, acting as though I didn't exist. Her eyes were glassy and out of focus.

"What are you looking at?"

"Is it my imagination, or are those robots coming for us?"

I whirled around and saw three humanoid robots making their way toward us. They were white all over, with glossy heads, bodies, and limbs, except for their eyes—they had blue circular interfaces as pupils, like hologram circles. In their artificial hands were scythes with blades that glowed turquoise.

"Harm!" I shouted. Yellow sparks shot from my scepter and flew toward the robots, but to my utter dismay, they bounced off their metallic skin and came boomeranging back at us. Grabbing Eileen's arm, I ducked as the sparks sailed over our heads.

Eileen gave her scepter a flick. Vines sprouted from the tip, glided through the air, and coiled themselves around the robots' torsos. However, no matter how tightly the vines curled around their steely chests, the robots kept marching forward, unfeeling and senseless.

"Run!" I seized Eileen's arm and bolted in the opposite direction.

"Eric! Stop!" Eileen screamed. "All the rooms here form a

circle, remember? The robots can easily block us from the other side if we—"

"Then what—?"

"The staircase!" Dragging me along with her, Eileen darted toward the staircase and made a run for the third floor. The clinks of metal behind us announced the proximity of the robots, who had followed us down.

Eileen and I hurtled past the white rooms. With a pang of astonishment, I noticed that the detonating devices were all gone.

"Ouch!" I tripped over an empty container lying on the floor and fell.

"Eric, are you—?"

"Go, Eileen! Just go! They're coming!"

Ignoring my protests, Eileen grabbed my arms and helped me up. I looked over my shoulder and saw that the robots were only a few feet away from us.

"We've got to do something! There!" I spotted the crate of rocket missiles right ahead of us and nodded at Eileen. The two of us dashed toward the box, grabbed a few missiles, and hurled them at the robots. I had never seen metal burning and smoking before, but the robots' steely white skin smoldered as the missiles erupted into flames.

"Well done, Eil—"

"There! There's more of them! They're coming in crowds!" she shrieked, pointing at the part of the staircase we could see.

Without thinking, I seized Eileen's hand and took off running. We dashed through room after room as we ran for our lives. The strange creatures in the aquarium tanks goggled at us as we hurtled past them, and the countless rows of potions became a colorful blur.

"Wait." I noticed the absence of the robots' clinking feet. "I reckon we've thrown them off. Listen, we need a safe place to hide, where they won't find us. Any doors or secret rooms here?"

The two of us looked around and caught sight of a door on the opposite wall.

"Let's try that one," Eileen tapped her scepter on the door. "Unlock and open."

The door swung open, leading us to the top floor of what seemed like a gigantic cubic building. Clear sunlight flooded through the glass walls. Eileen slammed the door shut and leaned against it, sliding toward the floor.

Behind the door, the clinks of metallic feet grew louder and louder, then faded into silence.

"That was a close call," I whispered.

"You know what's so scary about them, those robots?" Eileen whispered back. "When they're programmed to do something, they won't stop until they achieve their goal. They're not going to let us go until they've destroyed us. The robots have no mercy for anyone, and to make things worse, it's almost impossible to destroy them."

I patted her on the shoulder. "It's all right, Eileen. We're safe now. What's this place, by the way? Some glass fortress?"

It looked very much like the exterior of the Control Center, with the same latticed glass, white steel, and transparent triangles, rhombuses and quadrilaterals. Ninety-foot living walls blanketed with plants were erected everywhere. Below us was a bountiful and diverse botanical collection of exotic trees, shrubs, bushes, and undergrowth, forming a fancy palette of green. Glass pipes trailed in the air, transporting water to the living walls and the plants on the ground floor. The pipes all led to a large pool suspended in midair by a floating glass tank. Elevated glass walkways with frameless balustrades weaved through the living walls and plants, almost invisible among the ubiquitous flora. Like arteries, they stretched everywhere in the cubic building, sometimes intertwining and splitting into narrower roads or merging with a wider path. One of the walkways stretched right before us, leading us into the maze of greenery.

"Looks like a conservatory," remarked Eileen.

"You're right. Since we can't go back and fight the robots, we must get to the ground floor. I bet there's another entrance to the Control Center down there, like the one we just came in through. Once we get back, we can find the others. Come." I took Eileen's hand and set foot on the glass walkway.

It was a huge, boundless museum of vegetation.

Everywhere we went, we were greeted by exotic flora I'd never seen before. We passed a gallery of blue flowers that yawned every five seconds, stretching their soft petals to their widest before shutting them. A family of palms waved at us as we walked by, shaking their large compound leaves. On our left side were tall bushes with small flowers shaped like kittenpillars that changed color with each glance. I could see lush green bushes and ferns dotting the garden below us through the floor. Ahead of us, the walkway split into two paths, the left one slanting upward into a graceful curve and almost meeting the ceiling of the cubic building, while the other dipped low, threading through a forest of giant pine trees.

"It's amazing, isn't it?" said Eileen, who had abandoned her fear. "How can they house so many plants that thrive in different climates?"

"Good question. Magic, I suppose."

Eileen nodded and scowled. "Hold on. What's that smell?"

Several smoking shrubs that gave off the unpleasant tang of something burning caught my attention. "The shrubs over there, on the right path."

"Let's take the left one, then. I suppose we can find a way to get to the ground floor later. The passages here are like a big elevated maze."

We hurried along the curving walkway, which led us to the highest point of the conservatory. A plant with fat turquoise leaves squirted yellow liquid at us. I dodged out of the way and leapt to the other side, pulling Eileen with me.

"What's that?" Eileen frowned at the plants. "Pus?"

"Poison, I guess. I don't think this conservatory was built here by accident. Alta must be inventing new species of plants as weapons and keeping them here."

We had reached the peak of the walkway. The trees, plants, and all the vertical gardens stretched below us like a map, a rhapsody of green hues mingling with one another. The elevated walkways, I noticed, were suspended in the air by magic, without poles, columns, or any form of support underneath. I traced my finger in the air as I studied the crisscrossing passages, figuring out how to reach the ground floor and leave.

Just then, a flash of turquoise light zoomed at me, narrowly missing my heart.

"Enjoying yourselves?" said an icy voice.

Eileen gasped. A few feet behind us was a figure with flaming red hair and a face etched with victorious delight that, if possible, made it seem even less human. It was Alta.

"Well, well, well, if it isn't my traitor of a son," she said in a silky voice. Her features screwed up in rage, and a murderous glint shone in her eyes. "How dare you stand in front of me, as bold as brass! Have you no shame? You are my son! You belong to me. You're mine!"

"I'm not yours! I'm *mine!*" I balled my hands into fists to prevent them from shaking. "And you will never control me again!" I hurled in as much hatred and contempt as I could in the last sentence.

A turquoise beam of light zapped at me at that moment, brushing past my arm. Without a moment of hesitation, I turned on my heels and tore along the walkway, racing past plant after plant.

"Slow down!" Eileen panted.

"We've got to keep going! Alta's right behind us!" I turned and hurled a turquoise fireball at Alta, but one of her bodyguards deflected it.

"Blast!" I shouted. A wave of golden sparks zoomed at them, and a few devils and devilines were thrown off their feet by the force.

Eileen and I went on running, and we came to a fork again. The walkway had split into three paths. This time, we took the right one. It snaked through an array of towering living walls, like a road skirting around skyscrapers in a city.

"Which road did they take?" Alta's sharp voice seemed to penetrate the air.

"I...no idea, my mistress," a second voice said.

Alta cursed. "Jones, Black, and Fletcher, you take the left path. Scott and Reynolds, take the middle one, and Miller, come with me. We'll take the right path."

"What do we do? They're going to—"

"I've got an idea," whispered Eileen. "I can try interacting with the living wall with my elemental magic and see if it can help us."

"Fine, but we've got to get out of here before they see us."

Eileen pointed her scepter at the living wall. "Rise!"

It was a magnificent sight. The plants sprung off the living wall and onto the walkway, blocking the path behind us; others stretched their branches all the way to the ground.

"There they are!" Alta screeched. She leapt over a fern plant and made a dive for Eileen and me. Right at that moment, a plant with tendrils as thick as arms seized Alta's wrists, hoisted her up into the air, and shook her. The same fate met Miller, the dogfish who came along with his mistress. The two of them struggled in a fruitless attempt to break free.

"Awesome," I said, grinning at Eileen. "Great thinking."

"Did Mistress Alta just call?" a voice asked.

Eileen and I spun around and saw a deviline and two dogfishes coming in the opposite direction. One of them barked at the sight of Alta, who was screaming and waving her arms in the air. The plants were tossing and catching her, juggling her as if she were a ball.

"M-m-mistress!" the deviline stuttered. "Who...? What...?"

"Don't just stand there like a fool, Jones, get them! The Otherworldians!"

The deviline and the two dogfishes advanced on us, but six more plants escaped the living wall, shielding us as they formed a great green barrier.

"What the—? Blast that thing apart!" Alta spat at her subordinates.

Eileen and I tried to run in the direction we had come from, but the plants were blocking our path, and it'd take forever to remove them.

"Eric! The glass pipes!" shouted Eileen. "It's wide enough for a person to climb in." She pointed her scepter at the tube beside the living wall. "Reverse."

"Have you gone mad? We can't—Eileen? Eileen!"

She had dived headfirst into the mouth of the pipe and was now skyrocketing toward the ceiling of the conservatory. At that moment, an arrow whizzed past me, grazing my cheek.

"Get him!" the deviline shrieked. They had somehow destroyed the plants and cleared the path.

The three of them hurtled toward me. Having no other option, I scrambled into the glass pipe, swinging my legs into the fat tube as quickly as I could manage. An unseen force that I knew was the suction yanked me upward like a gravitational force. In a fraction of a moment, I was zooming past a sea of green plants and flying feet-first toward the ceiling, going at such an extreme speed I felt as if my face were peeling off. I saw the black bottom of Eileen's boots far ahead of me.

"Eileen, are you okay?" I yelled.

"Never better!" she hollered. "It's like magic!"

I watched the plants below grow smaller and smaller, blending into an endless canvas of green. Anticipation and excitement coursed through my veins as I felt my heart hammering in my chest and blood thundering in my brain. A group of devils and devilines stood on the walkways, hurling weapons and shooting arrows at the glass pipes, attempting to sabotage them. Bearnixes spat fireballs, and dogfishes tossed icicles at me, but miraculously, the ammunition bounced off the glass tubes.

"Blithering idiots!" Alta, who was still stuck on the living wall, screamed at the top of her lungs. I could hear her shrill, penetrating voice, although I was confined to the tubes. "The glass pipes are unbreakable! Nothing can penetrate them! You've got to wait until they come out—ouch!" The plant with fat turquoise leaves squirted yellow liquid at her. In less than five seconds, her hands and arms were gloved with blisters.

The pipes stopped climbing, and I was now soaring across the ceiling in a lying position, a missile speeding through the air.

"Where does this pipe lead to?" I yelled to Eileen.

"The floating glass tank of water down there, I guess! It was supposed to transport water to the living walls, remember? I did a 'reverse' spell on it, and now it's going to transport us there instead of the other way round."

"Genius! Even Brian or Helen couldn't have done a better job."

"Quick wits, that's all," said Eileen with a chuckle. "Oh, I think we're going down. Close your eyes!"

I obeyed, bracing myself for a sudden drop in altitude. Before I knew it, velocity took me. A rushing sound of white noise filled my eardrums as the wind slapped my face. I was going down, down, down, almost plummeting into—

Then I stopped falling. I opened my eyes and surveyed my surroundings. Eileen and I were still zooming past plants of all shapes and sizes, only this time, we were slowing down. The pipe swerved through the glass walkways; bearnixes and dogfishes thrust me wrathful glares of venom as I shot through the tube, appearing and disappearing right under their noses.

"So long, fools!" I called out to them, unable to suppress a grin.

We then passed a family of ferns covered with spikes, a tall mistletoe with turquoise berries, a bush with leaves that chomped at the air, reminding me of the biting roses in front of Mors Manor. Finally, we passed a frosty tree with bare branches. As Eileen and I zoomed past the tree, pale blue and ivory roses bloomed on its limbs.

"We're going to land in the tank soon," said Eileen.

Moments later, I was engulfed by the freezing waters of the pool. I kicked and waved my arms, inhaling lungfuls of fresh air. "Eileen?"

"I'm here!" she squeaked.

"There! The Otherworldians! In the floating pool! Blast them apart, Scott!"

"But the glass—"

"THE TANK ISN'T MADE OF UNBREAKABLE GLASS, YOU IDIOT! BLAST THEM! NOW!"

Eileen pointed her scepter at the living wall beside us. "Descend!"

Two leafy vines sprouted from one of the plants, increasing in length and trailing down into the pool. Eileen and I seized one each, swung ourselves out of the water, and landed on the ground.

"Now, we've got to find the exit," said Eileen. "Where might—?"

"They've escaped!" Alta roared from above.

My stomach gave a terrible jolt as I saw Alta sitting on the back of a unibird, now circling above us.

"Smash them!" she commanded.

I made the mistake of looking up again, and a vial of blue liquid landed right before my feet.

"What the—?"

"They're attacking us with potions!" Eileen yelled. "Run!"

The two of us scampered through the bushes and plants, diving behind one and taking refuge for a few seconds from time to time. Jars and vials of colorful potions rained over us, smashing left and right ahead and behind us as we ran. One landed right beside my heel, and another brushed past my left cheek before crashing to the floor. I wholeheartedly regretted the decision of coming down here in the first place. The devils and devilines now had the advantage of the higher ground, and they were playing to their full strength. Plus, the bearnixes and dogfishes were pelting us with everything they had. Something icy and watery hit the back of my head; one of the slushballs had soaked my hair. I looked up, just in time to see a dogfish toss a green flask of potion at Eileen. I grabbed a fistful of her cloak and yanked her out of harm's way.

Dozens of icicles and ice boulders rained down from the overhanging walkways in front of us.

"Watch out!" I yelled. Eileen and I leapt over the mound of boulders, narrowly avoided a purple vial, and ducked as a sizzling fireball sailed over our heads.

All of a sudden, a stinging sensation erupted throughout my body, and I fell to my knees—an icicle had pierced into my leg. I cried out in pain, and Eileen crouched down beside me. Wincing, I removed the icicle from my wound; blood was streaming from it. I had a vial of healing ointment in my pocket, but we couldn't afford to stop.

"Eric, you can't go on running—"

"I have to! We all have to!"

A million vials of potions in every color of the spectrum dropped from the passages above us. One glance told me we were not going to make it. All the terrifying effects of those concoctions would be enough to kill ten people, let alone two. I tried to move, but my leg was immobilizing me. With every last bit of strength I had, I pushed Eileen out of the way and braced myself for death.

Nothing.

Confused, I opened my eyes and blinked. A unibird with a blond head and a fluorescent-yellow body had flown out from nowhere and slapped the potions away with its wings. The Underworldians were no longer tossing potions or ammunition at us. I looked over my shoulder and saw glowing bearnixes, dogfishes, and kittenpillars hurtling through the glass walkways and chomping at Alta's minions.

"Oh, Eric!" exclaimed Eileen, flinging her arms around me. "You saved me!"

"Not really," I said, smiling.

"Eric! Eileen!"

The figures of Alexandria, Brian, and Evonne emerged from behind a tree with orange leaves. Dragging my injured leg, I hurried over to the three of them, half-leaning on Eileen. "Where have you been?"

"On the second floor, freeing the genetically modified animals," said Evonne, a grin splitting her lips.

"And spending a few minutes to convince them not to eat us alive," added Brian.

"Yeah, that too," admitted Evonne. "But anyway, they've agreed to fight for us."

"That's great news!" Eileen cried.

"I gave the animals on our side half of the potions I stole. Look…." Brian pointed to a trio of glowing dogfishes who pelted a bearnix with vials of glittery black substance. A shower of vomit drenched a dogfish below that I recognized as Alta's subordinate, Miller.

"How did you guys get here?" I asked, bending down to apply some ointment on my leg.

"Brian saw a funny little door by the dogfish tank, and it took us here," explained Alexandria. "Any idea where this is?"

"Some kind of conservatory with strange plants," I replied. "Looks like— "

"Hold on," Evonne cut in. "Eric, Eileen, have you two seen Helen and Zack?"

A horrible feeling sank to the pit of my stomach. I lowered my head.

Alexandria's expression darkened. "Is that a no?"

Eileen shook her head.

Brian and Evonne exchanged worried glances. "You don't think—you don't think that they're—?"

"Wait!" cried Alexandria. "Is that them I see over there? Helen and Zack?"

I whirled around and saw two tiny figures, one purple and the other black, dashing across the elevated walkway on the other side of the conservatory.

"Look! Isn't that the one that leads to the third floor of the Control Center?" Eileen asked. "I think they went the same route as we did. They seem to be running away from something. What are they—?"

To my utmost horror, a group of robots barged into the conservatory and charged after Helen and Zack. What's more, half of the robots had mechanical wings; some of them flew off the walkway and swooped down on the fighters on the ground floor.

"Run!" Alexandria grabbed my hand and sprinted in the opposite direction.

Pandemonium reigned; pure pandemonium. It was as if the end of the world had come.

"We must find a place to hide," Alexandria turned to us. "Then we can come up with a plan to save the others."

"Duck!" I hollered as a robot came soaring at us.

Eileen conjured a self-running-flesh-eating-Venus-flytrap and waved her scepter to automate it. The flytrap chomped on the robot's arm, but it was no match for the metallic monster, who sliced the plant's jaws apart with the blades on its wings.

"Get down!" shrieked Alexandria. The three of us stooped, and right at that moment, a dozen ice boulders and fireballs sailed through the air and bonked the robot on the head, buying us time.

With Eileen bringing up the lead, we rounded two living walls, dodged three oak trees and a fat shrub, and took refuge behind a rosemary bush until we were sure we had lost the robots.

"Phew, that was a close call," said Eileen.

"Right, let's figure out—What's that?" I spotted something white and steely by the bush. It was a metal plaque that had come loose.

"*Spherical Steerer. Made of unbreakable glass,*" I read aloud.

"Unbreakable glass?" Alexandria asked.

"Weapon-proof and elemental magic-proof," I said. "But why is this thing—?"

"Wait a second," Eileen interrupted. "You remember the white rooms upstairs? Every single invention had a metal plaque with its name and a short introduction. What if this Spherical Steerer thing is an invention? What if it's right here, in this conservatory? All we need to do is to find this thing and work out how to steer it, then we can bail the others out and get out of the Control Center."

"Brilliant," breathed Alexandria. "Now, let's go look for this Spherical Steerer. Remember, it's round like a ball, made of glass, and probably big enough to fit several people. It might look like the Control Center in miniature—Watch out there, Eric!"

I barely dived out of the way as a potion with limpid contents zoomed in my direction. Cursing, I flung a turquoise fireball at the deviline who had attacked me, and she collapsed.

The three of us hurried through the innumerable rows of plants, looking for the Spherical Steerer and at the same time chucking ammunition at the sneaky Underworldians who were lurking behind trees and bushes and trying to ambush us. I blasted a shrub apart and tossed a fireball at the unibird hiding behind it, just as an angry devil whacked me in the back with his huge horns and knocked me down.

"Get off him!" Alexandria yelled. She put up a fight with

the monster and stabbed her spear into his belly.

"Keep going." Eileen seized my arm, and we hurried through the ocean of plants, Alexandria on our heels.

Just then, something shiny and glistening piqued my attention, something perched under a bearded willow tree.

"Look," I said to the others. Curious, the three of us approached it, our scepters raised just in case an enemy was lurking around. It was a spherical contraption made entirely out of glass, big enough to fit ten people. Alexandria, Eileen, and I edged closer to the giant bubble, and I saw two transparent doors, one on each side.

Alexandria shot me an excited look. "The Spherical Steerer—this is it."

"Just what we needed," Eileen said. "It's like a car."

I had no time to stop and ask what a "car" was. "Whatever this is, it may be our only hope of making it out of this place alive. Open," I said, pointing my scepter at the Spherical Steerer. The doors obeyed, revealing an empty circular space inside. "Come on, let's get in." The three of us clambered in and shut the doors.

"Suppose we're safe in here," said Eileen, sitting cross-legged on the floor. "Now, how do we activate this thing?"

"Reveal." I pointed my scepter at the bubble.

Nothing happened. "What about...activate?"

A screen formed on the wall of glass before us.

*Password?*

My heart sank. "Uh...." I looked helplessly at Alexandria and Eileen.

"Try the one that helped us into the Control Center. One zero four zero six seven," said Alexandria.

*Incorrect.*

Alexandria let out a groan of frustration. Eileen and I exchanged nervous looks.

"What should we do?" moaned Alexandria. "It'll take us forever to decode this thing."

"Wait." I closed my eyes, trying to recall something from earlier. "Do you remember the wrong password Anderson gave us? You don't think he made it up, do you?" Seeing the blank expressions on their faces, I added impatiently, "What if Anderson was trying to tell a convincing lie and blurted out the first password he thought of? What if it's the password to activate the Spherical Steerer?"

"But what if it's not?"

"Zero six zero two three seven," I said to the Spherical Steerer.

*Correct.*

I grinned at the surprised looks on Alexandria and Eileen's faces. "How can we steer this?" I asked the bubble.

*Give commands. Up, down, left, right, forward, or backward. You can also choose to state the name of your destination.*

"What the—? This bubble thing can fly?"

"I'll give it a try," Eileen volunteered. "Up."

The bubble contraption rose up into the air, now hovering three feet above the ground.

"Wonderful." Eileen beamed. "I think I've mastered this. Let's go and save the others. Do you see any of them?"

I stared at the plants below us, which blurred into a green field as I observed it through the glassy floor of the Spherical Steerer.

"Evonne," said Alexandria, pointing at a little lilac figure on the ground floor who was running away from a robot.

"Down and forward." The bubble descended to the ground and zoomed toward her.

Evonne looked up and saw us. Her face was pale and clammy with terror or fatigue. I wasn't sure which. "What are you three—?"

"Get in," said Alexandria, moving closer to the door.

"No, don't open it!" I shouted, grabbing her hand. "We've got to kill the robot then save her. Evonne, could you lure it to the floating water tank over there?"

"What are you—?"

"Just do it!" I yelled, trying not to feel bad for bossing Evonne around when she was already in such a stressful situation. "And Eileen, fly us over to the water tank."

"Will do," she said.

As our bubble hovered in the air, I watched the robot dash after Evonne under the water tank.

"Blast!" I pointed my scepter at the tank as soon as Evonne was out of harm's way. It shattered right below us, water and broken shards of glass splashing everywhere. Drenched, the robot froze on the spot and collapsed.

"Fly us to Evonne," said Eileen. She opened the door, grabbed Evonne's hand, and pulled her up into our bubble.

"Thanks," gasped Evonne, wiping the sweat on her forehead with her handkerchief. "Where are the others?"

We gained height, and I looked down at the conservatory, scrutinizing the labyrinth of transparent passages to see if the others were there. A wingless robot was chasing after two devils, while another was running in pursuit of Brian, Helen, and Zack.

"I see them. Eileen, fly us down there, and we can—"

"It's too risky," she said. "We have to wait until they're a few feet away from the robots, or they might get into our bubble."

Evonne took a sharp intake of breath. "Oh no!"

Zack had tripped over a fallen branch. A robot caught up with the three of them and snatched him by the arm, flinging him away like a frisbee. He crashed, landing a few feet away from the others. His ankle was bleeding, crimson drops staining his brown boots and dotting the glass floor beside him. Helen dashed over to his side, and the robot, who seemed to think two were better than one, left Brian alone and ran in pursuit of Helen.

Eileen descended our bubble right next to Brian, who gaped at us.

"Are you all right?"

"I...I think so," said Brian shakily. "I would've died if I hadn't had the potions with me. I got away by chucking them at the enemies and distracting them. What's that you're driving?"

"Get in, and I'll explain later."

Brian scrambled into the bubble, and we steered our way toward Helen and Zack.

"Don't touch him!" Helen yelled at the robot, throwing herself in front of Zack. The robot made a lunge for her but missed. The blades on its fingers scarred her, leaving three bloody gashes on her neck.

Brian groped in his pouch and chucked an orange vial at the robot, bonking it on the back of its head to distract it. The robot spun around to check who the assailant was, and we seized our opportunity.

"Here!" Alexandria opened the door and helped Helen and Zack into our bubble.

Just then, Alta's unibird came soaring at us. Gloating and grinning, she chucked a white vial of potion at Alexandria; the latter caught the potion with her right hand and flung it at the robot, who was still searching for its attacker. Alta's expression melted into one of rage. An inarticulate roar of fury and frustration escaped her.

"Up!" Eileen shouted, and we rose up into the air once again. "How do we leave the conservatory?"

"Detonating devices," said Brian, producing a jar of orange liquid from his pouch. He opened the door and chucked it at the wall of latticed glass. It exploded and formed a hole. "Is this big enough?"

"No, too small!" I said, though I wasn't sure. All I knew was that I didn't want to risk breaking our bubble.

Alexandria screamed; a winged robot was jetting towards us. "Hurry up, Brian!"

Brian flung another detonating device at our escape route. More fragments spilled as the hole widened. "Is this okay?"

"I think so," said Eileen. "Out of the Control Center. To the Kenzania River," she told the bubble.

We zoomed out of the conservatory for what I hoped was the first as well as the final time in our lives. I looked over my shoulder, watching the massive glass cube grow smaller and smaller until it faded away in the distance.

"Brian, have you nicked any healing potions from the Chemistry Inventions Room?" Helen asked.

"I think—Yes." He handed her a vial of pink liquid, and she poured a few drops on Zack's wounded ankle. The effect was a lot better than the healing ointment. The skin mended itself, and the blood faded away.

"Thank you," said Zack. "Helen, you're hurt as well."

Helen poured a few drops on her hand and dabbed at the gashes on her neck. "Anyone else needs this? We've got another battle to fight as soon as we get back to the Otherworld."

"Please," I said, taking the little bottle from her and mending my leg before passing it on to Brian.

"Thanks," he said. "Disastrous, wasn't it? Everything that happened today. We barely made it out alive."

"I think I'd rather fight the snout monster again than go back to the Control Center," agreed Alexandria.

"On the bright side, though, we've got the terrains and everything recorded down." Helen examined her notebook with an air of satisfaction.

"You're wonderful, Helen," said Evonne. "Thank goodness we didn't take the shortcut. We'd all be dead by now if we'd done that."

"Your idea bought us enough time to explore the inventions," agreed Brian, grinning at the potions and gadgets he had stolen from the Control Center.

"What happened after we split?" Zack asked. "I wonder what everyone's versions of events was."

"Oh, don't even get me started on that," I said with a weak chuckle. "I've been trying to wipe those memories away ever since we escaped from the conservatory."

This was so true that everyone laughed, except for Alexandria.

"Why so quiet, Alexandria?" asked Zack.

"I'm thinking about what Alta said. About the spy, you know."

The atmosphere tensed. We all glanced at Helen to see her reaction.

"I don't think there is one," she said. "Alta's just trying to make us fight amongst ourselves. You don't believe the nonsense she's making up, do you?"

"You're forgetting something," Alexandria reminded her. "The scout, remember? The scout in my dream. The scout I mentioned yesterday, who knew we'd figured out the non-changing terrains of the Underworld."

Nobody spoke. There was too much truth in Alexandria's words to be ignored.

Helen sighed. "Why did I forget that? You're right. I take back what I said about the spy."

"Wait a second," Eileen chimed in. "Eric, do you remember the oath you swore on the last mission before becoming an Otherworldian?"

"Yeah, of course, I do. What do you...?"

"The oath," she continued. "Zack said it would take your life if you broke it, right?"

I nodded. "So?"

"Do all Elders have to pledge an oath to King Patrick and Queen Marianne on the initiation ceremony?"

"Of course."

"Would the Elders die if they broke the oath?"

"I see where you're coming from," I said glumly. "But the oath new Elders pledge on the ceremony is different from the one I pledged to Helen before joining the Otherworld. It's not a binding contract, and it has no restrictions. The new recruits do it simply for formality's sake. They won't die if they break it, which means we'll have a very hard time figuring out who the spy is."

"So, what's our next step?" asked Zack.

"I stick by what I said yesterday," replied Helen. "I'll report everything to King Patrick and Queen Marianne and suggest they investigate in secret. None of the Elders should know about the investigation."

A frown creased Brian's forehead. "Do you think it's a good idea to handle this quietly? We've got a battle to fight as soon as we get back to the Otherworld, and now there's this problem of a spy hiding among us."

"It's like I said." Helen raised her voice. "I won't permit them to question every single Elder and make a list of suspects. The Otherworld's already in danger. I can't imagine what will happen if we keep suspecting each other of leaking information to Alta and Alto. Plus, we might inadvertently alarm the spy if we make a big deal out of this. They might find other ways to sneak information out of the palace, and that'll make it harder for us to catch them."

"And what if the rulers are determined to warn every Elder about the spy?" Evonne asked.

"I'll do my best to persuade them not to, in that case." Helen stared at the snowy fields and glaciers below us, her expression inscrutable.

A few minutes passed in silence before our bubble jolted to a stop. I looked down and saw that we were hovering above a river. The waves were incandescent under the afternoon sunlight.

"Kenzania River, here we are." I opened the door. "Ready to jump?"

Everyone nodded. "After you," said Eileen.

Knowing an endless fall awaited me, I took a deep breath and dived into the water below, chilly air rushing in my ears and blanketing my body in a cloak of coolness.

# Chapter Thirteen

## CONFLAGRATION (ERIC)

*Splash*!

Like on our last mission, we were transported to the fountain in the middle of the courtyard, but unlike last time, the courtyard was anything but peaceful. Roars of fury and cries for mercy were audible from the upper floors, penetrating the walls and echoing in our ears.

Eileen caught my eye, and I gave her hand a quick squeeze. "I'm here," I whispered.

Just then, there was a loud bang. I whirled around and saw that the second-floor corridor had exploded. The wall was blasted apart, chunks of debris showering the hedges and bushes in the courtyard.

"Now what? Where are they fighting? What should we do?"

"We've got to fight in teams," decided Helen. "Zack, Evonne, you will both join me in patrolling the palace and fighting."

"What about the rest of us?" I asked.

"Eric, Brian, take Alexandria and Eileen to the lobby. Patrol the passages as well. Eric, do you have the map of the palace with you?"

I checked my pocket and felt a wrinkled piece of paper. "Yes."

"Good. Your job is to maim or drive away any Underworldians in the lobby or the courtyard. Help anyone on our side."

"Got it," I said.

"You may now take the others and go. Do not leave the lobby no matter what," warned Helen.

Brian exchanged a look with me, and we both nodded. "Come on," I said to the others.

***

I had expected to see a mess in the lobby, but surprisingly, there were no signs of destruction, not even the tiniest bit of evidence that a battle was raging on the other side of the palace. All we heard in the massive hall was ringing silence.

"Alexandria, guard that passage, the one on the left side of the balcony," ordered Brian. "I'll take the right one. Eric, Eileen, go to the double doors down there." He pointed to the entrance of the hall.

I nodded. "Got it. Eileen, come along."

Eileen and I hurried down the imperial staircase. "Look, the carpet's been cleaned, and the chandelier's been repaired," she observed.

"What?" I shot her a puzzled look.

"Don't you remember—? Oh right, you weren't there."

"So what happened?"

Eileen smiled. "During that invasion two weeks ago, I was down here battling a group of monsters with Lilith and Evonne, and just when we were about to lose, Zack and Alexandria, who were both up there," she pointed at the balcony, "did a severing charm and made the chandelier crash on top of the monsters. Although it was dangerous, I think it was a pretty creative idea. Anyway, nobody on our side got hurt in the end."

"Wicked!" I said. "Pity I wasn't there to witness it."

"Eric? Eileen?" a squeaky voice sounded from nowhere.

"Gidget?"

The tiny figure of Gidget knocked on the door, or to be

more accurate, pounded on the door with her tiny fists. "Willy and Cameron are also here. Could you let us in?"

"Sure." I opened the door to admit them.

"Eric, Eileen," said Willy, grinning. "Good to see that you're all back. How was your mission?"

"Pretty successful," I said. "We've found out all about the terrains and—"

"Really? Have you?" Gidget's eyes were as round as coins.

I nodded. "We now know everything about the Underworld."

"How did you manage to do it in three days?" Willy asked.

Eileen beamed with pride. "We scaled the west peak of Mount Maravillas and went to—"

"Wait, wait, wait. You guys went mountain climbing?" Cameron asked, a glint of mischief twinkling in his eyes.

"Don't get too jealous, Cam. It hasn't been much of a vacation," I said. "We had to survive in—"

"Let me finish," interrupted Eileen. "We climbed Mount Maravillas to get to the Control Center. It's a place where all the secrets of the Underworld are hidden. It's got all sorts of technological weapons, gadgets, and instruments."

"Really? What did you see there?" asked Gidget.

"Glowing animals, robots, mirror-gateways, an anti-gravity waterfall...," I counted them off my fingers.

"And there's the Control Room," said Eileen. "There's a big screen in a—"

"The Control Panel," I explained.

"It's sort of like an artificial intelligence data-storing machine," said Eileen. "We can see all the terrains and their exact positions in the Underworld."

"Which is actually a very large world," I added. "Turns out that the portals only lead us to different parts of Mirabilia District, one of the three districts in the Underworld. We also know—"

But a howl of shrill laughter cut across me. I turned, and a shudder ran through my body as I found myself face-to-face with my furry yellow nightmare—the Chirpy Bird. A quartet of devils and devilines leapt out from behind the bird, and Gidget, Willy, and Cameron charged at them.

"I noticed two of your friends are missing!" the bird shrieked. "Have they both gone running back to their mommies and daddies like cowards? Have they forgotten about the pathetic Otherworld? Or are they already dead?"

"How dare you!" Alexandria sped down the staircase and made a slashing movement with her scepter. Fireballs and lavabricks zoomed at the Chirpy Bird.

"Ha!" the Chirpy Bird shouted, dodging Alexandria's missiles with great ease. "I remember you, little princess! Have you and your traitor cousin come to avenge your friend?"

"Clarissa may have died, but she's still with us, in spirit and in power," I declared, raising the scepter and sword I had inherited from her.

The Chirpy Bird guffawed. "What fairytale are you talking about? Or is this a figment of your imagination? Your little friend's elemental magic died with her when I killed her!"

"Well, you're wrong, aren't you?" I said, my voice triumphant. "Before Clarissa died, she gave me her scepter, allowing me to inherit her elemental magic." I gave it a wave. Golden sparks emitted from the tip and zoomed at the Chirpy Bird.

An expression of horror and shock was displayed on the bird's face, but it soon wore out. "Well, little hero.... Then let's see if you can beat me with those magical powers you inherited."

The Chirpy Bird whipped out a sword and advanced on me.

"No!" Eileen shrieked.

"Out of my way, idiot girl!" The Chirpy Bird made a snatch for Eileen but missed.

She bolted up to the balcony to join Alexandria, and the two of them exchanged urgent whispers. "Eric, keep the bird busy for a few moments. We've got a plan."

I had no time to ask for details. Waving my scepter, I did my best to harm the Chirpy Bird by firing sparks of lightning at its eyes. The bird leapt out of the way and gave me a violent shove. The force knocked me off balance, and I fell to my knees, my legs screaming in pain.

"A wonderful position for my last takedown," snarled the Chirpy Bird, madness blazing in its eyes. "I like it this way better, Eric Williams, you kneeling down and begging for my mercy, rather than the foolish girl last time who waved her sword at me and caused her blade to rebound. You see, I don't like it when my enemies die so quickly. What's the fun in that? No, no.... They must endure pain beyond death before I wipe them out myself. I want to torture them into insanity and hear their screams of agony; I want to see their helplessness, see them writhing and struggling on the ground; I want to see them kneeling before me, begging me to kill them once and for all. Now, prepare to endure—"

Gathering all my remaining strength, I forced myself onto my feet, regardless of the bruises on my legs. If I was going to die today, I would die standing up, fighting and clinging onto my last shred of dignity before death took me, rather than kneeling down before my enemy and pleading for mercy. I could not and would not give the Chirpy Bird the satisfaction of watching me, crumpled and broken, imploring for death before its feet.

*The Chirpy Bird was the one who took Clarissa's life,* I thought, glaring into its wicked yellow eyes. Perhaps I imagined it, but I saw images of the past flickering in front of me. I saw Clarissa laughing and chatting with me; saw the sympathy in her eyes when I mentioned my first love Bella; saw her arguing with Alexandria, vouching for me and insisting it was wrong to reject me because of my parentage; saw her risking her life and flying a cloud to save me from the sand-tsunami in the desert; saw her leading everyone in the final assault during our rehearsal battle, our ammunition pouring from the clouds as we claimed our well-earned victory....

"Well? Do you want to join her?" said the Chirpy Bird. "I'd be more than happy to oblige you."

It hit me. The Chirpy Bird had been trying to manipulate me, displaying the images of Clarissa and perhaps tampering with my mind and making me beg for death.

No. I was not going to die like a coward, yielding to the Chirpy Bird and obeying it like a puppet. I would not give it the pride and pleasure of killing me while I stood there, not even bothering to defend myself in any way. Gritting my teeth, I slashed my scepter at the Chirpy Bird and summoned all my willpower to attack it with lightning. The bird roared and smacked me in the face with a shield. I fell to the ground, and my concentration broke. From the corner of my eye, I saw two devilines sprinting toward me, their horns sticking out. I dived behind the Chirpy Bird at the last moment, and the two devilines slammed into the bird's stomach. The bird let out a howl of frustration, blood oozing from its belly. Seizing my opportunity when the Chirpy Bird was distracted, I slashed my scepter at the bird again, struggling to stay focused. Finally, a blinding streak of lightning burst from it and struck the target. The bird slammed to the ground, where it lay as still and motionless as a fallen statue. I exhaled with relief and turned to assist the others—

"HA!" A deafening roar of triumph shattered my eardrums. Before I knew it, I was lifted bodily up into the air. The Chirpy Bird grinned at me, eyes crazed with malice. "You made the huge mistake of underestimating my—"

"Get away from my cousin!" a voice hollered.

The Chirpy Bird dropped me. Landing on the floor not-so-gracefully, I looked up and saw a verdant vine stretching from the balustrade of the balcony to the other side of the hall like a zipline. A figure, grasping the vine, zoomed toward the Chirpy Bird. It was Alexandria. Her vivid sheet of red hair flowed behind her like a waterfall of lava.

"Take that!" Alexandria delivered a sharp jab to the Chirpy Bird's eye with her scepter and flung a large fireball at it. The bird yowled and shrieked, clutching its bleeding eye.

"Alexandria?" I called out in amazement.

The Chirpy Bird made a snatch for me, but Alexandria tossed a lavabrick at the bird's injured eye before it could succeed. Howling and shrieking in agony, the giant bird sank to the floor.

Alexandria stuffed her scepter back into her pocket, let go of the vine, and landed on her feet like a cat. "Eric, you all right?"

"Yeah, I'm fine. How did you build the zipline?"

"Some help from Eileen. We had a plan and—"

"Alexandria, I'm going to automate the flytrap now!" Eileen yelled from the balcony.

"Wait for us! Come." Alexandria dragged me by the arm, and we raced upstairs to join her.

"Behind me," ordered Eileen, poking her scepter at a nasty-looking Venus flytrap. "Now, go!" With a furious swish of her scepter, she sent the self-running-flesh-eating-Venus-flytrap sprinting down the staircase and after the Chirpy Bird, who was still yelling its head off.

The three of us hurried to the balustrade and looked down at the chaotic battlefield. The Chirpy Bird was zooming around frantically, dodging the snapping jaws of the Venus flytrap. I hurled a ball of turquoise fire at the bird but missed.

"What are you doing?" whispered Alexandria.

"Trying to injure it and slow it down," I replied.

"I'll do it." Eileen fired a spiky rose at the bird and hit the target.

It worked. Pressing a wing to its eye, the Chirpy Bird uttered an unearthly scream. Right at that moment, the Venus flytrap, who had caught up with the bird, chomped into its furry rump.

"Well done," whispered Alexandria to Eileen. I gave them both a thumbs-up.

*Boom.* The Chirpy Bird ran headfirst into a floor window, and shards of glass splashed everywhere.

"What's wrong with it?" Eileen asked.

"YOU—YOU MONSTER! YOU MADE ME BLIND IN ONE EYE!" shrieked the Chirpy Bird.

"Look out, Eileen! Duck!" I yelled.

A shield hurtled through the air, aiming for Eileen. I grabbed her hand and forced her out of harm's way at the very last moment.

"You'll pay for that!" Leaning against the balustrade, Alexandria drew a circle in the air with her scepter, trapping and encircling the Chirpy Bird in a ring of fire.

"What's this gimmick?" the bird snarled.

Alexandria tightened her grasp on her scepter and gave it a twirl. The ring of flames grew in height and became a tall, sizzling column of fire, a spectacular sight to behold. With a bellow of anger, the Chirpy Bird dissolved into thin air.

"Is it dead?" I whispered to Alexandria, who shook her head and donned a bitter expression.

"No. The coward escaped right on the spot," said Alexandria, looking furious with herself. "I should've acted quicker." She twirled her scepter, and the column of fire vanished.

"Eric? Alexandria? Eileen?" Zack's voice called out to us. "Oh, there you are. Eric, take Eileen and Alexandria to the village now."

"What? Why? Aren't we supposed to be guarding the palace?" I asked.

"We just saw—" began Zack.

"The Underworldians dropped ten liquid detonating devices on the village, and it's in flames," Helen, who emerged from behind him, interrupted. "Go evacuate the Otherworldians. Take all the survivors to the residents' activity center."

"But we'll need—"

"Wait, hold on for a moment!" a new yet familiar voice shouted. "What have I missed?"

I spun around and saw Daphne jogging toward us. "Great, just the one. Daphne, we need your help. Now more than ever."

***

The four of us bolted across the front lawn. On our way out, we saw Noir and Bessie, each leading a large group of fighters. Elders, bearnixes, unibirds, kittenpillars, and dogfishes dotted the palace grounds, battling in pairs and some in threes.

I took a sharp intake of breath.

"What?" said Eileen.

"Conflagration." I jerked my head in the direction of the village. Angry orange flames lit the night, consuming the residential area. "We've got no time to waste."

It was my first time to summon and fly a cloud, but I knew the theory well enough. Concentrating on my goal, I pointed my scepter at a cloud above us, and it descended to the ground. "Climb on."

The closer we got to the village, the worse the visibility became. A thick film of smoke enveloped the houses and buildings up ahead. The cloud beneath us was invisible, and it looked as though we were flying through the gray mist with nothing below to support our weight.

Just then, a scream echoed in the distance.

"What was that?" Eileen, looking terrified, clutched my sleeve.

"Might be someone calling for help. I think it came from there." Alexandria pointed at a pale yellow house a few feet ahead of us. "Eric, I see a balcony or something behind it, if only you could land us...."

I lowered our cloud onto the balcony, and we were immediately engulfed by the smothering heat that came from the lower floors. Smoke burned in my vision, making my eyes dry and swollen. I could feel tears streaming down my cheeks.

"Now what?" I heard Eileen ask.

"I'm immune to fire. I'll go first," Alexandria piped up. "Daphne, after me. Extinguish the flames with your magic, and Eric and Eileen can follow—"

"But Alexandria," I cut in. "We've got a bigger problem to deal with—the smoke. Perhaps you and Daphne could go in and rescue the survivors while Eileen and I wait for you outside."

Alexandria hesitated for a few moments. "All right, but be careful."

"You'll need this." Eileen withdrew two small limpid orbs from the pouch of her cloak. "Oxygen-producing bubbles. They can guarantee you an endless supply of oxygen for a hundred minutes."

"An hour and forty minutes," Daphne calculated. "Perfect."

"Are those the ones we nicked from the Control Center?" said Alexandria. Daphne opened her mouth and closed it as if wanting to ask us what the Control Center was but decided now wasn't the best time for questions.

Eileen nodded. "You'd better get going. Take care."

We watched Daphne smash a window with an ice boulder and disappear into the house with Alexandria.

"Come on," I said to Eileen, clambering back onto my cloud. "Let's go and see if we can help— "

A deafening shriek split the air, followed by a maniacal roar of laughter.

"What's going on?" Eileen asked, her eyes darting and searching for the source of the cry.

I lowered us to ground level, and we disembarked from the cloud. There, right in front of us, were two devils. On the ground before their feet was a kittenpillar whose white fur was stained with scarlet. I took a closer look at the kittenpillar, and my stomach lurched—it was Ella. A deviline was waving a scythe at Ella as she dodged the blade, writhing and thrashing in agony. The two bystander devils jeered and smirked, deriving immense pleasure from watching the tortured kittenpillar struggle.

"Let go of her, stop it!" hollered Eileen. She raced up to them and flung herself between the deviline and Ella, covering the latter with her arms to shield her from further harm.

"Out of my way, girl!" snarled the deviline. "She's just a kittenpillar, not worth saving. Anyway, it wouldn't make a huge difference if I killed her. Now, go away, or you'll meet the same sticky end as the kitten— "

But Eileen, yelling abuse at the deviline, refused to budge. The blade of the scythe struck her like a whip, and a piercing scream exploded from her throat. I advanced on the deviline and pinned her to the ground, knocking the blade out of her hand. She whipped out a knife and made a slashing movement, aiming for my chest. I rolled out of the way at the last moment.

"Leave him alone!" shouted Eileen, her scepter raised. "Don't you dare— "

A jet of turquoise light struck her cheek, and she keeled over sideways.

Scepter grasped in my sweaty hand, I did my best to fight the devils and deviline, but it was impossible for me to shut my mind and concentrate on anything. I felt someone seize me by the shoulders, and something icy and metallic kissed my throat.

"I got him!" the devil who had caught me yelled in triumph. He pressed the long hilt of his spear against my neck.

"Well done." The deviline got to her feet and walked to me. "Well, well, it's Mistress Alta's son."

"The traitor boy, Eric Williams?" the other devil asked, his voice trembling with eagerness.

"Yup. That's the one."

"What should we do with him? Take him back to Mistress Alta?"

"No," said the deviline, a grin spreading across her face. "I hate people who are disloyal to Mistress Alta. Let's give this traitor boy what he deserves and watch him crack under the pressure. Hand me the scythe."

A strangled yell broke from me. I squirmed and wriggled in a fruitless attempt to escape.

"Now, stop moving." There was a twisted smile of sadistic pleasure on the deviline's face, highly reminiscent of Alta. She pressed the scythe to my right arm. A sea of flames assailed me as the scalding blade made contact with my flesh. The pain was excruciating. A searing sensation flooded my senses; it was as though every inch of me was on fire. Before I knew it, I was screaming myself hoarse. I felt my face contorting in agony and tears pouring from my eyes; I felt my entrails and lungs and stomach burning; I felt my vision blackening, my consciousness slipping away, my mind unknowing, unfeeling....

"Eric, you okay?"

I opened my eyes, and Eileen's scarred face came into view. "Eileen?" I croaked.

"We've got to get back to the palace right away," replied Eileen. "Ella's hurt, and I think you've got a second-degree burn."

I looked at my right arm. It was red, raw, and numb with pain.

"Can you stand?"

"I think so." I managed to get into a sitting position and onto my feet, but the next second, my knees gave in, and I grabbed Eileen's shoulder for support.

"Be careful." Eileen wrapped an arm around me.

Half-leaning on her, I clutched her shoulder with my uninjured hand and stood up. Eileen helped me to the cloud, which was hovering a few inches above the ground. From the corner of my eye, I saw the devils and devilines all sprawled beside each other, immobilized by sticky vines. They glared at us, hatred oozing from their unblinking eyes.

"Thanks, Eileen. You were wonderful," I grunted.

"Stay here, Eric. I'll go get Ella."

Scooping the kittenpillar up into her arms and wrapping her in her cloak, Eileen hurried back to our cloud. "Don't forget, we've got to pick up Alexandria and Daphne."

"Oh, right. Levitate," I commanded. "To...to Alexandria and Daphne, wherever they are," I told my cloud, hoping this was a valid command.

As our cloud drifted on, Eileen crawled over to me, got out a little vial of healing ointment, and dabbed the golden paste on my arm.

I felt my forehead break out in a sweat. "Ouch, it's burning," I moaned.

"Don't move. It'll heal soon," whispered Eileen.

"What about you? I saw the deviline hitting you with—"

"I'm fine," she assured me, patting me on the back. "You feeling better?"

I nodded. "You could try applying some ointment on Ella's burns, too."

Eileen shot the kittenpillar a worried look. "I'm not sure if this can be used on a kittenpillar. I think I'd better leave her to Roxanne."

Meanwhile, we had arrived at the balcony where we had dropped Alexandria and Daphne off. I could make out two blurry figures in the dense smoke.

"Eric, it's us!" Daphne's voice shouted. She and Alexandria were waving to us on the balcony. Alexandria's face was blackened with soot, and Daphne's blue ponytail was scorched. Their jaws dropped open as they saw Ella.

"Holy— Is that Ella? What happened to her?"

"The Underworldians were torturing her," explained Eileen. "How did you do?"

"Daphne and I have evacuated all the Otherworldians." Alexandria wiped the beads of sweat from her forehead. "Let's go back to the palace. The invasion isn't over yet."

***

Strangely, we found ourselves greeted by eerie, ominous silence as we landed on the front lawn. One by one, Alexandria, Daphne, and I clambered off our cloud. Eileen lifted Ella up into her arms, and the four of us hurried across the dark lawn and up the steps.

I tapped my scepter on the double doors to open them. Two people were standing on the balcony, conversing in urgent whispers. "Willy? Sheldon?"

The two of them froze in their tracks and stared at us. "Where have you been?"

"Evacuating the villagers," said Alexandria. We hurried up the staircase and approached the Elders.

"What happened after we left?" I asked, surveying the dim lobby. "Where have all the Underworldians gone?"

"Left the Otherworld half an hour ago," replied Sheldon. The sleeves of his jacket were torn. "Alta retreated her forces, saying this invasion was just a second taster."

I swore under my breath. "Fooling with us, is she? What on earth is she playing at?"

"Where are the others?" Alexandria asked. "Helen and Zack and everyone in the Inner Circle?"

"Helen's been summoned by King Patrick and Queen Marianne, and I think Zack's with her. She asked the members of the Inner Circle to gather in her room before she comes back. Let's go. The others are already there."

"But I've got to take Ella to the infirmary," said Eileen. "She was tortured by a devil and—"

"All right," Sheldon cut in, "but be careful on your way."

"No, she can't go all by herself," insisted Willy. "It's a bad idea to walk around alone on the palace grounds, especially after an invasion. How about this? I'll take the others to Room 699 while you walk Eileen to the infirmary. Meet us in Helen's room afterwards."

"Good plan." Sheldon nodded and left, Eileen tagging along behind him.

Willy turned to Alexandria, Daphne, and me. "Follow me." He guided us into the passages of purple flames.

"Here's a map," I offered, producing the wrinkled piece of paper from my pocket.

"Thanks, Eric, but I know the way."

"Anyone hurt in the invasion?" asked Alexandria in a timid voice.

"Gidget tried to take on Alto single-handedly, and she's been hospitalized," said Willy in a small voice. "Not to worry, she'll be fine," he added as Alexandria's forehead creased in anxiety. "And we haven't heard from Lilith and Evonne since Alta's forces retreated."

My stomach clenched, and I felt Alexandria tense.

"Anyone else we know?"

"Well...Cameron...he died," Willy answered in an even smaller voice.

Alexandria, Daphne, and I exchanged horrorstruck looks. "Who killed him?"

"Alto," whispered Willy.

"Does Connie know?"

Willy nodded, his expression grim. "She's devastated."

I felt as though part of me was missing. Connie and Cameron.... I knew them. I knew how much they had suffered in the past, how they had lost their triplet brother Colin. I could not fathom why fate was so cruel to them.

Without another word, we proceeded up the familiar spiral staircase and followed Willy all the way up to the sixth floor. Since my room neighbored the stairs, I never had the chance to explore the corridors that wove through the fancy rooms beyond mine. They were blanketed in plush mauve carpets, and large, colorful tapestries of magical creatures were sprawled across the walls. However, I didn't have the heart to stop and admire them.

After a few twists and turns, Willy came to a halt.

"Room 699," he said, knocking on a door beside us.

I had never been in Helen's room before. It was way larger than I had expected. The walls were draped with violet curtains, and the floor was carpeted in the same stately hue. In the middle of three velvet couches perched a tufted white table. A small crystal chandelier dangled beneath the ceiling, flames flickering on the candles.

"Eric." Brian was the first one to notice our arrival. He was huddled in the corner of a couch. Dianthus and Juniper were also here, trepidation written across their faces. Willy sat down beside Brian, and we joined them.

"Any updates?" asked Willy. "How many Elders—?"

Brian shook his head. "Helen's not back yet. Suppose she'll have news later. Where's Eileen?"

"Tending to Ella the kittenpillar in the infirmary," I said. "We found her when we were evacuating the villagers. The Underworldians tortured her with a burning scythe, and she was hurt."

Dianthus gasped. "Oh no.... Gidget and I saw Ella wriggling out of sight while we were fighting a group of bearnixes in the courtyard. Perhaps she was caught by the invaders while trying to escape from the palace."

"It's not your fault," I said. "Nobody could have known where she went."

"How could they do that? It's just brutal." Brian shook his head in indignation. "I would've blasted the little scoundrels into smithereens and fed them to a flock of unibirds."

The door opened, and in came Helen and Zack, both looking careworn and distressed.

"I've reported everything to the king and queen," said Helen. She exchanged a look with Alexandria in silence, and I knew she was referring to the spy.

"What did King Patrick say?" Brian asked.

"That it's been an unexpected attack, a great calamity that befell the Otherworld," replied Helen mechanically. I assumed she was repeating King Patrick's words.

"How many Elders—?"

"Noir and Bessie will report to us when they're done counting," said Helen.

"Anything else?"

"We're going to have to train every day, starting next week, and I mean serious training," added Zack. "King Patrick and Queen Marianne both believe the final war will take place anytime."

A knock on the door interrupted our conversation. "Lady Helen, it's me, Noir. Bessie and I are here to report the casualties and injuries."

"Come in."

Noir and Bessie breezed in, both scarred and exhausted. There were innumerable cuts on Noir's fish body, and Bessie's left eye was puffy and swollen.

"Here." Helen handed them each a pink vial of healing potion we had stolen from the Control Center. "Apply this to your wounds."

Noir and Bessie nodded to show their gratitude.

"How many Elders?" asked Helen, her lips pursed.

"Fifteen Elders were found dead, forty-one injured, and two missing."

"Missing? Who?" said Zack.

"Lady Lilith and Lady Evonne."

Helen dropped into the nearest chair, absolute horror written across her face. A nervous ripple of murmur erupted throughout the Elders.

"We're still searching for them," said Bessie, looking uneasy.

"Let me go with you," Helen begged. "I want to help find them."

"My lady, King Patrick and Queen Marianne, has requested all the Elders to remain in their rooms," replied Noir. "Roaming the palace after an invasion would—"

"Then promise me you'll do your best to find them. Please." Helen's voice was brittle.

"Yes, my lady. We'll keep you updated with our progress." Noir bowed, and Bessie saluted. "We will take our leave, then."

Alexandria exchanged a fearful look with me. "Do you think Lilith and Evonne will...?" she murmured in an undertone.

I shrugged. "No idea. The Elders look very upset, though," I mouthed back.

Willy was wringing his hands in anxiety; Juniper was staring at the wall with glassy eyes; Dianthus had his face buried in his palms, and Helen looked miserable and stricken. I registered the absence of her pearl bracelet and wondered if she lost it by accident during the assault. She placed a hand on her bare wrist, and this new tragedy added a grim twist to her lips.

Zack laid a hand on her shoulder. "It'll be all right. Lilith and Evonne...." He gave an awkward pause.

"Are both clever and skilled at fighting," Brian finished his sentence. "They'll survive."

"Eric, where's Eileen?" Zack asked, steering the conversation away from the topic of Lilith and Evonne.

"She went—"

"I'm here," said Eileen, who emerged at the doorway with Sheldon behind her. "We were just sending Ella to the infirmary."

Zack raised his eyebrows. "Ella the kittenpillar? I thought you went to the village to evacuate the Otherworldians."

"We did, and we saw the Underworldians abusing her," I explained.

"They were torturing her with a burning scythe, the devils and the deviline," said Eileen through gritted teeth. Her ponytail quivered with rage. "They didn't think it was a big deal because she was a kittenpillar and wasn't worth saving."

"The devils and devilines have always considered themselves superior to the other creatures," said Sheldon, his jaw clenching. "Alta used to have her minion devils torture the bearnixes, unibirds, kittenpillars, and dogfishes."

"Why?"

"Perversity. Torturing them just for the sake of it."

"That's awful!" exclaimed Eileen, looking aghast. "How could they? You should've seen Ella writhing on the ground while the deviline whipped her with the scythe." She shook her head. "Discriminating against kittenpillars. I could've strangled that—"

"Enough!" snapped Helen, who had remained quiet all along.

Stunned by her sudden outburst, everyone fell silent at once.

"How can you have the heart to debate about kittenpillars when Cameron's dead and Lilith and Evonne have gone missing?!"

Although Helen's tone was furious and somewhat scathing, the unshed tears that glazed her eyes betrayed her true emotions. Fighting them back, she fixed her gaze on the golden candelabra on the table and said no more.

Both Eileen and Sheldon devoted their attention to the carpet, looking abashed.

The next half hour dragged by in palpable tension. I watched the candles get shorter as the lilac pool of melting wax grew larger, reflecting the mounting anxiety in all of us.

A gentle rapping on the door made me snap out of my trance. Letting a stream of cold air escape, Noir the dogfish glided into the room like a ghost, unseen, unnoticed.

"Noir?" I addressed him. The others stirred in their seats and turned to look at him.

Helen stood up. "Any news of Lilith and Evonne?"

Noir bowed his head and apologized. "Please excuse me for barging in without—"

"Never mind that just tell me if Lilith and Evonne are fine."

Looking flustered, Noir's gaze dropped to the ground. "They...they're still searching for Lady Lilith...and...."

Noir cast a fearful look at me, and I knew what had happened before he confirmed my worst suspicion.

"Lady Evonne...has been found dead."

# Chapter Fourteen

## A Mourning Morning
## (Alexandria)

I felt as though a part of me was going...going...gone. *No. No, it couldn't be. There was a mistake.* I denied the dreadful, appalling news with all my might. *Yes, as long as I refuse to believe this lie, Evonne will come back to us, healthy, well, and alive.*

I was aware of the others' reactions, though in a queer, detached way as if they were merely actors in a movie. Overwhelmed with shock, the remaining color drained from Helen's face, and her knees buckled. With trembling hands, Zack helped her into a chair before she could collapse. Both Eric and Eileen looked dumbfounded, and Brian's bottom lip trembled. The others lowered their heads, tears streaking their cheeks. Noir, looking awkward, bowed and left the room.

Grief lingered in the air. Silence reigned; uncomfortable, ringing silence that seemed to last forever. Everyone was lost in their own thoughts, or perhaps, wallowing in misery and sorrow.

"I always knew that Evonne, like any other Elder, had a chance of falling in battle," said Helen, her voice shaky. "But I never thought.... I never imagined...."

"Neither have any of us," replied Brian in a hollow voice. "It's all my fault. I should never have left her side when we were fighting."

"It isn't your fault, Brian," I assured him. "Nobody knows what could happen in a battle."

"Don't say that," Zack pleaded. "With Evonne dead and Lilith gone, I can't stand the thought of losing another...." He drew in a staggering breath, and a tear trekked down the length of his cheek.

Looking very somber, Helen laced an arm around his shoulders. That was how quick she was, snapping out of the shock of losing Evonne and sewing herself back together, re-assuming her usual strong, stoic character.

Nobody spoke. The eerie, haunting, suffocating silence drew upon us once again as though foreshadowing an unpredictable future for everyone.

***

Five gloomy, endless days drifted by. To me, they seemed to drag on for an eternity. Like last time, all the events and meetings were either cancelled or postponed.

The morning sky was a dull, dismal gray, as though mourning for the Otherworld's loss. We headed to the training grounds behind the palace, solemn-mannered and decently dressed for the occasion. It seemed as though the whole population of the Otherworld was congregated there. Countless rows of seats were set on the lawn, facing sixteen purple sarcophaguses. It was hard to digest the fact that Evonne, who had been laughing and chatting with us five days ago, was now lying in one of them, decaying, dissolving, deteriorating. Evonne without Evonne.

We approached the altar to join Helen, who was in charge of the funeral today. Like all the other Elders, she was bedecked in a stiff black gown instead of her usual magnificent one. Helen was staring into the distance, her face pale, her gaze weary, and her expression vulnerable. She clung to her composure as if it were a lifeline. Nothing about her suggested even a hint of emotion. But still, I could see the heaviness in her eyes, the heaviness of the acknowledgement and realization that nothing would ever be the same again. Anyone who knew her well could tell she had cried out every tear she had.

"Lilith couldn't make it, then?" Helen asked as she noticed

us.

"Roxanne wouldn't let her," replied Zack.

Helen nodded, looking a little absentminded. "I see King Patrick and Queen Marianne coming. You'd better take your seats."

To everyone's great relief, Lilith turned up two days after the invasion. According to her, Alta's minions had attacked her with a Coma Potion and dragged her into the maze of hedges behind the palace, where nobody could find her. Fortunately, she made her way back as soon as she came round. Although Lilith was badly shaken and had to stay in the infirmary to recover, she had wanted to come along with us and attend the funeral. However, Roxanne insisted that she was still fragile in health and wasn't supposed to leave the infirmary.

King Patrick and Queen Marianne's gazes roamed the audience as they took the podium. "Dear Elders, friends, and families, we are gathered here to commemorate...."

As the funeral began, the rulers and Helen all gave lengthy speeches of lament, paying their condolences to the ones who had fallen in battle. Many Elders delivered eulogies and recounted the memories they shared with their deceased friends. As much as I used to despise and dislike the Elders, I couldn't help feeling a wave of pity for their loss. I knew and shared their profound pain, as I, too, had lost not one but two of my friends during the past month.

I glanced at the others. Eileen waved her scepter, making as little movement as she could while whispering commands and conjuring wreaths of green lilies and white daisies. Eric was holding Eileen's other hand. Daphne was listening half-heartedly, her eyes staring into space. Zack lowered his head, tears spilling from his eyes and splattering onto his lap. I knew he had been close to Evonne, and her death was a huge blow to him. A few rows behind us, I saw the ashen, tear-streaked faces of Mr. and Mrs. Fitzgerald and Edward, Evonne's parents and brother. It was obvious their grief was beyond tears, beyond articulation, beyond any form of expression.

"...remember those heroes who have left us. Remember

what they died for. We will not let their sacrifice be in vain. From now on, we will all continue to fight the Underworld bravely. We are all of us, and all of us are one. We will rise again. We will honor their memories. We will make them proud. Together," King Patrick delivered his closing remarks.

He then cast a look at Eileen, who understood. She got to her feet and raised her scepter. The wreaths she had conjured rose into the air; each of them floated to one of the sarcophaguses. A lone lily petal dropped like a tear and got carried away by the wind. My eyes followed its progress as it vanished into and assimilated with the lush lawns around us.

Eileen returned to her seat, biting her lip. Eric patted her and draped an arm around her. Daphne blinked furiously, and Zack gulped down a sob.

Gathering myself, I tried not to contemplate the possibilities of how many funerals I would have to attend in the future. *The future....* That would not be long for me. With Alta and Alto and their determination to destroy the Otherworld, I myself could be dying anytime....

***

After the funeral, Eileen, Daphne, Brian, and I followed the Elders into the Elders' Lounge, a spacious room full of tufted chaises, couches, and ottomans located on the third floor. The bright flames on the candelabras seemed to mock our misery. Brian chose a random couch and sat down, and the rest of us followed suit. Most of the Elders were reclining in chaises and listening to a piece of gossip about Liam, another Elder. Moments later, they broke into a peal of shrill laughter.

"It's all they care about, isn't it?" I said, annoyed. "Laughing and chatting when so many of their fellow Elders are dead."

Brian, too, was frowning at the group of Elders. "Right you are."

"What do they do besides that?"

"Quarrel over pointless topics spread rumors about their peers and tarnish their reputations.... Don't be surprised, Alexandria. They've always been this superficial."

"Oh, thanks a lot. I'm starting to have second thoughts

about joining the Elders," I grumbled.

"Well, you've still got us, haven't you? Your two friends, Eric, Helen, Zack, Lilith, Sheldon, Gidget...oh, and me."

"Good thing I've got a few trustworthy friends here," I said. "Where are the others, by the way? I don't see Helen and Zack."

"I don't see them, either." Daphne winced, placing a hand on her ribs. "Ouch, I guess they haven't fully healed yet."

"The Representative Elder and the Elite Elders will follow the king and queen to the royal cemetery by the palace for the burial after each funeral," said Brian. "To pay their final respects."

At that moment, Noir, the dogfish, entered the lounge and caught sight of us. "Lord Brian, Your Highness, Miss Spencer, and Miss Sinclair," he said, bowing.

"Hello, Noir."

"Your Highness, King Patrick and Queen Marianne invite you and your fellow heiresses to stay in the Otherworld until the final war's over."

"Well...," I sighed. "I'd be lying if I said I hadn't been expecting that. But Eileen, Daphne." I turned to look at them. "Things are getting more and more dangerous and unstable than before, and this is a huge risk, staying in the—"

"So that's why you need us, isn't it?" Daphne cut in. "You're not in this alone."

"I'm also staying," said Eileen. "For the Otherworld."

Slightly taken aback, I looked at the two of them, meeting their gazes of earnestness. Torrents of emotions swirled in me like a vortex of clouds. "Thanks," I said, struggling to put my gratitude into words. "Thanks," I repeated, pouring all the unsaid feelings into this one word.

"I'm positive you'd do the same for us," affirmed Daphne.

"Yes," I nodded. "Definitely."

"Where in the world have you been?" Eileen called out to Eric, who had entered the Elders' Lounge and was making his way toward us. For some reason, he looked strangely excited.

"Why are you looking so...?"

"I've got news."

"News?"

"You're not going to believe it," Eric said, shaking his head as though he himself was denying the news. "You won't believe it."

"Believe what?"

"Zack...." Eric gave a dramatic pause. "Zack proposed to Helen."

"What?" Speechless, I did not know what to make of this shocking piece of news.

A hush fell upon the five of us. As if nobody had understood, everyone gaped at Eric, flabbergasted and at a loss for words. Eileen's mouth dropped open in astonishment. Daphne's eyebrows joined in the middle.

"When? And who told you that?" Daphne was the first to come to her senses.

"A few moments ago. I witnessed it. They were strolling in the courtyard after they'd returned from the—No, I wasn't spying on them!" Eric clarified as Brian opened his mouth to interrupt. "I just happened to pass by, and I saw Zack down on one knee, so I lingered a little longer. Wouldn't have believed it if I hadn't seen it with my own eyes."

"This is insane," said Brian, shaking his head. "Of course, I've always had my assumptions, but this is just—"

"Too abrupt. Way too abrupt," Daphne finished his sentence for him. "How did she react when—?"

"Wait, wait. Hold your questions," I cut in. "Did Helen accept his proposal?"

"Well, uh...."

"She *accepted*?" Eileen asked, her eyes widening.

Eric shook his head. "Rejected...sort of. Helen confessed that she also loved him, but she's still refusing because she—" He shifted his weight from one foot to the other in uneasiness. "She thinks she might.... You know, follow Evonne's footsteps." Seeing the looks of puzzlement on our faces, he explained. "You know what I mean, fall in battle. Helen also told Zack she wanted to focus on fighting rather than romance, or at least for now. Meaning she's putting her duties as the Representative Elder ahead of everything."

"What about Zack? He wasn't too disappointed, was he?" said Eileen.

"No. He promised Helen he'd wait for her until she was ready," Eric replied. "You know, we're lucky to have a dutiful Representative Elder like Helen who makes decisions for the bigger picture instead of her own happiness. She cares about her responsibilities and the future of the Otherworld more than anything else."

"Right." Brian nodded with fierce approval.

"Honestly, I can't believe this. What was Zack thinking in the first place?" I shook my head. "Couldn't he be just a bit more sensible? There's an imminent war, the Underworld's launching attacks every now and then, Elders are getting hurt, Evonne's dead, Lilith got taken by Alta's minion and barely got away, and who knows what's in store for us in the future?"

"Which is exactly why Zack's choosing to propose now," Brian chimed in. "He wants to seize his opportunity, to court Helen and propose when he can, when he's still...." The last word got stuck in his throat.

"Alive," Eileen completed his sentence. "That's quite understandable."

"It is," said Brian. "The frequent attacks make everyone realize how fragile and fleeting life can be, taking the lives of people we love when we least expect it."

I shrugged. "Fine. Justified. But I still wish he could be more sensible."

"Um, Alexandria?"

I turned and saw my two other cousins, Jacob and his little sister Samantha. "Hi, Jacob. Hey, Samantha," I greeted them, forcing a smile. "What brings you here?" I added, taking notice of their grave expressions.

"You...remember we told you about our detective agency last year?" said Jacob gingerly.

I sighed. "Please, Jacob. Now's not the time to discuss things like that," I snapped, sounding a little harsher than I had meant to.

"In fact, it is," replied Jacob. "We discovered something appalling. It's about Lady Evonne's death. It was murder."

The five of us exchanged looks of skepticism.

"And where's the evidence?" demanded Brian.

"Evonne didn't die in battle, you know? Noir discovered her body in one of the passages in the basement at a quarter past ten p.m. on the day of the invasion. He immediately suspected something was wrong."

The five of us looked at one another, racking our brains to try and recall when we had been told that, only to realize we hadn't.

"You wouldn't know," Jacob said at once, as though he could read our minds. "King Patrick and Queen Marianne ordered Samantha, Noir, and me to keep the news sealed. They didn't want to cause panic among the Elders. However, I thought it would be wise to consult some trustworthy...acquaintances."

He looked at me, and then Eric, who nodded. Sincerity, unsaid but true, passed between the three of us.

"Please go on, Jacob," I said.

"My parents have a cordial friendship with Noir, and he knew all about me and my sister. I guess he was pretty desperate for help, for he contacted us straight away. Samantha and I answered his call and came to the scene of the crime. Judging from the clues, we're positive it was murder."

"But who?" Eileen looked anxious. "We all know Evonne. She wouldn't hurt even a fly. Who would've hated her so much they wanted her dead?"

"No idea," said Samantha in a hollow voice that sounded unlike her usual self. "Jacob and I have been trying to figure out who did it."

"Any clues?" I asked.

"According to Noir, the battle ended at around nine in the evening," began Jacob. "Noir discovered Evonne's body at a quarter past ten and immediately got in touch with us. Samantha and I heard about the invasion at nine. We were so worried about our parents that we went straight to the palace to check on them, which is why we were able to answer Noir's call as soon as he reached us. We—Samantha, Noir, and I—arrived at the scene of the crime about two minutes after Noir had called us. Evonne's body was still warm then."

"Hold on, the heat hadn't left her body yet?" Brian asked.

Jacob and Samantha nodded.

"This can only mean she was killed moments before Noir found her," Brian concluded. "So Evonne did survive the battle. She was murdered afterwards."

Jacob nodded and pressed on. "Exactly. Evonne had no weapons with her, and—"

"How did she die?" I asked.

"Someone slit her throat with...I guess it was a knife, though it could've been a dagger, a sword, or anything with a blade. Evonne was lying face-up, and judging from the blood spatters at the crime scene, she wasn't running away from her murderer before being killed. Samantha and I also checked her hands. There were no cuts or scars. We think Evonne didn't fight back—or didn't have time to fight back. The murderer could've been standing right behind Evonne before bringing the blade to her throat."

"And where is the weapon that killed her?"

"Gone. We didn't see anything with a blade at the scene of the crime. Like I said, one, Evonne had no weapons with her. Two, the murderer slit her throat and was probably standing behind her. I think Evonne had let her guard down at that moment. Now, look at all the facts I've just laid out. Put two and two together. I think the murderer is someone Evonne knew well. Someone she was close to."

Everyone exchanged dark looks with each other.

"Anything else?" I asked.

"We found a crumpled note a few inches away from Evonne's head." Samantha withdrew a piece of paper from her pocket and handed it to me.

"It's wet," I noticed.

"That's because we used a bottle of fingerprint-revealing potion on it. Nothing happened."

Eileen, Daphne, and Brian skirted closer. I smoothed the

wrinkled paper, trying to make the text more discernible.

*Meet me in the secret passage in the basement at ten fifteen.*

"Ten fifteen," I muttered. "Ten fifteen.... Didn't Noir discover her body at ten fifteen?"

"Either Evonne got there earlier and was killed, or Noir arrived at the crime scene one or two minutes after ten fifteen. He didn't see anyone in the basement."

"Or the murderer escaped on hearing Noir's footsteps," Daphne suggested. "Any footprints on the crime scene?"

"No. I think the murderer removed the footprints by magic."

"But where could this murderer have gone?" questioned Eric.

Daphne said nothing and shrugged. "Who wrote it?" she asked suddenly. "The handwriting on the note. If we could track down the person—"

Jacob shook his head. "Evonne wrote it herself. We've confirmed the handwriting."

"So, what does this mean?" I asked, confused. "Why would Evonne write...?"

"I've got a theory here which makes sense," said Jacob. "Evonne wanted to talk to this murderer and wrote him or her the note."

"How come she didn't sign her name?" said Eileen.

"Maybe she asked someone to take it to the recipient and tell them it was from her. And when they met in the basement, they argued, and the murderer killed her. As for why the note was left at the crime scene, I think the murderer may have dropped it there by accident and forgot to destroy the evidence."

"He or she forgot to destroy the evidence?" I said. "But if that's true, why weren't there any fingerprints on the note?"

"Alexandria's right," said Eric. "Only a fingerprint-removing charm could have done—"

"Wait a second, stop," Brian interrupted. "What if...what if there were no fingerprints at all? What if the culprit never even left a fingerprint on the note?"

"How is that possible?"

Brian pointed to the gloves on my hands. "That's the answer. Gloves. The murderer must have been wearing gloves. Only women wear gloves in the palace, so I think it's a *she*."

"Now, Brian, we shouldn't jump to conclusions about anything," said Jacob. "Anyone could go to the boutique and buy a pair of gloves, men or women, right? The Elder who killed Evonne could even borrow a pair of gloves from a friend. There are too many possibilities. I do think that everyone in the palace is a suspect, but let's forget about the rulers first. They couldn't have killed their own advisor, could they? So now it's all about the Elders."

"The Elders," I repeated, my mind spinning. "How can you be so certain it was an Elder who murdered Evonne?"

"The place," Jacob reminded me. "The basement. Nobody knew there were basements beneath the palace, except for the Elders."

"Wait, what basement are we talking about here? There are twelve basements, right? The vaults, or—?"

"No, no," Brian cut in. "The basement we're talking about is the one below the vaults. As Elders, we refer to the first twelve basements as 'vaults' and not 'basements.' The basement in question is basement thirteen. Only the Elders know about it."

"I didn't know the difference between the vaults and basement thirteen," I admitted. "Not until you mentioned it."

"Neither did I," Eileen added.

"Well, I knew all about basement thirteen, but that's because I'm an Elder," said Eric, looking nervous. "You're not going to suspect me for that, are you?"

"Of course, we don't suspect you," answered Jacob vaguely.

"Perhaps an Elder forced a bearnix, unibird, kittenpillar, or dogfish to murder Evonne?" surmised Daphne.

"Good point." Jacob scribbled something on a notebook. He sighed and looked up at us. "I hate having to do this, but there's something I ought to show you." He cast a dark look at his sister, "Samantha, show them."

Looking hesitant, Samantha produced a pearl bracelet from her small purse. "Evonne was clutching this in her hand when she was found. No fingerprints on it, except for her own."

My heart turned over as I saw the bracelet. "It's Helen's. I've seen her wearing it before." Dread and panic flooded me, and I shook my head in denial. "No, it couldn't have been her. She wouldn't—"

"Many women have similar bracelets," agreed Eric. "Like Lilith, Gidget, Juniper—"

Jacob pointed to a name engraved on one of the pearls: *Helen.*

Eric fell silent and developed a sudden interest in the glossy beige tiles.

"Well, hard to admit Helen's on the list of suspects," said Brian matter-of-factly. "The evidence is mounting, and everything's pretty much against her. Someone close to Evonne, someone who wore gloves, an Elder who knew about the basement, and her bracelet—"

"Brian," Daphne said, a piercing look in her eyes. "Do you think Helen would kill Evonne?"

Everyone turned to stare at Brian.

"No, I—I was just saying the evidence...," Brian stuttered, looking mortified. "I didn't believe—didn't think she'd—"

"Evonne had been Helen's apprentice," Eric reminded him. "Don't forget, she was heartbroken when Evonne lost her memory last year."

"Eric's right. Helen didn't have a motive," I agreed. "They got along very well, Helen and Evonne. They were like sisters."

"But Brian's got a point," Samantha piped up. "The evidence is all there."

"The real culprit could've given Evonne the bracelet on purpose before killing her off. He or she could have asked Evonne to return the bracelet to Helen, then walked up behind her and killed her while she was distracted. That way, he or she could frame Helen for Evonne's death. Yeah, that's happened before. A lot of Elders have framed Helen for things she hadn't done, just because they were jealous of her and wanted to replace her as the

Representative Elder." Jacob frowned. "Hmm.... Did Helen have an alibi then?"

"Yes," I said. "The murder occurred at ten fifteen. We were all gathered in her room then. Me, Eric, Eileen—"

"But hold on, you're forgetting what Daphne said," Samantha pointed out. "Someone could've threatened a bearnix, unibird, kittenpillar, or dogfish to do the dirty work. Just because they had an alibi doesn't mean they couldn't have forced someone else to do it."

"Maybe," murmured Eileen. "The murderer could've threatened a fellow Elder, too."

"Right. We mustn't rule out any possibilities," Jacob agreed, jotting down more notes. "This isn't an easy case, but Samantha and I will do our best and begin our investigation right away. Now, all we can do is to interrogate the workers in the palace and ask them if they know anything about the murder or anyone who might have done it. However, I have no way of knowing whether they're telling the truth or not. I wish I do, though."

The sound of rustling satin and clicking heels announced the arrival of two figures in black; it was no other than Helen and Zack.

"What are you all talking about?"

"Greetings, Lady Helen, Lord Zack." Jacob and Samantha bowed and curtsied at the sight of them. "Samantha and I have been investigating the murder of Lady Evonne."

"Murder?" Zack repeated, his eyebrows raised. "I don't understand."

It took forever for Jacob and Samantha to clarify everything. By the time they had finished, Helen was already white with horror and Zack frozen with fear.

"Lady Helen, Evonne was holding this in her hand when she was found," said Jacob as gently as possible, showing her the bracelet. "I'm sorry, but I can't return it to you. It's part of the evidence."

Helen said nothing. She stared at it, spellbound. Moments later, I saw a teardrop strike a pearl on the bracelet.

"Helen?" I asked.

Ignoring my question, Helen turned on her heels and hurried out of the room.

"I'm going after her," said Zack at once. "Thanks for notifying us, Jacob and Samantha. Excuse me." He breezed out of the room and sped after Helen.

The seven of us looked at one another, at a loss for words.

"Didn't you see Helen's reaction? How appalled she looked when Jacob was recounting the details?" Brian asked. "I mean, she is a potential—"

"Brian, we're not going over that again," Daphne said with a firm touch of finality, her resemblance to Queen Marianne striking.

"I'm on Daphne's side," I said, as Eileen nodded. "Helen looked very upset and was—"

"Because they found her bracelet—" cut in Brian.

"Because she lost her former apprentice—" I interrupted in an even louder voice.

"Because she was involved—"

"Brian!" I almost shouted. "Why do you think—?"

"Stop contradicting me, all right? I didn't say Helen killed Evonne. I'm just suggesting there's a possibility."

"You just want her to have killed Evonne, don't you?"

Before I knew it, I was on my feet. Sparks of fire danced on my fingertips.

Brian stood up, too. He glared into my eyes. "Stop having a go at me."

"Unless you drop it—"

"I'm just stating a fact!" Our noses were only one inch apart.

"That's enough," said Jacob in a stern, Helen-like manner. "Listen, we shouldn't start fighting amongst ourselves."

Glowering at each other, Brian and I sat down.

"I agree with Brian," remarked Jacob, earning frowns from Eric, Eileen, and Daphne. I opened my mouth to protest, but Jacob raised his hand to silence me. "I'm sorry, but we cannot rule anyone out. I don't care who's got a motive or who doesn't.

Like it or not, all the Elders are suspects. We can't let any personal opinions color our judgment."

"Yeah, but what Jacob said." Eric put on a brooding expression. "Fighting amongst ourselves—it rings like a bell. Ah, yes. You remember the spy we talked about on our way back to the Otherworld on our last mission? Might it be the same person that killed Evonne?"

"That's possible," said Eileen. "But the million-dollar question is, who?"

My stomach gave an unpleasant jolt as the dream I had on the first night of our mission occurred to my mind again. Alta had addressed Zack as "my old friend." I had had the same doubts when we were discussing this topic the following day. Could he possibly be the spy, as well as the one who killed Evonne? But if my assumption was true, why would Zack do that? Did he have a reason to hurt Evonne, yet unbeknownst to us? And why would Evonne be clutching Helen's bracelet moments before her death? Too many questions, but not even one answer. Desperate for evidence to contradict this possibility, I racked my brains to recall everything Jacob had said about the scene of the crime. "Do you think...?" I mumbled. "Maybe—"

"Think. Yeah, all right. Let's think," Daphne cut in, her tone mocking. "Who do we know hates Helen and doesn't give a toot about the Otherworld?"

Everyone remained silent.

"Oh, come on, isn't it obvious?" Daphne plowed on. "Juniper Richardson?"

Jacob stiffened. "My mother? A murderer? Daphne Sinclair, are you suggesting that my mother killed Evonne?"

"There's a possibility—"

"No way. I know my mother. She can be a bit sharp-tongued sometimes, but taking someone else's life? She'd never do anything like—"

"Well, you're one to talk!" Daphne retorted, disbelief and indignation working their way through her features. "Who said 'like it or not, all the Elders are suspects'? Who insisted not to rule anyone out?"

Jacob was about to defend himself when—

"Jacob Richardson, Samantha Richardson." A harsh female voice sounded from behind us.

I swiveled in my seat and saw Juniper towering right behind us, her wrathful gaze implying danger. The dress she was wearing, a bright orange gown adorned with lace, frills, and a pale gold sash clashed more horribly with her green braid than ever.

"Good morning, Aunt Juniper," I murmured, pretending to be polite and determined not to give her a reason to yell at me.

She ignored my greeting and instead laid a warning hand on Jacob's shoulder.

"Mommy!" said Samantha. "Why have you—?" Her voice faltered as she caught sight of her mother's icy expression.

"Mother?" Jacob asked, looking anxious.

"Jacob Richardson, I am here to warn you to stop intervening in the Inner Circle's business. Do you hear me?"

"What do you mean by that?"

A very ugly look was displayed on Juniper Richardson's face. "I should have made my meaning clearer. Evonne Fitzgerald's death has nothing to do with you, and therefore, I forbid you and Samantha to investigate further. Am I making myself clear?"

"Mother, how can you?" Jacob said in a voice of restrained fury. "After being in the Circle for almost a month! Evonne Fitzgerald was your colleague. And she was only twenty-five when she died. What's more, judging from the evidence and her body, it was no ordinary accident. It was *murder.* How can you make me stand aside and—?"

"I'm not asking you to stand aside," Juniper Richardson cut in. Her raised voice had attracted a crowd of Elders. "I'm asking you to stop providing assistance to the Inner Circle. The Inner Circle has proved to be a pathetic, useless organization that can do nothing to stop the attacks. Figuring out the positions of the terrains, eh? Well, that hasn't stopped us from losing members. Clarissa Dawson died, Cameron Miller followed her footsteps, and now Evonne Fitzgerald's also dead. What good has joining the Circle done them? I've had enough of it. I'm quitting."

"But Mom—" Samantha said.

"Quiet!" Juniper snarled at her daughter before turning to face her son. "As for you, young man, I am very disappointed in you."

Jacob goggled at his mom. "Mother, you can't say that. You have to—"

"When will you be sensible and stop arguing with me?" Juniper was near hysterics.

Jacob drew himself to his full height, and this was such an outstanding move that everyone in the Elders' Lounge turned to look at him.

"Fine." When he spoke, his voice was surprisingly calm. "Leave the Circle if you like. I'm filling in for you. And I'm going to find out the truth. I *will* get to the bottom of this."

It was his mother's turn to gawk at him. "How dare you—? I won't allow it!" she shrieked, almost waving her fists at her son.

"That," replied Jacob in a serene manner, "will be a matter of whether Helen Edmunds allows it or not. Goodbye." And then, he took his sister's hand and marched out of the Elders' Lounge, his shoulders squared, and his head held high. Fuming, Juniper stormed out of the room after her son.

"How could Juniper Richardson say that?!" Daphne pummeled her fist into her knee. "She's such an old cow— Sorry, Alexandria, didn't mean to insult your aunt."

"No, it's fine. You're right. She's a foul, attention-seeking, nasty old hag," I said, glaring at the silver draperies across from us.

"*She* did it," said Eric. "I'm almost convinced. It was Juniper. She gave Evonne that bracelet and killed her to frame Helen. And now, she's trying to stop the detectives from investigating the crime."

"No, I don't think it was Juniper," said Brian. "Being mean is in her nature, but I don't think she'd—" He broke off in mid-sentence. "Look, I'm sorry for saying those things about Helen," he said in a little voice. "But Evonne was murdered. And we, any of us, could come to the same sticky end if the culprit strikes again."

I registered his trepidation, and for some reason, it thawed me. "No, Brian. I understand. I'm sorry for accusing you earlier. You were just being your usual sensible self. I'm sure you didn't mean it."

"It's all right," replied Brian in a low voice. "What do you think, Alexandria? Do you reckon Juniper Richardson did it?"

I pondered on this for a while and shook my head. "I don't think so."

"What?" Eric and Eileen gaped at me.

"I know Juniper tried to stop Jacob and Samantha from investigating the murder, but I agree with Brian. Look, I'm not saying this because she's my aunt. You all know I don't like her at all. But I think Jacob's got a point. Juniper's bitter, but at least she's quite straightforward. Also, I don't think she's horrible enough to commit a murder. She just doesn't seem like the type. I have a feeling it isn't her."

"But—" Eric started.

"We can talk later. Now, excuse me while I go check on Helen," I said, standing up to leave.

I exited the Elders' Lounge and set foot on the spiral staircase. Jacob's words occurred to me: *We cannot rule anyone out. I don't care who's got a motive or who doesn't. Like it or not, all the Elders are –*

I froze in my tracks, certain I heard someone crying. Curious, I followed the source of the sobbing up the stairs and to the conference room where the Inner Circle held meetings. With a pang of astonishment, I spotted Helen, who was weeping with her head pillowed in her arms.

"Why Evonne? What did she do to deserve this...?" Her voice trailed off.

Zack draped an arm around Helen's shoulder and snuggled her closer and tighter to him. He did not reply, for he, too, was choked with grief. His eyes were rimmed with red, and his shoulders shook with anguish. The two of them conversed no more but wept silently in each other's arms.

The thought of approaching and comforting Helen and Zack flashed across my mind, but I knew, deep down, that my sudden disturbance would only upset them even more. The last thing either of them would want was an intruder to witness their vulnerability. Plus, all they needed was each other at this moment.

With a heavy heart, I turned to leave, only to hear a familiar voice and brassy laughter issuing from upstairs. Raising my scepter, I tiptoed up to the fifth floor and saw a group of Elders, including Kerry Jenkins.

"Funny how King Patrick and Queen Marianne regard the members of the Inner Circle as heroes, praising them for their bravery," said an Elder in a navy-blue tuxedo, smirking.

"I don't call that bravery, Galen. Foolishness, that's what," replied Jenkins, a spiteful expression on her face. "The king and queen look upon them as heroes because Saint Alexandria's in the Inner Circle."

"She's no saint. She relishes her fame, being worshipped and placed on a pedestal," spat one of the others. "The Elders in the Inner Circle are fawning on her because she's the princess. Disgusting lot of hypocrites, if you ask me. The sage, sanctimonious members of the Inner Circle. Makes me sick to even think about it."

I felt myself brimming up with venom.

"The problem with the insufferable kid is that she should be perfecting her appearance and socializing with aristocrats instead of fighting and going on adventures," remarked Jenkins. "For a prince, that's no big deal. But for a princess? That's just pathetic. Her destiny is to love and marry, not to fight. The way I see it, no man in their right mind would court someone as rebellious as she. What a disgrace to the Otherworld. I pity her."

"You're wrong."

The group of Elders gaped at me. It was the panic and shock written on their faces that calmed me, filling me with a savage sort of pleasure.

"You'll never know the importance of staying true to yourselves, and that's even more pathetic," I said in an unfazed manner, knowing my nonchalance and placidity would anger them even more. "I pity you."

Without another word, I turned and glided up the spiral staircase.

***

The unibird-shaped medallion twinkled on the lacquered purple table in my room as I shone it with my handkerchief, light playing on its shiny surface. It was a souvenir of the mission I had gone on last year.

*The mission last year....* It seemed so far away an event, so faint a memory. Everything was so perfect, so wonderful, so full of hope and joy then. We all survived the mission; Eric found a new home; Evonne was healed and revived....

However, the past was in the past. Now, everything seemed so bleak, dreary, and hopeless, as though all the color had faded from the world. There was a spy among the Elders; there was a murderer hiding among us; there was the lurking threat of the Underworld, a hibernating bear waiting to attack anytime. Our fates were as intangible as air, as fluctuant as water. After all the trials we'd been through, our carefree minds were now marred with the knowledge that nothing in our life was permanent or guaranteed.

Eileen, Daphne, and Eric, who were all sitting beside me, gazed at the medallion, lost in their own thoughts as well.

I closed my eyes, and the cheery faces of Clarissa and Evonne floated to the surface of my mind. Moments later, I opened them, just as the cruel reality dawned over me again, this time harsher and more brutal than ever.

"Clarissa, Evonne, rest in peace. Your sacrifice won't be in vain."

For some reason, I half-expected to see Evonne's smile or hear Clarissa's voice. I still could not digest the fact they were gone forever, even after attending their funerals in person.

"Clarissa, Evonne, I promise you." These words I said, hoping for a reply, a smile, or any proof that Clarissa and Evonne weren't figments of my imagination, that they had existed before.

Only to find my words greeted by the iciest, loudest,

hollowest silence.

"It's not over yet, Alexandria," said Eric. "You're not alone. We've still got each other, haven't we?"

Eileen and Daphne both nodded.

"No matter what happens in the future, we'll face it together."

The setting sun grinned in the distance, casting a veil of golden light over us.

"Together...," I echoed Eric.

It was not until then that I realized how powerful a word it was.

# Otherworld Trilogy

## Now Available

## Coming Soon

Hermione Lee was born and raised in Taiwan, where everyone and everything in her life stimulated her rich imagination and inspired her to write. Although she prefers writing stories in her grandma's quaint, cozy home, she writes anytime and anywhere. To her, words are portals that whisk her to whimsical worlds of magic. When Hermione isn't writing, she indulges herself in epic tales of fantasy, horror, and adventure; but mostly, dwelling in her reverie.

Hermione's life motto says a lot about her stories: *Fight for what you believe in; believe in what you fight for.* This sentence best represents her journey of becoming a writer. She waged a constant war against invisible enemies— self-doubt, self-discrimination, and of course, countless rejections. However, these struggles only strengthened her will to succeed and pursue her ambition. Along the way, Hermione learned to stick to her goals, have humility and perseverance, and stay loyal to her own beliefs. Her personality is strongly projected on the characters she created; firm, unyielding, and with a thirst to prove themselves.

When Hermione first started writing, she had eyes for only the fame and recognition accompanied by success; however,

her opinions have matured greatly during the past few years. She continues to write stories nowadays, but out of sheer interest and passion rather than gaining profit.
https://authorhermionelee.cms.webnode.com

CPSIA information can be obtained
at www.ICGtesting.com
Printed in the USA
LVHW032119290322
714723LV00006B/429

9 781956 788686